I Hear the Clattering of the Dreams)

"These stories will haunt you. They are savage and visceral, full of vivid imagery that leaves no question as to what Stewart wanted you to see. There is gore for those who seek it, along with terror, blistering action, and suspense. Stewart cuts not only to the chase but to the bone with these stories, but it's not all blood and gore. There are also moments that feel quite personal and heartfelt, proving that the intensities of both horror and the heart are not as distant as one might believe."

Michael R. Goodwin
Author of *How Good It Feels to Burn* and *Smolder*

"Consider this a warning: Jamie's brand of horror has a way of getting under your skin. It's like you've taken the wrong road, and ended up somewhere familiar and yet wholly strange. Where things are off-kilter, just to the left or right of normal. He takes you to places where the improbable feels possible, where honest sentiment and the inhumane commingle, and walks you through the horror with a disarming sensitivity."

Christopher Robertson
Author of *My Zombie Sweetheart* and
The October Society

"Stewart's prose is as capable as it is evocative.

Although the collection maintains a simple, straightforward style, there is plenty of vivid imagery and description to hold any reader's interest. It certainly held mine. I read the whole book in one sitting."

Briana Morgan
Author of *Unboxed*, *The Tricker-Treater* and *Mouth Full of Ashes*

Price Manor

"Not since Shirley Jackson's *The Haunting of Hill House* have I seen such fully realised characters bought together in a strange house. Just as Jackson did with her character Eleanor, you feel for these hapless creatures as they stumble through the darkness of their own desires. The House That Bleeds is, I believe, a masterpiece of horror."

Spencer Hamilton
Author of *The Fear, Sister Funtime* and *Welcome to Smileyland*

"This is, without question, the best of anything I've read from Stewart. The expressiveness of his prose, the poignancy and pain conveyed in such a rapidly progressing plot, the constant unease and drive toward a finale that was gratifying and perfectly executed...this book is modern gothic horror done right."

Michael R. Goodwin
Author of *How Good It Feels to Burn* and *Smolder*

Montague's Carnival of Delights and Terror

Montague's Carnival of Delights and Terror offers fun, but you'll find there's nothing fair about what's happening on the Ghost Ride. This book is an absolute roller coaster; pulling you in slowly, raising the tension, and dropping you full speed into twists that leave you screaming. It's a funhouse mirror, distorting your views of what you think you know about the genre. It'll leave you breathless, shaking, and begging to go right back and do it again.

James Sabata
Author of Fat Camp and The Cassowary

Starting as an exploration of trauma and ending on what exactly makes a monster monstrous, Jamie Stewart's novel reads at an amazing fast pace and questions our childhood memories of carnival delights to bring us up close to the terror of real life.

Catarina Prata
Author of The Last Dive

What Jamie has achieved here is nothing short of incredible; a 100,000 beast of a novel that has a fine cast of characters chocked full of heroes, villains, and those in between, plus some terrific set pieces that will have your heart thumping and keep you turning those pages. The big reveal comes with still a quarter of the book to play out - it's a wild ride!

Perhaps most impressive is the scope, scale and sheer size of this work. Very few indie authors out there are likely to attempt something even approaching this, and the dexterity and panache Jamie shows to keep the story moving - with multiple plates spinning at times - and to pull it all together for a powerful and satisfying ending really shows his prowess as a writer. You're also left in no doubt of how much Jamie loves his craft - the enthusiasm and passion he shows every day on his social feeds is reflected in his writing here. He's having fun, he's enjoying you being around to listen, and he's confident that what he's got to say is worth your time. And, trust me, it is.

Dave Musson
Author of Mirrored

Copyright © 2022 Jamie Stewart

All rights reserved. No part of this publication may be reproduced, stored in a retrieval system, or transmitted, in any form or by any means, electronic, mechanical, photocopying, recording or otherwise, without the prior permission of the copyright owner.

This book is a work of fiction. Names, characters, places, and incidents either are the products of the author's imagination or are used fictitiously, and any resemblance to actual events or persons, living or dead, is entirely coincidental.

By Jamie Stewart

Mr. Jones
I Hear The Clattering of the Keys (And Other Fever Dreams)
Price Manor: The House That Bleeds

Co-editor anthologies

Welcome to the Funhouse from Blood Rites Horror
The Sacrament from Dark Lit Press

Reading the Fairway.

What you hold in your hand is not a book.
In every possible way it may appear to be one, but make no mistake, it's as deceptive as your chance at winning a prize at one of Montague's games.

No, this right here is a love letter - a stunning, epic 100,000 word ode to a bygone era. Before you get to Jamie's tribute, though, allow me to sing his praises like a ballying barker building a tip.

My introduction to Jamie was through an act of kindness on his part. He, alongside the book's editor Kelly Brocklehurst, selected my phantasmagorial fairy tale for their carnival-themed anthology *Welcome to the Funhouse*. That single act of inclusion was like a kind ride operator handing me a free ticket to a ride I couldn't afford, and it's one I haven't gotten off since. That generosity and uplifting spirit Jamie showed me is something he does daily for many others in this strange little world of indie horror. To write a foreword for him, for what I genuinely believe is Jamie's best work, is beyond an honour.

It's funny: carnival horror is what brought us together, and it's something we both share a deep love of - without knowledge of each other's projects, both Jamie and I produced full-length carnival horror novels. However, like the man himself, Jamie's work is far more mature.

Jamie calls these books "tombstones", chunky horror epics you'd typically see the names Laymon, King, Koontz, Simmons, Straub, and other legends carved on. The format may have gone out of vogue these days, but these big ones will always have a special place for many of us,

9

especially with Jamie. If you've never heard him talk about his love of these types of books, then check out one of his many podcast appearances or his reviews of Stephen King's bibliography, "Books That Shine", for Horror Oasis.

By the time you got to the end of say *Ghost Story* or *The Stand*, you felt like you'd conquered something alongside the heroes, sharing in their triumph, and that's something Jamie truly captures here. You genuinely feel like Joe Cage can't battle the evil forces swelling against him without your help, turning the page and pushing him on.

I said before this book is deceptive, and I mean that in the best possible way. While Jamie pays loving homage to the giants who came before us, this ride's no jaunty carousel; it ain't no zamp. It's a magnet-powered rocket-ride dressed up like an old-school wooden coaster tearing through the pages like it's hungry.

And while the enigmatic Montague's name may be on the cover and heading up the carnival pulling into the small Kansas town of Marybell as you read this, he's but the showman. Jamie's the actual operator here, running a show that reaches as far as The Whirl and thrills more than a Journey Through The Crypt.

Anyway, I'm blowing my pipes raw here, and - look, the lights are coming on, the music's playing, and that's a ticket to one hell of a ride in your hands. See you on the other side. Maybe.

Christopher Robertson (author of Virgin Night).

Montague's Carnival of Delights and Terror

This book is dedicated to Stephen King, whose work made me a reader.

It is also dedicated to the horror novels of the 70s and 80s - novels that I refer to as 'tombstone books' on account of their vast size and the world building within them. Montague's Carnival is a homage to those type of stories, as you'll soon see.

Book One

Kansas, 1983

Prologue

1

Sheriff Timothy Jackson arrived at the Teal farm to find that the farmer, who everyone in town considered to be the king of tall complaints, was telling the truth for once. A Teal interaction was a monthly occurrence, mostly due to drunken teenagers scaring his cattle at night. While the majority of Marybell's Police Department found this irritating, suspecting that Philip Teal actually relished complaining to them, Jackson had a lot of time for the farmer.

Anyone who chose to work the land had his respect.

Yes, the days were lovely now that the summer was beginning, but in winter when the ground froze and the sky glared down from above with icy hate and the road to town became impassable because of the snow, and the cold could still be felt no matter how many quilts you lay under, it was hard.

People like Philip Teal could complain as much as they wanted as far as Jackson was concerned; they had earned it.

Thinking such thoughts caused his mind to drift back to the young man with the bruised face. He had been hard with him, though not unnecessarily.

This had been outside Bob's Roadside Diner a few miles back. He had pulled in for a morning coffee to find a stranger sitting alongside the usual suspects – retired farmers with nothing better to do.

The topic of conversation naturally had been the carnival that had come to town. Jackson witnessed the young man, who he automatically thought of as a drifter on account of his dirty clothes and the stuffed backpack by his feet, engaging with the old-timers, asking about the fair, asking about work.

Jackson hadn't said anything then, just grabbed his coffee from Meryl Grey at the counter and waited in the parking lot. By then the old-timers had sped off to do whatever it was such men did with their time.

'Hey, kid.'

The young man glanced over his shoulder at him, the purple swelling that marked the left side of his face visible even in the day's wavering heat. He had been staring at the township sign reading "Welcome to Marybell" that someone had decided to use for target practice with a .22.

'That's one hell of a shiner you've got there. Mind telling me how you got it?'

'Just an accident is all,' he had replied.

'Is that right? I suppose it's one of those falls-in-the-shower type of accidents that I hear about all the time. Come over here and chat with me a second; I'm sure you've got a few spare. I see that pack on your back and I know it isn't full of school books so it isn't like I'm going to be keeping you from any college classes, is it? Not that there's any college in these parts. Come on over, kid. I'm not going to ask a third time.'

The kid had strolled towards him, his boots scraping over the gravel that made up the diner's parking lot. Not once did his brown eyes leave Jackson's, hidden behind his silver sunglasses. There was suspicion in his eyes, and a little fear too. He noted that the kid rubbed absently at his right wrist with his left hand as if readying the flesh there for his handcuffs.

He wondered if Meryl Grey, the diner's waitress, was watching them from inside. She had a kind heart and been friendly towards this stranger when he had stepped inside, the doorbell announcing him with a chime.

'What can I do for you?' asked the stranger, still rubbing his wrist.

'First off, what's your name?'

'Joe Cage.'

'Marybell is not so small a place that I know everyone by name. That being said, I know a stranger's face when I see one, especially one that spells trouble, just as your bruised one does.'

'I can promise you, sir, I don't look for trouble.'

He had nodded at this, his eyes scrutinising Joe behind his glasses.

'What if trouble is looking for you?'

The stranger named Joe frowned at this. The swollen lower left-hand side of his face looked like some sort of tumour feeding off of him.

'I'm going to offer you some free advice, which you should take not just because it will be good for you, but also because nothing comes free nowadays: keep walking. When you walk down that road, when you walk into town just keep… on… walking. Marybell is not a kind place for strangers.'

Hard. But not unnecessary, he concluded. Yet as Jackson recognised the ease at which he travelled down the dirt lane to the Teal place, a shadow entered his mind, hanging over his heart. He would not treat Philip Teal with that same aggressive tenacity.

Marybell is not a kind place for strangers.
What exactly did I mean by that?

The voice asking was not his own; instead it rang with sleazy curiosity. Jackson's thick fingers tightened over the steering wheel's leather. The Teal farmhouse was dead ahead now, painted sunflower yellow beyond a square dooryard of dust and several outbuildings, including a barn the colour of a rooster's feathers and a steel grain silo. The gravel road churned beneath the Chevrolet Blazer's wheels, filling the big car's interior with sound and drilling the beginnings of a headache in his temple as he pondered his words. There was a certain level of honesty in them that made his beige uniform itch against his skin.

I was simply looking out for him, he responded to the voice in his head.

Why? it asked. *What was he in danger of?*

His knuckles were white on the wheel now. He knew the reason he had harshly sworn the young man off. Sometimes things went wrong for travelers in his town; not all the time, not to the man and his wife who happened to be driving through. But to those who maybe only had one change of clothes, sometimes things went wrong for them if they stayed too long.

That's not true though, is it? said the firm, accusing voice in Jackson's head.

Emotion wormed in the muscles along his jaw.

Anthony Eke had more than one change of clothes on him; he had been travelling across the country to visit his sister in a brand-new pickup, except he pulled over because Miriam Black, the minister's wife, had blown a tyre. He tried to help her, and a few boys with a few too many beers in them hadn't liked the idea of a black man helping a white woman, so they shot him in the back of his head as he was crouched over her tyre iron.

Jackson's hands hummed with tension on the wheel. There was a waterfall of sweat running down his spine, dampening his shirt. Anthony Eke had been on his mind when he talked to Joe Cage by the diner.

Marybell was a community, a nice one for those within it, yet the darker side underneath it caused Jackson to wonder on more than one occasion as to whether he actually liked the place. However, he had little time for further ruminating on the subject, spotting Teal. He was running across the dooryard at the Blazer, his sun worn face distraught.

2

'Sheriff, Sheriff!' cried Teal as Jackson slammed on the brakes.

The Blazer's wheels dug into the gravel, stopping just before the vehicle's grill would have struck the farmer, who showed no signs of noticing this. A flare went up inside the Sheriff's head: something was wrong here.

'Christ, Phil, I could have run you down.'

'Never mind that,' he gasped.

Jackson heaved himself out of the police vehicle, causing it to lurch on its suspension. He was a big guy, only he didn't feel so big now; maybe it was his sudden remembrance of the Eke incident or seeing the emotion in Teal's leathery, creased face, or both. He felt small and ill-prepared.

'My cows,' exhaled Teal, waving behind him with his right arm.

'Slow down now,' he said soothingly, gripping the farmer by the shoulder. The skin beneath the man's plaid shirt was as damp as his own. It soaked through the cloth and greased Jackson's fingers. 'Tell me what happened.'

The farmer's mouth opened and closed like a goldfish; his eyes unable to latch onto Jackson's gaze. After several seconds of this, he suggested, 'Show me then, if you can't get it out,' which was how he ended up following Teal across the dooryard, dust feathering their heels, towards the fence line.

As they moved, Teal seemed to regain his voice.

'The boys and I were just starting for the day when we discovered how they were. We couldn't believe it...how we could all have slept through it... The animals must have been going crazy. I don't understand it. Not even my youngest, Arlene, heard anything and she's normally up four times a night going to the bathroom. She's inside now with her mother; the poor thing is in tears.'

Jackson listened to all this as they marched through an open gate into a much greener land. He spied Teal's son, Andrew, sitting atop the fence along with the other workers the farmer employed. The colour had left his skin, making it look like pasty, grey dough. There was a puddle of vomit at his feet.

As he walked by, Andrew's blue eyes met his. His stare was sterile, yet hostile, causing Jackson's uniform to itch even more.

There's something really wrong here.

He continued to follow Teal, climbing a section where the land rose into a hill that obscured the rest of the property. As he huffed for breath it dawned on him that he should be hearing the farmer's herd by now. The air around him should be ringing with the sound of mooing, munching cattle.

It wasn't.

As Jackson crested the hill he became aware of a buzzing drone that he couldn't place at first. He noted another thing as the day's heat pressed against him. The smell of cow shit wasn't as strong as it should be. Today, there was no stench, but there was a coppery scent floating in the air.

They reached the top of the hill.

Black clouds of flies, all rippling with activity, draped the carcasses that littered the field as far as Jackson could see, the grass coated red in their blood. In various places, he made out the white tooth of a rib and the staring jelly of a dead eye beneath the mass of droning insects as he stared, open-mouthed, at the massacre before him.

Teal's field had become an abattoir.

3

Teal's cattle, two dozen of them they would later discover, hadn't just been slaughtered. They had been mutilated, their flesh stripped from their bones and scattered across the field the way a toddler discards their toys.

Later they would discover large portions of each animal missing. These were never found, but the rest of the herd was, huddled together inside one of the outbuildings, trembling. Several lay dead on the floor. Autopsies would show that their hearts had exploded. The cows that were alive made no sound when they were discovered. Nor did they for the next few days, as if each one was afraid that whoever or whatever had killed the others would eventually return.

4

Jackson was aware that Teal was crying beside him. He made no move or said anything to comfort the farmer, as he too distracted by the contents of his stomach surging upward. He bent over and vomited on his black boots.

It wasn't the sight that had done it; he had seen some nasty scenes, particularly the mess left behind in road accidents. Nor was it the drone of the flies. It was the smell, the rich, hot stink of blood and meat cooking in the midday sun like hot pennies and sweet, rotten fruit.

'Holy shit,' he gasped, chest hitching for breath. The inside of his mouth tasted rank. He looked to the farmer. 'Phil, tell me what happened. Tell me everything.'

'I dunno, Sheriff,' replied Teal. 'Like I said, we slept through the whole thing, and I dunno how that's even possible. Whoever did this tore my animals apart forty feet from my house, and we didn't hear a thing.'

Chapter One

Montague's Carnival of Delights and Terror

1

Joe Cage had considered the sheriff's words. He had thought about the empty wallet in the front of his jeans, of his bruised face, of fights in parking lots, of cheering crowds drunk on booze and the notion of seeing blood fly, of waking that morning between the roots of a maple tree, waking to dawn light and the desire to seize upon whatever the western road had to offer him.

He thought about the officer's words and turned towards the town.

2

The directions the waitress, Meryl, had given him proved accurate. He followed the road as it became the main street of a town that was little more than a grid of shops, bars, and homes until he was out the other side. It was there that he discovered where the carnival had been set up in a field by the roadside. Meryl had referred to it as Launder's Field.

Other than the small break walking through Marybell, his view had been of the flat, green Kansas landscape that seemed to stretch into the horizon. Seeing the fair for the first time was like a hallelujah moment for his mind. What impressed him most was its size, even seeing it mid-construction.

He had expected a few patchwork tents, not this.

The word legitimate sprung into his mind upon seeing the line of vividly painted wooden stalls and mechanical rides that formed a crucifix around a grassy avenue. At the crown of the crucifix rose a grand Ferris wheel, the colour of a shark's tooth. Its circumference was ringed with what looked like glass pods rather than the simple bench-like seats that he remembered being squashed into when he was a teenager.

Joe felt compelled to seek out a ride on it, to take it to the top, and having tipped the operator a few bucks, have it stop there so he could enjoy the view from what was surely the tallest structure for miles around. His chest ballooned with a floating, tingling sensation as he observed it, a mix of excitement and fear that was half memory of other rides. He could hear the calliope music that would play later when the place was ready for customers, that strange, slightly sinister jangling sound that all amusement parks blast out from unseen speakers.

Yes, he wanted to ride the Ferris wheel. More so than he wanted a job that would fill his wallet right now. But maybe there was a way to hit two birds with one stone and with that thought, Joe stepped across the field.

3

There was a gaggle of boys trying and failing to hold up a wooden archway long enough so the supporting posts could be nailed in, to the delight of the onlooking crowd. It seemed the rest of Marybell was picnicking in the field, drawn by the sudden change in the town's ecosystem: the arrival of the fair.

As Joe drew closer, grass swishing at his ankles, he heard one voice above the cacophony of hammers, generators, and laughter.

'FOR FUCK'S SAKE, STAY STILL!'

It belonged to a carny, shouting instructions so fast that the boys had little time to implement them. He wore a pair of grey trousers with red suspenders that roped over the wiry muscles of his naked torso, the colour of chestnut from too much time in the sun. Atop his head rested a grey trilby hat at a jaunty angle and on his feet was a grass-stained set of Nike Airs.

'RIGHT SIDE! YES, YOU GUYS! STOP MOVING. NOW LEFT SIDE TAKE A FEW STEPS BACK SO THIS DOESN'T LOOK LIKE A PIG'S ASS.'

Joe found himself joining the onlookers in snickering at him, though he couldn't help suspect that it was a show for the crowd, one that had been performed numerous times.

'TAKE A FEW STEPS MORE,' he yelled.

The loudest laughs were coming from a group of teenage girls at the front of the crowd, causing vague, giddy looks in their male counterparts.

'JUST A FEW STEPS MORE,' yelled the carny.

The boys holding the arch on the left-hand side shuffled backward. Joe saw the collapse coming in the slow motion rise of one of the girls. Her dress, a blue number decorated with a white flower print, billowed around her legs as she stood. Glancing back down at her friends, she smiled and giggled. Her hair was brown and honey in the golden sunlight as it spilled over her shoulders like something from a Bruce Springsteen song. She clutched something tight against her belly: a Polaroid camera.

The Springsteen girl raced out into the unoccupied grass in front of the archway, dropping to one knee like a soldier about to take a shot. Joe's legs were already moving by then, propelling him into a sprint.

The boys had enough time to register what the girl was doing. They collided against one another in a bid to strike the best pose for the picture, all of them forgetting what they held.

'WHAT ARE YOU DOING?!'

There was no humour in the carny's voice now.

A scream came from the crowd as several people rose to their feet. The archway was teetering forward. Its shadow stretched across the grass, enveloping the Springsteen girl waving the photograph her Polaroid had just ejected. Her expression slackened as the huge arch loomed over her.

Joe slammed his shoulder into her hip, sweeping her feet off the ground, his arms hugging her close while he twisted his body mid-air.

The arch hit the ground behind them with a sombre thud, kicking up a cloud of dust.

4

He had just enough time to ask, 'Are you okay?' and see her nod before the crowd smothered them. They had rolled several feet from the fallen archway and now lay in the grass, gathering breath. Then hands gripped his back, his shoulders, pulling him up, pulling him off of the Springsteen girl.

'Damn boy, that was some display of speed. You're a goddam hero,' said a man into his face while holding his arms.

It was the bare-chested carny.

'Thanks,' Joe muttered, his eyes searching the tide of bodies for the girl.

He saw her being pulled into the group of friends that she had been sitting with, some of who were crying hysterically into her dazed face. Dust coated her. He wasn't surprised to see she had lost her camera in their tumble, but the photograph was still pinched between her fingers.

'Seriously, man, that was a fine thing you did there,' said the carny.

'He wouldn't have had to do it if you had been doing your job right,' shouted a member of the crowd.

This seemed to gain a cry of agreement from those encircling him. Glancing around, Joe discovered he was trapped alongside the carny. His eyes flashed from face to face, reading hostility in each one, feeling the hair on his arms stiffen as if an electric current had passed over them. And there was a current, though not of the electric kind, that was emitting from the crowd and it was aimed at them, the carny and him. The words spoken by the town sheriff returned to his mind.

Marybell is not a kind place for strangers.

The carny hooked his thumbs into the beltline of his trousers, staring at the man who had accused him. The local stared back, dressed in dungarees and a white t-shirt yellowed with sweat, his bare shoulders burnt lobster red.

'I can only do the best I can with what I'm given,' said the carny, 'and what I was given was a bunch of boys.'

A murmur rippled through the crowd as Joe watched the accuser's blue eyes twitch in the direction of boys. It made him wonder if he had a son in that bunch.

'Now I'm not pointing fingers at anyone, especially when everyone makes mistakes,' proclaimed the carny. 'But I wasn't handling this thing when it fell; if you all recall, I was simply instructing those that were and I did not, at any point, tell them to drop it.'

The murmur was louder this time; the hostility that Joe had read before in many of the surrounding faces was dissipating. Even some of them, the girls and dungaree man included, had started drifting away.

'Now if you folks don't mind, there is a task that still needs to be completed.'

As the crowd continued to disperse, Joe addressed the carny in a whisper.

'I think you could use some help with that task,' he said.

The carny looked at him shrewdly, his eyes dark jewels underneath the brim of his trilby hat. Joe got a mental flash of how he must look, denim jeans and jacket, black boots, and a backpack coated in road dust. He hoped it hid his bruises.

'I think you might be right there,' said the carny, offering his hand. 'Arnold Kauffman, Arnie for short.'

'Joe Cage,' he said, accepting his hand.

'Callouses,' remarked Arnie as they shook. 'Good ones too; you've seen some hard labour. Think you can kick them townie boys into shape?'

'I think I can manage.'

He unslung his backpack and set to work.

5

It didn't take long in the end. Arnie Kauffman was no longer interested in putting on a show for the crowd and the townie boys were scared white. They heaved the wooden arch into the air without complaining about being bossed by him, bracing it against the support beams as he nailed it into place. A light applause erupted from the crowd as the last hammer stroke fell.

Joe stepped back to marvel at their work, wiping his hands together. Beyond it lay the rest of the carnival, all hustle and bustle, with the mighty Ferris wheel standing tall like a throne at the rear. The sight of it, a good hundred feet tall, pulled at a part of him. A part that lived in his chest and seemed to stem straight from his childhood; just for a second he caught a mental glimpse of a sun-bleached sky that was fading to pale blue, smelled fresh grass and heard a boy's laughter against a din of calliope music and knew that it had belonged to him. The imagined scent of sugared apples, salted popcorn, and fried meat sprung upon him as he stared, his vision blurring at the tug of memory.

Joe did not think of his past often - he made an effort not to - but sometimes the past came back at the smallest of sights or sounds. The carnival was not a small sight but one that threatened to torpedo the dam he had built in his mind over the past few months on the road. It shocked him to learn that there were good feelings behind him, even if they were distant and vague.

One of the boys approached him, his hair a spill of dark copper, yanking Joe out of his daydream.

'Thanks, mister, for saving our Karen,' he said.

Joe noticed that there were similarities to the Springsteen girl in the boy's freckled face. Before he could reply, the boy darted off.

A harsh jet of air shot out through Joe's lips. His left hand crept to his face, brushing along his jaw with trembling fingers.

He could feel it all: his past like some unfathomable violent tempest crashing against the barrier in his mind, relentless. Despite the good the carnival conjured up in him, there were bad things that existed behind there, memories that, if free, could flatten him. Even now he could feel his throat closing, making it harder to draw air as his past beat to be free.

Joe blinked rapidly, a stone weight in his stomach as he forced the imagery away and down, away and down, thinking only of a black canvas as he sucked dusty air through his narrow windpipe. The bodies in the crowd around him reduced to ghosts on the edges of his senses.

Eventually, by sheer force of will, the panic that had been rising in him began to seep away. His trachea relaxed, allowing him to drink air once more.

He shot a glance in the carny's direction. Arnie was finished having bills snatched out of his hands by the boys and was wandering over.

Be cool, he thought, his nerves electrified. *Be cool. You need the work, so don't blow this by coming off as a nut job.*

The carny joined him in admiring their handy work. 'Welcome to Montague's Carnival of Delights and Terror,' he said, reading the writing that was stamped in gold on the arch.

'Who's Montague?'

'He would be the leader of our little family,' replied Arnie.

Joe could feel the man's eyes on him, scrutinising, assessing him. This was another part of the drifting game that he thought of as begging for scraps.

'You're a townie,' said the carny, 'but you're not from this town. Nor are you from Kansas.'

Joe's head snapped around to stare, seeing a small mischievous grin on his face.

'When you've traveled this fair country as much as I have, you learn how to tell these things. Heck, I've been around so much I can tell a person's surname sometimes just by looking at them.'

I hope that's not true, he thought. *I hope you can't tell where I'm from and if you can, please don't ask about it, because I won't answer you. I'll just walk away, no matter how much I need the money.*

'I suppose you're looking for a job?'

'I am.'

'Well,' he said and tipped the brim of his trilby back, 'we have a strict hiring policy here. We don't mind taking on a few lads and lasses wherever we camp to help out with the few odd jobs, like putting this son of a bitch up. But for taking someone on for the more in-depth work, we are pickier. That being said, after what you did today, not only saving that young girl's life - which is what you did, don't get bashful about that now - you also saved our necks. I'll still have to talk to the boss man about it, but I think I can guarantee you some work, just as long as you tell me honestly about that shiner you're sporting.'

Joe let out a snort of laughter, his eyes leaving Arnie's to stare through the entrance at the fair. As he did, he thought about that memory, that honey-glazed sky. It was safe to think such thoughts now; the ocean of memory still churned threateningly but it did so deep within him.

Joe found he wanted the work. He always did when begging for scraps; there was something in him that ached to prove himself, even to people like the owner of the roadhouse in the next town

31

over who had watched with everyone else as two redneck boys had taken him on with their fists.

Yet it was more than that this time.

Staring at that Ferris wheel, its metal as white as a shark's tooth, he wanted to be part of this carnival. His desire was simple and urgent.

Later on, Joe would be able to articulate internally that what he wanted was to be closer to his memory of attending such a place. But in the moment, he was lost to his want and so turned to the carny and answered him honestly.

'I got into a fight with a couple of young boys in the next town over,' he said. 'I didn't start it, just finished it. This was when I was working at Dylan's Roadhouse, pulling drinks, mopping up the messes people leave behind, you know, that sort of thing. Nothing major. Those two boys came in every weekend, just eyeing me and drinking too much. I guess they didn't like what they saw or knew I was from out of town and took offense to me serving the local crowd.'

'Did no one try to step in and put a stop to it?' asked Arnie.

His question caught Joe by surprise, mostly because he had never thought to think someone would.

'No, sir,' he answered. 'Friday night fisticuffs seemed to be a tradition for the place. The owner used to have me wade in when someone couldn't stand anymore. I guess after four weeks, it was my turn in the ring, though I was the only guy who worked there in that time that was ever in a fight.'

'Hate and fear, kid, that's what it's called,' said Arnie, his dark eyes glinting once more from beneath his hat. 'Most people are scared of the unknown and most people are stupid. They get to hate their place in the world and what stops them from hating themselves is to hate those that stick out from them. You learn all about it in this line of work, believe me. We've been bum-rushed out of so many hick towns I've lost count. Anyway, that's glum talk, and we're in the business of bringing a little delight into the world. Grab your stuff and follow me, we're going to meet the boss.'

6

Arnold led him under the arch and along the avenue of grass that split the carnival. To Joe's right and left were finished stalls sporting names such as 'The Ring Toss', 'Shoot The Star', and 'The Duck Pond'. Each one was painted in flamboyant colours and jeweled in multicoloured lights. In his need to see them all, he almost collided with two carnies carrying a wooden beam.

'Watch it,' snapped one of them.

Joe apologized even though the pair had already vanished into the hubbub. Arnie slipped him a sly grin over his shoulder.

'We've got two major rides here,' he said. 'I'm sure you've already noticed The Whirl and Journey Through the Crypt. Despite being in charge of that little show out front, looking after the second ride is my real job; she's my ride and she is one bad motherfucker. Most customers favor The Whirl, especially those looking for a bit of heavy petting; you can keep her, that's what I say. I prefer my rides to instill a little terror in the customers. There she is.'

They were halfway down the fair now and Joe had already noticed the structure that Arnie was guiding him to. It was a rectangular building painted a dark, jungle green with a ramp at the front that snaked back on itself, leading to a platform where there were several carts. One of the carts rocketed forward into the yawning mouth of a fanged clown on the left-hand side of the platform, doing so with a squeal of hydraulics and a whoosh of air.

'Beautiful, isn't she?'

Joe agreed, though he felt a small squeeze of terror in his heart at seeing the massive ride. He had never been good with rollercoasters or ghost trains.

Arnie led him to an RV parked behind the base of The Whirl, which according to him served as the owner, Montague's, mobile home and office. There were similar RVs and even several forty-foot lorries positioned behind the fairground proper. Beyond them was the rest of Launder's Field, occupied by several derelict-looking farm buildings and one well-kept house off to the eastern side. Woodlands bordered the field behind The Whirl.

Joe felt a pang of disappointment in leaving the fairgrounds. Transitioning behind the scenes was like exiting Narnia, but instead of returning to the world he knew, he was able to see how the magic worked. Close by a generator puttered, filling the air with the cloying scent of burning fuel. Carnies walked here and there, their attentions elsewhere.

'Montague is known for having a bit of a silver tongue,' Arnie informed him. 'Be honest the way you were with me about that shiner of yours and you'll be fine. The man may talk all poetic, but he can smell bullshit from a mile off.'

That was all the advice Arnie had for him before Joe found himself thrust inside the RV. He just had time to recognise that this particular motor home was much grander in appearance and size than the others dotted about.

They were welcomed by the bellow of a raised voice.

'I did not let my field out to the entire population of Marybell,' yelled the unknown speaker.

It took a few moments for Joe's eyes to adjust to the gloomy interior. The light was dim even though there were several lamps on, their glow the colour of weak tea. The walls were lined with what looked like movie posters; on closer inspection, he realised they were past advertisements for the carnival. Smoky blue trails clouded the air, making his throat dry; through it, he made out two figures.

One sat behind a desk on the other side of the RV, facing Arnie and Joe. The other stood before it, a squat, barrel-shaped man in a white shirt and dark trousers.

The man shot them a glance, allowing them a brief look at his mustached face. His cheeks and the bald pate of his head gleamed with sweat from the RV's sultry interior. His nose looked like a burst raspberry.

'Well, Montague,' said the man, returning his gaze to the man behind the desk. 'What do you have to say for yourself?'

If the man's tone offended Montague, he gave no sign. Even Arnie continued to stand nonchalantly, though Joe sensed something tighten within the carny, as if he was offended by the man's raised voice.

'I'm sorry, Mr. Launder,' said Montague. 'I'm confused as to what matter you're referring to, exactly.'

The carnival owner's voice was polite and cordial.

35

'The entire town is out there trampling up and down on my land. They're ruining it,' said Launder, casting one arm out to the RV wall.

'Mr. Launder, the people of Marybell are excited,' said Montague cheerfully. He reclined back in his seat, his grey eyes twinkling alongside the silver in his beard reminding Joe of a jolly store Santa. He wore a slate-coloured suit, not expensive, but not too shabby either.

'We can hardly be blamed for the actions of the townspeople. They've come to see us, to see the rides, the stalls, and that's no bad thing. It means commerce for us, and not just of the financial kind. Montague's Carnival of Delights and Terror is more than just the exchange of money for a few cheap thrills. My company aims to create memories that will last a lifetime for those who visit, and you get to be part of that memory, Mr. Launder. Years from now, your people will associate those memories with you.'

Time seemed to stretch as Launder considered his words. Words that were so similar in sentiment to those that Arnie had used to describe his ride, that Joe wondered if they were part of some sort of rehearsed statement.

He already had an opinion of Launder and that opinion was not positive. The man reeked of sleazy motivations. It was the raised voice he had used as they had entered the RV. The anger in it had not rung entirely true; there was a falseness to it and something more, a searching type of greed underneath.

Was there falseness in Montague's speech?

He didn't think so; he thought the carnival owner truly believed what he had said. But he also thought that Montague had Launder's character pegged even more than he did. He was appealing

36

to his ego in a specific way that Joe fumbled over in his mind. It didn't take him long to understand.

He had only been in the same room with Launder for five minutes and thought of him as a sleaze. What did the rest of the town think of him?

An image sprung on him of dull eyes staring out of enraged faces. It was the memory of the crowd earlier when they had formed a ring around Arnie and him. The flesh of his arms crawled with unease in remembering.

All it had taken was a few seconds and a mistake made by a couple of young boys that had left every face rejoicing in the summer afternoon sun slack and lifeless. It bought to mind a Ray Bradbury story he had read as a teenager called 'The Crowd'. At the time, he had not found the images of a staring crowd frightening.

Now he did.

And it made him wonder what it would be like for a person like Launder to live in such a town, where people's expressions can flip on a dime. Where their energy could change from joyous celebration to threatening hostility.

He looked to Arnie, who continued to stare at the two men, a smug smile on his face. What Launder said next caused it to sag at the corners.

'And do you think I care about the daydreams of some dumb cowpokes?' asked Launder, before laughing.

The good humour disappeared from Montague's face.

'You are most definitely a gypsy with that sly talk of yours. The only other men I heard can talk as sweet as gypsies are the sissy kind that lives in the big cities nowadays. Say, you're not one of them, are you?'

Montague simply stared at Launder, ruefully grinning back at him. It no longer touched his eyes, which had grown dim.

'Doesn't matter, nor do the hicks in this town. It's money that matters.'

'I was under the impression that you do not use the land. That you are the owner of several chicken farms and you outsource the running of those farms to others elsewhere,' said Montague.

'I see you've done your research,' replied Launder. 'You're smarter than you pretend to be. I am exactly what you say, but I may come to sell this place in the future, and I don't want to be disadvantaged by you lot being here.'

'Carnies,' corrected Montague.

'Huh?' said Launder.

'We are carnies not "you lot" or "gypsies".' The humour was back in his voice but there was a barb within it now. 'How much money would cover the potential damages, do you think?'

Launder must have recognised the carnival owner's tone because when he spoke again it was without his previous brashness.

'Well...I think another hundred dollars should be enough to cover it.'

'A hundred it is.'

The carnival owner tossed several bills from a drawer to Launder's side of the desk. The stout man snatched them up, counted them, and shoved his prize inside his trouser pocket.

'That certainly puts my mind at ease,' Launder said.

'I'm sure it does,' replied Montague. 'Please see yourself out.' Joe watched Launder pause, his mouth open, his body swaying on the balls of his feet. There was a sense that something had been achieved here, but not by him. That despite his success in gaining the money, the loss of his confidence towards Montague made the victory bitter. In the end, he seemed to decide it wasn't worth it, for his mouth clamped shut and he exited the RV without a backward glance.

'Slimy piece of shit,' said Arnie as soon as the door was closed.

'Truer words have never been spoken,' said Montague.

'I wanted to rip that guy's throat out,' snarled Arnie.

Montague let out a hiccup-like laugh.

'Now, now...you should pity those that put all their value in fragile pieces of paper. Launder knows nothing about living. Anyway, who have you brought into my home today and why?'

Joe held the carnival owner's grey eyes and tried to appear job-worthy.

'His name is Joe Cage and he's looking for work,' explained Arnie, then went on to add, 'He's not from town.'

'Aren't we all,' said Montague. 'And what skills do you possess that make you a desirable employee?'

'For one, he's quick on his feet,' Arnie interrupted. 'Joe has already saved us from a scandal and being bum-rushed out of this town.'

The two silver caterpillars that Montague had for eyebrows rose as Arnie explained.

'I was in the right place to see what was going to happen,' said Joe, his face burning red.

'Having seen the crowd out there this morning, I'm sure there were a few who were able to see what was going to happen,' remarked Montague.

'Yep, they were, but Joe here was the only one that moved his ass to do anything about it,' added Arnie.

'Did he now?'

Joe opened his mouth to speak and found he had no clue as to what to say.

Arnie looked from him to Montague with a smirk, and Joe felt part of his brain twang. It did so with a lightness that rippled throughout his entire skull as he watched the two men stare at one other, seeming to continue their dialogue wordlessly. When Arnie turned back to him, the feeling was gone.

'What? Are you seriously trying to stop me bragging about you? Do you want the job or not?' he said.

Joe shook his head from side to side, trying to clear the cobwebs that seemed to fill it.

'I want the job,' he said. 'Mr. Montague, I'm a hard worker. I'm good with my hands; I worked on building sites in Jefferson City and I can pretty much guarantee you that there isn't anything I can't help construct, and if there is, I'm willing to learn how to do so, sir.'

Again, another look passed between the two that left him feeling light-headed.

'Jefferson City, I know that neck of the woods,' said Montague. 'There are a good lot of miles between there and here. You hitching, or do you have a car?'

'Hitching, though mainly I've been walking the last few days.'

'And where exactly are you hitching to, Mr. Cage?'

It was a question no other employer had ever asked him. They had wanted to know where he had come from just to be sure that he wasn't running from the law or anything. But as to where he was going, they didn't care. They only cared about how much work they could get out of him before he moved on.

Joe was used to lying about his past, but he had never before stopped to consider where he was going.

'I dunno…I guess I'll stop walking when there's no more land in front of me.'

The two carnies stared at him contemplatively and he tensed, waiting for them to break into laughter. They didn't, but he still jumped when Montague slammed the palm of his right hand on the desk.

'Now that's something I haven't seen in this country for an age…Pioneer spirit,' he said. '"I'll stop walking when there's no more land in front of me." I couldn't have said it better myself. That's exactly how I feel about this place. I don't think there's much further to discuss. It seems to me that you have impressed Arnold here and with that, I might add you have also impressed me. You're hired. Though, just one last thing, how did you come by that bruise?

Joe's eyes glanced at Arnie, whose face betrayed nothing.

'I got jumped at my last job working in a bar in the town over. The locals there didn't take too kindly to strangers,' he answered.

He stood waiting for the guillotine to drop.

'Arnold and I know all about that kind of thing,' said Montague. 'I like you, Joe. You interest me. The job pays nineteen dollars a day plus food and accommodation. Arnold will show you the ropes and if you're good enough when we've turned a profit in this little town, you might be welcome to join us as we move on. We look after one another here at the carnival; it allows us to stay out of trouble from narrow-minded townies such as whoever it was that did that to your eye. Maybe you'll want to join us when the time comes to leave.'

Joe recalled all he had seen walking through the fair earlier. He already didn't want to leave.

Chapter Two

Shadow People

1

After radioing it in, Jackson prodded down the hill with knees that wanted to fold in on themselves. The reek of spoiled meat stalked him, burning in his nostrils; it seemed to be stitched into his clothes. His stomach did another somersault, though thankfully this time without spewing. Still, he had to grab hold of the fence post once he had reached it and breathe deeply.

When the nausea passed, he raised his head to find Andrew Teal and the other employees observing him. All shared the same expressions of disillusioned horror and what he had come to recognise as a "What now?" look. A look anyone in any position of authority knew.

Being on the receiving end of it made him suck up what he was feeling and stand straighter. The action alone sent an echo reverberating within his skull back to his previous thoughts about the young man on the road.

'Is everyone okay?'

The older employees, all neighbours of Teal's, nodded their heads. Andrew did not; his stare remained aggressively blank.

You're nicer to them, accused the voice in his head. He ignored it, squishing it down inside, telling himself he had a job to do.

'Okay, the land beyond that hill is effectively a crime scene, so I don't want anyone going up there. In the meantime, I'm going to need statements from all of you as to your part in the events leading up to the discovery of the cattle until right now. So start thinking of what you did and when you did it.'

'Sheriff, we didn't have anything to do with it,' whined one of them.

'I know you didn't, Dave, but it's procedure,' he shot back.

Still, Andrew persisted to stare.

'You sure you're okay, kid?'

What Teal's son said next caused the flesh of his back to crawl. The sensation was unnaturally cold in contrast to the day's phenomenal heat.

'Arlene saw something last night.' The sixteen-year old's voice was a croak.

Jackson's gaze drifted to the sunflower-coloured farmhouse, then back to Andrew. 'Your dad said she didn't hear anything.'

'She did, she was just too upset to say anything this morning,' replied Andrew.

2

Arlene Teal was a lanky eight-year-old with the same Teal-blonde hair, except hers was all corkscrews. She had a notepad in her lap as she sat on the sofa in the living room of the spacious farmhouse, her mother, Angela, beside her. She had the same corkscrew curls as her daughter.

Like most children, she struggled to look him in the eye; he was a stranger, after all. The rest of the family observed the scene from the kitchen, including the young girl's grandparents, who lived under the same roof. They kept their conversation to a dull murmur.

'Your brother said you saw something last night,' said Jackson in the best leading voice he could summon.

Arlene squirmed in her seat, looking to her mother.

'Go on, tell the sheriff now.'

'I don't want to be in trouble,' replied Arlene, her voice regressing to that of a much younger child.

'Why would you be in trouble?' Jackson smiled. 'Do you think I'm going to arrest you?'

'No,' sniggered Arlene. 'My daddy would stop you.'

This caused her grandparents to chuckle.

'She means because she was out of bed at night. We try to persuade her from getting up because Phil's mom, Maura, is a light sleeper, on account of her condition.'

It was well known in Marybell that Maura Teal suffered from a chronic illness that left her in a wheelchair and in constant pain. A condition she embraced with the good humour she had expressed throughout her life. She was considered a saint community wide.

'You won't be in any trouble, dear,' assured Angela. 'Tell the sheriff what you saw.'

'I saw this.'

Arlene Teal presented her notepad to him, the pages of which were filled with drawings, some in colour, some not. The one she showed him was done in lead.

For the second time that day, he felt his skin crawl, even as he struggled to understand what the girl had made. At first he thought he was looking at a hill with a flat top, only there were holes dotted around the base. The longer he looked, the more he realised he was seeing bodies, bodies all piled on top of one another as if they were all clambering for a prize, like something from a cartoon. Only this didn't look funny; maybe it was the grey lead pencil that had been used to draw the scene against the stark background of the white page, but it looked haunting. There was a captured sense of frenzy about it.

'Where did you see this from?'

'From the bathroom window,' replied Arlene

'Are these people? Did you recognise any of them?'

Even as he asked this second question, the girl was shaking her head.

'No, they were shadows, shadow people.'

Chapter Three

Big Sissy

1

Joe Cage didn't believe in fate; life as he saw it was a stream of random bullshit. After May 10, 1983 – the day the Greys came to the carnival – he started to reconsider his philosophy; that the random bullshit, both good and bad, wasn't so random after all. That would all come later, as the terror coursed through him, when it was too late to change anything.

2

He met them underneath the archway where he was exchanging cash for tickets, recognising Meryl from the diner instantly by her copper hair. His head ached from a hangover gained from drinking around the campfire the night before. One of the best evenings in recent memory as he got to know Arnie and some of the other carnies, listening to their fiendish banter.

'Kid, if you want a future in this business, you'll stick with me,' said Arnie, his speech slurred slightly.

'Don't listen to this old donkey, he's a fool,' said Carmen Garcia, the carnival's fortune teller and the most beautiful woman Joe had ever seen.

'Hung like a donkey is what I am,' replied Arnie.

'Aye, one with a lame dick, you dirty fucker,' Carmen shot back.

This had sent everyone sat around the campfire into howls of laughter.

It seemed poetic to him then that as he worked with this growing feeling of thankfulness that he should meet Meryl – the woman who had helped by directing him to the carnival. She had been kind to him in a way that was small, yet rare, so rare he realised it was the only kindness he had been shown in his entire time on the road.

He had been speechless, sat on his stool at the diner's counter. And in seeing her wade towards him, her attention on the sullen-looking teenage boy accompanying her, while restraining a set of blonde twins from running off, he decided to repay it with his own kindness.

'Henry, it's not going to happen,' Joe heard her say, speaking to the teen. 'No matter how much you moan and groan, it doesn't change the fact that we can't afford … *Ben stop doing that.*'

Joe ignored all this and focused on the family member who was leading the party. She was perhaps five years old, with hair like straw tumbleweed, skin as fair as milk, and big royal blue eyes. She held a ragged teddy bear in the crook of her left elbow while showing no signs of unease as she stepped purposely ahead of her family to meet him.

'Hello, little lady, are you excited to go on some rides?' Joe asked, squatting down to her level.

She did not recoil as most children that morning had when being addressed by a stranger. Instead, her lips parted in a smile, revealing a missing front tooth.

'I am,' she giggled.

Her family noticed her reply and immediately stopped squabbling.

'And what ride are you looking most forward to?' he asked.

'The ghost ride,' she said in a hushed voice full of vehemence.

A frown creased Joe's brow. Before his feelings could articulate themselves into understandable thoughts, the twins delivered a high-pitched chant.

'Big sissy, big sissy, big sissy.'

Gooseflesh erupted at the nape of Joe's neck at the recurrence of the phrase Launder had used the day before; especially hearing the twins reciting it in their strange singsong voices was like getting a bucket of ice thrown over his head. It chilled his skin even with the day's scorching heat.

The girl scowled and stamped her right foot.

'No, I am not,' she yelled.

'Boys,' hissed their mother, 'what did I say about teasing your sister?'

The twins fell silent, stealing a glance at each other and grinning. Meryl's eyes found Joe's and she gave him an embarrassed grin.

It communicated to him in a plea, *'I'm a good mother. I'm doing my best.'*

'Well, look at you,' she said. 'You made it.'

'Yeah, I did.'

He was aware that Arnie was probably listening close by.

'I was worried the sheriff had said something to you to put you off our little town,' said Meryl.

Joe's smile didn't falter but inside his head, he felt a twist of discomfort. It had been an entire twenty-four hours since he had last thought about the sheriff's words, the contentment he had felt for his place making him forget.

'Not at all.'

49

'It seemed pretty serious,' she probed.

'He was just making sure that I wasn't a serial killer or anything,' said Joe, laughing.

Meryl joined him while her children looked on in bewilderment. She caught her daughter's gaze and said, 'Lily, this is...'

'Joe, Joe Cage.'

'Lily, this is Joe, someone I served yesterday at work,' Meryl said to her family. 'And this is Ben, Clay, and Henry. We're the Greys.'

'Nice to meet you all, and your mom did more than that yesterday,' he told them. 'She pointed me in the direction of this place.'

'So it wasn't just me who recognised your worthiness,' said Arnie. 'Oh, I'm sorry did I say worthy, I meant worthlessness.'

The family chuckled; even the teenager managed a flicker of a smile.

'I just felt sorry for him,' remarked Meryl.

'As did I,' added Arnie.

'There was just something so... sad about him,' Meryl added.

This time everyone laughed and as they did, Joe felt the chill begin to leave him. The day was too hot, too bright, and their laughter too full of promise to wallow on such morbid feelings.

'Okay, okay, okay,' said Joe. 'Are you going to buy tickets, or are you going to abuse me all day long?'

Meryl bought five tickets that amounted to nine dollars. As Joe handed her back a dollar change he said to Lily, 'I can't speak for the ghost ride myself – it's not my cup of tea, as the English say – but I heavily recommend The Whirl.'

Joe swept his arms around – *ta da* – to showcase the grandiose Ferris wheel at the carnival's rear.

'That's because Joe here is a big sissy,' said Arnie.

The children all giggled together, even the stroppy teenager. However, Meryl's face had brightened with awe and suddenly he saw the young woman she used to be, perhaps one whose yearly calendar was spent in anticipation of the fairs that came to town.

'Now that's something,' she said in a half-whisper.

'Speaking from personal experience...it is,' said Joe.

Arnie had claimed drunkenly that a ride on The Whirl was part of every new recruit's initialisation process. So he had enjoyed taking a turn around the ring's wheel alongside Daisy Hill, another new employee, as the sun set.

'The test is whether you survive,' Arnie had said at the time. 'Who knows if they've built the damn thing right?'

They weren't the greatest words of encouragement for Joe, but he took it as a good sign that Arnie, Carmen, and Montague would be joining them on the ride's inaugural spin. The land had been dark by then, the horizon a mosaic of scarlets, oranges, and yellows. The jovial conversation that had followed them into one of The Whirl's cabins fell mute at the sight of it, the horizon like something from a child's dream.

It would have been a perfect moment if not for Montague.

'Can't beat a Kansan sunset. Is this your first time seeing such a sight, Joe? As Arnie says, you're a townie, but not from this town'.

He had been asking similar, not-so-subtle questions all night and Joe had managed to avoid divulging too much, yet at that moment, his head

51

experiencing that lightheaded feeling, he had answered truthfully.

'No, it's not, though it's the first time I've seen the sunset from this height.'

It was a simple enough answer that hardly gave away anything. Still, Joe had not liked how easily it had spilled out of him, as if in his distracted state Montague had gotten past the defences in his mind.

'Thank you,' Meryl said in a conspiratorial whisper as she passed him.

Joe blinked, realised where he was, and smiled at the kind woman.

'You're welcome,' he returned.

'Lily's heard nothing but talk about that ghost ride for a week from my boys and between you and me, I think it's a little too old for her. Mentioning the wheel might save me from a crying match'.

She was gone, trotting after her three youngest who had exploded in separate directions. Joe watched them, his mind still on Montague's inquires.

'You did well there,' said Arnie, lighting his pipe. 'You don't fake it and you're respectful; customers appreciate that. Though the real praise should go to the genius that hired you.'

'According to Carmen, that genius is nothing but a fraud,' said Joe.

'She said that, did she?' replied Arnie.

'Yep, and a drunk,' added Joe. The humour in his voice betrayed him.

'Well, I must say, I have misjudged you,' said Arnie. 'You clearly are a bastard.'

His lips curled into a smile around the end of his pipe's mouthpiece. His dark eyes flashed at him underneath his trilby. Joe laughed at him heartedly.

'Listen, it's slacking off here,' said Arnie. 'I better go see if the boys at my ride need a hand; usually they do. Plus I want to make sure everything is running smoothly for that little girl. Why don't you pop in with Lou at the Toss, just to make sure everything's okay? He's a lazy shit and will have left all the work for that new girl, Daisy.'

Joe nodded and with the enthusiasm of the newly hired, sped off.

3

Joe knew guys like Lou Fritz in every job he had ever had. Despite only being employed at the carnival for twenty-four hours, he had already pinpointed Lou as such an individual. That Daisy Hill had been assigned to work with him had made Joe wince.

Lou had not only abstained from riding on The Whirl with them, but he had also vacated the campfire last night. This was after he had welcomed Joe by glaring over the firelight and saying, 'So you're one of the fresh meat? A little word of advice, stay the fuck away from me. I've got no time or patience to take you by the hand when you fuck up, and you will fuck up, fresh meat.'

With that he had lurched off into the dark, clutching a bottle of Jim Beam.

The grass that had slushed at Joe's ankles yesterday was trampled flat today as he made his way up the Fairway - the name the carnies called the main avenue throughout the carnival. The day was hot and made hotter by the tight press of bodies. Yet that cold sensation returned to his neck.

Perhaps it was in remembering Lou's sneering face as firelight danced in his eyes. Or the memory of Lily's brothers, their voices calling as if trapped at the bottom of a well, cold and cruel, saying, *'Big sissy, big sissy.'*

What had they been harping on about? It was the ride, the ghost ride. You're just freaked out because Lily talked about it, the one you don't like.

It was true he had no love for Journey Through the Crypt after having reluctantly endured its two minute and forty-three second ride time with his eyes shut. Unfortunately, this had been with Daisy Hill, who had screamed and whooped for its entire duration. She had hopped out of the coffin-themed cart used to propel them around the track like a ballerina. He had staggered, his body feeling like a closed fist.

But it was more than that, an internal voice whispered to him.

That was true. There was simply something threatening about how the ride seemed to loom over the Fairway. It felt alive and watchful and forever hungry.

Plus those twins were as freaky-looking as those two in that Kubrick film.

This thought made Joe chuckle. As he did, he felt whatever bind in those remembered words loosen again. Nightmares could be laughed at in the sunlight. It was in the dead of night, when you were alone in the open space of the Kansas farmland, that made what was once laughable feel real.

'Roll up, roll up, folks,' catcalled Daisy Hill's familiar voice.

With a smirk, he squeezed down a gap between two stalls, his shoulders brushing their tarp skins. The smell and taste of ancient dust became displaced by his presence, making him cough.

54

Once through, Joe entered The Ring Toss by the rear entrance.

Lou Fritz sat reading a wrinkled copy of Playboy in the Toss's backroom, despite the noise from the crowd outside. He was dressed as he had been last night, like someone from The Ramones. His lanky body reminded Joe of a grasshopper, especially his legs, which were strangely long and thin inside his tight jeans.

He did not look up as Joe swept by; instead, his horse-like face remained concentrated on whatever bliss the magazine offered.

Do you read that for the articles? thought Joe.

The sun blinded him as he stepped onto The Ring Toss's stage.

'This is my unglamorous assistant,' proclaimed Daisy Hill's voice somewhere to his left. 'He's all we could afford.'

A scatter of chuckles followed her words.

As his vision adjusted, he saw that the people were three lines deep before the stall, their faces amused and eager. Daisy stood to his left, beaming a smile that was as bright as the sun.

'That's it, wave to the lovely people,' Daisy instructed.

Without realising it, he had raised his left hand, palm outward.

'He's a little slow,' she remarked.

The audience laughed louder this time. Remarkably, he found he was grinning to the point where his cheeks hurt.

'So, who is gonna step up and try their luck?' challenged Daisy.

Five children leaped forward and slapped their parents' change on the counter. Daisy spoke to each of them, joking that they were trying to pull one over her by not having enough coins. They in

55

turn fell enchanted with this adult who somehow possessed a kindred youthful spirit.

Lily was amongst them. She waved to Joe after Daisy passed her. He returned it and internally wished her luck.

'What are you doing here?' whispered Daisy.

The kids had started to toss rings as their parents cheered encouragement.

'Arnie thought you might need a hand,' he whispered back.

'As if,' was her response.

Joe liked Daisy immensely. It was hard not to. Like him, she had come out of the great emptiness of the American highways. By luck, they had separately happened upon Marybell and employment with the carnival.

For the next twenty minutes, they worked together. Joe followed her lead, learning exactly why she was given this job. She put on a pantomime for her customers, where she was the beautiful and mystical conductor, her dreadlocks like fine gold sweeping her shoulders and neck with each strut of the stage, whereas he was the clumsy assistant, the Igor to her Frankenstein, trudging behind. As he counted coins, she would claim he was miscounting or even stealing before slapping his butt, to the audience's delight.

The result was over thirty dollars in change.

'Not too bad,' Joe commented.

'Think they'll pay us by the commission?'

As if by magic, Lou appeared from behind the scenes. 'Not likely,' he said and swept the tin of change from them. Then he was gone back to the gloomy back room.

'Friendly as ever,' said Joe, though not too loudly.

Their audience had already moved further up the Fairway, allowing them a reprieve. Still, he didn't want Lou to hear him. The man seemed like the type to take it personally. Usually, he would have said nothing, only Daisy was someone he felt he could be genuine with.

Joe liked to think that's why he lingered at the stall. That it had nothing to do with the small piece of dread he felt about joining Arnie at The Crypt. Being with Daisy was like working in sunlight, only if that sunlight teased him constantly.

'I better get back to Arnie,' he said eventually.

'Sure thing,' replied Daisy, her eyes on the customers.

Joe wanted to say more to her then, to make up for his silence last night at the campfire. Daisy had taken over the conversation then.

'I'm from Tennessee originally,' she had informed them all. 'I walked out of there the day my momma married and invited my step-daddy to live with us. I never knew who my real daddy was; my guess is he got tired of her. The reason I say that he got tired of her and not us both is because I grew up around her. I won't say the woman raised me; more like she put up with me. Momma was too busy living the nightlife and bar crawling to be much of a parent. I can't imagine her being much of a wife. So I felt no great loss when I left, especially seeing as how my step-daddy's eyes followed me about the room before he moved in. He's fifteen years her junior, which made him four years older than me. So I shoved my stuff into a bag, took what savings I had, and put on these cowboy boots and started walking. Been on the road now for two years and it's mostly been great. Met a few men with eyes like my step-daddy, but

I've always had a gift for knowing when to move on from a place, so life hasn't been too bad to me.'

Joe had stared over at her from across the campfire, his mouth dry at the casual way she had spoken. It was as if her past was something she could shrug off with no lingering effects, no scars. Her attitude fascinated him.

Nor was he the only one that was impressed.

Montague had leaned closer to the edge of the fire, his eyes on Daisy with a smug quality that Joe had not seen in then before. It did not belong to the person he had met in the RV, a man who had presented himself like Father Christmas.

No one else had seen it; the carnies were too busy fawning over Daisy. It was like he had caught Montague in the middle of a private revelry.

Then the carny king's eyes had flicked onto him.

The red muscle in Joe's core had tightened even though Montague's gaze was gentle. Still, his face had told Joe it was his turn to tell his story. As if by some telepathic cue, all the others had begun looking to him.

'What about you, Joe?' Montague had asked. 'What's your story?'

Joe had told them nothing more than he already had. It had been difficult, for the lightheadedness was upon him as he parried and deflected each question the carnies asked, but he had refused to allow the dam that he had created in his head to be breached. When that became clear to the carnies, they had ended their interrogations, leaving an awkward air over the campfire.

Carmen had rallied them down another conversational avenue. As their attentions turned away, he felt a set of eyes on him. Daisy's eyes, staring at him with a look of sorrow that said she understood his need for privacy.

Joe Cage opened his mouth and found he could not articulate the thoughts in his head about that look she had given him the night before. Daisy did not notice; her attention was on the passing flow of customers.

'Listen,' he said, coughing. 'Fancy grabbing some lunch later on?'

'With you, okay, but if Youssef The Strongman asks me, you're eating by yourself,' she said. 'That's one ride I'm eager to try.'

Joe left the stall laughing and only little put out. Daisy's catcalls followed him as he trundled down the Fairway.

4

Something was wrong. Lily knew it was by how her stomach felt like bruised thunderclouds. She was finally at the ride, the ride she thought of as hers: Journey Through the Crypt. But it wasn't how she had imagined it.

The air, which had been scented with a thousand sweet things, now smelled greased and electrified. It caught in her throat as she swayed from foot to foot. Her view was all jeans and legs. She could hear shouts and the clump of machinery through the jangle of Jack In The Box music, which blared at a volume that made her head hurt.

Her Momma's hand held hers, its grip hot and sweaty.

Looking up, her Momma's face seemed a hundred feet away. It had that red-faced look like a blister about to explode.

59

'It goes at a hundred miles an hour,' Ben had announced at the kitchen table that morning.

'That's like, swoosh,' Clay, his twin, said, emphasising the sound by swinging his fist through the air.

'I know... and... and you know it does loop-to-loops.'

'No way!' exclaimed Clay with holy relevance.

'That's nice, dear,' said Momma in her distracted voice. She was frying bacon for their father, who had yet to rise from their bed.

Lily had smelled the familiar stink of beer in their bedroom on the way past that morning. It was a yellow smell that made her think of rotten food.

She loved her Momma and Daddy, but she didn't like that smell. There was something untrustworthy about it to her. So she did what she had always done on such mornings, which was to concentrate on something else.

Loop-to-loops.

Lily's brain latched onto the idea of Journey Through The Crypt, imagining the rush of cool air over her body as she rode the ride, her arms aloft like a set of wings while she screamed joyously until her tummy hurt.

She couldn't scream now, though.

Standing in the sweltering queue beside her family, her throat grew tight, like someone had gripped her there and was beginning to squeeze. Lily could feel her heart beating rapidly in her chest, her temples, and even at the ends of her fingertips. The world of legs around her seemed to grow closer, to shrink against her. The lights overhead, flashing yellows and reds, became blurred. Using the muscles in her shoulders and tummy, she attempted to suck in what small

60

amount of oily air she could. She did this in a series of hitching breathes while tugging at her mother's hand, tears welling in her eyes.

5

The queue for the Crypt snaked back on itself. Joe scanned it; various expressions of excitement and apprehension beamed back.

Why not? he thought. *The carnival has come to town.*

That thought alone was a paradox to him. In the last couple of months, Joe had learned that small towns resented, even feared, outsiders. He hadn't needed the sheriff of Marybell to tell him that.

Except the carnival was different.

Looking into the faces in the queue, seeing the emotions there said that the carnival wasn't tolerated, it was embraced. And why wouldn't it be? It brought entertainment and thrills, delights and terror, as Montague had said to him.

The carnival broke the monotony of small-town life.

He was also aware of how quickly that could change. He had seen as much yesterday when Arnie was being harassed for the near disaster with the entrance arch. Even though the carnival provided a service, it was one provided by outsiders. Outsiders whose pasts were unknown, unlike those who lived in the town, where their history could be charted back to when they stepped off the boat centuries ago.

Joe could testify to that, having been part of a similar community. He had always been excited when the fairs had come to town and yet he had always been slightly fearful of the people that ran them. He could not see in their faces where they were from or whom they were related to. They were strangers, and strangers were to be feared.

Everyone in America knew that from an early age.

'That will be a dollar each,' he said to the young couple at the head of the line.

The boy handed him two crumpled bills while the girl giggled nervously.

Joe unhooked the rope that separated the end of the queue from the platform used to climb into the ride, letting the couple pass. He did this for another two passengers before replacing the rope. As the queue moved forward, he spotted the Grey family in it.

What he saw caused him to frown; Lily Grey was wrenching furiously on her mother's arm, a panicked look upon her young face.

6

'Momma,' Lily cried between each hitching breath.

Meryl Grey bent down so she was face-to-face with her daughter. This was no easy feat with the queue being such a cluster of bodies, but she descended slowly, carefully. Her knees popped like dry sticks being broken in half.

'What is it, dear?' she asked.

Lily's face was sunburnt red with sheer hysteria. Snot bubbled in the child's nostrils.

'I'm scared. I don't wanna go on,' she said, shaking her head and hugging her teddy bear to her.

Before Meryl knew what to say, Lily began to chant, 'I don't wanna go on, I don't wanna go on.'

Meryl's eyes, which had narrowed as she strained to hear her child over the shouts of carnies and the whirls of machinery, widened. Her head inclined backward as if Lily had swatted at her the way a cat will swat at a toy.

Before she could even think to respond, the man behind them in the queue spoke.

'Are you coming or going, lady?' he said. 'The queue is moving'.

Meryl scowled at him, then turned to look the other way. The man was right, the queue had moved forward and now there was space ahead of them.

She couldn't let him pass. The line was entrenched between two metal barriers and no one would have been able to squeeze around her.

She glanced once more at the man, noting he was holding the hand of a small girl and that the girl showed no signs of unease. She was craning her neck and standing on her tiptoes to see around them, to see the ride.

The sight of that caused Meryl to bite her bottom lip.

'Lily,' she said. 'This is the ride you've been talking about all morning. This is the one you wanted to go on.'

She sounded like she was pleading with her daughter and she despaired on hearing the desperation in her voice. It reminded her of the night before, how she had tried to persuade her husband, Len, to stop at six beers. He hadn't.

Her already hot face bloomed with feverish heat.

'I don't wanna go now, Momma,' cried Lily. Her lips were trembling.

Meryl's grip on her daughter's shoulders grew tighter. She could feel the eyes of the crowd upon her and the flesh between her shoulders prickled.

'We are waiting,' said the man behind her. He was tapping his foot on the metal ramp that they all found themselves on. 'Come on, lady, if the little girl doesn't want to go, move aside.'

'I am speaking to my daughter,' she snapped at him.

He blinked and fell silent.

The last twelve hours replayed through Meryl's head as she stood stiffly, gripping her daughter's left hand. *This was supposed to be a happy family day*, she thought. They had planned it for weeks after learning when the fair was coming to town. Despite those plans, Len was at home nursing off his hangover from last night while she struggled to shepherd the kids.

'Come on,' she barked.

The twins, who had been watching with intense glee, rocked on their heels. She marched them up the slight incline of the ramp behind the other queued families. Even her eldest, Henry, kept quiet on hearing the anger in her voice.

And she was angry. She was angry with Len, angry that Lily had made her sound so desperate, and at the way the man behind her had spoken to her. She was even angry at the day's temperature, which was so hot it seemed to sap her strength. She was so angry that she ignored her daughter's further pleas as the queue marched forward.

7

Joe had observed this all from his position at the ticket podium. He intended to say to Meryl Grey as her family reached the head of the queue that Lily could wait with him while they went on the ride. However, before he could speak, an alarm squawked from above, followed by a low dissipating whine.

The ride had stopped. A unanimous groan rose from the queue.

'No need to panic, folks!' yelled Arnie in his best pitchman tone.

No one could sound jollier than Arnie, Joe believed. The carny thumped him on the back as he passed him on the way to the control booth.

8

Lily Grey was at the front of the queue, her hand in her mother's greasy grip. The nice man from the entrance to the carnival had his back turned to her, watching the carnies work. That's what her father had called them. Well, he had called them 'fucking carnies', but she wasn't allowed to say Bad Words.

The carnies were darting about a railway trench where several carts, their bodies glossy and shining under the overhead lights, had stopped. Lily sniffed back the snot that trailed to her upper lip and stared. She didn't know that she had stopped crying, had even stopped feeling scared.

The carts looked funny to her. They looked like the empty mining carts that belonged to Ben and Clay's train set.

'Sorry about this,' said the nice man named Joe to her mother.

Her mother let go of her hand to fold her arms across her chest.

Something tugged on Lily's arm. It was Ben.

'You're a big sissy,' he said, jabbing a chubby finger at her.

Clay stuck both his thumbs in his ears and proceeded to hop from foot to foot while repeating, 'Big sissy, big sissy, big sissy,' in a voice that was high and whiny.

'No, I am not,' she snapped at them.

'You were crying,' said Ben.

'So?' she said.

'Like a crybaby,' added Clay.

'Only big sissies and crybabies cry,' said Ben, lifting his chin. It seemed to point at her.

It was true. She had cried. She was five years old and had cried. Her brothers were seven and had not. She crossed her arms, stamped her right foot, and pouted.

Both boys cringed from her. Despite their two-year age gap, there had always been something frightening about Lily, as if she possessed some authority beyond them. If they were completely honest, there were moments when she scared them in the way their mother did when she was mad. Yet they couldn't help teasing her; she was a girl, after all.

'Bet you won't even go on it,' said Ben.

'Yeah, I bet you'll like wimp out, big sissy,' Clay told her.

'I will not,' she snapped and both boys flinched. 'So take a chill pill, alright?'

Both brothers looked at one another with identical grins of conspiratorial mirth.

9

Journey Through The Crypt awoke with a noise somewhere between a lion's roar and an engine turning over. Arnie strolled from the control booth, arms outstretched, as applause cheered from the crowd.

As he drew close to Joe, he whispered in his ear.

'We would have certainly been in deep shit with the Boss if she hadn't started, especially on the first day. Perfection: that is what the Boss wants on every first day; remember that, ace.'

This was followed by another thump to Joe's back.

'Journey Through The Crypt will be recommencing in a few seconds, folks,' Arnie announced to the crowd, who cheered once more.

'Won't be long now,' Joe said to Meryl Grey.

She gave him a strained smile, her face deeply red and tired-looking.

'Have you been enjoying yourself so far?' asked Joe.

He knew this was a silly question, but he had found that giving people a chance to speak usually diffused them of any hostility they felt. He was proven right as she drew a deep breath, relaxed her features, and began to talk.

'Just trying to keep up with these guys, especially this one,' she said, inclining her head to Lily.

Joe flashed a smile down to her. There was no trace of the tears he had seen on her face earlier. Instead, her face was flushed as equally red as her mother's. She looked so determined, he chuckled.

'I understand that,' he said. 'I have a younger sister who's forever getting into trouble'.

'You do?' said Meryl.

'Yes, ma'am,' said Joe. 'She'd be a little older than Lily here'.

The nice man talked funny. He sounded sad to Lily, but she said nothing. Her brothers were behind her and whispering amongst themselves.

Their voices were like needles in her ears.

Lily was watching the railway line that the glossy carts rode on. An empty one had pulled up behind the nice man, its safety bars pointed to the roof.

The frown that had creased Lily's brow softened in seeing it.

'Tester cart going first, folks!' shouted the carny in charge to the crowd.

Lily turned to her brothers with triumph in her red face.

'Would a big sissy do this?' she whispered to her brothers.

Their voices silenced when she spoke to them. They witnessed with ever-widening eyes as their sister slipped under the rope before them and past the man their mother was talking to. Both adults were too distracted by their conversation to notice, plus Lily was only as tall as the man's hips.

'Radical,' breathed Ben.

Lily tiptoed up to the empty cart and looked left, then right. Even though she was visible to the people in the queue, none of the carnies saw her. She was simply too small and they were all preoccupied with the impatient eyes of the crowd.

Someone in the throng, a man, shouted a loud 'Yeeoo!' in seeing her.

The carnies' gazes all snapped on him rather than looking to what he was cheering at. By now, several crowd members had spotted the tiny girl who was alone on the platform and looked on with amused expressions. She wasn't their child, after all.

Only one person, an elderly woman, cried out, 'Good lord, that child!'

It was these words that caught the attention of Joe and Meryl; however, as the words resonated from the queue, they both looked in that direction rather than to the platform where Lily stood. It was only when their eyes followed the pointing fingers of several crowd members that they noticed her for the first time.

By then it was too late; Lily had already leaped into the cart.

'Gnarly,' said both twins in unison.

Lily shot them a thumb's up as the safety bar lowered over her lap. It was the last exchange she would ever have with them.

The cart began to move; sliding forward with such fluidity it was magical to her. This was more down to her young mind, which viewed the world through imagination-tinted eyes, as any child's mind does.

She gripped the safety bar with one hand. The other was wrapped around her bear, clutching it under her right armpit.

'Lily!' called Meryl, her voice shrill.

Her daughter only turned her head in her direction and waved, her lips smiling in delight.

Lily shifted her butt from side to side, becoming comfortable in the seat, as her eyes noticed the track beneath her. It stretched into the open maw of a massive clown head, its surface as glossy as the cart she was in. The clown's lips were ruby red; its white teeth like stalactites and stalagmites over the ride's entrance.

She looked up at its eyes, which were opal-shaped and lunatic in their gaze, her heart fluttering inside her. Then she looked down at the track and seeing it disappear into the darkness at the thing's throat, screamed, 'Momma!'

The cart that contained her shot forward, gaining speed.

Chapter Four

Journey Through The Crypt

1

The cart was a pinball being injected into a game.

I'm being swallowed, Lily thought. *This machine is alive, it's one big monster, and it's eating me.*

And it was.

The daylight had already faded, replaced by infinite darkness, along with all the sights and sounds of outside. Lily could no longer hear the voices of the crowd or the shouts and hollers of the carnies or even the insane calliope music. She was alone and screaming at the darkness, at the tunnel of noise and wind that the track had become as her cart rose and dipped over a series of bumps. Lily clamped her eyelids shut, her body as rigid as a stone as the hydraulics underneath her let out a high-pitched murderous squeal.

She couldn't afford to keep them shut for long. With each rise and dip, Lily found herself being hurled into the lap bar hard enough to bring tears to her eyes. She managed to get her teddy bear between her and the bar the third time this happened. It did not stop the pain in her, which was exquisitely sharp, but it did dull it to some degree.

The track seemed to straighten out after the third bump; the wind that whipped at her straw-coloured hair diminished as the cart slowed. Lily braved a peek at her surroundings, clutching her teddy tight as she spied out of her right eye.

The first thing she noticed was that the darkness was not absolute anymore - that she could see, and what she could see was fog. Her cart was driving into a shroud made pearlescent by an unseen light source from above.

As Lily was submerged into it, she shivered, her bare skin immediately forgetting that beyond the walls of the ghost ride, it was summer.

The fog was as blinding initially as the darkness had been. As she traveled farther along, Lily began to discern vague objects floating within the silver greyness. They were rectangular with curved tops.

Lily squinted at each one as they passed by, her brow furrowed in the same way as when her brothers had teased her.

A gasp escaped her as she spotted writing on the surface of one of the passing objects. The cart had been moving too fast for her to read what it had said, but she suddenly understood what they were.

Gravestones.

As if aware of her realisation, the cloud began to thin, revealing that the track was taking her through a graveyard. Lily saw a mausoleum in the distance, as white as bone, against a nighttime backdrop of what looked like the countryside. Stars twinkled down from within the black abyss above her head. There was even a scythe-like moon, although it was yellowed and poisoned-looking.

Nothing stirred amongst the helter-skelter rows of headstones. Not a sound rose from them, even the cart beneath her gliding along soundlessly for a change. It made it hard for her to believe this wasn't real.

Lily had already forgotten about the carnival, about her family outside, or even her

72

reasoning for jumping into the cart. She was in a real graveyard; her mind that still believed in Santa Claus and the Tooth Fairy confirmed this.

A small, dry moan escaped her. Her cart had slowed to a stop.

2

On her right, the land grew steep, becoming a platform at her eye level. A coffin, its wood dark brown and its handles gleaming gold, crowned it.

Lily's head rotated on her neck in quick, jerking motions as she looked around. Nothing seemed to have changed. Her surroundings remained as dead as the bodies she imagined were buried around her.

Satisfied that no one or nothing was creeping up behind her, her eyes returned to the coffin and bulged. Sweat dewed the flesh between her nose and upper lip. Her breathing grew shallow and quick, her throat and chest tight again.

She stared at the coffin, her upper body bending in the middle, her neck stretching as she leaned closer.

The coffin lid exploded upward, falling with a thump.

Lily screamed, her fingers clawing into the flesh of her lower lip and chin. The coffin lid had been dislodged with enough force that it had leaped into the air before landing askew. Emerald light, the colour of radiation, of cancer she knew from TV, splashed out from within it across her face.

But that wasn't the worst thing. The worst thing, the thing that made her bladder let go while she screamed, was the hand of the corpse.

It rocketed out from within the coffin, rotten and gangrenous, its dead fingers flexing at her, wanting to rend into her soft flesh. The tips she could see were black bone and even further back, at the wrist, she spied the tattered remains of its sleeve.

Lily threw herself against the far side of her seat. Her eyes were horror-movie wide and all white as her head shook from side to side. In the second before the cart took off once more, zooming forward by some graceful power, Lily imagined the occupant of that coffin pulling itself out from within. It moved stiffly, like her granddad used to when he tried to stand after taking a nap in his favourite armchair. Only what stepped out from the coffin didn't look like her granddad; it was a rotting skeleton in the remains of its burial clothes, black holes in the place where its eyes had been.

This never happened - the cart had already whipped Lily away - yet if she had lived, she would have told her brothers that a skeleton had come for her.

3

'Get her back,' demanded Meryl Grey.

The strained look in her eyes told Joe there would be no arguing.

He wheeled to his left to find Arnie already strolling over, grinning his best showcase grin. Whatever brief relief Joe felt at seeing his friend disappeared. His grin held too many teeth and its humour did not reach his eyes as it usually did; instead, the skin around them was pinched.

'She's a little devil climbing in uninvited',' said Arnie, speaking low so the rest of the queue wouldn't hear. 'I suppose you let her sneak past and all. In cahoots, were you?' Arnie said to Joe.

'No, I didn't... she just sneaked past,' spluttered Joe, surprised by the carny's slightly threatening tone.

Arnie raised his hand as if to provide Joe with his signature thump on the back. A gesture that would have said everything was okay. His hand settled on Joe's right shoulder instead, its presence instantly discomforting.

If Arnie noticed how Joe's shoulders had tensed, he didn't show it.

'Ma'am, don't worry. The ride doesn't last long,' he said to Meryl. 'If you'd like to step past the line here, I'll take you to where your daughter is going to come out.'

Meryl's response to Arnie's soothing tone was to speak through her teeth.

'Get her back now.'

Arnie blinked, his expression one of surprise beneath his trilby. 'Ma'am, I can assure you your daughter is perfectly safe.'

Meryl's hands gripped the edge of the podium Joe stood behind, her knuckles blanching white. Her twin boys gaped up at her from below with a look of reverent awe while worry flickered across her teenage son's face.

'You were supposed to send a tester round, not send my daughter round on it,' she said and though her eyes were transfixed upon Arnie's, a pang of guilt hit Joe like a sickness in his stomach. 'How do you know the ride's safe if you hadn't tested it?'

Arnie's cheeks flushed as the muscles of his jaws worked, his eyes darting to the crowd watching their entire exchange, behind Meryl.

'Mom, she'll be alright,' said Meryl's teenage son. 'The ride's not going to break on her.'

'Henry,' Meryl warned.

Her face was pale, doll-like except for two dots of apple red colour in her cheeks. Her coppery hair blazed in the noontime sun.

'So what if it scares her a little?' her son carried on, oblivious to his mother's fury. 'It's her fault for sneaking onto the thing in the first place.'

'Henry, shut up,' she snapped, with a ferocity that made Joe cringe.

He looked to Henry to see the boy's lips turn white as his mouth snapped closed. *I'd hate to be in her bad books,* thought Joe. *The thing, is I am. Lily slipped by me.*

'If we stop the ride, someone will have to walk the track and go in after her,' said Arnie, as if in explaining this, Meryl would concede to his point of view.

'I'll go,' Joe announced.

Arnie's attention rounded to him, his expression unreadable.

'I don't care how you do it, just do it,' said Meryl.

'Hey man, stop the ride and go get the little girl!' shouted a man from within the queue. His words gained a murmur of approval from the crowd.

Joe felt like he had been in this situation before, with Arnie nonetheless, only this time he wasn't on the carny's side. Yesterday, he had been a stranger wandering into a strange land in search of employment; the aggression he had witnessed towards Arnie from the townspeople at the near accident involving the entrance arch had led him to automatically be on the carny's side, being an outsider himself. Today was different,

76

maybe because he knew and liked the Greys. They were plucky and endearing.

Are you going to do the right thing? he thought, staring at Arnie.

As if he had spoken those words out loud the carnies eyes snapped back to his. They were dark and wondering.

Ever since Arnie had placed his hand on his shoulder, he had been uncomfortable. Now, staring into his almost slate grey eyes, Joe felt the balance of power shift in his favor.

'MOMMA' screamed a voice from inside the ghost ride.

It belonged to Lily Grey.

5

Lily Grey screamed for her mother.

The cart had accelerated again as it hurtled along the snaking track, forcing her back into the seat. She was past the graveyard and aiming for what looked like another tunnel, this one illuminated by a sporadically flashing light.

The light flashed, almost blinding her, and in its spotlight, she saw what reached from the walls of the corridor. Hands, thousands of them, their dead ruined fingers twitching to seize her like the one that had thrust from inside the coffin in the last room.

Lily clapped her hands over her eyes, no longer screaming, but crying.

The light winked out. It winked back on and the hands were closer, inches away. She shifted into the middle of the seat. It was no good; she could feel the air around her beginning to move as their presence filled it.

6

'Alright, switch it off,' Arnie ordered the carny in the control booth.

The machinery whined as it began to slow, a sound Lily registered inside along with the overall slowing down of the cart she occupied. She blinked several times, discovering that the light had stopped flashing and remained constant.

'Joe, grab a flashlight and go in after her,' instructed Arnie, though he was already moving in the direction of the ride's entrance.

'Ma'am, if you and your family would like to come with me, we will wait by the ride exit for Joe to bring your daughter to you,' said Arnie, unhooking the rope barrier.

7

In the harsh, ceaseless spotlight, the corridor of hands did not look the same. Lily reached out and gave the nearest one a tentative flick. The thing that she had dreaded twanged dully, signifying that it was made of rubber.

'Oh,' she said.

A small sound escaped her that was somewhere between a giggle and a hum. The ride had stopped. Lily collapsed back into the seat of the cart, relief washing over her like a wave, leaving her body tired and her eyelids heavy.

As her eyes began to droop, an alarmed sounded, startling her.

Lily's head pivoted on her neck, looking behind her and then forward. The safety bar was rising from its previous position over her lap.

She was free.

With the light on, she could see that there were walkways on either side of the track.

I could walk to the end, she thought, thinking of her brothers. *I could walk to the end and pretend I made it all the way through. I'd say it was boring and not scary at all and I don't want to go on it again because it wasn't scary enough.*

This made her to grin.

They would think she was some sort of hero.

She wiped her wet face with her teddy bear and reached for the edge of the walkway. Its surface was grimy to touch but she heaved herself upward with little effort until she was lying flat across it. When she stood, she discovered under the fluorescents that her outfit had become filthy. It had that electrified grease smell that she had smelled outside, only stronger.

Momma is not going to be happy about this, she thought.

Lily attempted to brush at her dirty clothes, smearing the black muck further. Shrugging, she started along the walkway, heading in the direction where the ride would have taken her had it not stopped.

8

Now that everything was going to be fine, Meryl felt bad about being rude to the carny. He stood beside her family as they waited at the ride's exit point, a cavernous hole decorated to look like a train tunnel, and she could feel his eyes on her. A part of her did want to apologize for being so forceful now that Joe had disappeared inside the mouth of the maniacal clown after Lily.

What held her back was shame.

Once in high school, she had made the mistake of removing her school top after physical education in the locker room. She hadn't even tossed the sweat-soaked fabric aside before the shrill catcalling of her peers ricocheted off the room's enamel tiles.

'Look at little Meryl Farber,' Sue Hargensen had announced. 'Or should I say "big Meryl Farber"? Look at the size of those things.'

Her right arm was extended out, her index finger pointed at Meryl's breasts.

Only her mother had ever commented on her body before and even then, that was in relation to buying clothes. She already knew her figure was fuller than the other girls; it was obvious and to have it become the attention of her entire class was initially confusing.

Surely, her mind had thought at the time, *we all have them.*

It was in seeing Sue Hargensen's face, gawking at her breasts with an amazed sort of hilarity while the rest of the girls sniggered on, that Meryl became mortified.

Thinking back on it all these years later, Meryl concluded that she wouldn't have even remembered the event if Sue had been a boy. At the time, the changes in both genders were unknown. Males her age had seemed to be on another planet to her and she to them. Even how to communicate with each other was so unknown that if a boy had gaped at her as Sue had done, Meryl would have shrugged it off as nothing.

It was just different because Sue was a girl.

Her actions and words contained an element of betrayal. Hadn't she been going through the same changes as Meryl, albeit with more grace? Sue was one of those girls in school that seemed to have a prissy type of capability when encountering any new social obstacle.

80

She had made Meryl feel like a sideshow freak, one that lived in a cage. She had made Meryl feel stupid.

'Look at them,' Sue had gone on. 'Have you seen the size of your boobs?'

Fourteen-year-old Meryl Farber had looked down at herself surrounded by a circle of her classmates, their faces relishing that this cruel singling out was not being inflicted upon them, and in seeing her breasts, felt stupid. As if their size had been a mistake she had made, like calling her teacher 'Mom' or 'Dad'. Yes, they were large, larger than anyone else's in the room, and by that fact Meryl Farber found they disgusted her.

Meryl Grey, now thirty-nine and four kids down the line, felt even more stupid than she had on that day twenty-five years ago. Because it wasn't just her that had made a mistake; it had been her daughter.

And like she had been back then, her family was on display before a crowd of onlookers. She could almost hear their thoughts.

'Look at them.'

'There's always one family that ruins all the fun for everyone else.'

'Dressed in their best and still looking like they get their clothes from Goodwill.'

'I would be mortified if I were that woman.'

'Where's her husband?'

She glanced in the direction of the carny, hoping to find some sort of support in his face, hoping that it would be open-looking enough for her to ask if they could move somewhere out of the public eye. What she saw there caused a shiver to run up her spine.

The carny had pushed his trilby hat back, providing Meryl a clear view. Never before had she seen such an animalistic leer of desire on a man's face, let alone one aimed solely at her. Her eyes darted to her kids, who were all so preoccupied with the tunnel exit that they hadn't noticed the carny's look.

He was hungry for her.

No, not possible, she thought, forcing her neck to turn in his direction. *No man has ever looked at me like that, not even Len when we were courting.*

Meryl stared into the carny's face, unperturbed of being noticed, with her sons' attention elsewhere and the public glaring into her back. All the muscles in his face were taut, his lips slightly parted, giving the hint of pristine white behind them. The leering look came from his slate-coloured eyes.

There was something in them that reminded Meryl of Sue Hargensen's gawking, a look that pinned a person to the spot. His eyes were like phantom fingers on her, caressing, massaging, and scraping her skin. She felt them, like the whisper of the softest breeze, trace the flesh of her belly before cupping her breasts. She felt phantom thumbs circle her nipples, making them hard, and phantom fingernails trace across her collar, neck, and jawline. She maneuvered her legs closer together until her thighs touched.

No man had ever looked at her like this.

Meryl told herself she was being silly. A person's gaze couldn't make someone feel like this, though her skin, hot and tingling with electricity, told her otherwise.

Was this what other women felt like? The Sue Hargensens of the world?

If it was, Meryl didn't like it. The slate grey eyes of the carny didn't make her feel desired, they made her feel like a piece of meat before a starving animal. Yet she could not for the life of her look away.

The carnies eyes did more than devour her; they held her hazel ones until they were all she could see, until she was drowning in their slate waters.

'She'll be alright, Ma,' said Henry's voice from far away.

Meryl felt his hand fill her own and it was this contact that jerked her out of her trance more than his voice. The last time Henry had taken her hand had been when his age was only single figures.

She looked at him as if she had just woken from a nap. Thankfully, he was too concerned about his little sister to notice, she saw.

''Course she will,' she said, a smile flickering across her face.

Meryl resumed her watch of the tunnel exit with the rest of her family. When she glanced back at the carny, she saw his face had changed.

He was grinning now.

9

The flashlight produced a feeble cone of illumination that stretched five feet in front of him. Joe could see the walkway on the left-hand side of the track and the left rail within the track's trench and no more.

Still, he pressed on, trying to ignore the tension in his guts at once more being inside The Crypt. His dislike of the carnival's ghost ride had been the furthest thing from his mind when he had volunteered to retrieve Lily Grey. Now, it was hard to ignore.

Joe glanced over his shoulder at the circle of light where he had come in. The plastic fangs of the ghoulish head framed the roof of the circle. In the dark, they looked like the bars of a cage that were about to drop down, imprisoning him. He was only ten feet or so along the walkway, and even then, the circle looked small and distant.

Joe swallowed, turning back to face the darkness.

The action alone seemed to muffle the noise of the crowd outside. Joe transferred the flashlight into his left hand, his right cramping from being so clenched.

Come on now. Don't be a chickenshit; you've got a girl to find.

That got him moving. He took a step forward. Then another. With each one, the noise from outside faded, faded and grew fainter still, then nothing.

He was alone in the dark: in darkness so deep it was like well darkness, like the darkness that existed beneath the earth, or the cosmic emptiness that exists between the stars. There was a heaviness to it that weighed at the bottom of his lungs, preventing them from fully expanding. His whole body was on high alert, as if anticipating some winged nightmare to come fluttering and screeching down at him from on high, teeth bared.

Another step. Then another.

He followed the walkway as it became a series of steps that rose and fell at three separate parts. The entrance light was now lost behind the rises.

There was something damnatory about losing sight of it.

Joe knew that if he reached out far enough, his hand would encounter the smooth plywood walls that acted as The Crypt's skin, or perhaps even one of the metal struts that served as its bones. His rational mind knew that. But his body said differently; the intelligence that lived in his nerve endings said that if he did that, he might not feel anything no matter how far he reached, or something might grab him by the wrist and haul him into the black abyss.

Joe did not like this ride, and that feeling did not have anything to do with his discomfort for fairground coasters. There was just something not right about it. He knew this in the same way he knew not to let his hand leave the illumination of the flashlight, by his nerve endings.

When he had first laid eyes upon the square building that housed the ride, he had experienced a sensation akin to what he believed an animal must feel when a predator is stealthily stalking it. It had been watching him then and it knew of him now as he traversed inside its bowels.

You're being fucking stupid now, a voice whispered to him.

Am I? Then why does my skin feel like it's crawling with insects? Why do I feel ready to squirt piss into my pants?

No answer.

Joe took another step.

White smog began to envelop him. Joe remembered this section of the ride and began to move forward faster through it. It limited the reach of his flashlight, the smoke reflecting the light at him, so that he wanted to get through it quickly.

When the first headstone appeared off to his left, he squatted down before it to read the inscription carved into the polystyrene. It had flown past at such speed last night that he hadn't had a chance to read it. The top line read 'Adam Kavaliar', and below this, '1253 - '.

Joe straightened, shining his light ahead, and moved on through the fog.

There were more headstones now, though he did not pause to inspect them until the tunnel he was in widened, revealing a graveyard at night. There was no sign of Lily.

'Hello?' he called out, shoulders flinching as he cracked the silence.

Seconds ticked by as he stared across the room, the air suddenly pregnant with anticipation after being disturbed. No response came back to him.

Joe exhaled, realising he had been holding his breath.

Why are you calling out? whispered the voice. *Are you expecting Lily to be hiding behind these gravestones or in that mausoleum over there?*

Arnie said that once the ride was stopped that the safety bar would be released on the cart. It's a fail-safe in case of a fire.

He began to cross the room, the floor beneath becoming spongy. Joe shone his flashlight down - despite no longer needing it, he found its light comforting - and saw that floor was carpeted with what looked like artificial grass.

By chance, its beam played across several of the headstones. Joe slowed to a halt, recognising one of the names. It was written on the headstone nearest to the track: 'Lou Fritz', and below, '1923 - '.

Despite his fear Joe chuckled at this, wondering if the headstone was some sort of inside joke amongst the carnies. His eyes lingered on the death year, or rather, the lack of one. There was no way the birth year was correct; Lou was haggard-looking as fuck, but he didn't look older than thirty.

Shaking his head, Joe moved on.

10

The next room contained a forest where the trees were as thick as a small car, their tops disappearing into the murky darkness overhead. Like the graveyard, a ground mist floated between the trunks of these mighty hulks.

Lily hummed the chorus to 'Billie Jean' as she followed the pathway that weaved through the forested area, teddy in the crook of her arm. She spotted a zombie, its arms outstretched, its clothes in tatters, its exposed skin mossy in places, as it attempted to tear its way through a bush. There was another, this one female, farther on down the path, trying to sneak around the trunk of a tree.

They weren't very frightening, Lily found, now that they couldn't move. They were a little sad, even.

It must be lonely with everyone passing by being frightened of them. The silliness of her thinking made her grin.

She hitched her shorts from their plastered position on her bum. She was going to have to sneak into a bathroom at some point and remove her pants when she got out.

I could claim there was a bit in the ride where I got sprayed by water.

Lily could see her brothers' faces staring at her with awe and reverence as she told her epic tale. She was editing her speech in her head when a loud metallic crash off to her left reverberated throughout the forest. Lily's head snapped in that direction, peering into the pockets of mist that swirled around the tree trunks.

She had stopped moving.

Maybe it's someone coming to rescue me; after all, the ride has stopped.

'Is anyone there?' Lily called out.

Despite the forest area's grand size, there was no echo. Her words seemed to fall lifelessly from her mouth into the air.

She continued to stare, breathing in the heavy aroma of pine. It smelled more like a car's air freshener than the real thing.

No shadow stirred between the trees.

Lily felt her fear return to her now, spilling into her system like a virus filtering into her bloodstream. She inhaled sharply, her chest tight once more.

Get moving. The quicker you move, the quicker you get out of this spooky place.

Lily nodded at these words and, squeezing her teddy, started forward. Her eyes were locked on the dark cavern that was the exit on the other side of the room. There was a flutter of movement to her left and above.

She skidded to a halt, her sneakers squeaking beneath her. To her left, one of the zombies was walloping as if something had knocked into it on the way by. Lily stiffened, staring at the male zombie in its frayed suit as it steadied. Its eyes were yellow in a head blackened by flame.

The fluttering sound came again, this time directly overhead. It sounded like a curtain rippling in a strong gale. Lily flinched from it, her eyes scanning the shadows above her, seeing nothing.

'Who's there?' she yelled.

No reply.

Only this time it wasn't because someone wasn't there. It was because whoever was there didn't want to let her know where they were.

Despite having already voided her bladder, Lily felt like something had a stranglehold on it. Her thighs inched closer together.

'Who's there?' she yelled out again, her heart a jackhammer.

This time, a branch snapped to her right.

Lily took off at a run, clutching her teddy to her. The exit tunnel yawned ahead, containing darkness. The fluttering movement resounded from behind her, giving chase. Her vision blurred as she began to weep.

She almost made it.

The tunnel was right in front of her, and her legs were readying to spring her forward into a leap like some action star in a movie when strong fingers clasped her throat from behind. Before the pain and the invading blackness, she felt the ground being torn away from her still-pedaling feet.

She screamed, but like her life, it was short-lived.

Chapter Five

Gone

1

Joe was investigating the empty cart in the corridor of hands when he heard the colossal crash from somewhere farther ahead. He yelled Lily's name, breaking into a run without thinking or assessing his surroundings. If he had, perhaps things would have played out differently, as Joe's left foot got tangled on one of the grasping hands that protruded from the walls.

Joe Cage fell like a sack of shit and met the floor with his left temple. His flashlight skidded away from him onto the track, its bulb shattering. A pool of blood began to collect around Joe's motionless body like a crimson halo.

2

When he woke, it was to a pulsating pain in his skull. A groan issued from him as he squinted at his surroundings, his head feeling full of wet cotton. It looked like he was still in the corridor of zombie hands, only now he was lying on the grimy walkway.

What the hell?

Joe made to push himself up only for the world to spin to grey. He sucked in air, taking deep, long draws like it was an elixir. Nausea struck him so hard he thought he was going to vomit his breakfast on the hands that held him.

If any of the others were to come along now, they'd think I'm doing some sort of weird push up and can't quite make it.

That thought got him laughing. Laughing distracted him from the urge to throw up until the world had stopped its spinning. When it did, Joe got a clear picture of the puddle between his hands at the same time he registered something slimy coating the left-hand side of his face.

Joe probed at his face gently, wincing at the flare of pain as his fingers came close to his left temple. His fingertips came away bloody.

'Shit,' he said, standing up.

He had to grope for the wall, his hands seizing on the dummy ones to stay upright. For a brief moment, greyness seeped back into his vision.

Joe shut his eyes and took deep breaths until he felt some strength return to his legs. When it did, he looked down, discovering his white t-shirt was stained red with his blood.

'Fuck,' he said.

As he assessed himself, he spotted the flashlight lying in the trench that held the miniature railway line used by The Crypt's carts. The glass that belonged to its bulb winked at him like diamonds under the harsh fluorescents. In seeing it, Joe suddenly remembered the reason why he was here.

Lily Grey.

His head snapped to the corridor ahead of him. How long had he been unconscious - long enough for Lily to walk to the end of the track and the outside world? He hoped so, but just in case she was still inside, Joe decided to continue forward, doing so at a plodding pace.

The inside of his skull still had that wet cotton feeling, as if his brains had turned to slush.

After several moments he had to stop, staggering to latch onto something to save himself from falling while the world spun and colours bled to grey. Eventually, when those moments passed, Joe pushed on, unaware that his gait had become that of a drunk wandering home after a night out.

Joe found no signs of Lily Grey during his journey through the carnival's ghost ride. His mind reassured himself that the child had simply done what he was doing and used the walkway to get out.

It was only when he stepped outside that he understood he was wrong.

The track curved hard in its last section before plunging into the bright afternoon sun. And that last curve was in darkness so dense it was like tar, leaving Joe squinting and holding up his hand to block the light as he left it.

Being unable to see the crowd, he could only hear their reaction to his bloody appearance. He heard them all inhale at the sight of him. There was a pause, in which he stood, his vision clearing from one brilliant strobe of white light to distinct colours. Then the screaming started.

It belonged to Meryl Grey and it didn't last long. She fainted shortly after her great lungs had expelled all their terror at the sight of his blood-slick figure. Luckily, Arnie's carnies caught her.

'I couldn't find her,' Joe said to Arnie, his tone desperate. 'I walked the whole length of the line and I couldn't find her.'

'It's okay, kid, it's okay,' Arnie soothed him, then turned to aid the others lowering Meryl gently to the platform floor.

The two Grey twins joined their mother on their knees, wailing loudly and shaking her. The way her body seemed to ripple effortlessly as they tugged at her brought flops of sweat out in Joe.

Her teenage son overlooked this scene wide-eyed, frozen to the spot, his face sickly pale. All the while, the calliope music jangled on overhead.

'Get this woman some water!' Arnie shouted to the others.

Several members of the crowd seemed to take this as an instruction and dashed off. The rest remained to feast on the evolving tragedy, their eyes just as wide as Meryl's sons', only lit by a hunger for drama.

One of Arnie's carnies, Joe observed, was already soaking her bandana in water from a jug she happened to have tied to her waist. She placed it on Meryl's forehead and begin giving reassurances to the two howling twins.

Arnie rose from his knees, indicating with a nod of the head that they speak away from this. Joe gladly followed him a few paces to the rear of the platform. As he did, he noticed Arnie's eyes were fixed on the mess of his forehead, making him wonder how much damage was there.

'Jesus, kid, you look like shit,' he said.

Joe didn't reply, reading something other than sympathy in Arnie's oily, tanned face. A horrifying epiphany struck Joe then like a lightning bolt. It obliterated the drunken soup between his ears, straightening him where he stood.

Does he think I did something to the kid?

The short answer was no, yet there was still suspicion in his face and something else, something like fear. In seeing Arnie's expression, Joe realised he had made a mistake by entering The Crypt after Lily.

The knack when drifting through America's highways and byways was to keep your head down, especially when bouncing from one job to the next. It was an exercise in not ruffling feathers, and he had just fucked up big time.

93

The carnies knew this rule better than anyone.

Joe's stomach felt like it had fallen into his pelvis. A tsunami of emotion, a cocktail mix of horror, despair, and anxiety, struck him then as he became aware of his vulnerability in this place - not only in the carnival, but in the town of Marybell itself.

Marybell is not a kind place for strangers.

The sheriff's words echoed back to him from the long, dark corridor of his memory. He remembered his musings half an hour ago about the fragile relationships that existed between townspeople and travelers, about how quickly they could change. Well, a missing child and a stranger covered in blood was one way to upset the apple cart.

Joe suddenly wished the earth would engulf him.

'What happened in there?' Arnie asked him in a hushed voice.

'I fell and hit my head,' Joe replied. 'I found the cart she was in, but it was empty and the safety bar was up. Then I heard something like a bang and I started to run, when I tripped on one of those fucking zombie hands.'

Arnie squinted at him, his eyes like flint sparkling in the blazing Kansas sun for a few seconds. Then the hard look softened. He clapped his hands on both Joe's shoulders, reminding Joe of the time his touch had been discomforting. It wasn't any longer; instead Joe took strength from it.

Whatever rapport existed between them, Joe hoped it was enough for Arnie to stand by him. He sent an internal prayer off that this man wouldn't throw him under the bus when the time came.

'Okay, keep that bit of information between us for now,' said Arnie. 'The boys and I are going to search the ride from one side to the next. I think the best thing for you to do is go see Carmen. She keeps a medical kit and is kind of our on-call nurse.'

Joe nodded his head and began to shuffle off, then turned back to the carny.

'I'm sorry, Arnie,' he said.

For a second, the hard-boiled light had returned to Arnie's eyes. *If there ever is a time when he thinks I have something to do with that girl, it's now,* thought Joe.

'Go on and look after yourself, Joe, we've got this,' Arnie eventually replied, the flint look gone.

The eyes of bystanders weighed on him. He took their weight as a sign of the trouble brewing for him, having broken the unspoken rule of vagabond survival. He had painted a target on himself, a bloody red one.

He had no clue as to how accurate his thinking was.

3

'The first day on the job and you've already made a mess of yourself,' said Carmen on seeing him.

'I was stupidly trying to appear eager,' Joe replied, dourly.

'Yes, well, enthusiasm can be a dangerous thing if it comes with a lack of thought. Come on over here and let me look at you.'

The interior of Madam Carmen's Fortunes was dimly lit and cluttered with cabinets and bookshelves supporting a treasure trove of bizarre objects. Its center was dominated by a majestic round table of rich mahogany that served as a plinth for a large crystal ball. Silk curtains hung from the ceiling like purple veils, their translucent nature giving the impression of secrecy.

Joe had entered the building that reminded him of the witch's house from the Hänsel and Gretel tale as a happy-looking customer was leaving. Word had spread fast about the beautiful mystic, he saw from the queue that ranged from the front of the building to the side. On seeing Joe's appearance, none of them protested as he skipped the line.

Joe wondered how long it would take for word to spread about the missing girl.

And there it is, he thought, catching himself. Missing. That was the word he had used. It preceded a black cramp of thought that he struggled to ignore.

'Let me see,' said Carmen.

She moved within the shadows of her cabin to him, her long, flowing dress swaying around her legs as she did. With the fingers of her right hand, she lifted the fringe above his left temple, inspecting the gash there. Joe noted that she wore several bracelets around each wrist and that her fingers were jeweled with many rings.

She caught him noticing and said, 'All part of the gimmick, sweetheart.'

Joe had no response for a change; he was too preoccupied with what Carmen was doing. She had never touched him before and she did so delicately, almost sensually, using only the tips of her fingers. His entire body felt like a tuning fork that's been rung. Joe stood at her mercy, every muscle stiff, his tongue dry, knowing that whatever boundaries existed between them were being overstepped.

He forgot about Lily Grey at that moment.

All his focus had narrowed to a single point, and that was Carmen. His body hummed with the knowledge that there were only a few inches of space between them; small enough that Joe could feel her breath on his neck, causing the skin there to erupt with gooseflesh. She was shorter than him and had to gaze up at his brow to see, doing so with eyes like black marbles with a hint of brown at their circumference. And while the interior of her building reeked of incense, she smelled of wildflowers and campfires. There were other things, too, that he noticed, like the way the boards sagged slightly under his feet; how the sound of the carnival had become muffled, indistinct inside Carmen's building; the tiny freckles that dotted Carmen's caramel cheeks; and the flecks of honey in her otherwise raven black hair.

Her eyes fell on his and held his gaze. She continued to do so as she retreated into shadow, placing her fingers in her mouth and tasting him.

'You'll be glad to know that it doesn't need stitches,' she said, giving him with a slightly feral look. 'I'll give you some ice in a rag to put to it and I'll check on you after. I have customers to see first. Take a pew outside, you'll be a good advert with this.' She pointed at his soaked top.

'Sure, I'll just wait outside,' he said, though he made no move to do so.

'It's not your fault,' Carmen told him. 'The girl going missing.'

Confusion broke through his current stunned mental state. He became aware of just how dazed he had been by his proximity to Carmen, as if he had been in a trance.

'How did you know a girl was missing?' he asked. 'I never mentioned it.'

'Word travels fast in the carny business,' Carmen replied, with a coldness Joe had never heard in her voice before.

On hearing her tone, all warmth that had existed in their previous exchange vanished and in its place was a second wave of despair. To him, Carmen's words seemed to communicate how alone he was in this situation. Alone in the sense that if the carnies decided it and Lily Grey wasn't found, he would be taking the blame for it.

Joe wheeled around, his boots scraping the wooden boards, and went outside. The sunlight wasn't as intense as it had been when he came out of The Crypt, though it still took his eyes a second to adjust after the dim interior. He took a seat on an old rocking chair off to the left. Carmen brought him a rag filled with ice and a bottle of Coke a few beats later.

'Thanks,' he said.

Carmen lingered, observing him as he sat.

'I'm sorry, I didn't mean for what I said to upset you,' she said.

Across the Fairway, The Crypt had been closed. Joe could see a chain had been linked across the entrance ramp and the crowd had dispersed.

'Don't worry,' she said, gripping his bicep. 'It will work out all right.'

Carmen took her next customer, a young woman, inside. Joe drank half the Coke in a few gulps.

He saw that Montague had arrived, dressed in the same silver/grey suit he wore yesterday, looking more like a used car salesman than ever. He was speaking with Meryl Grey, who was now standing beside her children, her face like a pale moon in the eye-watering Kansas sun.

There was a remarkable similarity in her features and those of her children.

He has one hell of a poker face, thought Joe of Montague. If the man was worried about the missing girl, Joe couldn't tell; his countenance only appeared placid and empathetic as he listened to Meryl speak. He was twenty feet away and could see them, but not hear them.

Why are you still here? Why haven't you grabbed your stuff from Arnie's RV and headed out of town? You know already that this is going to turn nasty, so why are you still here? Isn't running away supposed to be your whole deal?

His fist tightened on the rag he held against his temple, causing the ice to shift inside. The area throbbed with a spike of familiar pain, reminding him of how his entire face had felt the night after the fight at the roadhouse.

You haven't even thought about it, have you?

Joe fingered the rim of the Coke bottle, staring across the Fairway. Arnie and his carnies still hadn't returned from their search for Lily Grey.

Why are you still here?

An image blinked in front of his mind's eye; it was of Lily, the missing girl with straw-coloured hair that was as messy as tumbleweeds. Only it wasn't quite right: her nose and her jawline were different, sharper than the real Lily's.

It was his sister's face, or his sister as she had looked when she was nine years old. She was going on fourteen now back in the part of the world that he had left behind.

STOP IT! he thought and the image blinked away.

'Here, I have this for you,' said Carmen.

Joe jumped in his seat, unaware she was beside him and that the line outside her cabin had disappeared. *We must look like a real frontier family with me sitting in this rocking chair and her in her long dress.*

Carmen offered him a fresh shirt, a blue and pink Hawaiian-style thing that reminded him of Tom Selleck. Joe accepted it, balling his ruined t-shirt into one of the back pockets of his jeans. 'Thanks.'

'What's going on now?' asked Carmen.

'Nothing yet,' he replied then noticed he had spoken too soon. Arnie and the carnies were emerging from inside The Crypt.

There was no sign of Lily Grey with them. Joe's heart didn't sink in seeing this; it was already wallowing, confirming to him that what the voice in his head had said was true: he had been expecting the worst.

4

Meryl let loose a wail at the sight of the childless men. It was the one thing Joe heard clearly from across the Fairway, and he wasn't alone. Customers turned to look; however, the surrounding cacophony soon distracted them.

It worked like magic, for as soon as Meryl's cry rang out, the noise of the carnival seemed to swell, as if someone in charge of the volume had turned the dial up. Game pitchers shouted, 'Roll up, roll up and try your luck!' Someone else hollered, 'Candy, get your candy!' There was a tinny ding as a cowbell rang from the Test Your Strength pavilion, where customers could compete against Youssef, The Mighty Russian. Joe could hear his booming voice challenging customers to 'Step right up and give it a try.' Farther down the Fairway, the screams and whoops of children riding the carousel grew louder as the ride itself seemed to accelerate, its music increasing in speed to lunacy. And underneath it all remained the low chugging noise of The Whirl's engines.

It was like it was entirely orchestrated through some sort of telepathy.

There was no signal, at least as far as he could see, that was given. Not one of the carnies ran from The Crypt to pass on a message saying, 'Turn everything up real loud. We've got a missing child and a hysterical family over here.' Nor did anyone seem to notice the subtle increase in the din.

But Joe did.

Perhaps it was because he was the only one looking. From Carmen's rocking chair, he had a panoramic view of the scene unfolding across the Fairway. It looked like it belonged on one of those melodramatic television shows with titles that give the premise away: 'The Destruction of a Family' or 'Missing'.

Joe didn't know what to make of what he just witnessed. It filled his head with a strange, tingling sensation that he immediately disregarded for later consideration. At present, his concern for the Greys took over.

'I'm going to go see if they need a hand,' Joe told Carmen.

'Aren't you tired of being the hero?' she responded with a smirk.

It warmed him to see she was being coy with him once more. Joe had no reply for her; instead, he stood, hands out, palms towards her.

'God you're sincere,' said Carmen, shaking her head. 'You are one of those innocent bystanders aren't you, in the wrong place at the wrong time?'

'I like to think of it as the right place at the right time; it's more hopeful,' he replied. 'Anyway,

I've got to clean up my mess. I was supposed to go in and find her.'

This time, Carmen was without words. She simply stared past him at The Crypt, her face like a brooding cloud.

5

'There, there,' said Montague into Meryl's ear, holding her as she sobbed into his collar.

Joe noted that her arms didn't reciprocate the hug; instead, they dangled limply at her sides, their flesh as pale as milk.

'Listen, this is what we are going to do: you and I are going to take a walk along the track for your daughter. My company will search the carnival for her, and we will contact the local authorities, okay?'

Montague's words were cool, calm, and well-spoken, with only the hint of an accent Joe couldn't place. It was when he had said the word 'carnival' that Joe caught an unusual cadence in his voice.

Meryl nodded meekly against his bearded cheek.

'Good, good,' he said, as if pacifying a distraught child.

In some ways, that's what Meryl had become, Joe saw. There was a vacancy about her that was completely different from the assertive, helpful waitress who he had first met at the diner. His heart went out to her.

'We'll need someone to run to Launder's to phone the sheriff,' Montague informed Arnie over Meryl's shoulder.

'I'll do it,' said Joe before anyone else could.

All eyes turned to him.

Arnie and those who worked The Crypt evaluated him, their eyes dull steel. Meryl's family continued to look confused and vague. Only Montague's lit upon seeing him.

'Joe, my dear boy, you've certainly earned your stripes today already and yet you're back for more,' exclaimed the carnival owner. 'Arnie told me what you did here today and I must say, I couldn't be prouder of an employee. I see you've sustained yourself another injury. This young man is injuring himself in the line of duty, Mrs. Grey.'

'You didn't see my Lily in there, did you?' asked Meryl Grey, as if deaf to Montague's jovial bullshit.

'No, Mrs. Grey, I didn't,' said Joe, unable to meet her eyes.

'Oh,' she said, then added, 'I'm sorry you hurt yourself.'

All the fibres in Joe's being seemed to have become weightless at Meryl's distant tone, except for his heart. It ached unbearably.

'Joe did his best to find your daughter, Mrs. Grey,' said Montague, sounding sincere. 'I assure you he did, and we will do our best now. If you'd like to come with me, we will take that walk now. Arnie will take the rest of your family to The Fill Up, where they can get something to eat.'

The pair started moving towards the hideous entrance of The Crypt, looking like two lovers out on a stroll.

Chapter Six

The Milk Has Gone Sour

1

Joe had seen the cluster of dilapidated farm buildings situated at the eastern corner of the field that the carnival occupied the day before and had learned from Arnie this was where Launder called home. A sense of urgency overwhelmed Joe now; it had been over an hour since Lily Grey had entered The Crypt.

An hour since she had last been seen alive.

No one had yet said the word 'body'. Joe had not even entertained the idea that they could be looking for one; instead, his mind had concluded two potential outcomes. Something had either happened to her or someone had happened to her.

2

The knowledge chilled his body and fired his adrenaline. Rather than wasting time using the ramp, Joe leaped from the platform's side into the grassy alleyway between The Crypt and the next stall. He landed on his right foot, took one large stride with the other, and began to sprint until the grass slushed rhythmically at his ankles.

The Launder home was directly ahead at a distance of less than a mile. In between Joe and it was the carnies' campground.

The blare of a horn raged as he came shooting out of the alleyway.

At the time, he had been running full speed, the source of the horn appearing as a gargantuan black blur in the left-hand side of his vision. There was no time to stop. Joe's arms struck out, flailing in an attempt to slow while his feet skidded over the earth. The big rig – or what he assumed was a big rig, judging by its horn – bore down on him.

If Lou Fritz had been driving the eighteen-wheeler any faster, Joe would have been pulverized against the thing's shining chrome grill. Thankfully, Lou had only just set off and was keeping the speed low while navigating the carnies' campground. The behemoth-sized lorry jolted to a stop right in front of Joe, its hydraulics hissing angrily.

In the cab, Lou was making all sorts of hand gestures. With his heart racing, Joe threw aside his work etiquette without a thought. His right hand shot up, his middle finger thrust to the sky and aimed at Lou.

'Oh, fuck you,' he said.

Lou froze inside the lorry's cab, his eyes bulging while his ratty face drained of colour. He reciprocated the hand gesture, then cranked the big rig into gear, tearing forward in a belch of oily fumes.

Joe watched him depart, laughing wildly at the sky. A young girl was missing, a young girl who reminded him so much of his sister, and Lou Fritz was still a dickhead. It was too much for him. He laughed until his eyes watered.

Eventually, he managed to move forward at a shambling kind of hop, then, as the giggles subsided, his stride lengthened. Joe raced through the maze of RVs, big rigs, and cars of the carnies' camping area. Lou's shocked, disgruntled expression stayed in his head the whole way. *At least,* he thought, *if there's one good thing to come out of today, it was putting that bastard in his place.*

3

He regained his breath before mounting the porch and knocking on the door. Joe had no intention of telling Launder why he needed to use his telephone, other than it was an emergency. A man like him would not be sympathetic. If he tried to make a big deal out of it, Joe would tell him to take it up with Montague.

It turned out that he need not have worried. The door opened a few inches and the heart-shaped face of a teenage girl appeared in the gap. Her eyes were the colour of milk chocolate and they held his firmly.

'I'm sorry, but Papa's not here,' she told him. 'He's gone into town with Ma for groceries.'

The fact that Launder had managed to find someone to reproduce with, let alone father such a stunning young woman, surprised Joe into silence. Even in the shade of the porch, Joe could see her skin held a tawny hue. She had a beauty mark above her lips, which were plump and pink, and he imagined that many of the local boys dreamed of kissing those lips and that dark spot.

'I'm not here to speak to your parents,' said Joe quickly, as the girl was about to shut the door. 'I'm from the carnival.'

The girl's eyebrows jumped and she clutched the golden crucifix hanging around her neck even tighter. He noted that the gap was closing again.

'There's been an accident. A girl has gone missing, and I need to phone the sheriff,' he blurted out.

The gap stopped closing as the girl stared at him. A young voice behind her said, 'Someone's gone missing? Let me see.'

The girl rolled her eyes, sweeping the door wide to reveal who Joe assumed was her younger brother dressed in jeans and a grey Nike top. They both stood in a dark hallway that seemed to stretch the length of the house.

'Who's gone missing?' asked the boy. Joe guessed he was about twelve.

'I'd rather tell the sheriff that,' he answered.

The boy scoffed and said, 'Don't let him in. Father will go nuts if you do.'

'We're not supposed to let anyone in who we don't know,' explained Launder's daughter, apologetically.

She was dressed in a demure black dress that started at her ankles and went all the way to her shoulders. Having met her father, Joe suspected wearing it was not entirely her choice.

'Okay, I get that, but this is an emergency. This young girl's family is distraught right now, plus God knows how scared she is.'

'Swear,' said the brother. 'He just took the Lord's name in vain; Father says that people who do that are filthy heathens.'

Launder's daughter's face blanched a deep crimson.

'Lovely,' Joe replied, then addressed Launder's daughter. 'My name's Joe Cage, and I'm not a filthy heathen. What I am is just a guy trying to do the right thing by alerting the local law.'

A crooked twist of a smirk played across the young woman's face.

'Well, Joe, I'm Olive and that's Daniel, and seeing as you're not a filthy heathen, I think we can let you use the phone line,' she said to him.

107

'You can't!' exclaimed Daniel. 'I'll tell Father and Mother about this, and you'll ...'

'If you so much as breathe a word to Dad and Mom, then I'll tell them what I saw you and Bobby-Dee doing in our barn with your pants down,' snapped Olive, without even turning in her brother's direction.

This time it was Daniel's turn to have his face bloom tomato red. Joe's eyebrows skyrocketed at this revelation.

'But... I... ' Daniel stammered, tears welling in his eyes.

Unable to articulate his fury, Daniel stamped his right foot and screamed at both of them. He continued screaming even as he stomped upstairs.

'They were examining each other's wieners. I don't know why,' Olive informed him. 'The phone is this way.'

'Thank you,' said Joe, stepping over the threshold.

'Just promise me this isn't an excuse to get inside the house because you're a murderer or something,' said Olive, leading him down the dark hallway.

Joe held his right hand up as if taking a vow. 'I promise I am not a murderer or a filthy heathen.' Olive laughed, a single bark. 'Yeah, I'm sorry about that, my parents are big into their religion and unfortunately, Daniel drinks their Kool-Aid,' she said.

The notion that Launder was a religious nut was laughable to Joe, having witnessed him swindling Montague yesterday. The dull tone Olive used to speak about her parents suggested that she knew the same.

'It's okay, I've had worse things said to me,' said Joe.

Olive guided him to the room at the end of the hallway, which turned out to be a finely-furnished kitchen. Despite the poor state of the farmhouse buildings, Launder's house was pristinely well-maintained.

Only the best for Launder, Joe mused.

'Something wrong?' asked Olive.

Joe had been staring at the phone, which hung from the kitchen wall in a plastic cradle. He had been reliving his conversation with Marybell's sheriff the day before and became very aware that as he had left the diner parking lot, he had done so with the determination to never see him again.

'It's nothing,' he said, sighing and reaching for the phone.

4

As Joe walked back across Launder's field, he felt a weight had been lifted off his shoulders after speaking with police dispatch. This was not because he had washed his hands of Lily Grey; there was simply comfort in hearing that crisp, calm voice on the other end of the phone line. Underneath it was the sense of a great machine gearing up to work. It said to him, 'Don't panic, the cavalry's on their way.' He hoped for the Greys' sake that it was true.

5

Joe found them in The Fill Up, the carnival's only sit-down eatery. Montague was speaking to Meryl Grey while the three children sat at one of the red picnic tables that filled the eatery. The twins, their hair a shade darker than Lily's straw colour, had their heads bowed. Henry

Grey's gaze kept switching from the twins to his mom, and Joe didn't blame him.

Meryl Grey looked catatonic. Her head belonged to a wax figurine, one that could be molded into any shape, while her eyes had all the life of a doll.

Joe did not doubt that whatever Montague was saying to her was falling on deaf ears. This did not seem to discourage the carnival owner.

'Jesus,' whispered Joe on seeing her.

'She's been like that for a while,' said a voice at his side.

Joe half jumped out of his skin, clutching at his heart.

'Easy there, tiger,' said Daisy Hill. 'I thought I'd take you up on your lunch offer. You're still my second choice, by the way; I couldn't find Youssef anywhere to ask him. How's your day going?' There was a gleeful light in Daisy's blue eyes.

'Something tells me you already know how my day is going,' he muttered.

'Rumour has it you've been slaying little girls and bathing in their blood,' remarked Daisy.

'Is that what people are saying?'

'Yep, well, this job was nice while it lasted. It's been one of the nicest places I've ever worked, even if it has been all of one day. I have you to thank for that - for screwing the pooch so to speak. I guess everyone will be moving on.'

'What are you talking about?' Joe asked wearily.

He wasn't in the mood for Daisy's sense of humour right now.

'You honestly think the carnival is going to keep working in this little shit berg when the rumors hit the town? They're all spread about the fair today so everyone in town will know tomorrow;

110

that's how it works in places like this. If the carnival is still here, they'll rush us out of town.'

Joe rubbed his eyelids, then swept his hands through his hair. When he was finished, he stared across the obstacle course of red chairs and picnic tables to the Grey family.

'You think it's going to come to that?' Joe asked Daisy.

'They might lynch us,' she said, her tone infuriatingly bright.

The tented roof fluttered above them, trapping the cloud of sizzling burger grease from the grills. To the right, they could see the white struts of The Whirl and to the left, they could see the carousel spinning, a kaleidoscope of gold and scarlet. Children's screams came from everywhere.

'Are you going to be leaving?'

Surprisingly, Joe found he was saddened at the idea of never seeing Daisy again. In his time traveling, there was no one who he had met that he could say he missed, but he learned then that he would miss Daisy when it came time for them to head their separate ways.

Not that Joe had made any decision to leave, despite how his sixth sense was telling him to pack his bags and move on. All drifters and runaways developed this alarm system after a time bouncing from place to place, he had found.

'If it comes to it, yeah, this job isn't my final destination. It's just a stop along the way,' said Daisy philosophically.

Even in his disappointment, Joe looked at her with admiration. Daisy had been on the road longer than him; her sixth sense for danger was sharper, having already come to a decision he was still debating.

Ignoring his alarm system in the past had proved disastrous for him. One time in particular stood out, and that was his last job working for Dylan Macintosh, the owner of Dylan's Roadhouse.

The bruises on his right knuckles had almost faded.

But that gig had gone sour long before that confrontation. It had soured some days before that when he had been working the bar alongside Dylan. Joe's job hadn't been to serve customers; Dylan reserved that pleasure for his collection of attractive female bartenders.

'They get the clientele to buy more,' he had told Joe on his first day. His slimy tongue flicked the toothpick that was forever lodged in his mouth back and forth. Several of his teeth were black tombstones.

'It's a womanly talent to get blood out of a stone, and that's what my women do to the clientele. They get them so hot under the collar long before they're even drunk that they'll buy anything; they even get some of the woman hot too. Your job, Joe, is to make sure my women don't run out of things to sell.'

The bar was empty at this point, seeing as it was only the morning. Still, the place was loud with the glassy crash of bottles being binned.

'Your job is to bring the kegs from the back, to make sure the fine stuff is always topped up, and to do a general sweep up of the tables of any empties. Think you can do that?'

Joe had said he could and that's what he had done. The only mistake he had made had been talking to Leah McCain, one of Dylan's bartenders.

It was an innocent sort of thing. Dylan's Roadhouse was full of farmers and farmhands after a long day's work, and it was all hands on deck. As Joe returned to the bar, hands full of empty glassware, Leah had said to him, 'Better hurry up now, we don't need any slowpokes working with us.'

She was a little older than he was, with strawberry blonde hair and one arm painted in tattoos up to her collar. Joe had had a good view of it thanks to the 'uniforms' Dylan made his 'women' wear.

'Don't you worry, no slow poking with me,' he had replied and Leah had burst into laughter.

That had been the start of it. They had no time to have any real conversation with the business of the bar; instead, they had passed teasing remarks whenever they were in orbit of one another. Sometime later, Joe had caught Dylan staring at him from his perch, a stool he kept behind the bar in the corner, his grey eyes dark, his toothpick wagging like a dog's tail.

The next night, Joe had been holding class in the parking lot with two of Dylan's friends. It wasn't the fight that his sixth sense had alarmed at; it was Dylan's piercing stare the night before. Joe had not heeded the warning.

Just like he was doing now.

'Hey, look, if it means anything, I don't think you did anything wrong,' Daisy said to him sincerely.

Joe blinked, realising his mind had taken him on one wild tangent.

'Why?'

'Because I don't think you can do anything wrong. Not like, you know, kidnapping a child. You're too much of a boy scout to be a creepy abductor.'

'Thanks, I always thought of myself as a bit of a badass, actually.'

113

Daisy punched his right arm playfully. 'No, you're a complete boy scout,' she said, then added, 'There are worse things to be.'

'When do you think you'll leave?'

'Probably tonight, after I get my pay for today,' Daisy told him. 'Until then I'm still on the clock.'

At that moment, Arnie entered The Fill Up and whispered something in Montague's ear. The carnival owner didn't take his gaze from Meryl the entire time.

'What exactly happened anyway?' Daisy asked.

By the time Joe had told her everything, Arnie had wandered over to them.

'The police are here. One of my guys is showing them around The Crypt,' he said begrudgingly.

He looked bone-tired to Joe, like he had had some of the life sucked out of him.

'Listen, kid, I'm sorry for being off with you earlier. It's just calling the local fuzz is the worst possible thing to have to do for a traveling company like us. You did the right thing, though; don't think I don't know that. The fuzz will want to talk to you; you just tell them what you told me, and you'll be fine.'

Bonds that Joe had not noticed fell away from him at Arnie's words. For a horrifying length of time, he had been thinking that the person he had gotten closest to suspected him of doing something foul.

Arnie would also be someone who he would miss.

He held no animosity towards the carny for being wary of him. If their roles had been reversed and it had been Arnie who emerged from The

114

Crypt covered in blood, he would have been concerned as well.

'Thanks, Arnie. That means a lot,' he said.

'Good. In the meantime, let's try and distract these kids by getting them something to eat,' Arnie said.

6

'You guys must be hungry,' Joe remarked to the Grey children.

The two twins looked up from their laps with identical baleful expressions.

'Arnie here is best friends with the chef. I'm sure he can get him to rustle you all up some grub.'

'I sure am and I'm sure I can and most importantly, it's on the house, all you can eat for free,' said Arnie, playing along.

'Gee, thanks,' said Henry, looking relieved at the intervention of the three adults.

Daisy drifted around the side of the picnic table, dropping down to the twins' level and offering them her hands.

'Do you want to come with me?' she asked.

Joe had never heard her speak so softly or with such concern. It gave him a glimpse of a different side to Daisy beyond her inappropriate humour.

All three Grey children followed them subserviently to the nearest grill being run by Earl Porter, the carny in charge of all the carnival's food.

There was something bearish about Earl to Joe. The chef wasn't tall by any means, yet there was a looming vastness about him, both in his width and his personality, which was soaked in sarcasm. He sported glasses with heavy frames on top and wire underneath in front of a set of mahogany-coloured eyes. His head was shaved bald while a huge, bushy beard of wiry ginger-brown hair coated his jaw. Joe expected to hear a loud, booming voice from this man, only to be surprised by his reedy deadpan.

'These young men are eating for free, Earl,' announced Arnie.

'Free,' huffed Earl. 'What are we doing here, Arnie? Running a charity service? Because this food didn't pay for itself.' Then he looked over the top of his grille at the two twins. His eyes were huge and bug-like behind his lenses. 'You all must be special young men if Arnie says you get to eat for free,' he told them. 'Arnie thinks to say the word free is to speak another language.'

Both twins giggled lamely. *At least it's a start*, Joe thought.

As the kids ordered, he saw that Arnie was looking behind them.

'What is it?'

'The police are talking to Montague, and it looks like they've found something,' said Arnie.

Their entire group spun on the spot. Joe immediately recognised Sheriff Jackson as he spoke with Montague and Meryl Grey. The man was just as mountainous as he remembered him to be. The only difference now was that he had removed his sunglasses and he was wearing gloves.

The gloves were the plastic kind Joe supposed surgeons wore to operate on people. *Or for police to pick up the evidence with,* the voice whispered to him.

Sure enough, Sheriff Jackson clutched a plastic evidence bag and was holding it out to

Meryl to see. The bag was see-through so they could all make out what was inside it.

'That's Lily's teddy bear,' said one of the twins.

The teddy bear's fur was tacky with blood.

Chapter Six

Dylan's Roadhouse

1

Outside, the crickets sang their maddening song. On quiet occasions such as tonight, when payday was tomorrow, their chirping penetrated the walls of the bar. Dylan Macintosh didn't mind; he had owned and operated the roadhouse for close to twenty years, and it was as much background noise to him as the jukebox or the clatter of glass.

The only clientele in the bar were three local boys sat around a high table in the right-hand corner of the building. Dylan knew two of them well; Adam Lowe and Peter Grant had attempted to help him teach a former employee by the name of Joe Cage a lesson last week.

They had failed miserably.

Even from the other side of the bar, Dylan could make out the cast on Adam's right arm. It was tattooed with signatures, some belonging to his staff.

At that moment, the trio burst into uproarious laughter, spilling their beer in the process. Dylan knew they were all underage, but he'd rather make some money than nothing tonight, and it kept them sweet should he ever need a favor.

There was a squeal of brakes outside, diverting Dylan's gaze to the view from the windows on his left. An eighteen-wheeler was pulling into the parking lot, its tyres crunching on the lot's gravel. Whoever was behind the wheel parked it alongside the building with a hiss of hydraulics.

The crickets continued to sing, unfazed.

With the big rig's engine off, Dylan heard the clump as both cab doors were slammed shut, followed by the scrape of boots. Leah McCain, the only barmaid on tonight, must have heard it too because she asked, 'You want me to serve these two first, or is okay if I go tinkle?'

'Nah, you go ahead and see to yourself,' said Dylan, thinking if he were nice enough now, perhaps Leah would stroke him off later.

The toothpick between his teeth began to wag even more enthusiastically over his bottom lip. Sometimes, he found he toyed with the toothpicks so damn much that he rubbed the skin there raw.

'Thanks,' Leah said, giving him a smile that made him hopeful.

Dylan watched her go, his eyes on her ass as she disappeared into the narrow corridor on the building's right-hand side. She didn't always jerk him off when he drove her home; a lot of times she flat-out refused, usually when she was dating someone, and they would sit in silence for the duration of the journey, his erection like a hot stone against his zipper.

Other times she was more amenable to him.

For example, when she wasn't interested in tugging him off she let him suckle at her nipples; she always tasted salty, her body dewed with sweat from a hard night's work, and faintly of beer. On one memorable occasion, in the summer after the air inside the roadhouse had become sultry under the baking heat and from the press of bodies inside, Leah had demanded that he pull the car over. She had straddled him in the driver's seat before the car had even stopped fully. They probably would have gone all the way then if, in his excitement, he hadn't unloaded his sack onto the soft jelly of her belly. It hadn't been a complete write-off; she had let him do other things to her.

Dylan could feel the old member stirring against his zipper at the memory. He inserted a quarter into the jukebox and selected 'You've Never Been This Far Before' by Conway Twitty. The three underage drunks in the corner raised their glasses and cheered. Dylan nodded in response to them.

As he did, the two truckers entered the bar through the swing door. His first thought of the two men was that they looked like no truckers he had never seen before, the trucker stereotype being a middle-aged white guy dressed in denim and plaid with a gut like an apron.

These guys looked nothing like that.

The first was the biggest, darkest man Dylan had ever seen, dressed in dark jeans and a coffee-coloured pullover. He had to hunch over to get through the doorway, his bald head gleaming in the bar's weak lights. The second was a beanpole in comparison to his companion, dressed like a New York rocker, his face rat-like with its narrow appearance and sharp, jutting jaw.

Dylan noted out of the corner of his eye his other clientele were surveying the new arrivals with quiet hostility.

'Evening, gents, what can I do for you?' asked Dylan.

The mountain strolled off in the direction of the toilets without a word.

'Two Budweisers, please,' said the beanpole.

As Dylan popped the tops, he glanced at the big rig outside. It was painted entirely black with no commercial tags or emblems on the side.

'That's two dollars each, or are you looking to start a tab?' asked Dylan.

The beanpole stared as he sipped his drink with eyes like grey steel. The toothpick in Dylan's mouth stopped dancing.

'Oh yes, I think we'll start a tab,' he answered. 'You know that's an awful bad compulsion you've got; it says you've got a restless mind.'

What the hell? thought Dylan.

The beanpole stepped away from his stool and headed after his companion. *I guess you have to tinkle too,* thought Dylan, watching him go.

His eyes caught the trio's in the corner. Dylan shrugged his shoulders while Peter Grant shook his head and mouthed, 'Faggots.'

The roadhouse owner's lips pulled into a smile that felt like a grimace. There was something weird about those two men. Dylan stretched his back, rotating his arms at the shoulders, attempting to lose the ruffled feather feeling he felt.

Like someone's walked over my grave, he thought. *And where the hell is Leah? The girl said she was going for a tinkle, not a dump.*

There was an unsettled emotion linked with those thoughts that led Dylan to realise that he was very much afraid. In that realisation, his brain was already computing facts that it pulled from all his five senses.

Never before had he considered just how isolated his roadhouse was. There wasn't another building for three miles in each direction; that was a fact he had always known and he even relished the idea that no nosy neighbours could pry into his business. Now the coin had flipped and he saw the other side of that fact; that he was alone with no one to rely on for help. There was the telephone, but the nearest cop shop was an additional six miles away.

Why would I need them, anyway?

Because I'm in fucking trouble here, he screamed back in his mind.

The inside of the bar felt electrified, the way the air goes before a tornado swirls into existence. The sensation pressed against him like a hot palm, drawing flop sweat from his pores. And it wasn't just him feeling this way; he observed that his other clientele had grown quiet and watchful of the restroom corridor.

They had a better view of it from their corner of the bar than he did.

They were three miles to the nearest homestead on unlit roads, three miles of only cornfields and the endless Kansas night sky. There had been times when he had appreciated the secrecy that vast sky offered when taking barmaids like Leah McCain home. It had felt like a hood where he could achieve his desires without the fear of being overlooked or stumbled upon. But there were bigger and fouler things in the world that liked to use such vast, empty spaces as their hunting ground. And Dylan suspected that two of them were using his restroom right now.

'I got to take a leak,' said Adam Lowe.

Dylan's senses had been heightened by his panicked thoughts so much that he heard him clearly from behind the bar.

'Want us to help you with that?' said Peter Grant, referring to Adam's casted arm.

Peter and the third person in their party, Sean Wilder, laughed like it was the funniest thing in the world. The sound of their hacking voices caused the hackles to rise on the top of Dylan's spine.

'Fuck off,' Adam shot back at them, disappearing into the corridor.

That was the last Dylan saw of him. He heard his steel toe-capped boots on the wooden floor as he progressed down the narrow corridor. It was a poorly lit cave because Dylan bought the cheapest light bulbs. Dylan could imagine the shadows crawling up and down Adam's broad shoulders as he moved from light to darkness.

The tread of his boots ended as he came upon the men's restroom door on the left-hand side. The corridor ended at the fire door with a vivid green exit sign situated above it. Dylan listened, straining, and heard the swish as Adam pushed open the restroom door which, like the entrance to the bar, swung both ways. Then nothing.

Leah, where the hell are you? he thought, without any fury. This time he was concerned.

Seconds ticked by, marked by the steady march of the Miller clock on the wall. Peter and Sean spoke to one another in low, hushed tones. Dylan stood like a sweating statue except for the toothpick in his mouth, wagging back and forth. His gaze was fixed on the two Budweisers on the counter, watching the condensation run in rivulets down their sides.

'He must be struggling to find it,' said Peter to Sean.

Dylan's eyes snapped in their direction. His stomach somersaulted at seeing Peter getting off his stool. He wanted to shout, 'No, don't!' but he couldn't get his throat to work.

I'm just being crazy. Those two guys are simply back there sucking each other off or something and Adam hasn't come back yet because he's struggling with that cast of his. That's all that's going on.

Peter looked to him as he passed the bar; the yellow bruises along his jaw from Joe Cage gave him a jaundiced appearance in the dim barroom light.

'Just going to see if he needs a hand,' he said. There was sweat on the skin above his upper lip.

Dylan nodded to him, and copying Peter's awkward feign of humour, said, 'He might need you to shake it for him.'

Neither of them laughed.

Peter stepped into the corridor, his footfalls lighter than his friend's. Dylan's feet began to tiptoe across the floor behind the bar, the chirping from the crickets outside seeming to increase in volume as he drew closer to where the bar ended, and he stepped out from behind it. This placed him directly in front of the corridor just as the men's restroom door swung shut, sealing against the frame with a flat hissing sound.

Dylan glanced over his shoulder at Sean, who was watching in silence from his stool, brow furrowed, a hand round his beer glass. Dylan turned back and peered down the dimly lit passage with its draping shadows. Sweat pooled in his pants from his shriveled balls. They begged to be readjusted, to be yanked into a better position, as they sometimes needed to be.

Dylan made no move to do so. Everyone knows that to give in to distraction was when the monsters got you.

A door swung wide inside the passageway and Dylan sucked air into his lungs, nearly choking on his toothpick. It was the ladies' room that had opened, and Leah was walking out. She stopped short when she saw the two men staring at her. She was still buckling her belt.

'What? I'm sorry I took a while. What's going on?' she said.

An arm, corded in muscle and black as tar, shot out from the men's bathroom and seized Leah McCain by the forearm. There was enough time for Dylan to see Leah's head snap down to where she was being grabbed and then back to him. She looked confused.

In the split second that that arm grabbed her, Dylan's mind told him it was not human. The nearest thing his mind associated it with was a tentacle; it did not look like one, yet the way it had seized Leah reminded him of one.

The arm yanked her soundlessly off her feet.

It was an expression Dylan had heard countless times in his life, but never actually seen until now. Leah McCain was yanked into the men's restroom with such force that both her feet were lifted off the ground.

The restroom door shut with a clap.

Before, there had been no sound after the last two people had gone inside; now, there was the sound of bodies fumbling about. Then screams. They were undoubtedly Leah's.

'Holy fuck!' yelled Sean behind him, followed by a clatter.

Dylan saw that in his haste to stand, he had spilled his beer. He saw this because he was running for the exit, a high keening noise escaping from his throat. He spat out his toothpick.

When he was halfway across the bar, he heard a familiar bang – a signal that meant one of the restroom doors had been thrown open. He didn't dare look back because whatever had caused it to do so had Sean Wilder screaming like a girl.

Sean backed up against the wall, his eyes seeming to fall out of his head at what he was seeing. As Dylan reached the exit, a black blur smashed into Sean at the speed of a locomotive, slamming him into the wall. The black shape smothered him, moving with freakish rigidity over his body, its head buried in Sean's neck. Sean's arms seemed to embrace it like a lover as his legs skittered to find balance.

There was a sound like a phone book being ripped in half. Suddenly the walls and the shape were being sprayed in blood, as if Sean's neck had become the world's most ferocious beer spigot. The beer-sour air reeked of pennies.

Outside, the cool night froze the sweat on Dylan as he dashed across the gravel lot to his Trans Am, chest heaving. He reached the driver's side door, hands rooting inside his jeans for his keys. The crickets, whose song was constant at the roadhouse and had risen to such a level they were buzzing like live wires, ceased with a finality that made Dylan believe he had gone deaf.

He spun on his heels, staring into the cornfields.

'Oh, God,' he whispered.

Dylan groped for his keys, facing the car once more. He felt their familiar metal and heard their familiar jingle when a dark figure landed upon the Trans Am roof with a thump, rocking the vehicle on its springs.

He sat down hard on his ass, the gravel stabbing into the small of his back where his shirt had ridden up. He didn't care; that high keening noise was shrieking from his throat as the thing on top of his car leaned over him.

Its eyes were as red as rubies, and it seemed to be smiling.

Book Two

Investigations of the Weird

Chapter One

Bloody Rag

1

As a shell-shocked Meryl Grey and her equally shell-shocked children were being escorted to the Marybell Police Station in Sheriff Jackson's Blazer, Len Grey was woken from a sleep that was like a black vacuum by the shrill sound of his doorbell. He woke to a world of pain, as if someone had stabbed a steel spike into his skull and swirled its contents around.

Ding-ding, ding-ding.

With a mighty sigh, Len heaved himself to the side of the bed, the world wobbling like he was its axis. His tongue felt furred in cigarette ash from all the chain smoking he did last night. Worse was the smell of the bedroom that breezed up his nostrils, a sour, toxic scent that oozed from his skin.

'Oh shit,' Len muttered, scrambling forward on legs that felt like stalks.

He hit the bathroom door ahead of him, causing it slam against the wall. He had no time to care, as whatever burning fluid was in his stomach rushed up his throat, spluttering out from his dry lips in a jet. The vomit, the colour of egg yolks, splashed across the turquoise toilet lid before his knees met the tiled floor with a thump on either side of the bowl.

Ding-ding, ding-ding.

I wasn't even that drunk, thought Len as his stomach jittered seismically. This was true; even earlier that morning when Meryl had been organising the kids for the fair, he hadn't felt that bad at all. He had, if he was being completely honest, played up his hangover when it occurred to him that he could have most of the day to himself, the image of a plate heaped high with fried breakfast food tempting him.

He could make that all for himself, he had thought. No kids running around pestering him for his attention, tugging at his arm as he tried to read the newspaper or listen to the game. No Meryl wanting to have an adult conversation after spending the week looking after the kids.

That stacked plate of food where the meats were all vivid pinks and browns and deep burgundies, where the scrambled eggs seemed to glow they were that yellow, was so real his mouth watered at the imagined wholesome smell of the thing. That plate symbolised peace to him. So he had lied.

What was making him sick was not the booze or even the yeasty after smell coming from his pores; it was the other smell. The smell of raw flesh that haunted him every night he returned from the chicken farms where he worked, although it had begun to feel like a place where he was wasting his life rather than earning a living for his family.

Ding-ding, ding-ding.

'Hold on, I'm coming!' he yelled, spitting into the toilet.

His throat burned with the acidic taste of his stomach. Len swept a hand through the silver corkscrews of the fringe matted to his brow.

He flushed, used the sink to regain his feet, and padded back through the bedroom, nose snorting at the foul odour. An odour he associated with Glen Launder, his abrasive sleaze of an employer. It repulsed him to even think about spending his day off on his employer's land close to the man.

I've already wasted enough of time with that man, he thought bitterly, descending the stairs in his bare feet.

Len reached for the front door without considering the two shadows on either side of the glass panes. His head rang with the doorbell's shriek as he yanked the door wide.

All ferocity behind such a movement wilted at the sight of the two police officers standing on his porch step. Marybell being a small place, he recognised both of them instantly, yet that's not what shocked him. What did was the expressions on their faces, of people building up to bad news.

I don't really recognise them at all, he thought, for their expressions made them look alien somehow.

'Elaine, Mitch,' he said, clutching his bathrobe tight.

The two officers exchanged a glance, Elaine's height and Mitch's lack of it making them look like comical polar opposites on his porch. The sun was beaming at their backs, catching fire in Elaine's blonde hair and reflecting off the sheen of Mitch's bald head.

'What is it?' Len choked. The fur on his tongue felt like it had crept down his throat, absorbing all the moisture. He didn't need them to reply; he knew something was wrong, knew by their faces, by the plunge his lower half seemed to have taken. 'Please tell me it's not the kids.'

'I think it's best if we have this conversation inside, Len,' said Mitch, his deep country drawl sounding to Len like the voice of the Grim Reaper.

2

This is a portion of the transcript from the interview of Meryl Grey conducted on Tuesday May 10th, 14:30 by Sheriff Timothy Jackson and Deputy Lloyd Herrick.

Meryl: It's all my fault.

Sheriff Jackson: I'm sorry, Mrs. Grey?

Meryl: It's my fault she's gone.

Sheriff Jackson: Mrs. Grey, Meryl, nobody in this office thinks that.

Meryl: I don't give a shit about your office, Tim. It's the whole town that will be thinking it. You don't have children, so don't pretend to know what it's like. Have you ever seen one of those children's beauty pageants?

Sheriff Jackson: No, but I know what you're talking about.

Meryl: Well, every day is like a beauty pageant for a mother, especially in this town. Everyone's a critic; everyone is looking to see you fail. Well, I failed. I failed at looking after my baby. It was just so hot in that damn queue and the twins were acting up and I was constantly having to separate them to stop them fighting, and Henry was in a mood like he always seems to be in these days, and I was doing all this alone because Len was at home nursing off last night's beers. And Lily, who I always rely on to be good, started whining about that stupid ghost ride. She was frightened. I thought, Not you, not now when everyone else can see. So I ignored her. I ignored them all while we stood waiting. Lily... she just... she slipped by... slipped by both of us.

Sheriff Jackson: Listen, I think we are getting ahead of ourselves here. Now, I know you already told me all this information earlier, but I need you to state it once again for the record, okay? What time did you arrive at the fair?

Meryl: Around eleven o'clock.

Sheriff Jackson: And who was with you at that time?

Meryl: My daughter, Lily, my twins, Ben and Clay, and my eldest, Henry.

Sheriff Jackson: You mentioned already that your husband was at home.

Meryl: Yes, he wasn't feeling well.

Sheriff Jackson: So you turn up at the fair at eleven o'clock. Did you notice anyone suspicious, anyone following you or anything like that?

Meryl: No, not at all.

Sheriff Jackson: And where did you go inside the fair?

Meryl: We went to The Ring Toss game first because there was a crowd there and the kids wanted to see what the fuss was. After that, we went straight to the ghost ride.

Sheriff Jackson: And what time would you say you got to the ghost ride?

Meryl: About eleven-twenty.

Sheriff Jackson: You said earlier when you were queued for the ride that she slipped by both of us; whom exactly are you referring to?

Meryl: Joe Cage, he's one of the carnies. No, that's not right, he isn't a carny, just someone who happened to get a job with them while they were in town. I served him yesterday at the diner and knew from his look that he needed work, so I sent him in their direction. He was in charge of letting people onto the platform to get onto the ghost ride. He was the one who offered to go in and get Lily.

Sheriff Jackson: You served this man at the place where you work, which would be Bob's Roadside Diner. Is that correct?

Meryl: Yes

Sheriff Jackson: When was this?

133

Meryl: Yesterday...Monday the 9th.

Sheriff Jackson: Did you mention anything about your family to him when you were giving him directions?

Meryl: No

Sheriff Jackson: Did this man, Joe, have any prior interactions with your daughter?

Meryl: Yes, he gave us our tickets at the entrance to the fair. Lily spoke to him about how much she wanted to get on the ghost ride.

Deputy Herrick: I thought you said he was working the entrance to the ghost ride, not the entrance to the fair itself?

Meryl: I did, and he was. He was working at both; I dunno why. I just assumed the carnies shift about to where they are needed most at the time.

Sheriff Jackson: And he interacted with your daughter as you were entering the fair.

Meryl: Yes, well, you see the twins were arguing so I was busy dealing with them, and Lily, she had wandered forward. She was keen to get inside, and Joe happened to be the one working the entrance alongside that other carny, the one with the hat. That one seemed to be in charge of the ghost ride because I saw him there later ordering everyone around. He also helped me... when Lily disappeared.

Sheriff Jackson: Okay. Did you happen to see Joe at any other point during your time within the fair?

Meryl: Now that you mention it, I guess we bumped into him a third time. This was at The Ring Toss game; he was working alongside a woman with the strangest hairstyle. Lily waved at him.

Deputy Herrick: Did he seem overall interested in Lily in any particular way?

134

Meryl: No… I mean… What do you mean?

Deputy Herrick: Was he interested in, say, speaking with her more than speaking with yourself or your other children?

Meryl: Well, they spoke, but he was nice, friendly.

Sheriff Jackson: As you've already stated Joe Cage was the person who went to search for Lily inside Journey Through The Crypt first?

Meryl: Yes, he seemed genuinely concerned.

Sheriff Jackson: And did he go in alone or with someone else?

Meryl: Alone. Nobody offered to go with him.

Sheriff Jackson: My understanding from the statement we took from you earlier was that Joe was gone for as long as half an hour. Do you still think that is an accurate estimate of time?

Meryl: Well, yes, I say he was gone for half an hour. Maybe forty minutes.

Sheriff Jackson: And in that time were you concerned at all for your daughter's safety?

Meryl: Of course I was. What type of question is that?

Sheriff Jackson: Was any of your concern directed towards Joe being alone with your daughter? I mean, he disappeared for some length of time, and nobody saw what he did inside the ride.

Meryl: No… I wasn't. He's a nice guy.

Deputy Herrick: He's a nice guy that gave you all quite a fright. I heard you fainted when he came out without your daughter.

Meryl: That's because he was covered in blood and I thought…

Sheriff Jackson: What did you think, Mrs. Grey?

Meryl: I thought it was Lily's blood, that he was painted in Lily's blood. That's why I fainted. When I came to, I saw Joe again and I saw the cut on his forehead. The blood was from that.

Sheriff Jackson: Did you see Joe's forehead bleeding?

Meryl: No.

Sheriff Jackson: So why did you think the blood on Joe was from the cut on his forehead?

Meryl: I… I can't remember.

Sheriff Jackson: Okay, let's talk about something else.

3

'I take it you both are heading back to Launder's field?' Jackson asked the Greys.

This was in the corridor at the eastern end of the police station, where the windows on the right-hand side had their blinds shut. Farther on down they were open, casting the carnies waiting to be interviewed in sunrays so bright they looked like a mirage. Jackson's head hurt looking at them in that light, thankful for the small sense of privacy the shaded area offered.

To speak to the Greys down there would be like putting on a show to him.

'Yes, I'm sorry if I lost the head in there,' Len replied, pointing to the interview room over his shoulder.

'It's okay,' assured Jackson before he could carry on.

Len nodded at him as if to say thank you. Jackson was pretty sure he was about to apologize again for not being at the carnival, as he had done in the interview room with his face looking like a slack, grey death mask. This was after the man had slammed his fist repeatedly on the table between them, tears flowing down his silver stubbled cheeks.

Instead, his face was like a closed fist now as he took his wife's arm. While that concerned him, Meryl's expression worried him even more; she looked like his father had when the senility had stripped him of every facet of his personality, like someone lost in a fog.

'We are going to get to the bottom of this,' he informed them in the firmest voice he could muster, aware that his deputy's eyes were on him, that all eyes were on him, including those of the carnies at the end of the hallway.

The feel of those eyes made his words seem like a lie.

'Listen, I've pulled the night crew to help with searching the carnival proper as well as doing vehicle searches for everyone there. If you find one of them, they can keep you up to date on all that's happening. No stone will go unturned, okay?'

As he was saying this, his umber eyes glancing between the two and he observed that Meryl's head had drifted from him to the figures down the corridor, perhaps because of the sweet scent of sweat and wood smoke that they bought with them, overriding the hallway's bleach odor. Jackson watched her stiffen, watched the veins in her neck become pronounced, like two thick avenues beneath muscles that had clenched.

What happened next Deputy Lloyd Herrick witnessed with a sense of familiar awe from Jackson's side. One of the straps of Meryl's handbag had fallen loose from the crook of her elbow on account of the sudden shift in her body. The whole thing was tipping sideways, the mouth of the leather bag widening, becoming to him like the mouth of a catfish as it spilled out its contents: lipstick, a hair brush, a cloud of used tissues.

Jackson was already moving before the detritus of the lady's bag splashed across the tiled floor, and it was this that caught Lloyd's attention. The sheriff moved with a grace and speed that was hard to believe in someone of his size, his body ducking at the knees, his hands shooting out, forming a cup below the flow of objects raining from the bag. He did this before either of the other two men had moved, managing to catch most of it.

'Oh shit,' cried Meryl, her eyes rolling back, becoming tearful.

'Not to worry,' said Jackson, straightening with what he had caught in hands the size of baseball gloves.

Meryl pulled the straps of her bag wide so that he could deposit his catch inside. Meanwhile, both Lloyd and Len picked up the rest.

'Thank you,' Meryl said to them all, her jade eyes squeezing shut as she spoke.

'I think we best be going now,' said Len, roping his arm through hers once more.

Len nodded, then escorted his wife down the corridor where the blazing Kansas sun streamed through the windows. Watching them go was like watching a funeral march, Lloyd thought. He could tell in the faces of the carnies observing them that they were thinking the same.

The sight made his heart ache, and he thought, how this could happen here in his town? He looked to Jackson, whose lips were crushed white, his jaw like something chiseled from stone as he stared at the Greys. He thought of the man's inexplicable grace, a marvel compared to his own natural clumsiness, and drew strength from that.

138

They would get through this, he thought, staring at the man everyone in the community regarded as a fixture of stability. Or so Lloyd liked to think.

'Lawrence Montague!' the sheriff shouted down the hall.

'It's your turn.'

4

A portion of the transcript from the interview of Lawrence Montague conducted on Tuesday May 10th, 16:00 by Sheriff Timothy Jackson and Deputy Lloyd Herrick.

Sheriff Jackson: For the recorder, can you state your name and occupation?

Montague: My name is Lawrence Montague and I am the proprietor of Montague's Carnival of Delights and Terror.

Sheriff Jackson: Where exactly are you from, Mr. Montague?

Montague: All over really, but if you're asking where I was born, I was born in Charlestown, South Carolina.

Sheriff Jackson: According to several eyewitnesses at the scene, Lily Grey was last seen entering into Journey Through The Crypt at around eleven-thirty this morning. Mr. Montague, where were you at that time?

Montague: I was working on The Whirl, the carnival's Ferris wheel.

Sheriff Jackson: Is that a hint of an accent I hear in your voice, Mr. Montague? You certainly don't sound like you're from South Carolina.

Montague: That is correct, Sheriff. My parents were from some tiny country in Eastern Europe that doesn't exist anymore and I'm afraid I sometimes slip into their old inflection on certain words.

Sheriff Jackson: Interesting. We will check up on that. Is working on the Ferris wheel something the proprietor of a fair does regularly?

Montague: Well, I can't speak for other carnival owners, only myself, and on the first day of business, it's become a traditional practice for me to operate The Whirl. Don't tell anyone, but it is secretly my favorite ride. Tradition gives confidence and assures people, wouldn't you agree?

Sheriff Jackson: I do. Mr. Montague, at what time and how did you find out that one of your customers had gone missing within one of your rides?

Montague: I'd say around about twelve-fifteen. Patricia Bean, one of the hands working on The Crypt today, came and told me.

Sheriff Jackson: Were you told at the time that one of your employees had entered into the ride after Lily Grey?

Montague: You are referring to Joe Cage, one of our new hires. Yes, Patricia informed me that he was quite distraught about the young girl's leaving her mother's side and wanted to get her back.

Sheriff Jackson: What can you tell me about Joe Cage as his employer?

Montague: Very little.

Sheriff Jackson: Come on now, you mean to tell me a smart, enterprising man like yourself would hire someone to work for them and not know anything about them?

Montague: Oh, no. You must forgive me. I didn't mean to convey that I knew nothing about Joe, only that I know very little. For example, I know that Joe left his previous employment because of a dispute with two disgruntled customers. This was at a bar called Dylan's Roadhouse, I believe. The two customers attempted to, shall we say, get the better of Joe, which is how he received the bruises to his face. From what Joe tells me, however, the two gentlemen made a mistake in confronting him and soon learned it. Now, I have no proof as to whether this is true other than Joe's words and from what I've learned from those in my company. Other than that, I know that Joe has been drifting from job to job for the last couple of months. I don't know if he's run away from home, I don't know what his previous situation was like, and I don't even know what he intends to do with himself. As you can see, I was correct when I said I know very little.

Sheriff Jackson: And why is that, Mr. Montague?

Montague: He keeps himself to himself. He seems a very private person.

5

A portion of the transcript from the interview of Arnold Kauffman conducted on Tuesday May 10th, 16:30 by Sheriff Timothy Jackson and Deputy Lloyd Herrick.

Sherriff Jackson: It's my understanding that you are in charge of the operation of the ride known as Journey Through The Crypt, sometimes referred to as The Crypt, is that correct?

Kauffman: That is correct, yes.

Sheriff Jackson: Where exactly are you from, Mr. Kauffman?

Kauffman: New York, born and raised. If you want to go further back, my family is one hundred percent Irish.

Deputy Herrick: Kauffman doesn't sound like a very Irish name.

Kauffman: No, sir, it's not. My father changed it when he came over, believing the Jews had a nicer image than that of the drunken potato eaters.

Sheriff Jackson: And how would you describe your duties within the fair?

Kauffman: Well, Montague describes me as his right-hand man, and I guess that's fairly accurate, seeing as how when he isn't around, everyone looks to me to tell them what to do. This tends to be simply making sure everyone knows what they are supposed to be doing, usually in packing things away or unpacking them. You'd be surprised how quickly people forget to do a thing even if they've done it a thousand times. On top of that, The Crypt is my sole responsibility, in terms of its maintenance, operation, and right through to transportation. That's how we do it at the carnival: all the rides or stalls either have one individual or a few responsible for them in that way.

Sheriff Jackson: Is the operation of The Crypt difficult?

Kauffman: It can be. She's over ten years old now - the ride, that is. We keep her well-maintained and she's passed all the required safety inspections.

Sheriff Jackson: Do you have a copy of those certificates with you?

Kauffman: I do.

A shuffle can be heard on the recording as Arnold Kauffman passes over the requested documents to Sheriff Jackson.

Sheriff Jackson: Did the ride function well today?

Kauffman: You're poking at the malfunction that happened.

Sheriff Jackson: Eyewitnesses stated that the ride broke down for some time.

Kauffman: Aye, it happens from time to time. Sometimes a circuit overloads and the ride has to be stopped until we figure out if it's something actually wrong or just a tripped switch. In the case of today, it was a tripped switch so we tried to send an empty cart around the ride to make sure it was safe. Lily Grey seemed to have other ideas. She got into the test cart we were sending round.

Sheriff Jackson: Do you not have something or someone in place to prevent a member of the public from just stepping onto the ride?

Kauffman: We do. We assign someone to stand at the head of the queue. For the most part, that person's job is to charge customers and keep them calm if the waits are a bit long. Joe Cage was working the head of the queue today.

Sheriff Jackson: Was Joe Cage working when Lily Grey got into the empty cart?

Kauffman: He was.

Sheriff Jackson: Had Joe worked in this position before?

Kauffman: No, Joe is a new hire. We sometimes take on new people if they seem eager and capable.

Sheriff Jackson: How exactly did Joe seem capable to you?

Kauffman: Sir, he is beyond the carny life, if you ask me. He's good with his hands, yes, but that kid has college brains in his head, if you ask me.

Sheriff Jackson: If he is as intelligent as you think he is, can you tell us of any reason why Joe would be seeking work with the traveling community?

Kauffman: I don't know Joe's situation. He's very private about where he's from or anything. All I know is that he's smart enough not to be on the road.

Sheriff Jackson: Your employer, Mr. Montague, stated that Joe had some problems with his last employer.

Kauffman: That's right, the kid has a hell of a shiner on his face. He said the last place he worked in was a bar that's customers weren't too kindly to strangers.

Sheriff Jackson: At the time that Lily Grey slipped into your ride, Mr. Kauffman, did you notice Joe taking an interest in the Greys?

Kauffman: Well, you have to understand I was busy trying to make sure the ride was up and running safely in good time. Though I will say that Joe knew the Greys; or at least, he appeared to. Before we were working on The Crypt, I was showing him the ropes at the carnival's entrance. The Greys bought their tickets from him. He spoke with the missing girl; about what, I couldn't say. I was busy.

Sheriff Jackson: When you noticed that Lily got on the ride, what did you do?

Kauffman: We stopped it. Now, that's not normal practice and we only did it because her mother was becoming hysterical and the ride hadn't been fully tested yet. The plan was to send someone along the ride to pick her up. The thing with The Crypt is that when it is stopped, the safety bars release, so we had to send someone.

Sheriff Jackson: Whom did you pick to send after Lily Grey?

Kauffman: I didn't pick anyone. Joe Cage volunteered.

A portion of the transcript from the interview of Carmen Garcia conducted on Tuesday May 10th, 17:00 by Sheriff Timothy Jackson and Deputy Lloyd Herrick.

Sheriff Jackson: Mrs. Garcia, you looked after Joe Cage after he came out of The Crypt without finding Lily Grey?

Garcia: It's Miss, and yes I did.

Sheriff Jackson: And why was he sent to you?

Garcia: Montague and the others think of me as the official nurse of the carnival, despite having no nursing training. I think it's because I'm a woman, if I'm honest with you.

Sheriff Jackson: And how did Joe seem to you?

Garcia: He seemed fine, other than being covered in blood. He made a joke about the cut on his head, about being too eager to make a good impression.

Sheriff Jackson: Were you aware that a child had gone missing inside one of the rides?

Garcia: I was. My cabin where I tell fortunes faces Journey Through The Crypt. I could tell that there was some sort of commotion going on from the fact that the ride appeared not to be running. It was one of my patrons who informed me about the missing girl.

Sheriff Jackson: You mentioned that Joe was covered in blood. Could you tell us exactly where he was covered?

Garcia: His face and his t-shirt. It was quite a lot.

Sheriff Jackson: And how big was the cut on his forehead?

Garcia: Not too big, not enough to require anything more than some ice for the swelling around it.

Sheriff Jackson: Did that amount of blood that was covering Joe seem appropriate for the wound on his head?

Garcia: I guess, but as I've said, I'm not a nurse.

7

A portion of the transcript from the interview of Joe Cage conducted on Tuesday May 10th, 20:45 by Sheriff Timothy Jackson and Deputy Mark Stone.

Sheriff Jackson: Let the record show that Joe Cage has willingly submitted a piece of evidence and that evidence is a white bloodstained t-shirt belonging to Mr. Cage. Why are you handing this to us?

Cage: Because you keep asking about it. If it helps you guys clarify anything, then I'm happy to hand it over.

Sheriff Jackson: Well, as you mentioned it, why don't you take us through what happened inside The Crypt again? Just for clarification.

Deputy Stone: According to Arnold Kauffman, you volunteered to go after Lily Grey; why is that? Did you know her particularly well?

Cage: No.

Sheriff Jackson: But you had met Meryl Grey before?

Cage: That's correct. I met her yesterday at her place of work.

Sheriff Jackson: Meryl must have made some impression then if you were ready to just drop everything and go searching for her missing daughter. Did you ever interact with Lily Grey before she disappeared?

Cage: I talked to her at the entrance of the carnival. I was the one who sold the family tickets to get inside. She told me she was excited to ride The Crypt.

Sheriff Jackson: I thought you said you didn't know her?

Cage: I didn't. I'm just telling you what she told me in the few minutes she spoke with me.

Sheriff Jackson: She spoke with you for a few minutes.

Deputy Stone: You can learn a lot about someone in a few minutes.

Sheriff Jackson: Try to be accurate. How long did you speak to Lily Grey?

Cage: I'd say less than five minutes.

Sheriff Jackson: And did you see her at any other point during the morning before her disappearance?

Cage: I saw her at The Ring Toss stall, then again at The Crypt.

Sheriff Jackson: How did she appear those times?

Cage: She was bright, all smiles at The Ring Toss. When she was at The Crypt, she looked panicked, scared.

Sheriff Jackson: Why do you think that was?

Cage: I think she was scared of the ride.

Deputy Stone: You think she was scared of the ride yet, she somehow got onto it by herself without anyone looking.

Cage does not respond.

Sheriff Jackson: So you went in after Lily Grey. Why?

Cage: It was my responsibility to keep people from getting on the platform when they weren't allowed, plus... Meryl looked like she was having a bad day, and seeing Lily vanish into The Crypt, I think, was another bad thing in a long list of bad things that had happened that day. I felt sorry for her.

Sheriff Jackson: For someone who says he doesn't know the Greys much, you seem to know a lot about them, Mr. Cage.

Cage: What would you have done, Sheriff? Would have just kept quiet and not done anything while Meryl was on the verge of tears? Or would you have done something? See, that badge on your chest makes me think you would have done the same thing I did.

Sheriff Jackson: But you don't have a badge on your chest, kid. That's why we are asking you these questions. Tell us what happened inside The Crypt.

Cage: I followed the walkway after Lily. I found the cart that she was on empty in this section of the corridor with all these fake hands sticking out of the walls. When I was looking over her cart, I heard a bang, like metal being hammered.

Deputy Stone: What, like someone drumming a saucepan?

Cage: No, louder than that. Anyway, it freaked me out and I started to run when my foot got caught on one of the dummy hands. I fell and hit my head; it must have knocked me out because I remember waking up covered in blood. I managed to walk to the end of the track, but I didn't see Lily.

Sheriff Jackson: You didn't hear anything else while inside the ride?

Cage: No.

Sheriff Jackson: Mr. Cage, are you aware that during our preliminary search within Journey

Through The Crypt we discovered an item belonging to Lily Grey?

Cage: Yes, I saw you with it at the fair.

Sheriff Jackson: That item was covered in blood. It's been sent to the state testing facility, the same facility that your t-shirt will be sent to, and they will be able to tell us whose blood it is. I want you to think long and hard about that, Mr. Cage, and tell me if there's anything you'd like to change about your statement here today.

Cage: No, there isn't.

Chapter Two

Ghost Town

1

They were escorting Joe Cage from the interview room when Phyllis Harding - the station receptionist and daytime dispatch operator - yelled from the front desk, 'Tim, come quick!' At the time, Jackson was explaining that he would be investigating the contacts Joe had provided. His voice cut off on hearing the shortened version of his first name, one people only seemed to use in times of distress. Both Jackson and Deputy Mark Stone abandoned Joe, sprinting down the now vacant corridor, their hands falling to their guns.

Watching them go, leather shoes clapping on the tile like some fast-paced march, just made everything even more surreal for Joe. All day he had felt like he was floating above his body, his consciousness a balloon observing everything around him, yet feeling none of it. The interview had yanked him back, the guiding questions, the stony, resentful attitude of the two officers opposite informing him that his deepest fears were true.

Their investigation was pointed at him.

What would they uncover? He had given them the number for his parents' home; what would they find upon phoning it? Unaware, Joe began to rub at his right wrist - the skin that encircled it was mottled, scarred and sandpaper rough - as he wandered down the hall lit by fluorescents after the officers, moving in a daze. He could smell the residue of the carnies in the air, the smell of fires extinguished, of smoke and ash, even though they were long gone. None had stayed behind to wait on him.

He could hear voices shouting ahead, coming from some great distance to his ears as he drifted internally. The ocean in his head was roaring, crashing against the dam he had built; its water the colour of coal, its high waves topped with green foam like it was curdling as it stormed. Cracks streaked through the concert of the wall as the torrent continued to pound on.

Joe squeezed his hazel eyes shut, his right hand reaching out, planting a palm against the cork surface of a bulletin board, his heart galloping in his chest, his temples.

'Pull it together,' he whispered. 'Don't go back there.'

More shouts from down the corridor. One voice caused his eye to snap open as he recognised who it belonged to with a spike of surprise.

2

'What is it?' asked Jackson, skidding into the square reception area.

Phyllis stood behind the chest-high desk, pointing her index finger with a nail that was extraordinary long and sharp looking, at the double glass doors leading to the station's parking lot. Mark pulled up beside him, his shoes squeaking over the linoleum as he came to a halt.

'Outside. There's some sort of fight going on,' she said to him.

And there was, too. Now that Phyllis had directed his attention, he became aware of the raised voices outside the station.

'Here, catch,' he said, tossing the evidence bag that contained Joe Cage's soiled t-shirt to her.

Phyllis caught the baggy in the cup of her hands as the two officers sprinted through the doors. Outside, darkness had combed over the sky, mystifying Jackson at how much time had passed since the day's chaos had begun. No stars could be seen through the sultry whiskey hue beaming down from the station's parking lights, giving Main Street, with its row of silent shops opposite, a hooded look as if a dull orange canvas had been thrown over it.

There was no one in sight beyond the parking lot. Jackson understood why, on a hot night like this when the air hangs still and dry and the darkness seems to press down from above, heavy and empty, there was a security in staying in, in having a roof over your head. Plus, standing on the tarmac, his eyes scanning the square area made by the lot around the station, the weight of Lily Grey's disappearance seemed to add to the oppressive air.

To the right of the door sat a battered station wagon, its colour lime green. A young, petite woman with a bizarre tangle of golden hair was standing before its ticking bonnet screaming into the face of Andrew Teal. He was flanked by two other young men Jackson recognised as his friends.

There were four bloody trails across Andrew's right cheek. Rake marks, he thought on seeing them.

'Your kind doesn't belong here, freak,' spat Andrew at the young woman with a viciousness that stopped Jackson in his tracks. There was desperation in his voice and also an anguish that seemed bizarre coming from the young man he only knew as a placid and respectful.

'You're nothing more than a plague. I know about you. You're all part of some satanic cult, aren't you? Going around slaughtering animals, stealing kids.'

Both Andrew's friends – linebackers on the high school football team – moved on either side of him, the meaty muscles in their shoulders flexing. If the woman noticed this, she didn't seem to be fazed.

'All that has nothing to do with us, you dumb fucking hick!' she shouted.

Despite being half a head taller and a good deal wider than the unknown woman, Andrew Teal moved for her, his fingers hooked into talons. His two friends, their suntanned brows heavy above eyes that glinted like grey diamonds, followed him, wading forward with their arms swinging.

The sight was like a gut punch to Jackson, who knew all three of them as never having any trouble with the law or their peers; yet here they were, ready to beat a woman because she was associated with the out-of-towners, the carnies. Gross. That was the word that vomited into his mind as he strode forward through the dry, hot night air into the fray. Gross.

'Heyheyheyheyheyhey!' he roared as he and Mark intercepted the boys.

'That's enough now; show's over,' Mark said.

To Jackson's further surprise, Andrew Teal pushed against him.

The kid didn't see the badge then; he didn't recognise his face as being from the town. His fury and disgust for this girl had blinded him. It didn't matter that Jackson could easily force the kid back; his inability to see beyond the outrage he was feeling disturbed and even frightened him.

How many people are sitting at home feeling the same outrage? Knowing that within their town limits a child has gone missing and the people responsible for the safety of that child are still here and worse, they're from out of town?

Gross. It was all just gross.

In all his years as an officer of the law, Jackson had only ever experienced one lynching. The victim had been found in the teeming rain strung from an oak tree on the outskirts of town, his head cocked at an unnatural angle, his tongue purple and protruding from his swollen face. It was later discovered that the man had nothing to do with the supposed crime he was murdered for, leaving Jackson and his fellow officers another case to solve.

Lynch mob mentality only turns the outraged into murderers.

'You're a fucking whore!' yelled Andrew, trying to swipe at her from around Jackson.

'Easy now, kid. You don't want to do that,' he responded, trying to calm him.

'You're trash, you're all just fucking trash.'

Jackson shoved Andrew back into the circle of his friends, realising he had made an error when the girl tried to squeeze between Mark and him, trying to get at all three of the boys. Her fingers scratched for purchase on his upper arms when she couldn't get through and instead tried to climb over him, her nails digging into his skin even beneath his uniform shirt.

'Oh yeah?' she yelled. 'And you're nothing but a couple of inbred fuckwits that couldn't get it hard unless their mother was in front of them.'

He had to give it to her – she could sure trash talk.

Andrew charged once more, a futile attempt as the two officers shoved him back into the arms of his friends with ease. The woman bullied at them to get by, then her nails were yanked from Jackson's arm from behind.

He spun, thinking that maybe Phyllis had decided to intervene even though she had not followed them outside into the hot night. He tasted and smelled that gritty odor that rises from tarmac after it's burned in the sun all day long, a sensation he knew well having grown up here.

To his surprise, Joe Cage held the scrambling woman aloft on his hip the way a mother holds a baby, his arms coiled around her waist. Even with this, her arms and legs continued to pedal at the trio of boys.

'Go fuck a pig!' she screamed at them.

'Daisy, Daisy, settle it down,' soothed Joe.

On hearing his voice, her struggles ceased.

'They attacked me,' she said to him as he set her down.

For a moment Jackson felt a touch of admiration towards Joe, at the calmness in his voice. That he had stepped in at all said a lot, seeing as Jackson and Mark had grilled him for over an hour. His admiration merged with the whirlwind of emotions he had experienced so far today, turning his core black with despair at the thought that Joe was their number one suspect.

'They were waiting around the corner when I got out of my car, said "you're the child stealer's friend" and shoved me.'

'Boys, get inside the station and wait at reception,' Jackson snapped at the trio.

They moved sluggishly, glaring all the while at Daisy and Joe. When they were gone, Mark Stone said to him, 'That was one hell of a catfight.'

He agreed with a raise of his eyebrows.

155

Daisy and Joe were resting against the station wagon's bonnet, draped in the whiskey glaze from above, Daisy with her arms crossed, her plump cheeks flushed scarlet, though in the light it made her looked jaundiced.

'Are you going to do anything about them?' she demanded.

Her eyes, their colour unreadable with the shadows under her brow, glared at him. He recalled the way her nails had felt under his uniform, knowing he could arrest her for assault; the intelligence in her eyes said she knew too and didn't care. The admiration that had bloomed in him for Joe grew to include her as well.

'Yes, I will,' he told her, 'but first I need to know what happened. How did this all kick off?'

'Just a couple of hick country boys waiting around to lynch someone.'

Her voice was indignant and ferocious. Jackson winced at the harshness of it, an image flashing in his mind of the dead man's swollen face, the bones of his jaw broken by the rope when it pulled taut round his neck. He could see his purple tongue and crimson lips; the rest of his complexion had been dust grey.

That had been five years ago.

'Is that the type of town you have here?'

'I hope it isn't, ma'am,' he replied. 'I really do.'

His honesty took the venom out of her look. Joe was scrutinising him with surprise, while he felt Mark's gaze on him doing the same.

'But there's a difference between the truth and hope. As I said to your friend there when I first met him coming into town, Marybell isn't a nice place for strangers.'

'We've done nothing wrong,' said Daisy.

'Someone has, though,' replied Jackson. 'I suggest you two get on out of here and head back to the fairground. Joe, I probably don't have to say this but I'm going to anyway: I expect you to stick around until this thing has all cleared up. I'll deal with those three idiots inside. For the next couple of days, I recommend you don't go anywhere in town unless you're part of a group.'

3

As soon as the station wagon's doors slammed closed, Daisy said to Joe, 'He thinks you've got something to do with that little girl going missing.'

'Yep,' said Joe, his vacant gaze on the doors of the police station.

'Fuck me, this is some serious shit,' said Daisy.

She turned the key in the ignition, causing the engine to purr into life. It seemed loud in comparison to the silence of the parking lot in the center of Marybell. Daisy reversed the car out of the space then drove to the lot exit, stopping more out of habit than caution. Main Street, a canyon of store fronts around a ribbon of tarmac, was still deserted. Joe read the names of the buildings, Denton Hardware, Green's, as Daisy pulled out.

'I thought you were planning on leaving tonight?'

'I was until I saw the others come back without you. They said you were still being interviewed, so I thought I'd swing by and pick you up,' she told him.

He glanced into the back where Daisy had converted the backseat and trunk space into a bed area by installing a mattress, complete with pink curtains on all the windows. He imagined they scraped on the rails whenever she braked or accelerated, and the thought brought some semblance of a smile to his lips. It smelled of fresh linen and peppermint, a scent he recognised as Daisy's.

'It looks like you were all packed up, too,' he said, seeing her bags.

Ignoring, him she said, 'Those guys were waiting for you.'

'Well, thank god they jumped you. If it had been me, I would have been a goner,' he said, trying to distract her.

Her eyes snapped from the road to him, assessing in the gloom of the car's interior. There was a hint of a smirk underneath the shadows on his face.

'That's true, I am a warrior,' said Daisy

Her eyes reverted back to the road, feeling a similar smirk on her own lips.

'Daisy Hill, the warrior woman,' said Joe and chuckled.

'You're goddamn right I am.'

'What do you think they were going on about slaughtered animals for?'

'Who the fuck knows what those inbred hicks were talking about?' Daisy replied swiftly.

Marybell's empty streets sailed by without sound. The only indication that there was life was a stray mongrel dog sniffing at a trash can. Jackson's words echoed in his head about the town and Joe felt something squeeze at his heart as the mongrel's head snapped in their direction, its eyes shining in the light, its black lips peeled back to bare its yellow teeth at them.

Jackson phoned Phil Teal and asked him to come to the station to pick up the trio. He had intended to rip them all a new one, when all three erupted into tears after he said, 'You realise that woman had nothing to do with Lily Grey or what happened at the Teal farm? And you could have gone to prison, where much harder men make toys out of young boys like you.'

He left them to weep in the plastic chairs that lined the corridor outside the interview rooms, disgusted.

'Phyllis, what are you still doing here?' he asked, seeing her still seated behind the wall of her high reception desk. The thing was like some wooden battlement the colour of weak tea. 'The night shift has started. Weren't you supposed to be finished at six?'

'I'm doing the same thing you are: my job, seeing as the world has gone to hell in a handbasket today,' she said to him, rising from her seat. Those at the station joked with her that it was her throne.

Jackson let out a sigh as he hugged the top of the desk, his arms wrapping around the cool wood as if it were a life raft at sea. Phyllis patted his left shoulder. At fifty-two years old, she was the oldest member of the department other than Mitch Collins, and as such took on the role of den mother.

'Anyway, I thought you'd want to know that I got through to the state police and they will be sending someone down tomorrow.'

'Just one?'

'That's what they said.'

Jackson groaned; his department specialised in breaking up drunken brawls on Saturday night, not missing persons, plus tonight had shown him that there was another element he had to consider: the townspeople.

Andrew and his thugs had made him aware that there was more than just the darkness of the night sky hanging over Marybell; there was an oppressive resentment in the air. He could feel it even now, chilling his flesh, and wondered how many more were sitting inside brooding over what had happened to the Greys at the fair today.

Thank god for the carnies, he thought and acknowledged the peculiar feeling such a thought created in him.

Montague had promised him that the fair, or carnival as he called it in his strange accent, would be closed tomorrow. He had then gone on to offer the services of his people to aid in the search effort that would take place tomorrow in the woods behind Launder's field.

'We'll provide food for everyone involved. We're fully stocked with goods that will all spoil if we don't get rid of them,' he had said with a shrug.

Jackson hoped that it would be the sign of goodwill the people of Marybell needed to soothe whatever tensions were building right now. It would be hard. Carnies were the epitome of outsiders to townspeople. They were considered sleazy and lawless.

'I'll be going home now,' said Phyllis, handbag hanging from the crook of her arm. 'Here's that piece of evidence you threw at me earlier. I'm sure you'll want it back before it goes missing.' She placed the evidence baggy on the desk beside his resting head.

'Thank you, Phyllis,' he chimed in a lackluster tone. The same way he would have responded to his mom as a kid when she'd ask him to do something he didn't want to do.

Phyllis clipped him on the side of his head with the palm of her hand. Jackson flinched then watched her strut around the desk, heels clapping, her hair a beehive of blue-grey, her mighty bosom like the bow of a ship. He found strength in seeing the stiff way she held her shoulders as she walked; it was an endearing and somehow comforting sight.

'If you're wondering where Elaine is, she's out on patrol.' Her lips had a puckered look about them that made him weary.

'Why would I want to know where Elaine is? I'm going home after these boys leave,' he said, gesturing with his thumb at the trio.

'Just in case you were wondering,' she said, deviously sweet.

'Goodnight, Phyllis,' he said, shaking his head.

5

Len Grey slid the ancient Ford pickup into the driveway. The living room curtains twitched at the sound of the engine, revealing Henry's face. He had waited for them, Len thought, with a loving ache in his heart.

He wondered if the twins were still up or if Henry had put them to bed. If so, he wondered what reassurances his sixteen-year-old had given them.

Len raised a hand in salute, signaling they'd be a minute. Henry nodded in understanding, his head ducking back behind the curtains, resetting them seamlessly.

The streetlight in front of their home only illuminated a portion of their garden. As result, darkness seemed to have crept up the front of their house and draped itself there. The space under the sagging porch roof was a cave. The windows looked filled with black ice. Overall it did not look like a home, it looked like a husk, something abandoned and left empty, left to rot.

Len killed the Ford's motor with a flick of the wrist. Neither he nor Meryl made any move to leave the vehicle. They were alone, the street surrounding them devoid of life. By some miracle, even the neighbour's Rottweiler was quiet.

There were tears in his eyes when he began to speak. 'Meryl, I'm sorry I wasn't there today.'

He sensed her head snap in his direction and found he could only look at her out of the corner of his eyes. Even then he could see the ruddy colour in her face deepen. She had been looking wide-eyed and flushed all day.

'Not now, Len,' she said to him, mournfully, tenderly. Like she was speaking to a child who she was too exhausted to scold.

Len, a thin reed of a man who loved his wife with all of his heart yet did so feeling like he was always falling short of the love she gave to him, flinched at her words. He bowed his head and nodded, hearing her fumble at the door latch.

The scent of sweet peas floated into the Ford as Meryl opened the passenger door. *She planted them while I had gone and left the porch to roof sag*, he thought, tears now running through the stubble on his cheeks.

'Come on inside, Len,' she said from the passenger doorway.

'Yeah, I guess I will,' he said, wiping his face with the back of his hand. He couldn't remember the last time he had cried real tears. He followed his wife inside their dark home; though he was forty-one, he walked with the shoulder-stooped appearance of someone much older.

6

Deputy Elaine Green plucked the radio from her belt on the bedroom floor, mooning the bed's occupant as she bent. She could feel his eyes on her, enjoying the view, and felt a wash of pride.

Why not? Despite her hiccups, she knew her figure was a fine one. Well, most days she did, and that was more and more because of him.

'You've been the best part of my day,' he sighed from the bed.

She stood six foot one in her bare feet and had been that tall since she was fourteen. Back then, her legs had sprouted up like stalks, making her a target for every wannabe school bully. She was thirty-two now and while the rest of her body had eventually matured, her mindset still received echoes from when she had been a tall, gangly teenager who just wanted to be invisible.

Thankfully, it was dark in the bedroom; the only light came from the streetlights outside and fell across her body in stripes. She felt comfortable in the dark. Not that she was uncomfortable around him; there was still just a difference in being with someone and standing stark naked before them.

Smirking, she depressed the black button on the radio's side. 'Mark, this is Elaine. I've just reached the Teal property and I'm circling back now. Nothing to report, over,' she said into the device.

A second later Deputy Mark Stone's voice issued from the radio. 'Copy that, over.'

Elaine left the radio on top of the cabinet where he kept his colognes and a jumble of the makeup that she had begun to leave there. The sight of her cosmetics in the dark, tubes of lipsticks and creams, made her pause, thinking they had not discussed her leaving things here, yet she had done so without any thought or remark from him.

A warmth erupted within her, shrouding her, at what that might mean.

'That gives us half an hour left,' she said over her shoulder.

Like her, he was nude, although with none of the reservation.

Her eyes pierced the shadow that draped over him, seeing everything. His body was huge, significantly in his shoulders, chest, and thighs, all well maintained and corded in muscle. His chest was coated in a pelt of black hair that she knew felt silky against her own.

'I didn't want to be one of those guys who played football in high school and you see two years later and all that work has just turned to fat,' he had said once. By then she didn't need to be told; she knew how strong he was from how he stripped her of her clothes, how he carried her, and held her.

'Only half an hour,' he said, stretching his arms until they trembled. 'I hate it when you're on the night shift.'

'At least it's quiet enough that I can sneak away to do this,' she told him. 'I hardly think we can sneak away during the day.'

'It's just, if we were on days together, you could spend the night here.'

'I guess you'll have to take that up with my boss,' she said, smirking.

He grinned at her, his teeth a white line in the dark.

Timothy Jackson had once been the star quarterback of Roffman High School; although he graduated before Elaine had attended, the girls in her class continued to swoon at his match photographs on the walls. The fact that she, the awkward nerd with the weird body, was bedding him all these years later was not lost on her. Not that it had been a huge ambition for her at the time; he had been just another photograph on the wall back then. Nor had it been her ambition when she joined the department over a year ago. They hadn't even flirted with one another. But she had caught him looking, admiring from afar, not at her legs or her butt or her breasts as so many other men did, but at her. She had caught him because she had been looking, too. And looking eventually led to a kiss.

They had been in his cruiser on a Saturday night in case they needed to break up a bar fight and the talk between them had been good, effortless as it always was, and then he leaned in and lightly touched her lips with his. Then he reclined back and said, 'I'm sorry, I just…'

Elaine had let him get no further, shocking herself at her longing, smothering his mouth with hers. And that had been their beginning. No one knew, although they suspected Phyllis Harding had guessed. They had yet to confront her about it, so for now it was their secret.

The past six months had been filled with nights such as this one. Tim would leave his double garage open for her to slide her car or the cruiser into, closing it as she made her way into the house via the back so none of his neighbours could see. Once she was inside they tangled together.

Sometimes Elaine worried it was just sex, usually when she was with her friends, listening to their unfolding dramas. What calmed her was looking at him, really looking and seeing the person he was.

She saw that this was not a fling for him. She saw that whatever they had, he thought of it as rare, that he was lonely and had been for some time. Elaine knew that from this big house of his with its too many empty bedrooms.

With that in mind, hearing the desperation in her girlfriends' talk made her realise that their relationship was better kept private. Marybell was her hometown and while she loved its small-town quaintness, she understood that for some people, high school hadn't ended and that schoolyard gossip had just become backyard gossip. That didn't stop her from wanting to phone the bitches from her high school and screaming at them, 'Hey, remember when you used to call me skyscraper? Well, I'm fucking Timothy Jackson now; what do you think about that?'

Elaine knew she never would; still, she enjoyed the pettiness of the fantasy.

'Tough day, then?' she said, slipping on top of the rumpled bedsheets beside him. Without thinking, she twined her long legs with his, their skin tanned from reading in the sun, back before all this mess came to town. His skin was fever hot from their previous exercise.

'Huh. It certainly has been one for the record books.'

'Phyllis told me you've already got a suspect,' she probed.

'His name's Joe Cage. He's twenty and a runaway from the sound of things…'

'Jackson, I'm not looking for his height and build; I'm asking if you think he did it,' she said, uneasy because she was scared. Scared because her town seemed to be the site of a horror movie in the last few days.

She recalled the nerve-wracking sound as thousands of flies buzzed over the area where Teal's cattle had been slaughtered last night, their bodies a withering cloud of brown-black in the headlights of police cars. This was after the carcasses had been removed; the flies were feasting on the dried blood that had stained the green grass all shades of red.

As one of the officers rotated onto night shift, it had been her job to guard the crime scene. The incessant drone of the flies' wings made her scratch at her skin, making sitting in her car the hardest thing she had ever had to endure on the job. There were still scarlet slash marks around her ears and biceps.

Elaine watched as Jackson stared at the ceiling from his bed of pillows.

'I don't know,' he said eventually. 'I mean, right now all the evidence says that he had something to do with girl's disappearance. He knew the family, he had met her, and we suspect he could have been the last one to see her alive. We suspect it; we don't know it because without Lily Grey, only he knows what happened inside that ghost ride. And if you take what he said to be true, he was knocked out for a while.'

'Wasn't he covered in blood?'

'Yeah, we're sending everything to the lab up state tomorrow along with the girl's teddy bear to see if the blood matches.'

'You sound like you don't think they will,' she remarked.

'The whole thing is just odd.'

'For example?'

'Like the fair itself. You should see inside that ride; it's like entering Narnia. Plus if you take into account that giant Ferris wheel and everything else, it screams money, a lot of it. Yet these are carnies we are talking about. Sure, the owner dresses well, but one of them was naked from the waist up when I arrived there today. As well as that, there's this thing with Teal's slaughtered herd.'

'That happened on the night after the fair arrived, didn't it?' said Elaine, frowning. 'What makes you think they're connected, other than the time frame?'

'I don't know,' he said. 'It's all madness.'

'I agree with you there,' she said. 'It's because it's Marybell, where the only thing that happens out of the ordinary is an accident at Launder's chicken farms or an altercation between spouses, not this. You still haven't answered my question, though. Do you think this Joe guy did it?'

Jackson paused again, his hand clasped across his barrel chest. Looking at his fingers made her aware of just how hot and humid the air smelled in the room. She could still feel the plastic slime of the condom inside her.

Heat bloomed in her as she observed his fingers, remembering how they felt on her.

'I think he's hiding something,' he repeated. 'I try not to think like some of the people in this town do; I try to give people the benefit of the doubt.'

'And?'

'I'm finding with this that I'm still thinking like a...townie. There's a part of me that already has this guy tried and convicted, enough that I want to grab him by the neck and throw him behind bars.'

'Why didn't you? You're the sheriff, you could have,' she asked.

'Because I don't want to think like that, I don't want to be tainted by presumptive thinking. I want to know without a doubt that he did it,' he said, speaking slowly, considering each word.

'Congratulations, you've just passed solving a crime 101,' she said.

He smiled, straightening himself so they were sitting shoulder-to-shoulder.

'You do know there is evidence to support that Joe didn't do it?' she informed him.

His gaze was on her toes – slightly square-–shaped - moving up, making her skin tingle.

'Like why would he walk out of the ride covered in blood in front of the Greys?'

His gaze had reached her tanned thighs, the tingling sensation ascending with his eyes, feeling like a softer version of pins and needles.

'I mean, he's not an idiot, is he?'

His eyes lingered on her pelvis and the fine black hair there, the opposite to the blonde of her head. They wandered higher to her chest, making her aware of her breathing, of how her chest rose and fell.

'No, he's not,' replied Jackson in a dreamy tone.

When his eyes found hers, she spoke.

'I think these thoughts and questions are for tomorrow. Tonight is tonight and we've got about ten minutes left,' she told him.

Jackson reached for her, his hands finding her waist. Her hands – smaller than his, their fingers long – found either side of his face, fingers splaying into his coal black hair as his lips latched onto hers. Her tongue flicked out to caress his. There was no condom this time; instead, he filled her with himself, just him.

Chapter Three

The Search Party

1

As the sun graced the horizon, turning the sky dust grey then pale blue, the campground in Launder's field began to stir, only without the usual fevered sense of activity it was accustomed to. There would be no more calliope music today, no more safety checks, or test rides. The Whirl's struts would not spin its lazy circle against the Kansas sky. Today, the carnival's operators woke resigned to participate in one task only: the search for Lily Grey.

2

Joe found Daisy waiting for him with the others in The Fill Up, the official gathering place for everyone taking part in the search. His gaze immediately honed onto the police presence - the mountainous Jackson in particular, whose eyes were once more hidden behind the silver reflection of his sunglasses, on the side of the eatery facing The Whirl. The fear he experienced last night having given over his contact details was a blade of ice against his spine now.

He wondered if the sheriff had made a call, if what he had left behind was now on the road coming for him like a chasing storm. Without being aware, the fingers of his left hand began to massage the scarred flesh of his right wrist. Running away had never felt more powerful to him than it did right then.

He turned his gaze away, scanning for a friendly face, and there was Daisy Hill, reclining against one of the tables, studying him.

'You decided to stay?' he said.

'Someone's got to watch your back,' she replied. 'Plus it felt wrong to leave knowing that little girl is missing.'

She wore her trademark cowboy boots, the brown leather faded to white in places, jeans and an off the shoulder sweatshirt. Her hair was a golden mix of dreadlocks and mess. Joe had never been happier to see her.

'Are you still wearing that thing?' she said. She was pointing to his Hawaiian shirt that Carmen had given him.

'Yes, why wouldn't I be? This thing is bitching,' he said, looking at its aqua blue colour and pattern of bright pink flowers.

As he took the seat beside her, the notion that they shared something returned. Not only were they both runaways, but they were also apart from the carnies who surrounding them, waiting on Jackson to speak.

Already, he had noticed several accusing stares from within the gathering crowd, some from carnies. Their agitation alerted him to something he had been trying to ignore after Daisy's confrontation with the three hillbilly teens the night before. Word had gotten out about his attempt to find Lily Grey inside The Crypt. He was now the town pariah.

Through the ever-moving crowd, Joe spotted Montague drifting over to them, his expression even now jovial in the early morning light. 'Good morning. How are we doing today?' he asked. He took the empty place on Joe's other side against the table.

'Pretty gnarly, all things considering,' said Daisy, her voice deadpan.

Joe couldn't hide his smirk and he turned his head in her direction so Montague wouldn't see. Daisy's iceberg blue eyes shot him a hard look, her lips twisted into a crooked smile.

'I didn't realise you had come in contact already with the town's sheriff,' said Montague, catching Joe unprepared. 'You must tell me what you two talked about.'

As his mind rapidly thought of what to say, not knowing why he automatically didn't want to tell Montague the truth, Jackson started to speak. A frown appeared on the carnival owner's brow that surprised him. It seemed to be the first genuine emotion he had ever read on the man's face.

When Joe turned his head back to Jackson, his stomach dropped.

Meryl Grey stood on his left-hand side; her face, which had been radiant with energy and purpose the day before, enough for him to see the young girl she had been, was now a pale moon, its flesh hanging like melted wax beneath eyebrows that fused together in a grim line. He could see the old maid she would become, shrouded in her grief and torment. Unkempt and unwell. He could see it by the way her blue polka-dotted blouse wasn't properly tucked into the belt line of her jeans, how strands of her coppery hair floated in the breezeless air outside of her ponytail, and how her eyes that seemed like colourless beads beneath her eyebrow roamed the crowd.

They stopped on each face, scanning, scrutinising, then moving on.

She's looking for the person who took her child, Joe thought and felt that blade of ice return to encapsulate all of him.

How will her face look when she sees me?

'Can I have your attention, please?' yelled Jackson over the hubbub.

A wave of silence rippled outward following his yell. Heads turned, bodies ceased moving, and suddenly Jackson found a hundred or more pairs of eyes on him. Never before had he been more aware of two people than he was right now of the Greys beside him.

Jackson knew this was going to be tricky. What he wanted to do was inform people without devastating the Greys even further, which is why he had a private conference with his officers before arriving today about the potential of finding Lily Grey alive. In some ways, that meeting had been the honest version of what he was trying to achieve here today.

Due to the length of time that Lily had been missing, there was a high certainty that they were looking for a body. His department all knew this, but it still had needed to be said to them so they could be prepared mentally.

This meant that the announcement that he was about to make was more of a formality in reassuring Marybell's population and the Greys. The trick was not to mislead them with hope without hinting to their greatest fears.

'The objective of today is to continue the search for Lily Grey,' he announced to the gathered people.

His people, he thought, remembering the behaviour of Andrew Teal and his friends the night before, and once again thinking one word: gross. Jackson had seen the kid's face in the crowd somewhere alongside his father's weathered one and hoped things wouldn't kick off again. He had also spied Joe Cage and Daisy Hill. All his officers had been informed to keep eyes on them.

'Yesterday, a search was conducted of the surrounding area known as Launder's field; it included all the buildings and motor vehicles on the premises. Today we will be expanding our search into the woodland area beyond the property line. The woods can be treacherous, so the aim today is to do this in the safest possible way. I don't want any broken ankles, and I don't want anyone getting lost. If I see or hear of anyone goofing around, I will have you immediately escorted back to town. To ensure that our search is carried out correctly, we will do so in groups of ten led by one of my deputies or a member of the local council. They will all have maps and radios to keep in touch with each other, so I recommend nobody goes tearing off on their own.'

'Why aren't the state troopers here?' asked Bill Denton. The question caused a murmur of conversation to ripple throughout the crowd. Jackson clenched at being interrupted; it was bad enough trying to do this without shepherding questions from the town nosy parkers.

'The state police have been informed and will join us as soon as they can,' Jackson responded.

This was a lie. The officer that was promised to them last night had not arrived this morning so far.

There was more he needed to say; however, Jackson never got a chance because it was at this point that Launder entered The Fill Up.

'Where is he?' bellowed a voice. It came from behind the people grouped on the eastern side of the carnival's eatery. All eyes spun there in hearing it, to see several people were being pushed aside as the shouter bullied his way into their midst. 'Get out of my way, get out... of... my... way!' yelled the man, which was followed by a woman's scream.

Launder emerged into the space; his face was as red as a tomato. Tufts of his black hair waved listlessly in the air under The Fill Up's tented roof from a scalp that sparkled with sweat. His beady, beetle black eyes raked the sea of faces surrounding him until they rested upon Montague.

'Get him out of here,' Jackson whispered to Lloyd.

The young deputy immediately took into the crowd but Jackson saw that he would never reach Launder in time to stop whatever upset he meant to cause. There were too many bodies crammed into the picnic area.

'You!' bellowed Launder, stabbing a finger in Montague's direction.

Joe, who was beside the carnival owner, heard him say, 'Oh my,' in an amused sort of way that made his head turn to him. There was a hint of a smile in the corner of Montague's lips and a gleam in his eyes that Joe recognised from the night around the campfire when he tried to pry him for information. It was not a kind look, more like a hungry one.

'You did this!' roared Launder, stabbing his finger with each word.

An audible gasp erupted from the surrounding figures. Joe saw Montague's bushy eyebrows leap.

'You caused this with your two-bit circus!' Launder roared. 'Police on my land, police entering my house, and that boy, you sent that

175

man who took that child into my house to endanger my innocent children.'

Joe's heart seized at being mentioned, immediately feeling Daisy's hand grip his left wrist. He remembered Launder's children. Daniel had been a grody cretin, and Olive – there had been a wildness in Olive's eyes that said she was aching to drop the façade her parents made her put on.

'Mr. Launder, I don't know what has got you saying these things,' said Montague, 'but I can assure you that my people and I would never intentionally bring any harm to you or your family.'

'It's all your fault, Montague,' said Launder, breathlessly. His previous bellowing seemed to have exhausted him. 'No more, I want you out. Take your flea bit fair and get the hell off my land.'

'It's a carnival, Mr. Launder,' Montague replied.

'It's a fucking shithole!' screamed Launder. His face flushed from tomato red to such an alarming shade of plum purple that Joe briefly feared for the man's heart.

Then he remembered who Launder was.

'Launder,' Jackson called from across The Fill Up. 'At this time, Montague and his people are not allowed to leave your property until the state police arrive and say different. They have to remain where they are.'

'You're taking their side…they're fucking scumbags. They're not even from around here!' His flabby chest heaved underneath his white shirt, its armpits damp with sweat stains. His beady eyes stared at Jackson with utter disbelief.

Despite the tented roof with so many bodies crammed together, Joe felt like they were all under a microscope. It was too warm, the air too close and smelling of too many bodies that, despite what morning rituals had been performed, were all beginning to perspire profusely. It caused an ache in his temples and a tightness in his throat.

'They will be staying put,' Jackson explained, his voice booming out, radiating authority. 'Montague and his people have already been very compliant with this investigation so far in agreeing to remain here, despite the financial losses that they may encounter. The most that we can do as a community in return is to accommodate them as best we can.'

'Accommodate them?' gasped Launder.

Joe noted that one of Jackson's deputies, the young lanky one, was nearing where he stood.

'You want me to accommodate them?' he said. His feeble voice grew to an aggressive roar once more. 'They're nothing but vermin!'

It was then that Launder spun and hurled the rock at Montague.

3

They had been so preoccupied with Launder's stabbing finger that they had all failed to see what the man had clutched in his other hand. The rock – a jagged piece of grey granite – hurtled through the air with phenomenal speed.

It slashed across Montague's left temple, striking the carnival owner with enough force to send him toppling backward onto the picnic table. Without thinking, Joe cast his right arm out, wrapping around Montague's shoulders, to prevent him from falling over completely. When he lifted him upright, his face was masked behind a curtain of bright red blood.

The Fill Up was in an uproar by then. Many people, including the deputy, had latched onto Launder. He would surely have fallen to the ground if not for the sheer number of bodies surrounding him.

One of the carnies, Youssef the Russian Strongman, was charging through the heated crowd, shoving those before him out of his way as he waded towards Montague's attacker. His size, which made even Jackson's build look small, and his bare torso showcasing muscles that looked carved from mahogany, reminded Joe of a soldier from some bygone age on a battlefield.

'Youssef!' yelled a voice by Joe's left ear.

It was Montague. His grey eyes, which had been dazed and rolling as Joe sat him upright, were now glaring at the Russian.

Youssef halted immediately, his bald head snapping around. Seeing Montague, the hate in his expression disappeared, replaced with concern and something else, something that looked like fear to Joe.

The carnival owner shook his head at him, his blood a crimson curtain over the left-hand side of his face. His grey eye on that side looked like it was staring out of some red hole. The silver hairs of his beard were soaked black with blood. He was a deadweight in Joe's hands.

'Lloyd!' bellowed Jackson. 'Take that fool back to the station and throw him in the drunk tank.'

'You're nothing more than a rat lover!' Launder shouted at him.

'And read him his rights.'

The young deputy pulled Launder forward, gripping his right forearm. His wrists were decorated with silver cuffs behind his back for them all to see.

178

Chapter Four

The Book of Daisy Hill

1

It took some time to calm everyone down before the first search parties set off. Youssef lifted Montague with ease from between Joe and Daisy, and with Carmen and Arnie in tow, the strongman took him to his RV to lie down.

The overall consensus from the townspeople was that Launder had acted fiendishly, especially considering the hospitality that Montague had shown towards everyone. A small group circled the carnival owner as he was carted off. Joe saw Bill Denton – the man who had questioned Jackson during his speech – was part of it, proclaiming that Launder should be jailed, while all around him townspeople were suddenly speaking passionately, apologetically with carnies, embracing them as they had never embraced them before.

They continued to stare at Joe as if he was a bad smell. It didn't surprise him; he was an outcast among outcasts. Still, he thought, something was changing, in throwing that rock Launder had caused those people to abandon their philosophy concerning outsiders.

2

An elderly woman was speaking with Daisy, telling her repeatedly, 'It's awful, so awful what he did.' She held Daisy's right hand while she spoke and shook it with each recital as if giving a benediction.

Joe glanced across The Fill Up, his neck doing a slow rotation. It wasn't until he had completed his scan that he saw he was not alone.

Len Grey, Lily's father, was standing beside him.

There was a shadow over his brow that prevented Joe from reading his intentions. His stomach muscles tensed in anticipation of a blow, something he even felt he deserved for not finding his daughter. Then the tented roof billowed above them, reshaping against the new flow of air and allowing the sun to wash away the shadows.

Joe saw that Len Grey's punching days were far behind him. He looked deflated: his craggy face too pale, his lips crushed into a thin scar, his shoulders slouched, his slate grey eyes forlorn. He looked like he had given up on life and was just passing time.

'I don't believe what Launder said about you,' he said. His voice was soft, almost lost among the cacophony surrounding them.

Joe stared, aware of the gritty air in his throat that had been kicked up from too many bodies stamping the grass to dust underneath their feet. He could feel the sweat on his brow, his collar, pits, and even on his stomach, as Len's grey eyes held his with an intense disaffected quality. He looked doped.

'I heard what you did, going after my daughter like that. It should have been me doing it. I'm glad she had someone like you around who at least tried to do something. I wanted to thank you for trying.'

There was no anger in his voice, or resentment, or anything. It was a voice belonging to someone going through the motions.

Len held out a calloused hand for Joe to shake. Joe stared at it for some time, not knowing what to do, aware of whispering voices belonging to people just outside of his peripheral vision who were watching. Their half heard words made Joe's skin itch.

'There's no need to thank me,' he said, his throat dry.

He accepted Len's hand. The man's shake was feeble; Joe did most of the work to pump it, smelling him for the first time. He smelled sour, like old beer, stale cigarettes and urine-soaked bed sheets.

It took all of Joe's will power not to cringe from it.

'It needs to be said,' Len went on, his voice monotone, barely audible.

'I hear you've been getting a hard time of it, and I won't have the person that tried to help my daughter thinking he did something wrong when he did something right.'

3

Meryl Grey moved to interrupt her husband; people were staring. Out of the corner of her eye she noticed that not everyone was watching Len. Her left arm froze mid-reach.

It was the one they called Arnie, who had leered at her the other day. He had returned from looking after his leader and stood only ten feet away, staring. No one else seemed to notice this, seemed to notice him. The crowd flowed around him the way water flows around a boulder in its stream.

His lecherous look was back, seeming to say to her *I know you see me*, his slate eyes boring at her while a twist of a smirk haunted his lips. It was a cruel look, desiring and hungry. The same one that had been in her dreams the night before, dreams that had left her body feverish with heat, her skin crawling with the sensation of a thousand exploring touches.

Once more, Meryl felt those phantom fingers caressing her as she stood behind her husband, this time around her pelvis just above her sex. They were little touches, barely there, yet enough to consume her attention to the point where the din around her grew mute, faraway. Even her vision changed, narrowing on the carny's eyes that shone like jewels above his lurid smile, until everything else around him became a blur.

She felt the pad of one invisible finger stroke her from the left hip down to her inner thigh, leaving a trail of heat that prickled. It was not an unpleasant sensation. New, hungry heat bloomed in her lower body for it.

Someone coughed loudly nearby, startling her.

Like that, the volume of the world returned all at once, filling her ears with the dull roar that was a hundred exchanges happening at once. Meryl's eyelids fluttered, attempting to deal with the sensory input while wondering what had just happened. When she opened them, she saw that Arnie had vanished and that her left arm was still extended towards her husband's shoulder.

A quick glance around informed her that no one was watching; all eyes were on the conversation between Len and Joe. She continued to stretch out her arm, resting her palm on Len's left shoulder.

'Len, I think Jackson wants to speak with us,' she said, in a not-quite-steady voice. Her eyes darted around, searching for the carny.

'Oh, does he? Okay.'

Meryl found that she wasn't as concerned about his absent tone as she used to be. She was thinking of that sensation on her inner thigh.

4

They weren't ten minutes beyond the tree line when Daisy took off. Their party had paused while Mitch Collins, the sergeant in charge, consulted the map, an ever-deepening frown sinking into his sweaty, pink face as he squinted at the creased paper, rotating it every so often. Daisy was the only one brave enough to say what everyone was thinking.

'Fuck this.'

Before Joe could think to say anything, she had crashed into the foliage. The sergeant, still engrossed in the map, didn't notice.

'What are you doing?' he hissed, chasing after her.

'Forging my path.'

'Aren't you afraid of getting lost?'

'Staying with Sergeant Doolittle is going to get us lost, not this, but if you feel more comfortable curling up beside The Man, you go ahead. I want to achieve something today. Plus with these, I won't be getting lost'.

Daisy stabbed her arms into the sky. In her left hand, she held a map. In her right hand, she held a large black device that sported an antenna.

'How did you get that?'

'Arnie gave it to me so we could keep in contact with each other.'

That hurt a little to hear. Last night Joe had passed out on Arnie's sofa like the night before, only this time things had been different. There had been a tension in the carny's RV, with its orange shag carpet, earwax beige cabinets, and wood effect countertops, that had not existed between them before. There was a tightness around Arnie's lips and dusk crow's feet that encircled his eyes as he spoke with him.

Daisy seemed to notice his silence and added, 'I bumped into him as Jackson was organising everyone into groups.'

'Did he say anything about how Montague was doing?'

'I asked and he said he's recovered from worse. He had more to say about Launder and not all of it was pretty. The man's lucky the police took him away.'

'Yes, I saw how your crush, Youssef, went for Launder.'

'As the kids say nowadays, gag me with a spoon. The Youssef ship has long since sailed,' said Daisy.

They were moving up a steep incline that required them to climb in single file, Daisy in the lead, gripping the dry branches of the trees to hoist themselves further. The day's heat was even worse beneath the emerald canopy of leaves overhead, their colour bleeding into the falling light, as the surrounding wilderness seemed to drink up whatever small amount of moisture there was in the air. It laced their throats with the sweet tang of sap.

They were both panting hard as they crested the top of the trail, not a tourist path but one made by the wildlife, their sweat sitting on them in beads. The pair turned to observe the incline behind them, astonished at the view from the high point over the woodland below, which stretched around them like a natural cathedral filled with that green-gold light. Birds twittered unseen in the heavens above as the place's choir.

184

Out of the blue, Daisy said, 'You know, you're not bad looking.'

'Where did that come from?'

The comment caught him off guard, his head snapping to his right to find Daisy was not enjoying the view as he was; she was scrutinising him with her blue eyes, hands on hips, her gold hair a shimmering halo in the light. He could see her diaphragm working beneath her sweatshirt, constricting and loosening the muscles of her slender torso.

Standing opposite, he couldn't help but think there was something wholesome and wild and present about her. It was a quality that captivated and intimated him in equal measure as he gazed at her, waiting for her to elaborate.

'You're attractive in that all-American way, or almost,' she told him, leaving his mind whirling. 'There's a little too much sensitivity in your face to be full-on all-American, but it works for you. I might as well tell you because, well, I might not be here tomorrow and I get the feeling if I were to wait around for you to make a move, I'd be waiting a while.'

'Would you?' Joe laughed. 'That's presuming I'm attracted to you.'

'Please, don't pretend like you weren't staring at my ass the entire time we were climbing up that thing.' Daisy laughed as his face turned red, wheeling from the viewpoint to follow the trail once more. He stumbled after, bumbling excuses out of his mouth. 'If I can offer up a little advice, you're very guarded,' she said as they fell into step beside each other.

The trail had widened enough to let them do so, yet it still seemed like they were walking on the spine of some fallen giant, with how the earth fell away from them on either side. The trees were smaller, thinner here as they tried to fight for life with their roots digging into the incline.

'It makes it hard to know if you're acting genuine, or you're acting to get by. In other words, it makes it hard for a girl to know where she stands.'

For some reason, perhaps because he felt put on the spot by Daisy's previous comment, he grew irritated. It burned in him; having his guarded nature referenced out loud fueled what frustrated anger had been building in him since being pulled into the cop shop and interviewed like embers stoked into a flame. What he said next, he said without thought.

'Okay, well, seeing as we are giving each other advice, perhaps it's not the best thing that you're so honest with everyone.'

'Ohhh...is that right?' cheered Daisy, hearing his turbulent emotion.

'Yes. Being on the road is dangerous, and giving up your whole history at the drop of a hat can get you into trouble.'

'This coming from the guy who has a town of people believing he is involved with a missing child,' Daisy countered.

He halted to stare at her in disbelief. She walked on, refusing to react to him, her golden dreads more like a lion's mane than hair.

'I thought you said you didn't think I had anything to do with it.'

'I don't, but the town does,' replied Daisy. 'Plus, did you ever think that the reason Montague has this little obsession with your past is because you refuse to give up any information about it? Haven't you ever thought that if you'd just spill the beans as I did, he'd leave you alone?'

The trail was widening now, the rest of the land rising to their level.

'Montague isn't obsessed with me.'

'He is,' said Daisy, spinning on her heels to face him while walking backward. 'He's already asked me a few times if you've said anything to me.'

'And what did you tell him?'

'The truth: that I don't know anything about Joe Cage,' she said.

All the whimsical humour that she had spoken with throughout this exchange was gone. Her bright blue eyes held his hazel ones, frank and damning.

Joe wanted her then, his longing so startling he was dumbstruck. It was like falling unexpectedly into a hot bath and being enveloped by the heat of the water. It was more than just attraction he felt; it was a desire to come clean to her, to put his trust in someone. The moment he realised that, he became aware of just how heavy a weight he had been carrying on his shoulders, not just from Lily Grey's disappearance, but everything.

'It's not that I don't want to,' Joe said in a small voice.

He watched how the muscles of her jaw rolled with his words as he stood in air that felt too hot, too dusty, too sickly sweet with hot sap. His body was flush with sweat like a second layer of greasy skin sticking to his clothes.

'You told those cops about yourself, I bet,' she said, moving forward with another heel spin. 'Whatever you had to say wasn't a confession to murder, seeing as you're still a free man. So what's the big secret?'

Joe's throat locked like a prison cell.

Yes, he had told Jackson about where he was from, about his family, but he had only been reciting facts like taking a history exam where you only needed to reel off dates and times. There was no emotion behind telling the officers his family's names, no confession; all that was safely locked away inside his head.

'There is none,' he murmured, rubbing at his right wrist absently.

'That's such bullshit,' scoffed Daisy. 'Why are you doing this?' She held her arms out in a gesture that was meant to encompass their surroundings. Surroundings that had changed once more, the inclines on either side of them disappearing as the earth rose up to the level of the path they were trudging on. Sunlight continued to filter through the trees, slashing across Daisy's figure like tiger stripes of light and shadow. Behind her, the trail snaked its way through a wall of brambles, their leaves a dark ivy colour shining silver as they caught the light, reminding him of snake scales. 'Why are you here now, looking for this missing girl who you met for five minutes? Why haven't you left town already? The police are hunting for any excuse to tie you to her disappearance and the town is gunning for you, so why the fuck are you still here? What's motivating you to stay?'

When he didn't reply Daisy spoke once again.

'You know there are other benefits to being honest. I know from your bruised face that you know about the shit side of being on the road. But you have no fucking idea what it's like doing it and being a woman. Where you see everyone who offers to help you as a potential rapist or serial killer, and some are. Some think of women as vulnerable little playthings that they can use and discard like rubbish. You criticised me for being honest, for attracting attention. Honesty is the book I live by. What you haven't thought of is maybe I do that because if I'm honest and I crack wise enough with the best of them, that will get men to stop thinking of me as a walking pussy, and other women, townie women with their husbands and their children, to stop thinking of me as some harlot looking to steal their precious men away from them. That's the life that I live on the road.'

There was fire in her cheeks and in her blue eyes, setting them ablaze to almost luminous qualities. Her speech had left her breathing hard, her diaphragm constricting and loosening, drinking in great lungfuls from the sultry air.

'I'm sorry, I only said that because I was trying to look out for you,' said Joe.

'Fuck you, you dick spout,' she shot at him, even more enraged. 'You know what? I take it back; I don't find you attractive. You know why? Your macho bullshit of I'm-just-trying-to-look-after-you. Fuck you, Joe. I'm doing a better job looking after myself than you are doing.

'You're the same as every man I've ever met. Too much TV; seeing that all the guys are heroes and all the girls are damsels in distress gives men this warped hero complex. In reality, men daydream and women get shit done.' She took off through the brambles, smacking the leafy branches out of her way as she did. Joe, his soul a well of remorse, took off after her. 'Daisy, hold up,' he said, no longer able to see her.

Inside the nest of brambles, it was as dark as cave. He was having less success traversing the trail than his friend; his wider shoulders brushed the leafy branches, their thorns – mud brown except for their pink tips – raking the exposed skin of his arms, leaving blood to well. One lashed across his right cheek, just under his eye. He clamped a hand to it.

That was how he exited the thicket, allowing Daisy to seize her chance. He stumbled out into sunlight and found himself before a lagoon that lay framed between grey stone, its waters clear and rippling slightly as it poured down a mound of more grey rock that towered above him.

'Wow,' said Joe, stepping towards the edge of the water.

'You know what, Joe, fuck you,' said Daisy behind him.

He felt her palms on his shoulder blades, heard her laugh, and then he was propelled forward. He just had time to gulp down a breath before he plunged beneath the water's surface. Cold soothed his hot skin, seeming to penetrate through and grasp at his heart as he kicked to the surface.

Daisy was laughing at him as he gasped for breath. It was good laughter, like the type that had filled her car on the way back from the station.

'That's what you get,' she shouted at him.

The lagoon was deep enough that he had to swim until his feet scraped the bottom. He waded to the shore, his jeans falling with the weight of the water. Daisy was laughing so hard she didn't think anything was amiss as he stumbled into her, his arms hugging her at the waist.

By the time she realised what he was doing, Joe had already lifted her, unclipping the radio and map from her back pockets, flinging them to the ground. Daisy screamed, 'No!' as he fell backward into the lagoon with a splash.

There was silence beneath the surface of the water. Or, almost silence as the pair kicked to the surface. Joe came up laughing.

'You asshole,' Daisy said, slapping water at him.

Joe grabbed her arms by the wrists to stop her from splashing him, pulling her close, all the while laughing. Wiping his eyes clear, he saw she was staring at him, her eyes a brilliant, blazing blue. There were only inches between them.

Daisy moved closer until their bellies rested against one another. Joe did the same, her face filling his vision along with the waterfall behind her. He kept looking from her eyes to her lips then to her eyes again. They were centimeters apart when he spied it beyond her shoulder.

'Daisy, get out of the water now,' he said with urgency.

He did not wait for her to respond but took her hand and guided her in a scramble onto land. When they looked back both saw that the pollutant in the water had spread further. Both recognised it for what it was. Blood.

5

The rocky outcrop was at least ten feet high, its sides framed by a steep climb of grey stones. Joe's and Daisy's feet plunged into them like they were sand, causing them to slide downward with each stride. They had to use their hands to claw their way to the top, leaving them coated in dust.

They saw the slaughtered thing straight away. It was not Lily Grey, but a stag. In seeing it, Joe felt like all the air had been punched out of him.

The animal's antlered head rested in the tiny stream, its hide a soft brown, the one eye they could see a black marble frozen in its socket. Blood oozed into the water from the exposed tendons of its neck. Its rear legs lay splayed on the dusty rock to the right. A space of six feet existed between them. The part of the animal that had connected these two pieces was nowhere to be seen. Instead, red gore and coils of intestines painted the ground, which was abuzz with flies in the hot, stinking air. It smelled coppery, like lightning storms.

'Fuck me,' said Daisy. 'Do we call this in? Do you think this has something to do with Lily?'

It was like she was speaking through syrup. His legs seemed to be losing all their strength. The world taking on a too bright resolution, all he could see was blood as scarlet as jewels and the shine of the sun off the water.

'I need to sit down,' he muttered, collapsing onto the stony floor.

'Hey, hey, what is it?' asked Daisy, bending to his aid.

She gripped his shoulders as he exhaled unsteadily, trying to slow his racing heart.

'I thought it was her. For a second, I thought it was her.'

6

Nothing else was found that day.

Chapter Five

The Cold Call

1

The sheriff observed him through the bars of his cage, his fingers toying with the cell keys. His skin was sun worn from the day's search and Launder could see the grim pouches of flesh under the man's eyes.

'I guess you didn't find what you were looking for?' he remarked.

'You're lucky, Mr. Launder, that Lawrence Montague doesn't want to press charges, charges that I would have fully supported after seeing your display today,' said Jackson, with no attempt to conceal his contempt.

If he was honest, the news surprised Launder, who had been sweating all day in his cell with thoughts of being sued for physical assault. He had given no thought to the idea that he could serve some time for his actions, only muddled over with ever-increasing fury at the chance that he might have to pay out some money. Rather than feeling relieved at Jackson's news, his mind had immediately begun to fret over what game Montague was playing.

'With everything that is going on, this community doesn't need someone like you starting fights. Mr. Montague has informed me that he has paid you for the use of your land for a week. You will honour that arrangement by allowing him and his employees to remain there until that time or until the state police say any different. Between now and then you will not interact with them, do you understand?'

Glen Launder crushed the feelings of injustice that swirled inside him like black, acidic bile, wanting to explode from his mouth in a volley of insults and curses until he had provoked the sheriff enough to make him wade into his cell with his fists raised. Such behaviour had worked for him in the past, but in this case he knew it would not serve him here.

Even with his impulsive tendencies to let his rage be known, there was a part of him, a cold, calculating part, that knew when it was time to pretend to be a meek yes man. It wasn't an act he often resorted to or found he could portray when his anger was so great. Yet he knew on this occasion that it was important to be cool; if not, the sheriff would undoubtedly keep him overnight. And he didn't want that, his mind having already begun formulating a plan.

I'll get them in the long grass, he said to his anger, as if it wasn't a part of him but a separate parasitic entity latched onto his soul.

'I understand, Sheriff. Those freaks won't see or hear from me,' said Launder, his voice cool and calm and as sweet as honey.

He smiled his best shit-eating grin through the bars of his cell, his mind picturing the pair of binoculars Shirley, his wife, had bought him for Christmas and the hunting rifle in his weapons cabinet.

2

Elaine entered his office after Jackson had made the first of two phone calls he intended to make before heading home. She was dressed in civilian clothes, a set of acid-wash jeans that showed her tanned ankles, white sneakers, and a salmon-coloured shirt. She was also carrying a wicker picnic basket.

The shock and joy of seeing her, of seeing her healthy, smiling, sun-touched face swept away the cobwebs that were gathering in his head. The phone call, which had lasted all of forty seconds, had been a strange one. It had simply enforced the bizarreness of the last few days that left Jackson feeling like he was trying to complete a puzzle with several pieces missing.

The surprise of seeing Elaine made him forget, at least for the moment, everything as he rose from his seat, his pecan-coloured eyes glancing over her shoulder through his office windows to see if anyone was watching. There was no one in the corridor beyond where the walls were decorated, like his office, with the same felt noticeboards the colour of old limes.

'Wow, you look incredible,' he said. 'What are you doing here? Not that I'm not happy to see you it's just...'

'It's the night shift, Tim,' she reminded him, leaning over his desk and planting a kiss on his stubbly cheek. She tasted the salt of his sweat and the lingering residue of Old Spice. 'The only one here is Mark Stone and he's on dispatch duty, reading, as usual. I think we will be safe. Plus I thought I'd bring you dinner. From what I heard about today, it sounded like you could use a woman's intervention.'

She placed the picnic basket on his desk, no easy thing considering the clutter of yellow notepads and pens on top of it.

'Woman's intervention? I call this saintly intervention.'

'Funny, how you refer to the woman you're sleeping with as saintly,' Elaine teased, dishing out the contents of the basket.

Jackson's eyes grew and grew, seeing potato salad, coleslaw, ham, several different slices of cheese, roast chicken, mustard, mayo, and more. His stomach rumbled thankfully.

'Speaking of saintly, you just missed Shirley Launder,' said Jackson.

'Lucky for me. Was she carrying?'

It was well known within the Marybell community that Shirley Launder was never seen without her black leather handbag that was said to contain three things: her wallet, a New American Bible, and a 38. revolver.

'She was. Picked up her nut job of a husband about ten minutes ago.'

'I heard about what he did from Phyllis,' she said, making a sandwich for herself while he made his own. 'You would think this town has enough to worry about without him kicking off.'

'That's what I said, more or less,' said Jackson after a swallowing a wad of his speedily made sandwich. 'This is incredible, by the way.'

Elaine took one of the two seats in front of his desk, which were also the colour of old limes, crossing her legs as she did.

'You're welcome,' she said, tearing bits of her sandwich off with one hand before popping them into her mouth. 'I also heard that Mitch Collins got his group lost in the woods.'

'Yes he did, and those poor people only got back to their cars two hours after everyone else,' said Jackson, chuckling, despite himself.

'I also heard you found something, just not who you were looking for.'

'Yep, a dead stag and guess who found it...Joe Cage and his girlfriend, Daisy Hill. Makes me think even more about what happened to Teal's butchered herd.'

Jackson watched Elaine's eyebrows jump under his office fluorescents.

'Have you uncovered anything more about him?'

His eyes darted back to the black phone on his desk.

The eerie sensation he had experienced on the call returned to him in the form of prickling at the nape of his neck. In the short time that the call had lasted, the individual on the other end of the line had only said five words. Aside from the six to eight seconds Jackson had used explaining himself, the connection had been filled with nothing other than the individual's slow, steady breathing.

As Jackson had listened to each inhalation and exhalation, a sense of place had overwhelmed him, envisioning each breath being transported at light speed from Hazel, Indiana to Marybell, Kansas under the earth via a network of cables like a giant octopus beneath the United States.

'I don't know,' he answered, staring at the phone.

Its black plastic coating gleamed at him in the light except where his fingers had left smudges.

'What's wrong?' asked Elaine.

'Before you came in, I was just on the phone with Joe's father. At least, it was the number he gave us for what he claimed was his parents' home address.'

'And what he did say?'

'Barely anything. I said who I was and that I was looking to speak to Joe's parents to confirm some things. He only said, "I don't have a son", then hung up.'

'Well, that's helpful. Do you think Joe gave you the wrong number?'

Jackson was looking at his phone again and the eerie sensation returned in full force. After spending all day in the summer heat, his body hummed with the temperature it had absorbed, his skin feeling as stiff and leathery as Shirley Launder's handbag. Now Jackson felt like he sat in a cold pocket, a dead zone where the temperature doesn't rise above crypt cold, mortuary cold. His balls had shriveled to tiny beads between his legs. The black hairs on his arm, the same deep coal black as his head, stood erect, like he was touching that weird electrical ball the carnies had at the fair.

'Jesus, Tim, look at your arms,' said Elaine, seeing them. She scooted forward, chair legs scraping the floor, and placed her palm over his right forearm. She felt deliciously warm. 'You're freezing. What's gotten into you?' she asked, alarmed.

'I don't think the kid gave me a wrong number,' he said to her. 'That was him, Joe's father. He didn't speak anything other than those five words, "I don't have a son", but you know when you call someone and you kind of get a sense of their mood? Do you what I'm talking about, or am I speaking Dutch?'

'No, I get what you're saying,' said Elaine, her voice high and slightly shrill. 'I experience it all the time when I'm speaking to my roommate, Sarah-Louise, who's never without boy trouble. She never comes out and says it, you have to guess with her, and you always can tell even over the phone that something's gone wrong again; there's a hesitance.'

'Yeah, well this was like that, but different,' said Jackson. 'It wasn't hesitance I was hearing on the line. It was hatred. I was hearing hate.'

Though that was entirely true, it didn't seem to convey completely the extent of the emotion Jackson had felt coming through the phone. It was like being close to one of those power stations, hearing the drone of the wires and feeling the fillings in your teeth reciprocate that ceaselessly buzzing sound. Only this had been blasting into his ear.

Jackson knew what hate was. He recognised it in Launder earlier when speaking to him through the cell bars. In that case, Launder's hate was a prissy, petty thing; it was something that made you pity the person who felt that way. The type of hate he heard over the phone was larger. It was an abyss in which there was no end, and it had frightened him.

'I never asked Joe why he was drifting,' said Jackson. 'I asked him everything else: where he had been, what jobs he had worked, but not why.'

'What are you thinking, Tim?'

'That the man on the phone is one bad guy.'

3

'I think we should pack this up and eat the rest at your place,' said Elaine. 'Nothing would make me happier,' he said, a tight smile flickering across his dusky face. His brown eyes looked half asleep. 'Especially if you're planning on staying.'

'I was always planning on staying,' Elaine told him with a confidence that suggested she had not expected him to protest.

Nor did it occur to Jackson that he would ever refuse her company. In the past few months, he had begun to notice things about his life that had not stood out so prominently before. Like the emptiness in his home, the quiet that seemed to exist within its rooms despite how loud he had the television on. These things seemed to make up a presence, a cold, stalking presence that shared the sofa with him as he channel surfed and joined him in bed at night as he stared at the ceiling, unable to switch the ticking clock of his mind off. He had begun to feel haunted in his own home.

Yet it was not a new feeling, only a magnified one. As a bachelor, he had encountered this discontent often and had learned to master suppressing it with exercise, with hobbies, with work. Those tricks did not work since Elaine had come into his life, because she filled the holes where that maddening, restless discontent lived in a way those past times hadn't.

He planned to ask her to move in with him. He loved her and knew she knew this even though he had never spoken the words out loud. He knew she loved him; it was part of the oddity that was their relationship, like the other night when he had left the garage door open and she had turned up later without either of them communicating to one another.

Their relationship seemed to exist with many unspoken expectations that made it unique and surreal from any others he had had in the past, where things had needed to almost be written down for either party to know what stage they were at. With Elaine, there was just…being. They were a fact; their equal affection and love for each other was a fact.

'I just have to make one last phone call first,' Jackson said to her.

'Okay,' she said, exhaling sharply through her nose.

Elaine had always admired his dedication to his job; however, sometimes she wished he delegated more, to not take on so much alone. She reclined back into her seat and began picking at her sandwich again, aware that Mark Stone at the dispatch desk was perfectly capable of making a phone call.

Sometimes she wondered if the others took advantage of Jackson's work ethic. Mitch Collins certainly did, a man who should have 'waiting to retire' stamped across his forehead with the amount of effort he put in.

Then she thought about him getting lost in the woods and chuckled.

'Hello, this is Sheriff Timothy Jackson from Marybell,' Jackson into the phone's receiver. 'I'm calling regarding an ongoing missing person case we have.'

'Yes, yes, I'll just go see if there's someone free,' said the woman on the other end of the line.

She left but didn't put him on hold, so he could hear the shuffle as she moved from her desk and then indistinct voices in the background. He glanced at Elaine sitting with her legs crossed, ankles on show. Eventually, there was another shuffle, and a male voice spoke in his ear in a gruff, cheerful tone. He reminded Jackson immediately of a gun-toting cowboy. 'Hi there, this is Detective Emmett Rook speaking.'

'Emmett, this is Tim Jackson. We spoke on the phone yesterday.'

'Tim? It's a bit late out in the boonies for a sheriff to be working, isn't it?' asked Rook.

To Jackson, he sounded like someone who is always close to erupting into laughter.

'I was just thinking the same thing about you. Isn't five o'clock bedtime for you boys?'

'Well, you're not wrong there,' said Rook, and this time he did laugh, though his humour quickly dissipated. 'We are just swamped with this new case. I've never seen anything like it, it's an absolute bloodbath. Plus we've got two guys out sick, which is why we haven't gotten anyone down to you yet.'

That tingling sensation began to needle at Jackson's neck again.

'Have you any new developments to report?' Rook asked.

'Not much, I'm afraid. We expanded the search surrounding Lily Grey's last known location, but the only thing we managed to find was a severely mutilated stag, which I wouldn't have bothered to tell you about except it's not the first mutilated animal to turn up in the last three days. A farmer by the name of Philip Teal reported that half of his cattle was slaughtered in the night, claims his family slept through the entire thing. And there's nothing back from the labs on the evidence we do have so far.'

There was a pause on the line, long enough that Jackson thought the connection had cut. Then Rook's voice came back, speaking this time without any trace of that gruff, good humour. 'Tell me about the cattle. Were they arranged in any specific sort of way?'

'Not particularly. If you want the truth, the entire field was full of scattered body parts. I had a veterinarian out to take a look at what was left. From her report, it looks like the animals were attacked by something. She found bite marks on the remains.'

Again, that tingling sensation persisted. This time it wasn't the wires beneath the ground that Jackson saw in his head, but Marybell sprawled out across the vast, flat American heartlands, a nest of twinkling lights, as the sun slowly slid over the curve of the earth, bleaching the sky bloodred. Quiet, sleepy, isolated Marybell, where the next town sat fifty plus miles away.

'You said you had the vet look at what was left. What did you mean by that?' Rook asked.

Suddenly Jackson thought, *Now I'm being interviewed.*

'Some parts, large parts, in fact, of each animal were missing. The same thing was found with the dead stag today.'

Elaine was watching him with eyes as big as saucers.

'Huh. Jackson, do you have photographs of each scene?'

'I do.'

'I know you boys are busy down there hunting for that little girl, but I'm wondering if you wouldn't mind bringing those photos and any documentation you have and meeting me at a little place up the road from you.'

'Do you think this has to do with your current case?'

'Well, I don't know what these events have to do with your missing girl, but the MO with those dead animals sounds mighty similar to what we are dealing with here, only it wasn't animals that we found.'

'You said earlier something about a bloodbath?' inquired Jackson, feeling it was his turn to ask questions and get some answers.

'Yep, it's like nothing I've ever seen,' said Rook. Now the good humour was gone from his voice; he sounded frayed.

'It's...Jesus. This thing is like a massacre, worse than that shooting in Texas in 66. I can't explain it over the phone.'

'Okay, give me the address and I'll be there,' said Jackson, grabbing the nearest pen and jotting down what Rook told him on a legal pad.

There was a little conversation that followed and soon the phone was back in its cradle. Elaine continued to stare for several minutes while Jackson reread what he had written. She read his words upside down.

'Dylan's Roadhouse. Isn't that...'

'That's the place where Joe Cage was employed before he came to Marybell,' confirmed Jackson.

Chapter Six

Confessions

1

Joe found her sitting on the rear door of her station wagon, its position reminding him of a pouting bottom lip. Shadows and orange light danced over her petite frame from the campfire she was staring into as music pumped from the wagon's tape deck, a groovy rock tune he couldn't place. Daisy's head bobbed to the beat, her gold dreadlocks swaying in sync with her body.

Joe watched from a distance, the bottle of Jack Daniel's he had swiped from Arnie's RV and the six pack of Cokes forgotten in his hands. It was enchanting to watch her, especially when she was spotlit by firelight; it seemed to be the type of light she was meant to be seen in.

Throat dry, he forced himself to go over. 'Mind if I join you?' he asked, trying to sound smooth.

He held up the bottle and the Coke as if submitting his gifts for inspection, thinking back to the way he had tightened up earlier when Daisy had questioned him. There was shame inside him for how he had deflected the conversation, manipulating it back onto her, and with it was that desire to be honest, to come clean to her. Holding her gaze, he felt the invisible burden of his secrets now more than ever on his shoulders, willing him to be quiet.

He realised that he wasn't going to, that if Daisy accepted him here, his secrets would spill out. He owed her that after everything. The thought of being open did not horrify him as it usually did. His fear was there, but it was drowned underneath a swell of calm acceptance that was almost serene.

She gazed back at him, stoic, her expression unreadable.

'If you say no, it means I have no one else to hang out with,' he told her after some time. 'Everyone else around here blames me for the carnival shutting down.'

'Are you saying I'm your only choice for not being alone?' Her blue eyes, now dark gems that glittered in the firelight, were as frank as ever.

'No, I'm just trying to make you pity me. Is it working?'

'Not really.' Her lips curled into a smirk.

'Well, if it means anything, even if I had the choice to hang out with anyone else, I'd still want to be here,' Joe said sincerely.

'Of course you'd want to hang out with me. Who wouldn't? I'm ... what is it you said about yourself? A badass,' she said.

Joe joined her on the wagon's back lip, their legs side by side.

'Shall I pour?' he asked.

'By all means.'

Joe unscrewed the bottle, pouring the drink into a teacup that was chipped and emblazoned with a blue teddy bear. He gave this to her while he poured his drink into a cup inscribed with the words "World's Best Boss". He added the Coke to both, which fizzed to the top.

They drank, gazing into the campfire, both enjoying the blazing trail the liquid left inside. Around them, the RVs stood silent, their windows dark. The only sounds were the logs cracking, unleashing a cloud of embers into the sky.

'So, what are we listening to tonight?'

Daisy's left arm whipped up, her fingers clasped around a cassette, the cover depicting a man playing a guitar outlined in golden light.

'T. Rex's Electric Warrior. This song is called Mambo Sun. Please tell me you're cool enough to have heard of them?'

'T. Rex? Isn't that a monster from that old B movie, Dinosaur?' said Joe.

'It is a dinosaur, not a monster, which is why the movie is called Dinosaur, but T. Rex is also the name of this bitching band,' Daisy informed him.

'They've got a nice groove to them,' he remarked, sipping his drink.

'Figures, you're not cool enough to know a band like T. Rex.'

Joe didn't reply; having Daisy insult him was as expected as getting wet while standing in the rain.

The bluesy, strutting song ended and was immediately followed by a mellow acoustic strum. Joe's tongue played along the back of his teeth as he listened, his secrets, his shame, ever present on his shoulders, threatening to sink him into the earth. He recalled how she had looked at him that first night under the campfire light when Montague had given up prying at him. The sympathetic look on her face indicating that somehow, she understood his need for privacy.

'I have a little sister named Harper back in Indiana,' said Joe, looking into his cup.

He kept his gaze on the dark liquid as Daisy's head snapped around. Part of her hair had fallen over the left-hand side of her face, her eyes glittering behind it in the corner of his vision. 'That's where I'm from, Indiana.'

'And he speaks at last,' she said. 'I've been through Indiana; I feel no need to go back.'

'Me either,' said Joe quickly. 'Hey, I'm only telling you this because I don't want you walking around thinking I'm some sort of meathead who won't let anyone in.'

'Aw, honey, I'm going to think that anyway,' she said with mock sincerity, nudging her shoulder against his so they swayed briefly together.

'You're not that bad. I've met worse. So, you have a little sister there, and here I was thinking you just fell out of the sky. Do you have parents too?'

'Yes, I do,' he said, finding it hard not to chuckle. Because it was Daisy, because she made him laugh, he continued. 'Lily reminded me of her, even though Harper's a good bit older. She's turning fourteen this year. We lived on a farm, but not a working one. Her favourite thing in the world to do is to play hide and seek in the haylofts, not that she's any good. She giggles too much.'

Daisy was quiet, sensing the fragility of this conversation. She prayed no one would come and disturb them because she knew that would mean the end of it, that whatever was allowing Joe to speak would crack like brittle glass and they would never get this moment back.

She found she wanted him to talk because she knew he needed to, that what he was saying were things that weighed on him and perhaps, she sensed, had become tangled with the guilt he felt for Lily Grey. There were things she wanted to do, like hold him, touch him, but she didn't dare in case it cracked the moment.

She kept still, she kept quiet, and she listened.

'My mother used to say we got lucky with her,' Joe carried on. 'She said that most girls that age don't have time for their big brothers.' There was a sorrowful smirk on his face, and though he wasn't crying, water trembled in his eyes.

'I think that's why I broke down earlier and I'm sorry for that,' he said with a deep frown that broke when he added, 'Lily looked so much like Harper did back when she was five. It's scary. I... I would go back to Indiana for her, but there are things there that I had to get away from. You know how when you read a book and a character in it just snaps and they do something completely unlike them? You know the way they write those things? I never really believed a person could snap... until I did. I snapped and I had to get out of there and I did it without even thinking of anything but get out, get out, get out. And I knew I couldn't think about what was behind me, so I built this dam in my head where everything from home sits, wanting to overwhelm me. And until now it's been fine. The only trouble I've had with it is when people like Montague, like Dylan who owed the roadhouse I worked at before here, ask me questions. I try to keep my head down, do my job, get paid and move on. Only with what's happening here, with Lily being taken by someone – and she has been taken – I was deluding myself that she was simply lost until we found that stag today, but no. Someone has taken her, and it makes me think about Harper and why I left Indiana and how I left her in the same shit I was dealing with. When I was there, she didn't get any of the bad things I did. And I took it because I was protecting her, but then I snapped.'

Tears were running down his face now. Daisy, unable to resist any longer, reached for him, her hands brushing over his chest, his collar, and his jaw until he was looking at her. One ran through his hair while the other gripped the collar of his Tom Selleck shirt. She pulled him close, her lips finding his, which first were firm then yielded to her touch.

She felt his tongue glide along her bottom lip.

When they broke apart, she nodded her head towards the inside of the station wagon at the space she had converted into a bed. She knew he was too chivalrous for his good, so she took his hand and said, 'Come on.'

2

Daisy led him inside, both of them butt-shuffling over the mattress she had installed for whenever she couldn't afford a motel, observing how he removed his shoes first, the way a person removes them before entering a home.

The curtains that she had installed were already closed, pale pink sheets that let the dancing light of the campfire in and nothing else. She doubted they would be disturbed tonight anyway; the campsite seemed to be dead. It was as if the place were in mourning, though whether that was for Lily Grey or being unable to carry on as business as usual, she didn't know.

They were the only ones who seemed exempt from the glum atmosphere, the anticipation of what they were about to share engulfing them in a repellant bubble. If they had been doing anything else, perhaps, Daisy would have considered the campsite silence as strange, maybe even sinister. All she felt was the same mellow understanding she had experienced as Joe had confessed to her, that they were sharing something intimate and fragile and new. She did not want to lose those feelings.

She closed the trunk door. T. Rex's Planet Queen was playing from the wagon's tape deck.

Joe was lying on his back in his jeans and shirt, propped up on his elbows. His eyes took her in.

She lifted her sweatshirt over her head and tossed it aside, leaving on the three chains of gold beads she wore, one reaching to her navel. The firelight withered over her skin, tanned from summer rays.

They sought each other's lips. After some time, he traced the line of her jaw, kissing the giddy beating pulse in her neck, stroking her right collar with his tongue before taking her right nipple in his mouth as she ran her fingers through his hair. A groan escaped her. She gripped his chin and mashed her mouth to his, kissing him hungrily now.

At one point he tried to sit up, his head colliding with the wagon's roof. She giggled at him, hand over her mouth, as he rubbed his crown.

Joe shrugged at her as if to say what now. Daisy started to unbutton her jeans as he removed his with a hard yank, then threw off his shirt. She lifted a knee and straddled him, naked except for the three chains of beads.

Her body found his soft and hard beneath her all at once.

She reached over his face, caressing his stubbly cheeks with her nails as she kissed him. The inside of the vehicle was furnace-hot now. Their bodies were dewed in sweat as they moved against one another. His penis a hard stone against her wet labia, laying straight, laying in the wrong position, not where her body demanded it to be.

Unexpectedly, his left hand let go of her hip and worked its way round to her front, his fingers caressing her there. Daisy's belly clenched hard enough to make her gasp, anticipating pain.

There was none, instead, there was only sweetness.

'You're good at that,' she moaned, her eyes closed, her hips gyrating slowly in sync with his fingers.

Her eye snapped wide as he slid effortlessly inside. Twin gasps of exhalation jetted from them both at this new sensation.

Daisy continued to rock her hips, gaining power with each rotation, her fingernails digging into the wagon's roof. He held her right hip, his fingers biting into the flesh of buttocks as the pleasure built, his eyes on her. Daisy's climax unified her body into one rigid muscle before erupting into convulsions. She rode it first, sitting atop of him, her muscles quaking, then when she could stand no more, she hugged him to her chest. Joe climaxed in watching this display, how her body shuddered, how her face contorted. They collapsed onto the mattress in a tangle, their sweat like oil on their skin, diaphragms working for air. The firelight continued to dance through the curtains, bathing them in flickering orange and red hues.

3

As he held her, Daisy realised that T. Rex had played out.

'Can we rewind the tape to the start and do that again?'

'Yes, please. Oh, god yes,' she answered, laughing.

The look in his face was younger, freer; he was unburdened, at least for now, of the things that haunted him. Their sex had something to do with it, but Daisy thought it had been the talking that made him look that way; he had pulled those dusty ghosts out from whatever shadows they had been hiding in and thrown them out into the light of day. There was still more in there, she sensed, but they could be exorcised later.

    Daisy knew then that she could fall in love with that face, and perhaps she had even fallen a bit already. The idea both scared and excited her. It had been a long time since she had cared enough about someone to want to stay around them. That's where her fear resonated; like Joe, she was too used to always moving on, to the next job, the next group of people.

    Whatever feelings were brewing in her for this man she knew they posed a threat to that rhythm. The excitement, however, told her to wise up. It conjured an image of having Joe in the wagon's passenger seat reading a map while she drove. Their destination: anywhere.

    It was an image that planted a seed of hope in her heart. It felt foolish and cheesy and immature to think of, yet a part of her clung to that image.

    She pushed all these thoughts away for later speculation. The time between them, their naked bodies side by side, was not for thinking.

Chapter Seven

The Man With The Wolfish Look

1

Henry Grey found his father sitting alone in their living room, his easy chair no longer aimed at the television, but at the bay window that looked out onto the street. It was open and a breeze filtered in, turning the white curtains into diaphanous spectral shapes that bulged and floated on either side of him.

From over the staircase banister, Henry could see that all of downstairs was in darkness. Despite the breeze the house still stank of smoke, of charred meat burned black from what had happened earlier in the kitchen.

'Dad,' he called, his voice timid.

His father showed no sign of having heard him. He sat brooding, his lower jaw making chewing motions, a mannerism that meant he was deep in thought as he continued to stare out into the night.

Seeing him like that made Henry want to turn and run for his room, slam the door closed, and lock it for good measure. He didn't. He had things that he wanted to say, things that itched in his mind even as he had read the twins their bedtime story with the hope that if he could articulate them right maybe the grey, listless despair that had encapsulated his family could be vanquished.

'Dad, can we talk?' Henry's voice was louder this time.

Leonard Grey grunted from his chair, his head twisting to see him. Henry spotted a Budweiser can in his right hand. 'Yeah,' he said eventually then added, 'what about?'

How you and Mom have been acting like zombies, he wanted to say. It was true. His father's eyes had been distant all day, as if the answer to the Lily-shaped hole in their lives existed inside him, while his mother seemed to be on an entirely different planet. Sometimes she jumped when spoken to; other times it seemed she had no concept of what was going on around her, like with what had happened in the kitchen.

'About the way Mom's been acting,' he told his father.

'Your mom's going through something, son.' His voice was sour. He turned back to the window. 'We all are.'

'I know, but she almost burned the house down tonight trying to cook Clay and Ben dinner. I had to snatch the frying pan out of her hands and take it out the back door. She acted like she had no clue why the kitchen was filled with smoke and the fire alarm was shrieking. All she said was the heat must have gotten away from her. This was in front of the twins.'

His father shifted in his easy chair. Henry got the distinct impression he didn't want to listen to this. He didn't care; it was like a faucet had broken inside him and it was all pouring out now.

'And where were you, by the way? I had to open all the windows to flap out that stink. I thought the neighbours were going to break into the house and ask what was going on. I told her I'd make the twins their dinner, and she just walked off, looking like a zombie.'

A part of him winced inside at finally saying the word out loud. Yet he kept going, seeing the way his brothers had gawked at their mother from the kitchen table, how wide with disbelief their eyes had been as they coughed, choking on the cloud of the blue-grey smoke lacing their throats.

'You've both been acting like that.'

The curtains ballooned as a sudden gust entered the house, sounding like half-whispered things just out of earshot. Henry stared at the transparent white sheets on either side of the bay window, chilled. The way they floated was how he imagined his mother's thoughts were right now.

'Where is Mom, anyway? She said she was going to take a nap.'

His words hung in the cold, stinking air as he waited for his father to reply.

'I don't know. She left about an hour ago, took the pickup with her.'

'Left! Left to go where?'

'As I said I don't know,' said his father, slurping from his beer can. His eyes never left the view from the window.

'I'm waiting for her to come home so we can go to bed.' Henry's fingers tightened on the banister until his knuckles grew white. 'Don't you think you should know where she is? What's going on with her, with you? Haven't you noticed how checked out she's been?'

He was shouting now, and it felt good to do so, it felt good to focus everything that was bottled up inside him and aim it at someone.

This time Len Grey tilted his head in his son's direction. 'Your sister is missing, that's what's going on, Henry,' he said in an absent tone. 'Your mother and I are very worried about her and I'm sorry if we can't be all sunbeams and rainbows right now for you, but we are going through something.'

'Then why aren't you doing anything about it? Why isn't anyone? Everyone is saying that carny, Joe Cage, did something. Andrew Teal told me he saw him coming out of the police station last night, said the police had been questioning him for ages. Why hasn't he been arrested? You spoke to him today, I saw you. You were all pals with him…'

'This town wants someone to blame is all,' mumbled his father in that absent tone, interrupting him. 'Blame them quick too so everyone can get back to pretending this is a nice place, where things like children disappearing would never happen. I know this town. I've known it a lot longer than you and I know the people inside it. They turn on a dime if it gets the bad taste out of their mouths. You know some blame me for not being there, that it's somehow my fault your sister disappeared because I wasn't there? They need someone to blame. Right now, that's Joe Cage because he's not from here, and it's me, and it's your mom because she should have stopped Lily from getting on that ride.'

'People don't think that,' said Henry, his voice weak now, whiny.

'They do,' replied his father. 'Joe Cage did not take our Lily; if he did, do you honestly think he would have walked out of that ride covered in blood? No, a guilty man does not do that, not if he's looking to cover his tracks.'

'Then who did?' Henry asked, mustering the power to shout.

'Why, someone who works at the carnival.'

His father's words silenced him.

'What?' he snorted. 'They've been so kind, they fed everyone today…'

'Aye, and you would have done the same in a place like Marybell. They greased the wheels so that they didn't get bum-rushed out of town or lynched in the night. Of course they did; they don't want to be associated with this mess, and it's working too. Everyone, including you, son, think that the carnival is just the place where Lily went missing. They don't think it could be one of them; they have Joe Cage for that. I fear for that young man in this town.'

This time Henry laughed; it was either that or go insane. What his father was suggesting called into question everything he knew about the place where he had grown up and everything that he heard in the last twenty-four hours. For some reason, the enraged Launder, his father's employer – the man he had cursed and complained about for years – came into his head. His expression was a beetroot mask of hate as his right arm whipped around his body, launching the piece of stone cupped in his palm. Henry found his own feelings mirrored Launder's fury at the carnival earlier; they boiled in his flesh at such an intensity that he felt ready to ignite into flame.

'All those years working in Launder's chicken farms has made you as crazy as him,' he remarked, knowing it would hurt his father, wanting it to.

More than anything Henry wanted him to rise from his chair and yell at him. However, Leonard Grey didn't reply. Instead, he returned his gaze to the street.

'I'm going to bed,' Henry sighed in frustration.

He ascended the stairs, his footfalls thunderous on the wood as tears ran down his cheeks. Below and behind, the curtains continued to float.

He had wanted to talk, he had wanted to fix things and instead, he felt like his family was even worse than he thought. His father was going insane with conspiracy theories and his mother... he didn't know where she was.

2

Meryl Grey stared over the Ford's steering wheel at the fairground, thinking about how creepy it looked at night.

Darkness cradled it, turning the stalls and the rides into vague shapes, some of which rippled in the wind. The sound was unsettling as she sat, reminding her of creatures with leathery wings. It was just the sort of noise she would associate with that leering face she kept recalling.

Why am I here? she thought.

The past twelve hours existed as a series of snapshots in her mind. Meryl could recall being mildly disconnected that morning, of her mind drifting into vague daydreams as she had dressed, repeatedly buttoning her blouse wrong as she thought about Lily, about whether she was alive or not. It was only when she arrived at the fair that her memory became fragmented. She remembered Len had been speaking with Joe, she remembered reaching out to her husband and seeing *him*.

He reminded her of the wolf in Little Red Riding Hood, a story she had recited to all her children at some point in their lives before bedtime, just as her mother had told it to her. It was the way his lips seemed to pull back over his white teeth, the way his cold eyes held hers, hungry and haunting.

The image of his sun worn face filled her head.

The next thing Meryl could recall was walking behind her husband in the woods with no clue as to how she had gotten there. Before she could even ask Len anything, her mind had floated off into another revelry.

They were inside what she imagined was Arnie's motorhome, a cluttered place with orange shag carpet. The place stank of stale smoke and another smell, an animal musk that made her nose flare with disgust while at the same time her nerves prickled with excitement all over in smelling it.

It's a rutting smell, she thought.

He stood in front of her, his trilby gone, revealing a buzzcut of black hair, but everything else was the same. The wiry muscle of his naked torso bulged and flexed under the sickly, tea-coloured interior lights of the RV, his dusky skin gleaming with perspiration in places as his cold eyes raked up and down her body. Behind him was a double bed stripped of its duvet.

In one swift swipe, he ripped her blouse open with one hand, tearing several of the buttons off in the process, making her cry out. The cups of her white bra could be seen through the slit he had created in her clothes, rising and falling with her breath as she stood, hyperventilating.

He circled her, a predator stalking its prey, his eyes ceaselessly running up and down her body. She could feel them as needles on her skin. Meryl remained looking forward, knew somehow that was what he wanted, and obeyed without protest.

In this dream, she seemed to have all the mental capacity of a doll. She wanted to protest, to say, 'I don't want this,' not because she was married, though that fact sat heavily in her mind. Her refusal was from having her body exposed. Meryl did not want him to see her, finding she could not remember the last time she had seen herself entirely naked.

It didn't matter anyway, because she had no voice in the dream. Nor did she seem to be able to act in any way that would resist him as he placed his hands on her shoulders. She was his toy.

Arnie seized her blouse and tore it off her body with arms that worked like pistons. It hurt, the whole thing constricting tight across her chest before the fabric gave, leaving two red marks on each collar.

She staggered backward because of the force he had used. Arnie made no move to help her regain her balance. He drifted around to her front, the two shreds of blue-polka dotted material in his sun-bleached hands.

Now topless except for her plain white bra (a married woman's bra is how she thought of it), she saw she looked the polar opposite of him. Her skin was as white as fresh linen sheets. Where he was hard and toned, she was rotund.

To her surprise, Meryl found she was not disgusted in seeing herself. She looked down at her nude torso and thought, *This belongs to a body that made and carried my four children. This body was also what caused Len to want to make those children with me. It caused the wolfish look in the carney's face.*

Meryl looked up into Arnie's eyes and saw him grin.

The dream stopped then. Meryl was in the next snapshot with once again no idea how she had gotten there. Sheriff Jackson was speaking with her; his voice seemed to be coming through the water. She felt Len's arm hug her, guiding her away, and saying to Jackson, 'We understand.'

Then reality drifted away as she submerged into fantasy.

She was on her back on the bed and Arnie was on top of her, his face no longer leering but lustful. His look and the way his body was posed over her, trapping her, frightened her. Yet it also thrilled her.

She wanted him to do all the things this wolfish expression promised, even if they were degrading or caused her pain. What he intended for her was not about love or intimacy, it was about a need: his need, not hers.

He wanted to exploit her, to devour her if he could.

She was completely naked beneath him and also beneath those sick yellow lights that hid nothing. The only form of sex Meryl knew was what she shared with her husband in the dark of their bedroom. The lights were never allowed on.

Sometimes, usually as they positioned themselves, she heard the voice of Sue Hargensen, shrill and mocking.

'Look at them! Have you seen the size of your boobs? Have you seen your belly, the one flopping against your husband's beer gut? The one you promised yourself you'd lose after the twins and never did?'

Len never wanted her like the thing in her dreams; his want was kind and loving. The man with the wolfish look didn't care about her hang-ups.

He liked what he saw and intended to act accordingly.

Meryl could protest, could demand that the lights be dosed, that the covers be pulled over them. It would do no good. The man wanted her, and part of that want was to see: to see the stretch

222

marks, the dimples, the rolls. And Meryl discovered something that excited her.

She liked seeing his want for her; she wanted him to see.

Tears slid down her cheeks only to be torn away by the wind. Meryl blinked, realising that she had left the safety of the Ford and was now standing by its driver's side door, staring at the fairground.

3

In the next snapshot, she recalled the blare of the kitchen fire alarm and coughing on the smoke hissing from the frying pan. Henry had been in that one, telling her that he would cook the twins' dinner.

Then more fantasy, more floating.

She remembered seizing the pickup's keys, but not the drive to Launder's Field. A panicked idea alarmed in Meryl's head. *I could have killed someone, and I wouldn't know it.*

The wind buffeted around her, pulling at her blue polka-dotted blouse like a hundred groping hands. Some of the wind's icy chill seemed to seep into her head, sharpening her thoughts.

Meryl looked around, unimpeded by the dull stupour that she had existed in for the first time that day, and saw that it was not quite full dark. The sky was instead slate grey. She also saw that despite being on the circumference of the carnies' campsite, she could see no one and hadn't seen anyone since she had arrived. Though she didn't trust her observational skills anymore.

The tented skins of the stalls continued to flap languidly. The long grass at her ankles rustled as she surveyed the dark carnival. There were no lights on there, no calliope music played. The Fairway, which had been a hive of activity a day ago, was now an empty throat for the wind to gale down. A piece of metal tapped dully against another at increasing and decreasing rates. At the rear, the mighty Ferris wheel sat, forlorn and grim.

In what felt like another lifetime, Meryl Grey couldn't wait to take a ride on that huge circle. It was bigger and grander than the ones Len had taken her on early in their courtship; still, she had wanted to ride it and see if it recreated the butterflies-in-her-stomach sensation that she felt back then for Len. Now, all she wanted to do was forget.

She knew now that she could have dispelled the dark fantasies that had plagued her all day long. It would have taken some effort, more than for any other daydream she had ever had, but she could have done it.

She simply hadn't wanted to.

Because it was better to float inside such a lurid world than be in this one. It was nicer to think about being pawed over by some perverse stranger than to think about her baby who was gone; not just gone, taken, taken somewhere by someone, and had God knows what done to her.

Meryl understood in thinking this that she was free from the fantasy of the man with the wolfish look. She tried to conjure him into her mind again and found she could not. She knew his name was Arnold Kauffman, that he wore a grey trilby hat and grey trousers with red suspenders but no top, so that his torso, all wiry muscle and dusky skin, was on show. Yet she couldn't see him.

She was free to leave, to get in the Ford and pick up her life where she had left it with her family in tatters, with the community whispering incessantly about what bad parents they were, and with her baby girl missing.

Meryl started across the field into the disorganised jumble of RVs. She did so seeking oblivion, feeling like she was going to her doom.

This did not slow her progress in the slightest; she started to hurry, passing a lime-coloured station wagon on her right. There was a small stone-encircled campfire at the rear of the wagon with only embers in it.

Not once did she see anyone. She followed the pull in her mind like following a leash back to her master.

The RV that she eventually stopped before was a nondescript Winnebago, its body cream with an orange stripe along its side. It was the only one she had encountered with its windows filled with soft, ocher light.

Twenty feet away from it, the door on the vehicle's side opened outward seemingly without assistance, spilling ocher light that seemed as thick as honey onto the grass. She could see a pair of boots at the top of the three steps of the Winnebago. Meryl knew who they belonged to.

She went to him willingly.

Chapter Eight

'I Think We Have A Problem Here'

1

Carmen Garcia only had to wait a few seconds after knocking before the Winnebago's door was ripped open. Arnie's naked figure filled the doorway, nothing she hadn't seen before, so she immediately disregarded it, choosing instead to lean over the threshold, trying to glimpse his companion tonight.

She already knew who it was; she just wanted to see what Arnie had done to her, however, from the lower angle looking in, all she could see were kitchen cabinets and the shag carpet.

'Having fun now that your roommate has found a new home?' she asked, leaning back.

In the time that she had tried to peek, Arnie had lit a cigarette and was smoking nonchalantly, his gaze on the starless sky.

'I was, what do you want?'

'Lou's back. Montague wants us,' she informed him.

The end of Arnie's cigarette flared red, then he pitched it into the grass.

'About time. Let me get dressed first.'

2

'Thank you both for coming,' said Montague from his desk chair.

As usual, his motorhome was lit by lamps that bathed only their surroundings in soft nicotine light, leaving pools of shadows to collect in various corners and spaces. Somewhere close by a cuckoo clock counted out the seconds. Arnie remembered buying it for him decades ago.

He reclined against the wall to Montague's right, while Carmen occupied the crimson sofa on the left, her legs crossed. Between them and before their leader's grand desk stood Lou Fritz, his hands clasped together at his waist, looking like a schoolboy who's been sent to the principal's office.

Except for his face, which portrayed a hint of a sneer.

'So, you finally decided to grace us with your presence,' remarked Arnie.

'Did you miss me? I'm touched,' replied Lou sarcastically.

'That's enough.'

Montague's chair squeaked as he moved farther into the lamplight. The skin of his left temple where Launder's rock had struck him was completely healed.

A lot had changed in the past two days, none of it good, and it showed in their employer's voice. He sounded wrung out and quick-tempered. There were bags under his eyes like purple-black bruises, which only stood out more in contrast to the fish belly whiteness of his skin.

'Lou, I sent you and Youssef off yesterday with the direct order that you were both to look after the cargo until you were relieved of that duty. I take it you did not encounter any problems?'

'No, sir,' replied Lou. The sarcasm he had previously shot at Arnie was gone.

'Then why did Youssef return this morning after I sent Valerie and Cynthia to relieve you both, and you're only returning now?'

227

'I stopped to get a bite to eat first is all,' answered Lou.

Montague's thick caterpillar eyebrows crushed together as he stared, the grey eyes beneath as sharp as flint. If Lou noticed his angered expression, he gave little sign; his face was stoic, his eyes staring at the wall above his employer's head, his body language that of a soldier at attention.

'Did you not think about the rest of us?' asked Carmen, her cheeks flushing red.

Slowly, almost stiffly, Lou's head rotated in her direction.

'No, I didn't,' he said in the same disaffected voice he used with Montague.

'With everything that is happening right now, I need everyone to do exactly as they are told. There are no exceptions,' lectured the carnival owner.

'Why? I mean, it's not like we have anything to fear,' said Lou.

There was exasperation in his voice.

'We have everything to fear. Our livelihood is at stake right now.'

'You mean this charade we pull everywhere we go. You're acting like we need this, we don't... '

'Enough!' bellowed Montague, rising from his seat.

Lou's mouth immediately snapped shut, his eyes downcast to the floor.

'This is not the time for discussion. This is the time for obeying orders without question. Can you do that, or do we have a bigger problem to solve?'

In a voice barely louder than a whisper, Lou replied, 'I can do that.'

'Good, now get out of my sight,' snapped Montague.

As Lou reached the exit, the carnival owner called to him.

'And I trust that you didn't leave a mess behind after your meal?'

The carny lingered, his hand on the door handle, before looking over his shoulder at them, his expression cruel delight.

'I left everything exactly as I found it,' he said, then walked outside.

'That boy is getting ideas above his station,' remarked Montague.

'It's more than that. He's been spouting off a lot lately,' Arnie informed him.

'About what?'

Arnie shared a glance with Carmen before answering.

'About how this life isn't the one you promised him when he joined us.'

Montague reclined into his chair, massaging his brow with his fingers.

'One problem at a time,' he said. 'For now, let's focus on enduring this mess, then when we move out of Kansas, we can deal with Mr. Fritz. Until then we keep helping the police. Carmen, would you mind seeing if that Deputy Herrick has any information about the investigation that we don't know already?'

'The one who looks like he should be in high school? I'm sure I can squeeze something out of him,' she replied. Her tone was all pride.

'Good, and normally I wouldn't inquire into your affairs, Arnold, but I believe we have a guest in our campground tonight? Shall I expect any repercussions from her visit?'

Arnie snorted, tapping a fresh cigarette from his packet. He inserted it between his lips but didn't move to light it.

'You know me, boss. I'm always careful.'

'Yes, but we are living under a microscope now. Will her husband and the rest of the family not become concerned?' Montague asked.

'Her husband is even more of a vegetable than she is,' said Carmen, coming to Arnie's aid. 'I introduced myself to him today and read nothing in him; same for his kid. That whole family is just walking around in a cloud of despair. Let Arnie have his fun; he's the only one getting some.'

'I had to ask,' said Montague. 'One can't be too sure these days, especially when one person's carelessness can put everyone at risk.'

'She won't be saying a thing to anyone,' Arnie said.

3

Even in his sleep, Len recognised the sound of his pickup's engine. He woke to a crippling pain in the small of his back, momentarily disorientated, to find that he was slumped in his easy chair. Dawn light, a dreary grey tinged with pale yellow, the reverse of twilight, had crept into the street outside.

He had fallen asleep downstairs waiting for his wife to come home.

When he had thumbed the sleep from his eyes, his body stiff and frozen having spent the night before the open windows, he saw her in the driveway staring back from behind their family vehicle. She stared at him with lost, tearful eyes within a face that was a pale, lined moon.

She made no move to exit the vehicle; instead she waved to him. Len watched her right hand, palm aimed at him, seesaw back and forth with languid slowness. He did not return her wave.

4

Elaine Green sped the department's 1980 Chevrolet K5 Blazer over the ruts in the dirt lane leading to the Teal property, bouncing in her seat every so often when she struck a big one. She wanted to drop off the documents for Teal's insurance company concerning his slaughtered cattle quickly so she could join the others at Launder's Field. With the facilities being offered by the carny folk, it was still deemed the best place to gather.

Tim had left before it was full light out, planting a firm kiss on her lips before departing to meet with the state detective. She knew from how he lingered on his doorstep, his brown eyes roaming her face while the sun splashed golden through his crow black hair as it scaled the horizon, that he didn't want to leave. That it was not just the town he was thinking about, but her as well. In his absence, leadership fell to Sergeant Collins, which because of his ineptitude was really like putting all the deputies in charge at once, as they tended not to listen to him.

With a scrape of his boots on the brick steps, he was gone without a word. Sometimes there is nothing to say, especially to someone you love.

All this swirled inside her head as the buildings on the horizon slowly grew through the Blazer's windshield. Turning off of the main road into the lane, she had been unable to even see the curved head of Teal's grain silo; now she made it out along with the red barn and the house painted the colour of sunflower petals.

They really are alone out here, she thought as the fields blurred by on either side of the Blazer like a green mirage. All deserted.

The land was flat and vast and unmarked except for the farm ahead. It made her shift in her seat as a sense of unease settled on her shoulders.

I'm getting like Tim, thinking too much, she thought.

5

The dirt lane expanded into a square yard, which Elaine guided the Blazer into. The red barn loomed to her left, casting its shadow halfway across the dusty space. She saw an iron wind vane perched atop of it with a rooster design at its peak. It was frozen in the still morning air.

The house sat in front of her behind a white picket fence that separated the lot from a lush garden complete with flowerboxes, all in bloom. No one came outside to greet her, which was strange. That she couldn't see anyone outside working was stranger.

She spotted Philip Teal's pickup sitting in the barn's shade. Though she wasn't a farmer herself she knew enough to know that on a property this size, a farmer did not go anywhere without his vehicle. That meant that Philip Teal must be here. Yet she saw no one in the house's windows; instead the place felt as lifeless as a graveyard in winter. There was a still, closed feeling about it.

I'm being silly; they're probably all inside waiting for me to knock on the door.

Switching the Blazer's engine off, she became aware of just how silent the farmyard was. Her unease grew, taking on a surreal nightmare-like quality as she stared out, waiting on what felt like a knife edge for something to happen, for something to burst the bubble of weirdness that seemed to envelope her surroundings with screams and violence.

Nothing did.

Nothing stirred outside the Blazer on the Teal property. And as time marched onward, that surreal sensation of tension only increased.

Something was wrong here.

Elaine could feel her heartbeat pulsing in her temples as her left hand hovered over the door latch. She pulled it, not opening the door yet, feeling the outside air seep in anyway. It was an oven, hot and stuffy, reminding her of dusty attic spaces that had been baked under the sun. Eventually, slowly, she stepped out of the vehicle, her right hand on the butt of her gun.

'Hello?' she called out, trying not to sound scared.

There was no echo; instead her words fell flat in the Teals' hotbox of a yard. She could already feel sweat beginning to collect in her armpits.

She glanced towards the barn; still the weather vane hadn't moved.

Elaine started marching towards the house, feet crunching on gravel. At the gate in the white picket fence, which only came up to her hip, she reached over and snapped the latch so it sprung open. She followed the stone path through the bountiful garden, her eyes on the windows of the house for any movement inside, until she got to the porch steps, which she mounted.

With one hand on the butt of her gun she knocked on the Teals' door. It swung ajar, hinges creaking, revealing in the gap between the door and its frame a portion of a dark wood-furnished hallway.

Whoever had closed the door last had not done so properly. Something Elaine didn't imagine any of the Teals doing.

When she called out hello for the second time and received no answer, she drew her gun from its holster.

6

There was no one inside. There were no signs of a struggle. All the rooms and halls inside the residence were neat, tidy, waiting on their owners to return and mess them in the way people do by simply occupying a space.

The kitchen floors reeked of bleach, as if Angela Teal had scrubbed them before Elaine had arrived. The dining room, with its long table, smelled of polish. All the beds were ready upstairs, awaiting people to sleep in them.

It was like the Teals had vanished into thin air.

The family car was still parked outside; the Teals only had one. It was five miles to Marybell. Some of them could have walked that distance.

Elaine knew that Philip's father, Michael, still performed light duties around the farm and was relatively fit for a man in his seventies. Philip's mother, Maura, on the other hand, was wheelchair-bound. Everyone in Marybell knew this and considered it an event when she came into town, as it was rare.

There was no sign of Maura's wheelchair in any of the rooms.

The evidence suggested they had all left for somewhere; however, the Teals were known as home birds. The idea that they all left the farm at the same time, especially as it was eight-thirty in the morning - working time - was unprecedented.

Elaine plucked her radio from her belt, depressing the button on the side and said, 'Sergeant Collins, this is Deputy Elaine Green. I'm at the Teal place. Do you copy?'

She released the button and had to wait an agonising ten seconds for a response. Ten seconds that were filled with the steady nightmare silence that occupied the rooms around her like an unwelcome guest, broken only by the random creak of settling floorboards after her exploration throughout the building.

'Copy, this is Collins. I'm a bit busy down here at Launder's right now. Is this urgent?' the sergeant's voice squawked from the radio.

It came out so abruptly that Elaine almost dropped the bulky device.

'Copy, Collins, I believe this is urgent. I think we have a problem here. We need some people over to the Teal place ASAP.' Then she added, despite the part of her brain that remembered her training, 'I can't find them.'

'Can't find whom?' came Collins's reply.

'The Teal family, all of them.'

Chapter Nine

Bloodbath

1

Jackson expected to arrive first, timekeeping being something he was meticulous with, only to be impressed on finding there was already another vehicle parked in front of the roadhouse. It also confirmed a notion he had felt over the phone: that whatever case Rook was working on had him rattled.

'I hope you weren't waiting long,' he said.

Rook had exited his vehicle as he had pulled off the main road and was striding towards him. They shook hands, smelling the dust burning off the gravel lot from the sun, which was hot enough for Jackson to feel sweat accumulating in his armpits. Both men observed that each held a collection of documents in their free hands.

'Not at all.'

The cowboy vibe still resonated with Jackson from the detective, spotting that instead of shoes, the man wore leather boots along with his grey suit. His hair was long, a mop of silver that had been brushed fashionably upward, and his eyes were tropical blue, lively and sharp. He was happy to see it, hoping it was a sign that the detective had recovered from their phone call. The eerie notion of feeling small and isolated still haunted him, along with a newer, more potent sensation: that of puzzle pieces fitting into place.

'You're not what I was expecting,' he said. 'I bet you played football in high school.'

'What were you expecting, some country boy in his dungarees, chewing a stand of hay?'

Rook let out a guffaw that made Jackson smile.

'I played a little in college, as well. I was a quarterback,' he added.

'Well, quarterback, I was just sitting in my car thinking I've asked you to come all this way without giving you much in the way of reasons to do so. With that in mind, I think it's best if I start first, if that's okay with you.'

Jackson agreed, liking the detective more and more.

'Good, that brings me to this place. Dylan's Roadhouse.'

Jackson surveyed the squat, single-storey building with its navy roof panels and neon lights. There was always something depressing about seeing places that were alive at night dead during the day. Yellow and black crime scene tape had been laced across its front door.

The building's contrast to the vast, flat expanse of green farmland surrounding the isolated state of Marybell and the people that lived there stuck him once again. Jackson shivered despite the day's muggy heat.

'One of its regulars, and by regulars, I mean a professional alcoholic by the name of Paul Flint, arrived at this place at around ten on Tuesday, May 11, to begin his drinking day. From what I have gathered, he knew the owner, Dylan Macintosh, quite well. Well enough to expect to be let in early.'

'From your tone I guess he didn't find what he was expecting.'

'You are correct, sir, though he did find Dylan Macintosh, or parts of him.'

Jackson, who had been eyeing the roadhouse, snapped his gaze to Rook.

The detective's blue eyes were shadowed over a heavy frown. He read confusion in that look, and fear. His palour greying some.

'Let's go inside, shall we.' All good-humour was gone from the detective's voice, replaced by a crisp, tense tone.

He's steeling himself, thought Jackson.

They crunched over to the crime scene-taped door, which Rook removed with a few quick swipes of his penknife before holding it open for Jackson. The inside of the building looked as dark as a miner's pit; still he entered, feeling the boards sag under his weight, his nostrils stinging from the chemicals the crime scene technicians had used and the more powerful smell underneath it, a coppery smell that reminded him of Teal's livestock. His stomach lurched.

Rook flicked on the overhead lights before presenting him with a single A4-sized photograph from the folder he held.

'This is what Paul Flint found.'

Jackson could discern that the photograph had been taken from the same spot where he stood. The bar was now pristinely clean; the mirror behind it reflected the image of him holding up the photo, with Rook at his side.

The image it had captured was very different. Four heads had been impaled on the bar's spigots used for on tap beer.

'Jesus,' whispered Jackson.

All four belonged to men, their faces twisted in agony. Their eyes were threaded with burst capillaries, making them look like red marbles, some looking in different directions. They had been impaled through their necks so that blood and flaps of tendon stained the bronze of

238

each spigot, pooling on the bar's cracked and potholed wood beneath. The flesh of their necks was jagged, signaling to him that whatever had been used to remove each head from its body hadn't been clean-cut; it had taken work to do it.

'That's not even the worst part,' Rook informed him as Jackson handed the photograph back.

Rook replaced it with another and jabbed his thumb at the left-hand corner of the bar. 'That was taken over there,' he said in a matter-of-fact tone.

Again, the left-hand corner was clean now. In the photo it showed that both walls were painted in dark, viscous blood where they joined.

'This was the pool table.'

Jackson glanced at it before looking at the photo; its green felt was bleached crimson. In the photo a body was laid spread eagle across it. *The first I've seen intact*, he thought, tasting bile.

The body belonged to a red-haired woman. She had been stripped of all her clothes; the flesh of her belly, pelvis and thighs looked severely white in the picture. Jackson could see the other areas of her body that had been hued or tanned by sunlight and realised he was in some way overstepping this woman's privacy in seeing the parts of her reserved for lovers.

'Her name was Leah McCain; she was one of Macintosh's employees and the only one working on the night of May 10 with Macintosh, according to the man's planner. There were abrasions on her throat that indicate choking, though the evidence suggests that this isn't what killed her. There were also abrasions on her right arm in the shape of fingers. Whoever did that has a hand the size of a dinner plate. We also found two types of semen inside her vagina and throat.

No matches yet. There were also teeth marks found.'

There looked at first to be little damage done to her in the photo. Her body was dirtied by blood in places, blood that did not seem to belong to her.

'How did she die?' he asked.

'As far as we can tell, her heart gave out as they raped her,' Rook said, speaking like a person with their walls up.

'Jesus,' Jackson said again.

Seeing the pictures, the eerie sensation returned to him in full force. He felt like he was standing too close to a set of live wires.

He looked at Leah McCain's slack face and felt the skin of his shoulder blades crawl. Like the men that had been impaled on the bar spigots, he could only see the whites of her eyes. Her neck was extended back as far as it would go, exposing the purple bruises around her throat to the camera.

'The worst of it happened in the men's restroom. Follow me.'

Rook moved towards a narrow corridor that was dark even with the lights on. Jackson reluctantly obeyed, wanting to get out this place that no longer stank of blood to him, but death and violence. He was imagining the screams that had filled it as whoever it was set about achieving this bloody sadism, knowing that they could take their time because it was a Monday night and business would be slow and there was no one around to hear the screams.

Rook slipped another photograph into his hand. It depicted the narrow cave of the corridor, only this time the floorboards were washed in blood.

The men's restroom door opened with a squeal and they stepped inside. The smell of chemicals and death were worse here. It wasn't so much burning his nostrils as tickling the back of his throat now and he had to fight the urge to vomit up the coffee he had had for breakfast.

Rook handed him the last photo, his fingers trembling slightly. In it were the two washing basins on the left and the two urinals on the right, with the one toilet stall farther back. At the moment, every surface was a white that had rotted to urine yellow. In the photograph, every surface was coated in red gore, not just blood but also ribbons of meat, and Jackson spied what looked like a heart in one of the basins: there were bite marks on it.

'They say an adult body contains only five pints of blood. Hard to believe when you see that. Only the men were ripped open. The woman was only bitten and in the places where she was, mostly around her genitals, her blood had been sucked at. We can tell by the impressions left on either side of the bites. Here's the thing - from the parts that we have been left with, we've discovered that whoever did this didn't use any cutting tools to take these people apart. We found that they were taken apart by hand, simply ripped open. From what I can tell, Tim, we are standing in the most horrific crime in America I've ever heard of.'

Rook turned to Jackson. 'That's why I asked you here. Now what do you have for me?'

2

They were in Jackson's Blazer. Rook was leafing through the file Jackson had brought, pausing now and then to scan a photograph or read a specific document, while Jackson stared thoughtfully at the roadhouse through the windscreen. His nostrils still burned with the smell of the place.

In his mind he saw each photograph again: the bar converted into a heinous trophy display; Leah McCain on the pool table like a pagan sacrifice to some cruel deity: the corridor that looked like a stagnant river of blood; and worst of all, the men's restroom that had been transformed into an abattoir. Did he think Joe Cage was capable of something like that?

Jackson thought hard even though the instinctive answer that came to him was no. Still, he approached it from every possible angle he could think of based on the evidence he had. The answer remained unchanged, which left Jackson with the original question: who took Lily Grey?

'You look worried, Tim,' Rook remarked, causing Jackson to jump.

He hadn't noticed that the detective had been watching him. Jackson studied Rook, wondering if he could be completely honest with him. What he read in the detective's face told him that if this man could offer help, he would.

'I'm worried,' he answered. 'I drove up here hoping you would have some piece of this puzzle that would help me solve who's behind our missing persons case. Instead, with the information you've given me, not only do I not have a clearer idea of the bigger picture, but it's muddled what little pieces I've worked out so far.'

'You mean to tell me that you think what happened here is linked to Lily Grey's disappearance?' asked Rook.

'Yes.'

'What makes you think that?'

242

It was the question that he hoped Rook wouldn't ask, knowing that any sane investigator would laugh on hearing his answer. Yet in the brief time that he had spent in Rook's company, he found he trusted the man.

'Everything from the butchered animals to this reeks of the same weirdness. Perhaps you don't feel that about Lily Grey because you guys haven't been down to Marybell yet, but if you were to come down there, you'd see for yourself. I have no evidence that suggests they are connected except the unexplainable nature in each situation. Don't you feel like we are missing something? That with all the evidence, we aren't approaching this thing from the right angle and if we found out what that angle was, it would be clear?'

Rook looked at Jackson shrewdly and then said, 'There's something you haven't told me, isn't there? You could have sent anyone up here with this evidence; you didn't have to come yourself. So why did you?'

Jackson sighed, his gaze floating back to the squat building that held so many horrors.

'Okay,' he said, 'but tell me first: do you suspect that whoever slaughtered Philip Teal's cattle is the same person who did this?'

'Well, what happened down in your neck of the woods is certainly similar to what happened here,' said Rook. 'Reading this, it sounds like these animals were all mutilated in the same style, though without the sadistic display with the remains. The only thing that's bothering me is the scale.'

'Our evidence suggests, despite how unbelievable, that this crime was conducted by two people. Fingerprints, semen, bite marks - all support that theory. Your crime scene suggests there were a lot more participants.'

Jackson nodded; it was one of the frustrating things about the Lily Grey case. If Joe Cage had had something to do with her disappearance, it would have required him to have an accomplice. They had been keeping close watch over him and the only friend he seemed to have was that elfin-looking runaway, Daisy Hill.

Why am I still thinking Joe Cage has something to do with this? The question gnawed in Jackson's mind as he replied to Rook.

'It works out though, in terms of time frame, doesn't it? Teal's cattle are slaughter on the night of May 8 or the morning of May 9, and these people were killed on the night of May 10 or the morning of May 11.'

'That's right,' Rook agreed.

'What if I was to tell you that our number one suspect for the abduction of Lily Grey worked at Dylan's Roadhouse for a few weeks before moving to Marybell and gaining employment with a travelling carnival?'

Rook's silver eyebrows leapt upward.

'What's his name?'

Jackson told him.

'There's no record of anyone by that name in Macintosh's books.'

'There wouldn't be. He's a runaway, and Macintosh paid in cash,' Jackson explained. 'Here's the thing: he was first seen in Marybell on May 9, and I can support this because I met the man at a diner just outside of town. He was going into Marybell from the direction of the Teal property.'

Rook's eyebrows did another leap.

'Where was he on the night of the tenth?'

'I had him in an interrogation room until ten o'clock. A friend by the name of Daisy Hill, another runaway employed in the same carnival, picked

244

him up from the station. I could find out his whereabouts for that evening, but I do know for a fact he was in Marybell on May 11 at around nine a.m. because he volunteered to help out with the search for Lily Grey.'

'Okay, what evidence do you have to support the theory that he abducted Lily Grey?'

'Well, he was the last person to see her alive... no, wait, that's wrong,' said Jackson, a frown creasing his brow.

Suddenly, in hearing himself speak those words, a memory exploded into the front of Jackson's mind, accompanied by the dawn of a new prospect.

'I'm sorry,' he said to Rook. 'He wasn't the last person to see her alive. I only said that because that's what those who were present at the time said.'

Who said it? he thought. It had been Arnie Kauffman, the carny that was supposedly in charge of Journey Through The Crypt - he was sure.

'But that makes no sense,' said Jackson slowly. 'Lily Grey disappeared inside a carnival ride and Joe was the first person that went in after her when her mother kicked up hysterics. He claims he never saw her inside so the last people to actually see her alive was everyone who was standing around the ride before she went in.'

Rook was silent, staring, understanding that Jackson was having an epiphany and that to disturb him could ruin whatever was stirring inside his head.

'Joe came out of the ride alone and covered in blood. He said that he had fallen inside, that he was knocked out and when he came to, he couldn't find any trace of Lily. We suspected him of being linked to her disappearance because he

245

found Lily's teddy bear covered in blood. Both the teddy and the clothes Joe had on have been sent to the lab for testing. We've had no results yet, but I have a feeling that they'll come back with no match.'

This time Rook couldn't help himself and asked, 'Why?'

'Because he does have a gash on his head that supports his story,' answered Jackson. 'Not only that but it's an injury that looks inflicted by a fall, not a scratch from, say, a child defending herself. Even more than that, he would require an accomplice to abduct Lily, but he's a loner.'

'What about the person who picked him up from the station?'

'Daisy Hill has a tight alibi for when Lily Grey vanished, and according to the carnies that both Joe and Daisy work for, they came into town separately and applied for jobs separately. I can support this because when I saw him for the first time he was travelling alone and on foot. Daisy Hill owns an old station wagon.'

'Perhaps they came into town separately on purpose so they wouldn't be suspected of knowing each other,' offered Rook.

The inside of Jackson's Blazer was hot now and not just from the sun. It was hot from that sensation of being on the edge of understanding something, of finding that missing puzzle piece that, once discovered, could bring an entirely different dimension to a case.

Rook had felt it before, though never as intense and not as often as he would like. He understood that what was bouncing between them was rare, maybe not as rare as finding gold on your land or winning the lottery, but it was still an elusive moment that sometimes provided a reward and sometimes fizzled out. Sat inside Jackson's

Blazer, he felt them circling a new angle to everything, only they couldn't quite grasp it yet.

'That's true, and they could have lied to everyone, even the carnies who claim they didn't know each other until finding jobs with them,' said Jackson.

'Here's the thing that I've been struggling with. I don't believe Joe Cage did it; seeing what you showed me today has finally made me realise that. I don't think he has it in him to commit any of these crimes. The evidence we have on him is entirely circumstantial, yet I couldn't help but focus on him. Why?'

'Well, his timelines fit these crimes,' remarked Rook.

'They do, but if you think about it, they're massively messed up. You've already said that evidence at Teal's farm and Dylan's Roadhouse are similar, yet it appears a lot more people participated at Teal's than at Dylan's. Joe is one guy, with one friend. And what? Where's his motive? Joe openly admits that things ended badly with Dylan. He told me so himself that night in the interrogation room; do you think that whoever killed Dylan would openly tell a police officer they didn't get along, then leave a police station and immediately travel forty miles to butcher him? Plus he has no motive for Teal and no motive for taking Lily.'

'Okay, let's cool it for a second,' said Rook. 'There is an argument to be made that not all these crimes are connected. The pattern at the Teal crime scene and the Dylan crime scene do not match your missing persons case.'

'Do you believe they aren't connected?' Jackson asked, staring hard into the detective's blue eyes.

247

Eventually Rook sighed, looking to the roadhouse outside.

'I think I'm going to have to ask to be taken off this case,' he said, 'because I do believe they're connected even though the evidence says otherwise. I think you hit the nail on the head when you said that all three are connected by a level of unexplainable strangeness I've never encountered before.'

'That's why I'm asking why I cannot get Joe Cage out of my head, despite believing he was just in the wrong place at the wrong time,' said Jackson.

'Well, he is the ideal suspect. He's a drifter; if there's a rumour about any drifter coming through any small town, then they're blamed for everything from stolen clothes off of washing lines to the reason why someone whales on their wife, you know that. They're the perfect scapegoat.'

Jackson stared at Rook, stared through him.

'Fuck me,' he breathed.

'What? Jackson, what is it?' Rook shouted, reaching out and gripping Jackson's bicep through his shirt.

He believed the big man opposite him was about to have a heart attack.

'You're right,' said Jackson, his voice dazed, his eyes still cloudy. 'He's the perfect scapegoat.'

Chapter Ten

Saboteur

1

Jackson held the Blazer's accelerator just above the floor, his hands gripping the steering wheel so hard they throbbed. The beige- and cream-coloured vehicle sped along the streak of tarmac that divided the surrounding cornfields at a steady eighty miles per hour. He was going back home, back to Marybell.

The thought alone made Jackson want to depress the pedal more, though he didn't trust the Blazer's tyres to keep him on the road. He kept seeing the town as a cluster of twinkling lights surrounded in darkness, how it would look to a bird if it flew over the town at night. It made him think of time - how much time he had wasted, and how much time he had left.

Two days.

Forty-eight hours.

That was how long Lily Grey had been missing, and what had he been doing in that time? Obsessing over one suspect. Why? Because he was the ideal suspect, because of small-town prejudice towards outsiders, even though he thought his worldview made him exempt from that, because the things that are ingrained in a person from an early age run deep and even hide.

Jackson knew he had fucked up big time; he had allowed himself to be blinded by one idea. Now his blinders were off and he felt like he was finally seeing the big picture. What he saw told him that he had been played, that they had used his prejudices to blindside him.

Who? Why, the carnies, of course.

It suddenly occurred to him that everything they had done had been to protect themselves: offering to feed everyone, offering to take part in the search for Lily Grey. Even in the interrogation room they had slyly turned his investigative spotlight to Joe. Not that he had needed much help there. In his head, Jackson replayed all the interviews that he had conducted, wincing at the focus of his questioning.

I was convinced the kid was responsible, he thought, his grip growing even tighter on the wheel. *Like Rook said, he was the ideal suspect.*

Jackson had left Rook at Dylan's Roadhouse with the documents he had brought with him. Lying in his passage seat was the thick folder the detective had given him; some of its photographs had spilled into the foot well.

One lay face up on the passenger seat. He glanced at it, saw that it was the brutal image of the four spiked heads.

That split second glance was also enough for him to veer into the oncoming lane. The eighteen-wheeler that had been heading in the opposite direction blared its horn, a sound that seemed to fill the world and squeezed Jackson's heart for good measure. He jerked the wheel to the right.

The Blazer's right wheels went spinning through the gravel on the road's shoulder, dragging the vehicle farther. Jackson slammed his foot down on the brake, trying to prevent the vehicle from flipping by making the smallest of corrections with the steering wheel.

The Blazer sailed along, left wheels on tarmac, right wheels on gravel, until it stopped. A tail of dust fifty-five feet long rose into the air behind it while the eighteen-wheeler's horn continued to blare, fading into the distance.

Jackson flopped over the steering wheel, his heart thundering through his skin, his flesh flushed with heat. As he rested there, his body heaving for air, a conspiring voice whispered to him.

Do you really have to go back?

I have to. I'm the sheriff, he replied.

What's the point? Even if you got back and somehow managed to save the day and returned Lily Grey to her parents, would anything change?

He thought about the self-righteous anger that Andrew Teal had shown as he had confronted Daisy Hill, about Glen Launder hurling that stone.

The answer was no: even if he did find Lily and the culprit who took her, nothing would change.

Those people are set on destroying each other over one belief or another.

He could turn around.

He could say fuck it to all of them.

It would be a blessing to get rid of the hornet's nest that his mind had become worrying over everything. He could move somewhere else, somewhere where he could just be another face in the crowd and not the person responsible for keeping the whole circus in line. He could abandon them all.

These thoughts had no emotion in them; they were cold and sterile. He did not think of the people he cared for or the woman he loved; instead, he saw the town as being one large brewing cauldron of prejudice.

His eyes caught the corner of the picture through the cradle of his arms. By some miraculous feat it had remained on the passenger seat.

He stared at each frozen expression of pain. His hands put the Blazer back into gear.

2

'Your department seems a little short on manpower today, Sergeant Collins,' remarked Montague.

They were wandering through the long grass on the edge of a lake of brownish water. Collins knew the area well, as it was one of his favourite fishing spots, so he felt little worry about being lost today. That didn't mean it couldn't happen; the grass was knee high in places, which meant that everyone was walking with their heads down, looking for any clues.

His neck already felt sore even though they had only restarted the search after lunch half an hour ago. The two cheeseburgers complete with fried onions and mushrooms he had gobbled up weighed heavily in him.

Montague's remark was an opportunity for him to look up and around. Collins did so, removing his Stetson to mop his sweaty brow. He saw that the eight other members within his search group were wandering far off to the left.

'I haven't seen Sheriff Jackson this morning, either. Is the man unwell?' asked Montague, his pompous voice nonchalant.

The carnival owner was bending down to investigate something in the grass; it turned out to be a discard boot. He tossed it back into the greenery.

'No, he's all well, he's just gone up state to speak with a few people about the case is all,' he answered, fanning himself with his hat. 'I think I better sit down for a bit; I'm not a young man anymore.'

'Yes, go ahead, don't mind me,' said Montague.

Resting on a nearby rock, Collins observed the carnival owner. While sweat seemed to be pouring out of him, there wasn't even a gleam on Montague's brow, despite wearing a waistcoat, shirt, and trousers. His face seemed thinner than usual, paler. There were bags under his eyes.

'I also saw you send that young deputy away this morning. What was that about?' asked Montague.

He was facing Collins now, giving him his full attention. Collins squinted up into the man's grey eyes, thinking it must be a trick of the light, because they no longer looked grey, but silver.

They seemed to shine down at him.

The sun was behind Montague, leaving his front in shadow except for that silver shine. Collins felt his jaw unhinge and gape as he stared into them, feeling no embarrassment or urge to snap it shut; in fact, he felt no urge to do anything as a mellowness descended over him. It was like he had slipped into a tranquil doze, one where his eyes must remain open.

'I sent him to the Teal property,' Collins told Montague in a voice that was vague and slow.

'Why did you do that?'

'Elaine Green radioed to say that the Teals were missing. She found the house empty and their pickup still in the driveway.'

Anger shifted behind Montague's eyes, threatening to destroy the harmonious state Collins was in. He cringed from it, frightened in a way that he hadn't felt since his older brothers had kept him up all night by whispering ghost stories to each other in the pitch black of their bedroom.

That had been almost fifty years ago, yet he remembered the way the terror squeezed at his heart as he lay awake long after his brothers had fallen asleep.

He felt that same dread now for the silver-eyed man opposite him. He felt his heart being squeezed by fear.

'Are you sure the Teals haven't just gone out of town? Maybe someone picked them up.'

Collins explained to him how unlikely that would be.

Sighing, Montague looked out to the lake of murky water. Collins still saw his silver eyes in his head like two stars that didn't twinkle, but blazed.

The sun had fallen behind a line of trees where the rest of the search party was, slowly bathing the area beside the lake in shade. A strong wind gusted through the air, causing Montague's clothes to ripple.

'Damn you, Lou,' he said, staring at the water.

Eventually, his attention returned to Collins. 'It seems I have a saboteur in my ranks.'

Collins nodded as if he understood, a string of saliva dangling from his lips.

'It's not easy being a leader is it, Sergeant Collins? I very much doubt that this is what you wanted to do with your day today, spending your time trudging through muck and mire. Yet here you are, doing just that. Why? Because in times of crisis, someone has to take charge, has to lead those that only look out for themselves. Am I right?'

Collins nodded once more.

'It is not an easy position to hold, especially when there are certain individuals who undermine you at every decision you make. Never to your face, but always whispering behind your back, waiting for you to fail. Some people are never happy to follow, it irks their souls, makes their minds crawl.'

'Bastards,' whispered Collins.

'It's funny. There was a time when I was the usurper, a time when I coveted this position of power. If I'd known then what I do now, perhaps I wouldn't have bothered with it. I often think about that when some youngling comes along with ideas above his station. I often wonder how can I teach them that the position they desire isn't what they think it is, that they would be ill-suited to the task because all they seek of it is power. Really being a leader is all about putting out fires, sometimes after the damage is done.'

Montague sighed again as the breeze wafted at his garments, causing them to flutter. It brought with it the smell of the lake, a soupy, muddy scent.

'Anyway, never mind my grievances. It has been quite pleasurable to communicate them to you. I must say, being in command is a lonely post to hold at times.'

'It's no problem, no problem at all,' mumbled the sergeant.

'One more thing - what exactly did those people up north have to speak to Jackson about concerning Lily Grey's disappearance?'

Collins told him without hesitation.

Montague pondered this information for a few seconds. As he did, several of the others called from the tree line, asking if they were coming.

'Thank you, Sergeant, for all your help'.

The silver light in his eyes dulled, leaving Collins blinking rapidly, his hands moving to his face as if to wipe sleep away.

'Must have fallen into a doze there,' he said with a chuckle.

'Yes, it's been a long day,' replied the carnival owner. 'I'm sure you're exhausted. Shall we move on and join the others?'

Collins heaved himself to his feet, sat his hat upon his head and smiled.

'Sure, can't let them have all the fun.'

3

Jackson didn't so much park the Blazer in front of the police station as abandon it. He wanted to change into a uniform before joining the search parties, with the aim to ask Montague and a few of his associates to come downtown with him at the end of the day. If he had gone home instead, the outcome of coming events might have ended differently; as it was, he met Phyllis when he went into the police building.

'Thank God you're back,' she said to him as he entered the building.

He had no time to process this, as she was coming around the chest-high reception desk, speaking to him in high-chipped manner.

'There's been another disappearance.'

4

'You've been quiet. You're doing that furrowed forehead thing that makes you look like you're trying to do hard math in your head,' remarked Daisy, pointing at him with a chili cheese fry.

They were sat in The Fill Up after another day of trekking, with nothing to show for it but sunburned faces, tired bodies, and empty stomachs. The mood, which had been glum that morning, was now complete despair; most of the townspeople had left, preferring to have dinner at home. Even the carnies were in short supply, having taken their meals back to their campers.

Only Sergeant Collins remained to eat. He sat some distance away while Earl Porter busied about cleaning fryers for the day.

'I don't think we are going to find her,' answered Joe.

'What makes you think that?'

Even Daisy's usually chirper tone was dour. Her blue eyes filled with sorrow on the other side of the plastic picnic table; like most things in the carnival, all the tables were painted a cartoonishly bright colour, in this case, fire engine red.

'Because if we were going to find something, we would have found it by now,' he replied. 'The police found her teddy bear by a broken fire door inside The Crypt. Whoever took her must have run through the campground to wherever they had their car parked and just drove off. If she's going to be found, it's not around here.'

'So these search parties are pointless?' asked Daisy, chili fry still in hand.

'Not in the beginning, but how many miles were covered in the last two days? Twenty, and we haven't found anything.'

'Well, what else can we do to help?'

Joe thought about the strange day that they had shared where everyone seemed to ignore them, some people even refusing to look in their direction as their boots scraped over rock and dirt in the woods, and how it didn't matter because of what they had shared last night, something they hadn't even discussed properly amongst themselves. It was like the bubble that

257

had protected them the night before had remained, cutting them off from the hostility on all sides. There had been no more secrets shared between them; that would come later, when they couldn't be overhead. This allowed him to think about what they were really achieving, if anything, with these search parties.

Earl slammed the lid down on one of the fryers, making a loud bonging sound that caused their heads to snap in his direction. Outside in the Fairway they spotted Arnie and Youssef strutting by, Arnie seemingly in the lead.

'I don't know if there is anything we can do,' said Joe.

5

'Where are you going tonight?' Len asked Meryl, as she stood with her right hand on the front door handle. In her left were the pickup's keys. 'To the same place or somewhere new?'

Meryl didn't turn, simply continued to stare ahead as she spoke the same words to him that she had said on the night Lily vanished.

'Not now, Len, please.'

It sounded to him in that too-quiet hallway like a mantra she was reciting.

'Are you going where I think you're going?' Len asked.

His speech seemed to shift through the drab molasses that had befallen it, rising, growing infuriated.

'I have a pretty good idea where that is. You came home with a love bite on your neck this morning, did you know that? I wonder what everyone who turned up to help look for our daughter thought of that today, while that silly hat-wearing fucker stared at you. Yes, that's right, I saw him.'

His speech reached a peak, causing him to shout the last sentence.

With Meryl facing forward, all he could discern about the impact of his words was from her shoulders, which had steadily grown more clenched. Only now, she was wheeling on him with a speed that made him step back, expecting her hand to whip out and slap him across the cheek.

She didn't. Instead she pinned him with her eyes.

Gone was the vacant look that had filled them for the last two days, making them look like marbles filled with water. Now they looked wild, their intent murderous. Len took another step back, floorboards creaking underfoot, raising his arms in a shielding gesture on reflex.

'Stay away from him,' Meryl hissed, not quite baring her teeth.

Her spittle struck his craggy cheeks in a spray, making his eyelids flutter. On regaining his vision, he saw she was tearing at the door, the floorboards underneath her becoming a choir of creaks. She stumbled through the ever-widening gap in an ungainly jog, pickup keys jingling in her hand and her left shoulder crashing into the door's wood, producing a shuddering twang.

He made no move to stop her now; he was paralysed by the plight he had read in her face. Not the anger that had shimmered on top, but the pleading fear he had seen in the corner of her lips and around the flesh of her eyes.

Footsteps thundered from above, the boards of the Grey family home putting in a fine performance tonight, he thought as Henry and the twins trooped to the top of the staircase behind him. He didn't turn, didn't need to; he could see their concerned, frightened expressions in his head and wondered for the first time in days what they must be thinking. It was a clear thought, one that considered people beyond the miasma of his own grief.

'Dad, what is going on?' Henry asked.

He didn't answer at first. Long ago he had come to terms with the fact that he was not an ideal husband and father. It pained him to know that even when he tried his best, much better than his own father had tried, there was still a part of him that was weak, that couldn't say no to another beer or ignoring a job like the sagging porch roof.

The idea that Meryl might be better suited to someone else was not new to him, to the point where he had often expected this moment: her interest in someone else. Standing, gazing out onto the front porch with his children's eyes on his back, he accepted her finding someone else the way someone can accept a bitter diagnosis after years of seeing the signs. The ocean of feelings inside him did not rage; they were calm, their only waves made of sorrow. Yet this was something different.

She had looked terrified, her words a warning.

Headlights flashed across the front of their house as the sound of the pickup's tires reversing out of the drive could be heard. There was a squeal as Meryl peeled away.

'It's nothing, Henry,' said Len, turning to face his boys. All three of them were clustered together on the top step of the staircase. The twins were on either side of Henry's tall, lanky form, all of them looking fearful.

'Listen, I need you to look after your brothers for a while, can you do that?' asked Len.

'Sure,' replied Henry.

Len was already moving into the living room, footfalls like a soldier's march, beyond their vision.

'Why? Where's Mom gone?' asked Henry.

He froze as his father returned, cradling the shotgun, a black twin pipe number with a stock of polished oak. The stock gleamed under the lights of the hallway, but the metal barrels remained dull and sinister-looking.

'She's gone back to the fairground,' said Len. 'I need you to look after your brothers for a few hours at the most, okay? Can you do that? I won't be long.'

Henry didn't answer, just stared at his father looking up at him with the shotgun in his arms. He saw no trace of the lethargy that had consumed him before. His countenance was that of someone with a task to do, a dangerous one that might take his life, but one he bore because it was necessary.

He looked like a hunter going out to seek food.

Henry nodded at him, his legs unsteady on the top step, his body perspiring at the formidable sight of his father, his heart hammering gladly in his chest.

6

With Daisy organising a trip into Marybell to do laundry, Joe found himself alone within the campground. He thought about hanging out with Arnie and was put off when he saw that the man's camper door, which usually stood ajar, was shut. So he wandered the maze of RVs instead.

Preoccupied by his thoughts about Lily, he never noticed where his feet were taking him until

The Crypt loomed above him. From the rear, it looked like a black box, its back wall a painted mural of rotten corpses rising from their graves, their flesh grisly grey parchment over their bones. Joe stared up into the black pits of their eyes, each leaking tar-like fluid down their sunken cheeks, feeling a coldness as he recalled what had occurred within these walls two days ago.

They're a little too frightening, he thought of the dead people, *a little too much for a touring carnival.*

He stretched out his left hand, touching the wall's surface. It had an awful, porous feel against his skin. Touching it recalled the metallic bong made by Earl in The Fill Up as he had slammed the lid of his fryer closed. His hand jerked from the mural as if he had received a static shock, He had heard that sound before, inside The Crypt.

His gaze found the only place where there was any indentation in the mural's surface: the fire door. It still couldn't be fully closed; there was a gap of a few inches between its frame and the door. Those few inches were as dark as the eyes of the creatures painted above him.

Yellow and black crime scene tape zigzagged over it.

Joe had no intention of displacing it, nor did he want to widen the gap to step inside the foul building. Still, thoughts cycled in his head, compelling him to move closer.

Without knowing why and feeling a spike of fear in seeing his left hand extend out, Joe reached into the gap. Sweat began to form on the skin above his lip and under his arms as he witnessed his hand disappearing into darkness. His nerves shot alarm bells to his brain, telling him that if something latched onto him from inside to pull back quickly. Nothing did. Instead, his hand felt along the door's locking mechanism, where the metal had been battered out of shape.

The metallic bong noise echoed in Joe's head once more. The fire door was one of those that could only be opened from the inside, not the outside. It was the sound he had heard as it had bounced off the interior wall. Whoever had done it had hit it with enough force to destroy the locking mechanism.

Joe gasped, retracting his hand. In the dying evening light, he saw he had cut himself on the metal. An inch-long slice ran diagonally across his palm.

He sucked at the blood welling there, the crash of the door echoing in him again and again and again. There was something else here, he knew it...then another noise entered his head from earlier. It was the hiss of the fryers in The Fill Up after being doused with water while still hot, sending plumes of steam into the air.

Suddenly, it came to Joe in a flood. This time the memory wasn't of what he had experience inside The Crypt, but of outside, in his run to the Launder residence to call the police. He had almost been killed, run over, and not twenty feet from where he now stood, by a black eighteen-wheeler.

Lou Fritz had been in the cab that day and had rained curses upon him for having to slam on the brakes. That hiss had come after, as the hydraulics of the big machine had seemed to scold him too.

He hadn't thought anything of it at the time; he had been too distracted by the task at hand. Now, all he could think about was that he hadn't seen that black eighteen-wheeler ever since. It was hard not to notice it, as it was the only vehicle in the carnival's collection that was painted that colour.

Where had Lou been the last couple of days? Joe tried to remember if he had seen him in any of the search parties and came up blank.

He thought about his previous conversation with Daisy, about how they weren't likely to find Lily Grey because whoever had taken her had most likely whisked her away in a vehicle of some kind. He had never considered the possibility that someone employed at the carnival could have been responsible. His thoughts had always been of a shadowy figure with no discernible features. Now, he saw Lou Fritz's smarmy, rat-like face.

The carny had even been at The Ring Toss when Lily had played, observing them from the back of the stall, observing the customers, all kids.

'It's a sad business, isn't it?' said a voice.

Joe spun to see Montague standing behind him.

7

'I suppose you can't get it out of your head,' remarked Montague, 'what with everything that's being said nowadays'.

Joe's mind was reeling from the possible revelation and he gave little thought to what he said next. 'What do you mean?'

'You know, son…the rumours about you and that little girl.'

Joe stared at the carnival owner, aware of a light-headed prickling at the back of his mind. Montague gazed back; it was still light enough for him to see the purple bags like bruises under the carny's grave eyes. His beard, which had always shone silver in the light, was dulled, as if the toll of the last few days was altering his physical appearance, diminishing it.

'I was actually out looking for Lou,' he lied. 'I haven't seen him recently and I found a few things in The Ring Toss that I thought might belong to him.'

Montague didn't reply, just continued to observe the broken door in front of Joe, his hands clasped together behind his back. The carnival owner had changed his clothes from earlier; he now wore a crisp suit the colour of coal, complete with a three-piece waistcoat. There was even a chain that belonged to a pocket watch trailing from one waistcoat pocket to the other.

The chain was silver.

'There is also another rumour going around that you are from Indiana,' offered Montague.

Joe's eyes widened. His first thought was that Daisy had told on him, and he felt a rush of heat at the idea. Then it occurred to him that Daisy had been with him all day and that Montague had come from a different direction than the campsite where she currently was.

'Who told you that?' he asked, trying to sound unperturbed.

Again, Joe felt the dam rise in his mind towards the carnival owner. There was just something about his jovial prying that rang false in his mind, as if his reason was insidious rather than genuine interest.

'I heard it from one of Jackson's people,' replied Montague. Then, when it was clear that Joe was not going to offer any further information, he sighed.

'You're an enigma, Joe,' he said. 'One I hope to solve someday, and I hope as well that you'll give me the chance to do so by considering joining our company more permanently once we leave here.'

'Really? I thought with everything that's happened...'

'Please.' Montague held both his palms towards Joe. 'I know you had nothing to do with that young girl vanishing. Trust me, Joe, we know all too well about the cruelty small town minds can inflict. I hope you consider staying with us. You've shown you're resourceful and practical. You would be an asset to the company, both of you would.'

'Both of us.'

'I'm going to make the same offer to Daisy when I see her next, so don't go worrying about the blooming romance between you two being cut short.'

Joe opened his mouth, intending to decline his offer, but the carnival owner was looking away from him. He followed his gaze and saw Len Grey marching towards them with a double-barrel shotgun in his hands.

8

'Where is my wife?' Len Grey bellowed, resting the stock of the gun on his shoulder. Its barrel was aimed at Montague's head.

'Why, Mr. Grey, I'm sure I have no idea where your wife is at this moment in time,' replied Montague.

He didn't even seem to regard the gun shoved at his face; his eyes were fixed on Grey's. Joe observed with dawning confusion that Montague had the same cruel, amused twist of a smirk on his lips that he had when Launder had ambushed them yesterday. *What the hell is wrong with him?* he thought.

He stood between the two and to the side, his head snapping back and forth, his hands raised as if the weapon were pointed at him, though Len didn't even seem to consider him; his eyes were only for Montague.

Taking advantage of that, Joe started to slide his right foot through the grass with agnosing slowness, bringing him closer to Lily Grey's father.

'Liar,' spat Len. 'Why has this town become an episode of the Twilight Zone ever since you and your ilk showed up? First my daughter vanishes, now my wife visits this place until the early hours of the morning. She comes to see that Arnie Kauffman, I know it. I've seen the way he looks at her.'

This news made Joe's head to snap to Montague, his progress towards Len temporarily forgotten. The carny's face gave nothing away, that cruel twist of a smirk still hauntingly apparent.

'I know nothing of this, Mr. Grey,' Montague told him, with what sounded to Joe like annoyance. 'What I do know is you coming here tonight and waving a gun around is not going to improve matters in this town.'

Grey was right-handed; he used his left hand to support the barrel of his gun, meaning his left shoulder obscured his view of Joe sliding closer. Angry tears ran down his stubbled cheeks from eyes that blazed.

'I just want my life back,' he whispered.

Joe watched the end of the shotgun sag slightly, pointing at the carnival owner's throat now. His boots slid another inch closer, then two.

'Mr. Grey, I can assure you...'

'I just want my life back!' Len yelled. His eyes came back up, the barrel of the gun following.

267

Joe darted forward and as he did, the shotgun roared.

Book Three

Reckoning

Chapter One

The Chain

1

They watched Collins pull away in his cruiser; its top bulbs still circulating silently, washing the grass, the carnival's archway, and them in scarlet. It did the same for Len Grey in the cruiser's back seat as he rested his head against the glass, his eyes mournful and unseeing.

Sergeant Collins had been the only officer still on site when Len discharged his shotgun. When he arrived at the scene, panting from the run, Grey was lying on his back on the ground and a portion of The Crypt's rear wall was smouldering from the spray of buckshot. Joe Cage stood nearby, with the offending weapon in his hands, its barrel still smoking.

Before Collins could draw his weapon Joe tossed the gun at his feet. As he did, Montague marched over to him, proclaiming that Cage had just saved his life. Collins got the whole story eventually.

There was one detail that captured his attention more than anything.

2

'How exactly did you disarm him?' Collins asked Joe.

He was looking at him over his notepad, his gleaming brow wrinkled with thin ravines.

'Well, Mr. Grey wasn't focused on me, more on Montague,' explained Joe. 'I was able to shuffle close to him while they spoke to each other without him noticing. When he went to fire, I shoved the barrel out of the way and planted a leg between Mr. Grey's legs. I then elbowed Mr. Grey in the face and turned so that he tripped over my leg as I pulled the gun away from him.'

'Where exactly did you learn some Bruce Lee shit like that'?

Joe could feel Montague's ears prick up at the question; he was standing only a few feet away.

'My father taught me,' he answered reluctantly.

'Is your father some sort of kung fu nut?'

'No, sir, he's just spent a lot of time in the military, sir.'

Despite this, Joe couldn't be too annoyed; if Jackson had been the one questioning them, then he would have required them all to come to the station to provide statements. Collins told them to swing by the station tomorrow to submit them instead.

Daisy, who had clung to him this entire time, spoke in a gentle whisper. 'Did you really do that?'

He looked down at her coiled against him and nodded. The strength with which she held him grew notably less as her eyes looked away. After Collins departed with Len handcuffed in the backseat, Daisy let go of him completely.

'I can't believe you'd be so stupid to risk your life like that,' she said to him, crossing her arms. 'You could have been killed.' Daisy stared at him, expecting an answer. He couldn't think of any.

'Find somewhere else to sleep tonight.'

271

She spat this last sentence at him before stalking off into the shadows. The only light left in the day was a streak of blood red on the horizon.

Joe called her name, but his legs were rooted to the spot. There had been little time to think about telling Collins his suspicions towards Lou Fritz in connection with Lily Grey, especially with Montague within earshot. Not that he felt he owed the carnival owner anything; his actions to save the man's life had been simply reflex. He kept mute in case he knew about Lou.

All of this was knocking around inside his head when the carnival owner landed a hand on his shoulder.

'The way the movies portray it, when a man acts like a hero, women swoon over him,' said Montague. 'Shows you just how much fiction they contain. Don't worry about her; she'll come around.'

Joe detested him then, mostly for the superiority in his voice.

'As far as mysteries go you're an intriguing one, Joe,' he carried on, shaking him by the shoulder. 'Your father is a military man. I told you I would solve the puzzle that is Joe Cage given time. I want to thank you for saving my life. That reminds me - Carmen wants to see you about something.'

3

The wind batted at the dead fairy lights that crisscrossed over the Fairway, making them rattle, a sound too similar to the one that lay behind the dam in his mind. Those memories seemed closer now, the dam less stable, after the adrenaline of confronting a murderous Len Grey.

Absently, Joe rubbed at his scarred wrist as he stood outside Madam Carmen's Fortunes after knocking on the door. The only light in the Fairway's dark avenue spilled from its two rectangle windows.

After a moment, the door to the gingerbread house swung wide.

'Hey there, Joe,' Carmen greeted him.

She was dressed in a pale blue bathrobe that reached down to her ankles.

'I'm sorry, is this a bad time?' asked Joe, seeing her in her bathrobe. 'Montague told me you wanted to see me and I just came over. I didn't think about the time.'

'No, it's fine,' she said, showing a line of pristinely white teeth. 'I asked him to tell you not that long ago. You're right on time.'

Carmen glided over to the round table that was the room's centerpiece. The glass ball was gone; in its place were plates piled high with food.

Even though he had eaten a few hours ago, his stomach growled ravenously as the food's aroma filled his nostrils. He saw creamy potatoes, carrots coated in honey, corn on the cob dripping in butter, and a plate of sirloin steaks.

'Don't forget to close the door behind you,' Carmen instructed.

It was only on hearing her words that he realised the sight had lured him over the threshold. He did as he was bid, the door to the gingerbread house shutting closed with a click.

'That lovely Deputy Lloyd Herrick bought the steaks for me. I suppose he was thinking that we could enjoy them together some night. I think he's kind of sweet on me. Anyway, after hearing Montague's news that he was going to offer you a permanent place with us, I thought it would be the perfect way to celebrate the occasion. Welcome to the company, Joe.'

'Carmen, I don't know what to say,' he stammered, realising he had never given Montague an answer to his proposal.

'It's nothing,' she said, swatting a hand at him. 'I know it's late and all, but come on and have a seat. This is your inauguration to the family, after all.'

Joe took a seat, still puzzled by Daisy's last words to him, and guided by the hungry growling in his belly. The only thing out of place was the buzz of a fly circling the yellow orb of a light overhead.

'I hope you don't mind if I lose this, it's a little hot tonight,' said Carmen, untying the strings of her bathrobe. Carmen shrugged off the light garment, tossing it onto the chair to Joe's right.

He stared at her, his body suddenly too hot in his clothing as she took the seat opposite him. She wore a white satin slip. Nothing else.

The skin of her body was the same caramel colour of her face, and suddenly he remembered the day they had been so close he could have counted all the freckles on her cheeks. She had smelled of wildflowers and campfires. He could smell that same scent now as he sat, his entire body clenched.

Does she know about Daisy and me?

Carmen smiled at him from across the table while beginning to dish food onto a plate that she then handed to him. He accepted it with numb fingers.

'Inauguration to the family?' he croaked, latching onto the first thing he could think of. 'What does that mean?'

His neck was beginning to throb from refusing to look anywhere else but into her eyes.

'Oh, it's just a little ceremonial I like to have whenever someone like yourself has been asked to join us,' Carmen answered.

Joe's eyes flicked to the left and right. The table had four seats, yet it had only been set for two.

'Montague's also going to ask Daisy to become permanent,' he said.

Carmen smiled at him, flashing her perfect white teeth once more while sawing into her steak. She did not offer an excuse as to why there wasn't a plate set for Daisy; instead, she said, 'I heard about what happened tonight.'

Joe frowned, the tension in his body transferring entirely to his spine. It made him feel like a scarecrow that's hooked onto a cross and planted in some field, except he was hooked into his seat.

'How could you have heard...'

'A shotgun was fired inside the campsite.'

A trail of red juice ran down from the corner of her mouth as she chewed. Her steak, which he hadn't noticed until now, was rare. It sat in a puddle of purple-red liquid on her plate. The sight made his stomach somersault.

'You know how fast stories spread in this place. I practically heard about it the second after it happened.' The meat in her mouth made squishy sounds as her jaws worked. 'That's why Montague is so keen on having you,' she informed him. 'You're one of those uniquely good-intentioned people.'

'I don't know about that,' he replied, thinking of his sister at home.

Again, the past seemed to be lurking just behind him. It felt like if he turned his neck to look he would just fall into an ocean of memories.

'I mean, the original plan was to feast on you and Daisy and dump your bodies in some ditch outside of town. But Montague changed his mind. And that is a rare thing; it takes a lot to impress him. He's seen how you've dealt with all the incriminating evidence stacked against you and how the townies are all baying for your blood and he is impressed. We should toast to that.'

Carmen raised her wine glass at him; its contents were a dark carmine colour.

'I'm sorry, what did you say?' Joe asked, confused.

The fly, which had been buzzing intermittently from place to place, landed on Carmen's right cheek. He watched it begin to crawl towards her grinning mouth, towards where the blood had stained her white teeth a vivid red.

They parted.

Her tongue wormed out with a dexterity that seemed impossible, stretching out horrendously to slap at the fly. It retracted back into her mouth with a slick smacking sound. Before it disappeared behind a wall of teeth he observed the fly, its legs withering on the pink, moist tip of her tongue.

Joe's cutlery dropped from his hands with a clatter.

Carmen continued to grin from across the table, only her grin was growing; the edges of her lips extended seamlessly through the flesh of her cheeks, exposing more teeth, sharp teeth, that reached halfway up her face.

He couldn't help staring at them.

'I want you to know I was never fully happy with that plan. I have always been your advocate,' she told him sweetly.

That was when Joe looked into her eyes. They were no longer the dark brown, almost black, that he had come to know. They were silver.

4

He had been afraid of drowning in an ocean of memories; now he was drowning in the silver blaze of Carmen's eyes.

'Don't worry,' she told him, her voice still sweet, but distant. 'This is all part of the fun.'

He nodded, sinking deeper and deeper and deeper into her eyes, noticing that the further he sank the more their light became like a mist that constantly stirred and shifted. He looked to its bottom and saw only emptiness.

The Carmen-thing pushed her seat back from the table and stood. Then one fingernail (like her grinning mouth, all her nails had grown) slid through the thin fabric of her slip from her breasts to her pelvis until it fell from her body.

'What do you think?' she asked. 'Do you like what you see?'

Never before had Joe seen a woman so fiercely beautiful and repulsive at the same time. Under the soft ocher glow from the overhead light, her body stood posed with ferocious assurance; however, there was no beauty in her face, which looked down at him as if from a tall, shadowy peak. What was there was made hideous by the hunger that spilled through her eyes.

He understood then that she was a dead thing, a hollow thing, made so by the insatiable void within her that demanded to be filled. This did not bother him; he was lost in the forever-shifting spell within her gaze.

'Do you want me?' she asked, sweeping round the table. Her eyes glared at him from its tall peak with crazed longing. 'Do you yearn for me?'

She was behind him now, her dead fingernails in his hair. Joe was powerless as she leaned close, until her mouth was at his ear.

'I want you,' she whispered.

He felt her teeth sink into him.

5

All his elation and want was set on fire by pain. Pain that was so severe, so all-consuming that he felt the barriers he had built in his mind crack. The rattling sound from earlier returned to him, no longer belonging to the carnival's fairy lights; it was the noise made by the chains in his family's barn.

6

'Come on in and see,' his father's voice called to him.

Joe stood at the entrance to the barn, peering in. It was late, almost bedtime, and the deepening night had turned the building's interior into a dark cave.

He could not see his father inside.

'What is it?' he asked.

'Just come on in and find out,' came his father's reply. It was accompanied with the chime of metal, a sweet sound because the metal was new.

Briefly, he hesitated, thinking back to the look his father had given him across the dinner table when he had refused to eat his broccoli. The muscles in his face had tensed, while his eyes had been wide and staring. There was something cartoonish about it that made Joe want to laugh.

He hadn't, but it had been close.

After that his father had spent the entire evening in the barn. His electric drill could be heard from their living room, whirling away.

'What's Dad doing?' he had finally asked his mother.

She was helping Harper colour in her colouring books.

'Tinkering,' was her response. 'You know your father, sometimes he just needs to be alone.'

Her words had struck him as being funny because he didn't know his father, not in the way he knew his mother, or his friends. His father spent too much time at the base where he worked, often overnight and for long periods of time. When he was home, he rarely spoke to him.

This revelation made Joe sad in a way that was unusual. So far his life had been one of contentment, in which he drifted along with no real purpose other than to find fun between the things his mother made him do.

Whenever he did encounter a moment of sorrow, it was fleeting. This feeling, however, felt vast and deep and unsettling. He intended to get rid of it by finding out what exactly his father was doing, which was why he pushed aside the memory of the dinner table and entered the barn.

'Where are you?'

'At the back. Here, I'll get the light.'

There was the scratch of a match and a flame bloomed, creating a globe of orange light at the rear of the barn. In its center was a lantern. His father stood to its left by one of the empty stalls. He was smiling.

Whatever he was working on must be in there, Joe thought, stepping over the barn's soft earth floor. His family had never used the building for its intended purpose, only for storage or in his case, a place to pretend. Most of his fantasies concerned the exploration of some long, lost tomb.

'What is it?' he asked as his father let him enter.

Lying across the floor like a dead snake was a chain of metal, the colour of coal, that ended in a bracket screwed into the barn wall by four screws. At the other end was an open manacle, small in comparison to the links of the chain. Joe tried to envision what possible use such a thing could be and why his dad was so excited about it.

'It's a teaching tool,' his father told him, his large hands resting on Joe's shoulders. 'Here, look.'

Before he knew what was happening, George Cage had guided him forward and closed the manacle over his right wrist, locking it with a tiny gold key. He slipped the key into his jeans pocket. Joe waved his trapped arm up and down, the chain making its sweet rattling sound once more.

It was heavy.

'Dad, what…'

The back of his father's hand came out of nowhere, causing his head to snap back while the cheek where it landed burned. He fell to his knees.

'You think it's funny to disrespect me?' roared his father.

He looked at him with tears in his unbelieving eyes.

The man who was little more than a ghost in his life towered above him, his chest heaving with rage, feet planted firmly apart, his eyes glaring.

'I don't know what sort of house your mother is running if you think you can disobey me, boy. I am your father and what I say goes, understand that?'

He nodded vehemently, tears splashing onto his clothes. His father slapped him across the other cheek.

This time he fell onto his left side and felt the chain pull taut.

'So when I tell you to eat, you eat. I work too damn hard for you just to go and waste my earnings by throwing things out.'

He kicked him with the toe of his boot, not hard, but enough for Joe to feel like his left kneecap had just exploded inside his jeans. He screamed then, his voice loud and high. His father hunkered down, his hands on his bent knees, his suntanned face oily with sweat underneath his grey buzz cut.

'In my job, boys older than yourself come to me with a lifetime of bad habits,' his father informed him. 'In order to teach them honor and discipline and respect for their betters, I have to break them first. I never thought I'd have to do that with my own son. I thought your mother would have known better. It seems that in my absence, as I fulfill my duty to my country, a duty you will one day take on as well, you have grown weak and undisciplined.'

Footsteps, running from outside into the barn.

'George, what's going on? I heard a scream...'

'This boy is learning a lesson, a lesson you should have taught him long ago.'

'Mom,' Joe wailed from the ground.

He could see her head above the stall. Darkness and light danced across the pale cheeks of her horrified face from the lantern's flame. She looked old then, the flesh of her face seeming to hang.

Her brown eyes looked to him then back to her husband.

'Go back inside, Audrey, I'll deal with you later!' he shouted at her.

Joe gaped up at her, pleading with all his will for her to come and scoop him into her arms, to save him. Instead, she never looked back, her gaze fixed on her husband's enraged expression. She eventually nodded to him.

Joe watched her turn and leave.

That was the first time. He had been ten.

Chapter Two

Half-Devoured

1

As Carmen's lips clamped over his flesh, sucking like a leech, the same hopeless despair that he had experienced on hearing the manacle's lock click into place overwhelmed him now. He convulsed against both the memory and the pain, dispelling the power her silver eyes had on him until he was free. Free to experience every single second of agony as Carmen leeched from him.

His legs scrabbled under the table as hot blood splashed down his neck. He could hear Carmen sucking it up and began to scream. His hands grabbed at her head, trying to pull her off, but to no avail. She was just too strong.

He groped at the table, disturbing plates and condiments until his left hand seized upon something long and cylindrical. Without thinking, he drove it into the creature he saw as only a blur in the left-hand side of his vision.

The effect was instantaneous.

Her jaws detached themselves from his neck as she let loose a shriek. His eardrums hummed with it as he slapped a hand over his spurting wound.

She staggered away from him, screaming in agony.

On the disheveled table were several napkins. Moving fast, he applied them to his neck. The pain, an excruciating sensation akin to being punctured by two hot needles, had dulled to a throb that followed his heartbeat. A dangerously slow rhythm, he realised. To make matters worse, drowsiness had descended, greying his vision, making his movements clumsy and slow.

Somehow Joe managed to vacate his chair by spilling to his knees. Half-crawling, half-skidding, he propelled himself into the nearest corner. Once there he spun, eyes scanning the room, braced for an attack.

Carmen was nowhere to be seen.

The walls of the gingerbread house were draped in shadows that his eyes couldn't penetrate. Above, the overhead light swung, its cable squeaking with each rotation as it revealed overturned furniture and even more darkness.

Her screams had stopped, preventing him from pinpointing her position.

He continued to stare, fighting the sleepiness that threatened to overcome him. His left hand pressed the napkins to his wounded neck, which soaked to crimson immediately.

Eventually, the light stopped rotating with a final squeak.

The scene before him remained unchanged. All he heard was his own haggard breathing, yet he wasn't alone. He could feel her eyes on him.

Carmen sprang onto the center table from the shadows opposite, landing on all fours. A growl like that of a wolf purred from her throat.

In the soft light, he saw that all her beauty was gone. Her nudity revealed only the coiling of her muscles as she prepared to pounce. A bib of blood, his own, had formed a U-shape between her breasts. He could smell it too, a heady, metallic scent that made him want to retch.

Worst of all was the steak knife protruding from her right eye.

It hadn't gone all the way in. Only half the blade had fully embedded into her eye socket, turning the eyeball into a running egg.

'I'm going to rip your fucking heart out!' she screamed at him.

Her two canines had elongated, reaching her bottom lip, caked red. The skin of her cheeks had parted, revealing crocodile-like teeth and red gums.

There was no time to think as her body uncoiled like a toad, leaping. He sprang forward, aware of the yawning maw that was her mouth growing wider and wider, a black hole ringed with teeth.

He forced his attention elsewhere, to the steak knife half-buried in her eye.

The effort to do this required so much focus he had no awareness of anything else. As he gripped the knife's handle, he thought her claws could be shredding him to pieces already.

It didn't matter, the knife did. The knife was his chance.

Their bodies thumped together.

2

They collapsed in a heap and were still. The power left his body a second after life left hers. He still held onto the knife; blood and goo now slicked his right hand. He had shoved it into her brain all the way to the handle.

'I guess that whole stake business is bullshit.'

He said this to her face, inches away from his. He had seen enough movies; he knew what she was as she began to transform. Vampire.

The fangs, which had threatened death and pain, had diminished to normal length. Her fingernails were no longer talons. Her nudity, though dirtied with his blood, was unremarkable. Even her expression had changed from hatred to what seemed like serenity.

She was his friend again, and she appeared at peace.

Grief constricted him like a python, suffocating him. Part of it was the surprise of seeing her revert back into the person he knew, for there was no hate in him towards her, only sorrow.

He let go of the knife, tears streaming down his cheeks, to lay her down. He swiped the cloth from the table, causing everything on it to crash, plates shattering into fragments on the floor, and covered her with it.

Stepping back to observe his work, he felt fury blossom in him, alongside his grief. Fury for being made a victim again the way his father made him one, for taking Carmen's life even though it was self-defence, and for breaking the walls he had built within his mind towards his past.

Joe could feel those memories even now wanting to overthrow him. What saved him was remembering Carmen's words from earlier. As they reeled through his mind, he spoke one word, his eyes shooting to the door.

'Daisy.'

3

Joe skidded to a halt after stumbling out of the gingerbread house. The carnival lights were on; not just the fairy lights above the Fairway, but every single light in the fairground. Calliope music churned from hidden speakers. All the stalls were illuminated as if for business. The recorded cackles for Journey To The Crypt brayed. Even The Whirl was spotlit.

'Oh, shit,' Joe said in seeing it all.

Out of nowhere he heard his father's voice speaking to him. His words were some of the last that he had said.

'A man doesn't run from his problems, even those that hurt.'

Joe spun on his heels, taking it all in, the cycling carousel, the red and white lollipop helter skelter, the reflecting mirrors of the funhouse..

The others did this, he thought. *It's part of the ceremony, of the inauguration.*

The hairs prickled on his neck, telling him that eyes unseen were watching.

Joe staggered into a run, aiming for the entrance archway with its rainbow of coloured orbs all casting light. The wound in his neck throbbed; he could feel the blood that had soaked past his makeshift bandage trailing down his chest as he ran in a lurching type of stagger. His vision was a teetering kaleidoscope of blurred darkness infringed with the lights of the carnival. As he got closer to the arch, he discerned a set of headlights trundling over the field towards the carnival and made for them, thinking perhaps whoever it was could help.

4

Sheriff Timothy Jackson guided his Blazer towards the bright lights of the carnival. It had been a long day and he could feel it now, making his eyelids heavy. Still, he proceeded on, mostly out of irritation towards Sergeant Collins, who had turned up at the station leading a handcuffed Len Grey inside.

Once he had heard the story, his response hadn't been civil.

'And you didn't think to radio for help, to bring them all in for an interview?'

Despite being twenty-four years his senior, Collins's face flushed.

Part of his frustration had been at being unable to drive out to the fairground himself due to the recent disappearances. It was only now as he drew closer to the place that had been on his mind all day that he felt ashamed of his reaction.

Even he hadn't followed protocol by being out here alone.

At least I'm here now, he thought. *And the cavalry is on its way tomorrow, courtesy of Detective Rook and the state police.*

It seemed they were finally going to make his town a priority after the disappearance of the entire Teal family. And Jackson hoped they'd have more luck than his department had today, because other than confirming that the Teals had gone somewhere and had done so without telling any of their closest friends, neighbours, or farmhands, his department had found nothing.

I'll have to make up to Mitch. I'll buy him a bottle of that bourbon he likes.

He had just finished that thought when a figure stumbled through the carnival's entrance archway towards him. Seeing the staggering person made him aware for the first time that the entire fairground was lit up.

'What now?' he said, slamming on the brakes.

He had to; the person running at him didn't seem to want to stop.

'Please, you've got to help me!' cried Joe Cage.

Jackson was already out of the vehicle and gripping the young man by his biceps, a sensation of déjà vu striking him. The man's white shirt-shirt was soaked red with blood that appeared to have spilled from a wound in his neck. It was covered with gauze that looked like a bloody sponge. Jackson cursed himself from coming here alone.

'Calm down, now. Start from the beginning and tell me what happened,' he said, trying to keep his voice steady.

In the glow thrown by the carnival lights, Joe's face was pale beneath his suntan. He kept glancing behind him, to the fair, with eyes that were too wide, the whites of them standing out like limestone in the night. The man jittered in his grip, greased with flop sweat as if he was infected with a fever.

'There's no time for that,' Joe snapped, jumping out of his grip. 'They might have Daisy.'

'Who might have Daisy?'

A voice full of pompous confidence and for the first time a touch of threat answered.

'I believe the young man is referring to us.'

He watched Joe's shoulders flinch in hearing it.

Montague stood on the grass in the beam of the Blazer's headlights in his usual stance, arms clasped behind his back. At his side and beyond the beam of light stood every member of the company, their features draped in darkness that seemed to rise up from the ground.

He could have sworn they had not been there a second before.

'Joe, you are a nuisance like no other,' sighed the carnival owner. 'I tried to do this the civilised way, put on a show, give the people a little delight, a little scare, something they might remember fondly for the rest of their meaningless lives and then take one or two of them with us as we go. Never anyone special or who would be missed. Every community has a few tumbleweeds like you, Joe, and your friend Daisy. We feed the towns and they feed us; that's the way it's worked for centuries. It seems it was not to be in this place. Fate, or whatever it is, wants me to do this the more barbaric way.'

Ignoring the man's insane ramblings, Jackson stepped forward. 'I want to know what's going on right now!'

His voice was steady, strong and loud, seeming to echo over the darkened land. He felt a sense of ending, of slotting the last puzzle piece into place and revealing the whole picture of whatever it was happening in his town. He marched forward until he was face-to-face with the carnival owner.

The man's expression was one of detached superiority, surveying him with eyes that glinted with silver shards in the dark.

'Sherriff Jackson, I must say I've grown tiresome of your constant interfering.'

Montague lurched forward and buried his teeth into Jackson's neck with a wet crunch. A fine red mist sprayed into the air, some of which landed on Joe, who stared as the carny seized the sheriff by the arms.

Jackson managed to draw his sidearm but failed to raise it. Instead, it discharged into the ground with a resonating thump.

Montague's head began to seesaw from side-to-side, shaking Jackson the way a terrier would shake the life out of a rat. Joe heard a frenzied slobbering noise, understood that he was witnessing the creature feeding, and more viciously than Carmen had tried to do with him.

Despite his smaller size, the carnival owner was lifting the sheriff off the ground now. Joe watched in horror, unable to move, knowing now it wasn't just one or two of them that were like Carmen, but all of them.

'See this.'

It was his father's voice again, speaking as if he were right by his ear. With it came a memory, a newer one, in which his father was older. His hair was greyer, his brown eyes encircled with more lines, yet he was no less fearsome. In it, he grasped the manacle around Joe's wrist and held it up the to his face.

'This will teach you not to run.'

Yet he had run in the end and was going to run now.

There was no helping the sheriff, he already knew that as his feet began to slide backward towards the Blazer's open door. Movement to his left and right made him aware that the others were stalking silently towards him, their bodies leaning low. Seeing them, he dived into the police vehicle.

As he yanked the door closed, he caught sight of Montague taking another bite out of Jackson's neck through the windscreen. The sheriff's body dropped to the ground as the carnival's king raised his decapitated head for Joe to see, his jaws smeared red while his eyes shone with alluring silver light.

Joe felt their pull ordering him to surrender.

Unlike before, he resisted it, recalling the unfathomable pain of Carmen's fangs as she buried them in his neck. As the other carnies scratched at the Blazer's doors he yanked the vehicle into reverse, slamming his right foot on the accelerator and causing the entire thing to shoot backward into the night.

Chapter Three

Siege

1

'Boss, was that wise?' asked Arnie.

Montague watched the Blazer's taillights dwindle then change direction, heading to town. He let the sheriff's head spill from his hands onto the ground, licking the salty residue of bodily fluids from his fingers as he did.

'I didn't have any choice,' he replied.

His eyes swept the others surrounding him, reading fear, shock, a need for guidance, and in a select few, glee. His family always loved seeing a bloody death, plus it had been years since they killed someone like Jackson. Someone people would remember and ask questions about it later.

'Lou, would you come here, please?'

Lou Fritz strutted forward, his rat-like face sneering with delight.

'Finally decided to uphold your promises,' he remarked.

Montague ignored him, turning his attention to everyone else.

'First off, I'm sorry you all had to see that,' he said. 'This is not our way; taking what we want when we want without being careful, without considering the consequences is dangerous. Many among you know why, yet from what I've been hearing it seems that some of you may have forgotten it. My hand was forced to act tonight because of Lou Fritz. It seems Lou has put us all in jeopardy by having a feast last night with the Teal family.'

An irritated and longing groan rippled through everyone.

'While we are all starving?' someone shouted.

'I cleaned everything up afterward,' Lou blabbered. 'I did it just like the old times, like Roanoke. No mess, no leftovers.'

'You're a fool,' Montague snapped at him. 'You can't make people like that disappear and expect everyone else not to notice. There will be investigations now, police.'

Another groan, this one was despairing.

'We have nothing to fear from them; they're cattle,' said Lou.

'Tell that to Carmen, she's dead,' said Montague. His cold, detached voice caused a gasp to erupt from the crowd. 'Murdered by one of the "cattle" you think so little of. We all know that Joe Cage has been keeping a close eye on us; well tonight, he discovered the truth about ourselves because certain individuals weren't being careful. He murdered Carmen Garcia.'

There wasn't a groan this time, but a ripple of outrage. A few started to openly weep. Arnie Kauffman looked to him with eyes that said *Tell me it isn't true'*. He did not bother to meet them, only stared at Lou.

The expression in Lou's ratty face was one of horror, horror and realisation. He knew now that he was in trouble, his ever-widening eyes scanning the crowd, his neck pivoting from face to face in quick, jerking motions.

'There is a reason why we live under the radar, going from town to town, never taking more than we need: because it's safe. Incidents like what happened in North Carolina bring attention and ultimately death. The humans to this day still remember Roanoke. They still write stories about us and put them in their movies for the whole world to see. The sheriff's arrival here tonight says that already stories have started to circulate within this tiny community. I do not doubt that his appearance here was to ask about any connection any of us had with the Teal family. That is why I acted as I did: because I had no other choice. It is why tonight, all of us will be doing the same. I don't know what's going to happen in the next couple of days. The humans have developed a phenomenal level of power in the last century, enough that if we were discovered, we could be eradicated. All I know is that we cannot be found out. Even if that means we must become legends once more, then so be it.'

'Are you saying what I think you're saying?' asked Earl Porter.

Montague looked at him dead in the eye. What he said next, he said in a voice as final as a coffin lid closing.

'We raze Marybell to the ground.'

A murmur of approval muttered from everyone. Arnie sidled up to him to whisper in his ear.

'This goes against everything we've been trying to achieve. Every rule you ever set.'

Arnie had been at Roanoke; more importantly, he had experienced the ramifications of their actions afterward and chosen to follow Montague when he suggested that they change their ways. He had stood at his side in the bitter battle that followed. He owed him honesty.

'What choice do we have? If we leave now, there will be questions, they'll come after us. Our only hope is to wipe the slate clean.'

'You're finally delivering what you promised me,' remarked Lou. 'To be gods above the cattle, above everything.'

Montague stepped over to him, taking his head lovingly between his hands as he stared into the man's face.

'Not for you,' he told him.

His hands began to squeeze.

'Wait.' Lou gripped Montague's hands with his own. 'Please, don't.'

He was clawing at Montague now, raking his flesh with his claws as he sank to his knees. No one moved to intervene; instead they watched in silence.

The area around Lou's left eye bulged with pressure as the bone cracked like old wood being snapped over a knee. The eyeball popped, spilling fluid down his cheek. His head caved in next, shooting a geyser of blood, bone, and grey matter from his crown.

Montague dropped him with no feelings of remorse or guilt. It had been a long time since he had felt anything remotely like those emotions.

'Let that be a lesson to anyone who endangers this family,' he said to the others. 'What we do tonight, we do because Lou Fritz left us no choice.'

'Youssef, I want you to go get Valerie and Cynthia and bring them back here along with the cargo. There's no point in us hiding anymore.'

Youssef nodded and disappeared into the night.

'What about them?' asked Earl, gesturing to the bodies.

'Dispose of Lou. As for the tiresome Jackson, well there's nothing wrong with us indulging in a little theatrics. Take him to The

Whirl. The rest of you, since this is hopefully the last time we have to do this, go have some fun.'

'What are you going to do?' asked Arnie.

'I think I'll pay Mr. Launder a visit.'

2

Mark Stone was in the corridor that contained the station's two jail cells, trying to talk to Grey through the bars. Elaine could hear him from the reception desk where she stood sharing a coffee with Phyllis. Collins sat at his desk off to the left, his features still rosy and his gaze far off; reliving Jackson's talking down, she thought.

Hell, we all are. It's why we're all stood here at ten o'clock and not home in our beds. We're waiting, waiting to see him walk through the door again along with Montague. The carnival owner won't be in handcuffs, but it will be clear that handcuffs could be an option if he doesn't cooperate.

She had never seen him this stressed before. He hadn't disclosed much about what he learned from the detective up the road, but she could tell it frightened him. And that frightened her.

Spending the day on the Teals' deserted property had felt like being inside a haunted house, though not like those in the gory movies, where everyone is running around half-naked. No. This was like a ghost story where something lurked constantly on the peripheral of her vision.

It made her wonder what exactly was going on in her town.

She was worried about him and her worry made the coffee she was drinking taste like nothing. It made her muscles throb with unreleased tension.

When she saw his Blazer pull up outside, she felt so relieved she didn't notice how the vehicle skidded to a halt. It was only when she saw someone else step out of the driver's side, someone in a white tee dirtied with blood, that all her worst imaginings threatened to overwhelm her.

'Collins, Stone, something's wrong,' she said, leaping towards the door.

3

In his cell, Len Grey spoke for the first time since his arrest. Mark, who was about to dart into the reception area after hearing Elaine, stopped.

'Are you any good with that gun?'

He looked at Grey, who was eyeing his sidearm through the bars. When he didn't reply, Grey spoke again, filling his veins with ice.

'You might want to get good, son. You might need to use that tonight.'

4

'You need to help me,' cried Joe Cage as he exploded into the station.

As Elaine reached him (dropping her coffee cup with a crash), the power left his legs, leaving him as deadweight in her arms. With Phyllis's help, they half-walked, half-carried him to a nearby seat. Glancing around for help, she saw Collins was still sat in his chair, frozen, watching them, his vast forehead furrowed like a hood over his eyes. She meant to shout at him to get off his ass, the words on her tongue, when her left hand readjusted its grip on Joe's upper arm and felt something slimy. This was as they were lowering him into one of the plastic chairs, its colour a faded red after years of seating individuals waiting to make reports or to pick up relatives from one of the cells after a night of rowdy drinking.

Her attention snapped back to Joe, seeing just how much of a red ruin his t-shirt was. The blood originated from a wound on the left-hand side of his neck, patched over with some indistinguishable material. Some of which was still wet, judging by the smear in the palm of her hand.

He smelled of it, a coppery stink that filled her nose.

Looking at her palm, she thought of how he had come alone, a chip of ice entering her heart as she thought, Where's Jackson? She rubbed at the blood with her thumb, its texture growing chalky as it dried against her skin.

'You have to help me find Daisy,' he said.

His eyes refused to meet theirs; instead they roamed the room, showing too much white.

'They have her... at the carnival...Daisy and maybe Meryl Grey, too.'

'Joe, where is Sheriff Jackson?' Elaine asked in her most soothing voice. 'You came in his car. I need to know where is he.'

His eyelids fluttered in response to her question. The muscles along his jaw began to quiver like a child's after they've experienced pain.

It was not a nice image to look at.

Joe's young and handsome face was made ugly by the emotions warring inside of him, which is why she believed him when he spoke next.

'Jackson's dead.'

There was a second's pause as Elaine felt Phyllis's eyes on her.

'Bullshit,' said Collins, rising from his desk chair.

It scattered away with a clatter from its wheels.

'He's dead. Montague killed him. He...he tore his fucking head off right in front of me.'

Joe practically yelled the last part.

Elaine's right hand, perched on Joe's shoulder, fell away. She took several steps back as Phyllis continued to console him, drinking in his image, memorising the blood and thinking, Is some of that his, the man she had thought of as being a sure thing after a decade of fizzle outs?

She felt emptied, scooped hollow by his news.

She did not doubt it, knowing in her bones that it was the truth because of the strangeness that had settled over her town. The same strangeness that made homes that were once warm and wholesome feel haunted. In such times, under such duress, any number of horrors seemed possible.

One of the doors to the station opened and closed, a sieving sound coming from the rubber seal in its frame. The newcomer took in the scene unfolding under the reception area fluorescents with a quick scan, smiling ruefully.

'I hope you're not misleading the law with your tales from the crypt,' remarked Arnie Kauffman, staring at Joe.

5

'How long do you think Dad is going to sit there?' Olive asked her mother.

They were in the kitchen. Despite the late hour, Shirley Launder had decided to bake, most likely because it gave her something to do while her husband held his watch over the fairground. He had done the same the night before after returning from the police station, refusing to go into work the next day, his hunting rifle across his lap and his binoculars close to hand.

Shirley intended to watch with him.

'Until we're safe from those travelers, honey,' was her reply. Her voice was as sweet as syrup.

'Now would you mind going downstairs and getting a jar of peaches for me, without the attitude?'

This last remark was directed at the sigh that had slipped out of Olive. She seemed to sigh a lot these days, usually at something her parents did.

Jars and cans were stored down in the cellar, a place that normally freaked Olive out. The air was always cold and damp and great weaves of cobwebs hung in the corners, but as she walked through the cellar door she heard her father announce from his post in the living room, 'Well, I don't believe it, that son of a bitch Montague is coming this way,' and she was glad of the task.

Her parents were big figures amongst Marybell's Catholic Church. Olive didn't sigh at this so much as scoff because both her parents seemed to live contradictory lives from its teachings. Teachings such as seeking the good of others, being compassionate and humble, or loving thy neighbour were the opposite of what she associated with their behavior.

Glen Launder owned the largest chicken farm in the county, as well as several hundred properties that happened to home his employees. Henry Grey once told her at school that, 'Your daddy might as well pay my dad half his wage because he takes half of it anyway as rent.'

His words, along with a dozen others who had made similar comments, made her take a real look at her father. She didn't like what she saw. She still loved him; he was her father after all, but she no longer accepted that everything he believed or did was right.

So Olive didn't mind descending the cellar's creaky staircase if it provided her with the opportunity to avoid the confrontation about to erupt. Montague, the man her father had cursed out, was probably on their doorstep to make peace. From what she had heard about town, having been forbidden from the carnival, the owner seemed to be a nice gentleman.

She heard her father's footfalls thunder towards the front door.

'Cripes,' she said, realising she had not propped the cellar door open.

The thing sat a few centimeters off the kitchen floor, causing it to forever swing shut. Olive could see this now as the light cast from the kitchen down the staircase was slowly being cut off by the door's closing shadow. She threw a glance behind her just in time to hear her father greet Montague.

'Well, well, well, it looks like someone's forgotten to stay away.'

Then the door shut, trapping her in darkness.

6

Joe's head pivoted in the direction of the newcomer.

Elaine recognised him from the search parties by his clothes, trousers with red suspenders draped over his naked, hairless torso, the skin muddy in colour from too much sun. A trilby hat crowned his head, tilted at a jaunty angle.

Joe's eyes, which had been wide before, now looked ready to fall out of his skull. For the second time, Elaine compared his reaction to that of a child's, thinking this was how he looked when he had been terrified of such things as monsters under the bed. It was a laughable thought, yet she felt no humour in it.

There was too much conviction in his expression for her liking. It made that small chip of ice in her heart seem to expand outward until her whole body shuddered with it, her skin once more erupting into goose bumps; it hurt.

Without thinking, her hand went to the butt of her revolver. Arnie's eyes flickered from her hand to her face.

'This can be easy,' he said.

His teeth seemed to grow under the bright fluorescents as he grinned.

'If you just give him to me no one has to get hurt. Plus, he wants to come with; he's just in shock is all. He wants to see Daisy. She's alive, Joe, and she's happier than she's ever been in her life. You don't know what it's like to be one of us. You've come into this story at the wrong time, a tragic time, and it's no surprise that you would react this way. We don't blame you for what happened to Carmen. Your actions were perfectly justifiable. It was wrong for us to put you in that position without fully explaining the situation. If we had, you would see what it looks like from our side.'

Elaine swayed on her feet to the cadence of Arnie's speech. His voice was like music, lulling her into the most relaxed form of being she had ever known, feeling no fear, or worry, or insecurity.

Even the sight of the carny's eyes shining with silver light didn't disturb her.

She was weightless and untethered. Whatever he was offering, she wanted to accept and float away with him.

'Come back with me and I will explain everything.'

There was a second's pause where Elaine, Phyllis, Collins, and Mark stood enraptured with Arnie's words as Joe stared into his shining eyes.

'Go fuck yourself,' he replied.

7

And like that the spell was broken. Later, she would like to think that she had come out of whatever trance Arnie had her under by herself, but she knew that wasn't true. They came out of it, all of them, because the carny had lost his temper. All rueful humour had vanished from his expression.

'He's not going anywhere with you,' snapped Phyllis, coming to her senses first.

She put herself between Joe and Arnie.

'He's staying right here and so are you until we get this mess sorted out.'

Elaine watched as Arnie dismissively looked away, rolling his eyes. It was a feint. His right hand whipped up and slashed through the air in front of Phyllis with fingernails that had elongated to talons.

Arterial blood sprayed the reception area, dosing Elaine, partially blinding her so that her vision was all red. It sprung from the slash in Phyllis's throat.

The woman she thought of as the mother of the Marybell police department clutched at the wound while staggering across the reception area.

Her hands stopped the shower of blood, but it continued to bleed through her fingers and down her front. Collins went to her, going down on one knee as she collapsed into his arms, producing sucking noises as she tried to breathe.

Elaine wiped at her face, still seeing red, wondering where Arnie was.

For a few brief moments, her senses were reduced to hearing alone because not only could she feel the blood on her, but she could also taste and smell it. She heard Len beating on the bars of his cell, yelling, 'Kill it, kill it, Stone!' She heard the jingle of the jail cell keys on Stone's belt. She could hear Collins muttering repeatedly, 'Oh god, oh god, oh god, oh sweet JESUS!'

She had no idea where Arnie was, or Joe.

Finally, she managed to wipe one eye clear enough to see, and through her blurred vision she saw that Arnie Kauffman had not moved. He stood before the double doors of the station, his eyes closed, his fanged mouth hanging wide as an inhumanly long tongue stretched out. His face was bliss.

By the time Elaine had her other eye clear, the tongue had retracted into his mouth with a smack. His gaze fell on her.

'That was nice,' he said.

Vampire, her mind spat at her.

Elaine drew her revolver only to find Collins was in the way, cradling Phyllis's now dead body. Arnie took advantage of this by seizing the Sergeant's head between his hands. There was a brutal snap of bone and suddenly she was staring into her colleague's face, his eyes wide with surprise.

Arnie had twisted Collins's head around the wrong way.

She screamed as her two colleagues slumped into a pile before her. The vampire smiled, stepping over them, coming for her with his hands held aloft like a preacher giving a sermon, his body painted in ropes of blood.

Mark watched all this from the doorway to the jail cells. He had a clear shot on the creature that was advancing towards his colleague, yet despite Len's urges, he couldn't draw his gun. He was frozen stiff at the sight of its horrendous mouth, the serene enjoyment on its face as it kept coming.

8

Olive could have walked back upstairs and propped the door open. If she had done that she might have been condemned to the same fate as the rest of her family. She was, however, used to the dark and the cold and the door shutting on her, plus she knew there was a flashlight on a shelf at the bottom of the stairs. So, taking it cautiously, she continued her descent.

'Yes, rules,' she heard the muffled voice of the carnival owner.

It sounded regal and somehow snobby to her.

Footfalls echoed above her that caused her to pause with both hands gripping the banisters on either side of her. Had Montague just walked into her home uninvited? As if to confirm her question she heard her father's voice.

'Wait, what are you doing? You can't just walk in here. Hey. HEY!'

A loud thud resonated from upstairs, above and to Olive's left where the front hall was.

'The rules have changed, Mr. Launder. There is no need for pretenses between us anymore.'

9

The revolver coughed in Elaine's hands. She had fired out of fear, not precision, and the slug passed over the creature's shoulder, shattering the glass of one of the station doors. He was at her before she could fire again.

His left hand enveloped her wrist, squeezing. Her bones screamed and so did she as they crunched within her.

Her revolver hit the linoleum with a thud.

The vampire grabbed her by the uniform, lifting her off the floor until her head dangled above its grinning mouth. Its fangs were like shark's teeth - diamond-shaped and many. Its breath was hot, moist, and putrid, reminding her of graveyard earth, blood, and dead things.

The creature started to lower her head towards its jaws.

Joe shoved his elbow through the glass case, aware of what was happening behind him. The emotion that had warred with him upon entering the station had been briefly swept aside as Arnie had attempted to seduce him.

Like Montague's try before, it had no effect on him.

He didn't understand why, only that instead of being hypnotised by this creature, he had seen him for what he truly was: a fiend. He had seen the smarmy attitude that existed in it, the same self-important superiority that it carried itself with as it murdered the clumsy Sergeant.

Observing this galvanised something in Joe. Something like bile burned up from his stomach into his throat. It was anger.

Moving fast, he pulled the fire axe from the glass case on the wall. Turning back, he saw that the creature he had thought of as his friend was paying him no mind. His attentions were entirely on the deputy he held above him.

The other deputy stood off to the left, stiff and white-faced. Useless.

'Hey, fuck face,' he called.

The creature's eyes, which were now red and bug-like, snapped to him.

Seizing the axe's shaft by the end, Joe charged forward. Arnie maintained his hold of the deputy while tensing for the attack.

At the last second, Joe dropped to the floor, sliding across the linoleum with a squeak, under Arnie's right arm, which had snatched at him. He cleaved the fire axe into the flesh above the creature's left ankle, feeling barely any resistance.

Arnie let out a shriek, dropping the deputy as he tried to maintain his balance on one good leg. He couldn't and began to topple forward.

Joe moved with a grace that he never knew he possessed. His legs propelled him into a stance while his arms continued to swing the axe, using the momentum from his slide in a circular motion above him. He completed the circle by bringing the blade down upon the back of Arnie's head. As the carny met the floor with his face, the axe chopped through his skull and brain until the blade sliced into the linoleum floor.

Her father's screams had stopped some time ago. Olive guessed he was either dead or knocked out. Her mother was still alive; she could hear her padding about the kitchen linoleum directly overhead while another, heavier, set of footfalls came after her around the kitchen table. She had no clue as to where her brother was and only prayed he had had the good sense to flee.

She had locked herself in the cellar's pantry room, hoping whatever it was upstairs didn't come down there and if it did, that it wouldn't notice the pantry door, which was identical in appearance to the walls of the cellar, an intended design by her father after he had read about safe rooms in some magazine.

As she had slid the bolt across the door, her eardrums had filled with the boom of her mother's .38, each one making her flinch as she stared at the floorboards above. That had been six shots ago. Now, she heard the gun clatter to the floor, empty. There was a moment of silence that hung heavy and pregnant with tension, as Olive stained to hear some sound that confirmed it was over.

'Thankfully, you're not much of a shot,' she heard Montague's voice say, stealing the air from her lungs. 'You almost got me there.'

'Get away from me, demon.'

Olive heard him utter a dry, mocking chuckle. Heavy footfalls echoed down from overhead, stalking steps that she followed, blinking away the dust they caused to rain down from the cracks between the floorboards.

'You believe that book will protect you?' he asked.

At his words, Olive knew then what her mother was doing. The .38 hadn't worked, so she had resorted to using her Bible. She could hear

309

her mother's steps, lighter than those of her stalker, off to the far right. Olive conjured up the kitchen with its yellow walls and linoleum floor in her mind; she saw her mother being backed into the corner where the countertops met, their dark wood cluttered with her mother's baking supplies.

'Get back. Leave this house. In the name of God, I command you.'

'Don't you dare think you can command me!' shouted Montague. 'My kind have existed long before yours decided to raise those icons. I spit on your crucifix, on your holy water, on your good book. All your talismans were invented just so your kind could curl up at night and feel safe from mine. It's how the human mind copes when it meets the real top of the food chain. You turn us into legends that have to be invited in. Well, Mrs. Launder, we aren't legends. We're flesh and blood like you, only hungrier.'

Her mother didn't scream as her father had. Olive guessed whatever the creature was hadn't given her the chance. Olive heard her feet tap dancing on the floor above instead, alongside wet ripping sounds.

12

The reception area was filled with the sound of hard breathing. From the cells, Len shouted, 'What was that? What happened? Someone talk to me!' No one did. They were too busy staring at the body, with its split skull.

Blood that was so dark it was almost purple was pooling underneath it.

Elaine, who had landed on her ass beside the grotesquery, butt-shuffled backward until she struck the reception desk. She looked to Joe standing above the body of the thing that had attacked them all. He had entered into the station in a shambling mess; now he stood posed for action, his chest expanding and shrinking in a steady rhythm as he stared at the dead thing.

He had saved her life, probably all of their lives.

'The carnies, they're like vampires,' he said, staring at the corpse. 'I think one of them got Lily Grey and the rest covered it up. They go from town to town putting on this play of being a carnival and hiring people to work, then when they leave town they take them with to feed on them. That's what they were going to do with Daisy and me, except it all got messed up when Lily went missing. When they look at you, really look at you, you can tell that they're hungry or thirsty or whatever. Not like us. They can't be satisfied.'

Elaine rose to her feet, nursing her injured hand against her chest. The pain in it was like a thousand wasp stings.

'That would explain what happened to the Teals.'

'We've got to call the police!' cried Mark, stumbling around the desk and seizing the phone.

'We are the police,' remarked Elaine.

'I mean the real police, with fucking SWAT teams and big ass guns!' he shouted back to her.

He looked like he was about to say more when a puzzled look fell over his panicked, sweaty face. He began mashing the phone repeatedly upon the receiver, returning it to his ear each time to listen.

'The lines are out,' he eventually said in a deflated tone. He let the phone drop to the linoleum. 'The fucking phones are out. What are we going to do?'

No one answered him.

Elaine had retrieved her revolver from the floor with her uninjured hand. She had stepped around Arnie's corpse to the bodies of her colleagues. If not for the sickening angle of Collins's head or Phyllis's bloody appearance, they would have looked like lovers who had fallen asleep in an embrace.

From the jail cells, they heard the sound of someone sobbing. It was Len Grey; he had heard everything Joe had said.

13

'Mark, unlock the jail cell and let Grey out,' Elaine ordered. 'Then go into the armory and unlock some of the Remingtons, one each. There could be more of these fuckers.'

Not caring that technically, he was the senior officer due to time served, Mark jogged into the cell area, keys rattling. All he wanted was to forget.

He wanted to forget and go home to Teresa, his wife, and James, his son, and board up all the windows in their house until morning came. But morning wouldn't matter, he realised, because he had seen these people in the day, he had worked with them across the fields and through the woods searching for a little girl's body. This was not a nightmare that could be dispelled by the daylight. This was a terror that lurked in the day as well as night, as real as the cancer that had taken his father, as the casual racism he experienced now and then.

There would be no escaping this, in the same way there would be no escaping those things unless something was done about it. Only Mark had joined the force for a reliable paycheck, not to be a hero. So when he heard Elaine Green say as he unlocked Grey's cell, 'We need to go after them,' his mind was already made up.

14

'They have Daisy and I think Meryl Grey,' said Joe, pulling the fire axe from the floor where the blade had eventually buried itself.

It came free with a scrape of metal on stone. As it did, the top of Arnie's head rolled onto its crown, exposing the wrinkled sponge of grey brain to the ceiling and allowing more blood to pool on the linoleum. His trilby hat remained on as if attached somehow.

We'll never get that out, thought Elaine. *Even if there is some industrial bleach strong enough, I'll never be able to walk into this place again without seeing the blood.*

She was at the station's front door beside Joe, feeling the wind as it churned outside through the shattered panel. She could smell the gritty aroma tarmac gives off after spending a day baking in the sun. She could hear the buzz of the streetlights, the tick of the Blazer's engine as it cooled nearby.

'Do you think he came alone?' she asked Joe, scanning the street.

From all appearances, it was deserted, nothing unusual for just after 10 p.m. on a Wednesday in Marybell. Still, it was quiet, even for the town.

Elaine realised that her body had once again erupted into goose bumps like it had at the Teals. She felt as she had then, that something was watching them just outside the peripheral of her vision.

'No,' Joe answered in that same hard voice she had marveled at earlier.

It had been fourteen minutes since he had burst inside the station, weeping like a child. In those fourteen minutes, a monster that looked like a man and shouldn't exist had slaughtered two of her colleagues. Now, Joe stood beside her with a fire axe in his hands and eyes that said he was ready to use it. She hoped it lasted, that he wouldn't regress to that sniveling version from earlier.

The lights winked out overhead.

15

'Mark!' Elaine shouted, fleeing down a corridor to the armory.

There were too many windows at the front of the building for her liking. She could hear Joe running behind her, still clutching the axe.

'I'm here!' Mark yelled as they entered the armory.

Mark and Grey were stuffing two backpacks with ammunition. They also had two Remington shotguns each.

'I can't use them,' said Elaine, holding up her injured hand.

Instead, she swapped her revolver for a Beretta. When Joe came forward to do the same, Mark asked him, 'Do you know how to use that?'

The two police officers exchanged a glance.

'I mean this guy was a suspect not five minutes ago.'

This was Mark to Elaine, speaking as if Joe didn't exist.

The station's armory had a small shooting range for the building with the department's weaponry confined to a set of gun cabinets. Joe retrieved a Beretta from the table the two men had been using, stepped over to one of the firing lanes, and aimed at the hanging silhouette some thirty feet away.

The dusty air filled with the roar of a firing handgun.

Joe fired eight shots in total, squeezing the trigger in a quick, yet controlled manner in sync with his breathing. There were four holes clustered in the torso of the paper target, another four grouped in its head.

'Holy cow,' muttered Grey, in awe.

The air was now singed with the explosive scent of gunfire.

'Who taught you to shoot like that?' Mark asked.

'My father was a military man,' Joe replied, replacing the Beretta's clip with a fresh one.

The trio looked to one another as this mysterious stranger who had entered the normality of their lives and upheaved them into chaos strapped a holster to his hip. Each of them sensed that there was the thread of a story there, each of them afraid to pull on it in case it invited further madness upon them.

Mark found he hated Joe then; after all, he brought the monster to them, introducing the concept that such unbelievable fantasies existed. As the young man armed himself, he couldn't help but glare at him with gritted teeth.

'Well, if those things think we slipped out the back before, they don't now,' commented Elaine on Joe's shooting.

'That's exactly what we need to be doing,' said Mark, tasting blood.

He turned, spat, observed that the teardrop of salvia that hit the cement floor was scarlet and turned back.

'This isn't a standoff like in some western where we all take the moral high ground by risking our lives for some cause. We have families to think about. Elaine, you have your parents. Len, you have yours.'

'I do; my eldest is at home looking after the twins. According to this one,' said Len, pointing at Joe, 'they have my wife at the carnival. If they do, then they'll surely know where we live. I'm not leaving them alone for those things.'

Grey gazed at them all with watery eyes, his jaw clenched, as if whatever warred within him, he was caging away.

'You can take one of the cruisers out front and go to them,' offered Elaine.

'Thank you. I need to take them somewhere safe, then I can think about going back for Meryl.'

'I think we should take a cruiser each and leave,' said Mark.

'We can't just slink away,' Elaine countered, outraged. 'This is our town, our station, our job. People will come here if they need help. What if they run into one of those things? For all we know, they could be everywhere.'

'He's right,' said Joe, speaking at last. 'We all should leave.'

Elaine wheeled on him only to see he wasn't sniveling. The hard look he had had out front was still in his face only, instead of it being injustice or contempt for those things, in his eyes there was fear.

Despair fell over her like a shroud in seeing that look.

'There's forty of them and four of us, we wouldn't have a hope in hell going up against them,' Joe told them all.

'They murdered my daughter,' Len spat at him. 'They murdered her. After all that time spent wandering through fields searching for some sign of what happened to her, now you're going to give up because you're scared of what you've found?'

'Yes,' replied Joe, his gaze meeting Len's glare, unflinching. 'I'm sorry about your daughter, about your wife, but I've seen what those things are. There's no way I'm going back there.'

'What about your little girlfriend?' Len spoke in almost a whisper, all of the fury burnt out, replaced with a loathing for the man opposite him.

'Daisy, what about her? You said she was still alive, are you going to leave her too?'

Joe Cage didn't answer. His gaze dropped from Len's.

'Coward,' said Len, in a croak.

'I'll help you get your wife back after we pick up your kids and my folks,' said Elaine. 'We'll take them to the Teals'; it's probably the safest place right now. No one will think to look there. Mark, you're welcome to bring your family, too. I'll see if I can find Daisy.'

Joe thought to tell her that it was hopeless, but as he opened his mouth to do so, the sound of glass shattering came from the front of the building.

'Let's see if we can get to the vehicles out front,' said Elaine, leading them to back to the reception area.

The window by Collins's desk had been broken by what looked like a Molotov cocktail. His desk and chair were in flames, along with several others.

'The bodies are gone,' said Mark.

It was true. The place where the bodies of Arnie, Phyllis, and Collins had lain showed only bloody stains. Seeing the vacant space they had occupied was somehow more terrifying for all four of them than the fire.

'We can't stay here,' said Grey, racketing his shotgun.

'Okay, let's be careful about this,' said Elaine, stepping outside, Beretta held in her uninjured hand.

The three followed her, leaving behind whatever little sanctuary the police station had offered.

16

Launder woke to find he was hanging upside down. The world was dark around him while his body ached from what he soon discovered were chains crisscrossed over him, pinning his arms to his sides, trapping his legs together. With a grunt of effort, he managed to lift his head enough to see the chains extended from his feet to loop around a wooden beam.

He was in the barn, which his family used for storage. The smell of ancient dust and bird droppings stung his nostrils.

'Ah, you're awake,' said a voice. 'That's good. I'm almost done with this one.'

Montague sat on top of a woodpile some ten feet from him. In his jaws, he held Daniel's limp body and was wringing him the way a person wrings a dishcloth to remove water. The carnival owner's mouth was embedded in the crook of the boy's left collar, his cheeks smeared red as if with jam. From the pale hue of his skin and the boneless way his limbs dangled in Montague's hands, Launder could tell he was dead.

'You fucking bastard.'

Launder revolted, his body lashing out as a worming entity, causing him to pendulum over the floor of the barn. Tears burned in his eyes.

Unperturbed, Montague tossed the boy's corpse to the side. His front was slick and tacky with blood. He brushed at it absently.

'So dramatic,' he remarked, gripping the chains that bound Launder, steadying him. 'There's no need for that now. It makes you look small'

'I'll fucking kill you,' Launder spat.

'Not likely,' replied Montague. 'Where's that lovely daughter of yours, Glen? I think I've earned the right to call you Glen now, seeing as I've murdered your wife and son. Yes, Shirley's dead too. I had her in the kitchen over the baking trays. But where's your daughter tonight? I couldn't find her anywhere. Tell me where she is and I might consider letting you walk free.'

Montague shoved him gently so that he swayed backward. The further he moved, the tighter the chains grew around his chest, making him wheeze.

'She's staying over at a friend's house.'

'Really, which friend?' asked Montague, grasping the back of his head with his dirtied fingers and raising it to look at him.

Launder saw that man's eyes had become two shining silver stars. A sensation of light-headedness gnawed at his mind, making him sleepy, seducing him into telling. Yet he could still smell the blood. He remembered how easily Montague had hurled him across the living room into the wall. He remembered his wife's screams and the sound of gunshots as he slipped into unconsciousness and thought, *Somehow Olive's gotten out.*

'I dunno which friend it is,' Launder answered. 'She's got a dozen and Shirley usually keeps track of them. Why don't you go ask her?'

Montague released his head with a sigh. The way Daniel's blood beaded the creature's beard reminded Launder of water on a rat's whiskers.

'Boss,' said another voice.

Launder's eyes snapped to the left, seeing two figures materialise out of the barn's darkness. One was tall and well-built, the other short and squat. He recognised the tall one as the man who had waded towards him after striking Montague with the rock.

'Yes?'

'Arnie's dead,' the tall one said.

There was nothing but silence as Montague stared at the two.

'Joe Cage killed him. He... '

The tall man's mouth shut with a clap as Montague let out a howl of rage that shook Launder's eardrums. He stamped his right foot, his eyes filling with crimson light, kicking up the earth from the barn's floor in a spray. The action was so like Daniel when he was throwing a tantrum that it filled Launder's heart with longing for his child, whose body lay not eight feet away. He wanted to crawl over to him and hug him against his chest tight, burying his face in his dark hair, which would smell of that boy scent, of shampoo and sunshine and earth and young imaginings.

Montague had ceased his anguished howl, his fingers relaxing and loosening into fists at his sides, staring at the two cowering men. Launder couldn't help himself. He understood he wasn't going to make it out of this situation alive and that most of his family was dead. He thought of Olive in that moment and how she had somehow evaded capture.

He prayed that she remained safe and then he spoke.

'Don't be so dramatic now. It makes you look small.'

Montague's red gaze snapped onto him. Launder committed his final act on Earth and sneered at him.

The carnival owner plunged his right hand into the man's chest, ripping out his heart with a meaty slap. Launder's body began to pendulum underneath the beam, chains jingling, his expression frozen in place, mocking him. Yelling, Montague tossed the heart aside and raked his claws across the man's face until it resembled red pulp and the air was misted with his blood.

When he was done, he was breathing hard, breathing in the man's life fluid.

'There's something else you should know,' said Earl.

'What?' he snapped, wheeling on them.

The two flinched once more as the news spilled out of Earl like water from a tap. When he was done, a grin spread across Montague's blood-caked face.

'He'll be coming home then. Tell everyone to come back to the campsite. I won't run the risk of losing anyone else tonight.'

Chapter Four

Runaway

1

The streets beyond the police station car park were deserted. Nothing stirred but the steady hum of electricity from the streetlights. The almost-soundless town gave the impression of peace and serenity.
Those exiting the station knew better.
'You take the Ford, Len, and we'll meet you at the Teals',' Elaine instructed.
As she did not instruct Joe and no one was motioning towards the sheriff's Blazer, it seemed it was his. Joe paused, one foot in the vehicle, one foot on the tarmac.
'Grey,' he called.
Lily Grey's father looked at him, his grey eyes like steel.
'I think it was Lou Fritz.'
Joe wanted to add more and couldn't, found he was incapable of explaining what needed to be explained. However, Len Grey, who had called him a coward minutes ago, nodded at him in understanding.
Joe heaved his tired body into the Blazer.

2

Joe glanced into the rearview mirror, looking to see the road behind him and instead seeing his bloody reflection. Unable to help himself, he used the mirror to examine his injured neck, which was bruised around two neat puncture marks. At least he hoped they were bruised, and not infected.

Will I turn into one of them?

Already, his mind whirled through the characteristics of vampires. Yes, vampires, that's what he had called them, and he guessed that was the closest definition to what they were. The only thing Joe knew about such creatures was from Hollywood, and the carnies didn't seem to be obeying the movie rules, such as being unable to walk in sunlight and sleeping in coffins.

Joe snorted at the thought; there was nothing else he could do.

Soon, he was laughing, shaking his head, thumping the steering wheel with his palm. The whole thing seemed ludicrous and insane.

The bite marks on his neck told a different story.

In seeing them, he heard the sound of a chain being pulled taut. If he were to ever tell his life story to anyone, surely they would think he was crazy for thinking up such a story. Yet the phantom sensation around his right wrist, like the bite marks, told him it wasn't some fantasy.

The carnies were vampires of a sort, as real as the nightmare figure in his past who had locked those chains around his wrists. And just like back then, he was reacting the same, by running away.

Joe heard Len Grey's voice calling him a coward. The word echoed in his head, making the hairs on his arms stand erect, making Marybell's barren streets seem even more hostile, making him feel even more alone.

No, I'm not a coward, I've just snapped is all. I've snapped like I did back in Indiana and now I'm running, running to save my skin.

323

His eyes glanced into the mirror and in that second when his eyes left the road, the Blazer's right wheel struck the curb, mounting it. A fire hydrant loomed beneath the whiskey-coloured streetlights and he imagined walking Marybell's empty streets without the protection the car offered. He yanked the wheel to the left, causing whatever Jackson had in the back to thud about.

When the Blazer was running straight and smooth, he once more risked another glance at the mirror. As he did, the memory of Len Grey's voice asked him, 'What about your little girlfriend?'

There was nothing I could do. I barely got out of there alive. I didn't have time to even think about her.

This did not change the molten ball of guilt in his stomach. Or the heart-wrenching pain knowing his memories of Daisy Hill would be placed behind another dam within his mind, to become ghosts that would haunt him, as those of his family had.

Once more, Len Grey told him he was a coward.

His reflection showed tears brimming in his eyes now as he left the last streetlight behind. His vision immediately reduced to the twenty-feet of tarmac illuminated before the Blazer's headlights. Everything else was in darkness, which seemed to flood through the windows as thick as tar.

His hands were sweating against the wheel's leather.

I should go back.

Tears rained down his grimy cheeks.

Daisy would have gone back for me.

That was true, he knew that in his bones. She was far tougher than him.

'Coward,' said Grey.

His tears glistened in the green glow from the dashboard dials. Sobs hitched in his chest. Whatever was in the trunk moved again.

Joe wiped at his wet cheeks, glancing in the mirror. Something in the corner of his reflection moved. He tilted the mirror for a better look of the back seat just in time to see a hand fall over the headrests.

3

Joe stomped onto the brakes, causing the tires to squeal as they dug for purchase. Everything inside the Blazer felt like it was attached to a bungee rope that was playing out. He could feel his nose getting closer and closer to the steering wheel. Then the whole vehicle jolted to a halt, his seatbelt biting into his torso, flinging him back into the seat as the thing in the trunk sailed past in a white blur before shattering through the windscreen.

4

Groaning, Joe groped for the seatbelt release as the Blazer's tires hissed with heat. A stripe of pain throbbed across his body where the belt had clamped down. Eventually, he unclipped it, allowing him to breathe the burned rubber scent with ease.

Joe didn't notice; his eyes were fixed on the figure lying face down on the tarmac. She was caught in the beam of the headlights, dressed not in the clothes that he had last seen her in, but in a white summer dress. Powdered glass surrounded her, glittering like crushed diamonds against the tarmac.

From the spill of her golden hair, he knew who she was.

This could be a trap, he thought, stepping out of the vehicle.

Joe spied into the rows between the corn stalks; the night's darkness was impenetrable as ever; he saw nothing.

They could be anywhere.

Glass crunched under his feet as he moved around the driver's door, his eyes flickering left and right. Suddenly, he found his shadow stretching out across the tarmac, draping over the motionless woman as he entered the beam of the vehicle's yellow headlights.

'Daisy,' he called, surprised at how quiet he sounded, how scared.

Joe stepped closer.

'Daisy.'

In the yellow spill of light, he saw her splayed fingers flex. There was the tinkle of glass as the woman in the white dress rolled onto her back.

Joe drew his Beretta from his holster.

Daisy, because he could see he had been right, sat up. This was accompanied by the sound of snapping bone.

Her left arm hung at an unnatural angle at the elbow. It was reconfiguring back into place in a series of sharp, jerking movements. The same thing happened with her face, which had been frayed when she skidded across the road's surface at high speed. The skin there seemed to knit back together as if no damage had ever been done.

In the yellow light, he saw two neat puncture marks on Daisy's neck. His insides, which had been squirming in revulsion, grew heavy.

Daisy was on her knees now, her eyes still closed, as they had been this entire time. Her dreadlocks were gone, replaced by flowing curls of gold that seemed more offensive than anything else did to Joe. He had always thought of her dreadlocks as a physical manifestation of Daisy's abrasive personality, a middle finger thrown at a suit and gown event.

Suddenly, the dam of memory crumbled and he was flooded with her. Daisy swimming in the lagoon inches from him. Daisy laughing in her unique way, throwing her head back, eyes squeezed shut. Daisy, with her body heat, sleeping beside him in her station wagon. And a hundred more memories tumbled within his skull, all threaded together by feelings of love.

It wasn't that he loved her then; it was that he had always loved her and was only just realising it. He loved this crazy, hurricane force of a woman who had entered his life, which made his heart tear even more as he placed the barrel of his gun in the middle of her forehead.

'I can smell the blood in your mouth,' she said, finally opening her eyes.

5

They weren't silver or red; they were the same arctic blue that he had come to know. They were Daisy's eyes, gazing up at him, filling with tears.

'They changed me,' she howled and the night air echoed with her anguish.

In a flutter of wings, birds jettisoned themselves from the corn to the sky. Joe flinched, his eyes squinting, his balls and everything else tightening.

There was humanity in her scream and it was outraged.

'Do it,' she told him. 'Do it, please. I don't want to be like them; they're so hollow. Please, kill me.'

His entire hand felt like it was cramping now.

'I can't.' The words heaved out of his chest, his throat shrinking to a pinpoint.

'I'm sorry...I just...can't.'

'You have to,' she said, grabbing his wrist so he couldn't drop the gun.

She moved like one of them, viper fast. Her fingers ground the bones in his wrist with little effort.

'I won't be one of them. Please.'

Joe's squeezed back on the Beretta's trigger, closing his eyelids.

'Montague did this to me. He came to see me after I left you, saying nice things, his eyes like something out of a dream. Then he bit and drank, but that wasn't the worst, the worst was...when he made me drink from him. I feel so...diseased! Please, Joe. I can't be like them.'

His eyelids had snapped wide at the mention of Montague's name.

'It's early yet. I'm still changing, but I feel their hunger. I felt it when he bit into me. There's an abyss inside of him that can never be filled. It just wants more and more and more. If I get like that, I won't let you end me; instead, I'll rip you apart and...and...feast.'

He stared out into the darkness beyond the beam of the headlights.

'Montague,' he muttered.

'Yes, Montague,' answered Daisy. 'He's their leader. They're all like him and they wanted us both to be like them, but somehow you got away. I don't remember much, it's all hazy. I do know they were mad at you…and Arnie and some of the others put me into the back of that car. He said I was a present for you.'

'They're so clever, aren't they?' said Joe, thinking of the smug look on Montague's face the first night by the campfire.

'This is what they want. They want me to kill you or for you to kill me. It's their plan.'

He made to remove the barrel from her brow and after some resistance, Daisy let him drop his arm to his side. If she wanted to rip him to pieces, now was her chance; he had seen how fast she had moved. She gazed up at him, confused by the faraway look in his eyes as they stared off.

'They're so superior, so frightening. I've known scarier things. That Montague is one smug bastard, though; I've known plenty of monsters like him. Dylan Macintosh was one. My father was another. He was the biggest one of them all, Daisy. Mr. Military Man, out to serve his country, only at home he was a fiend. He…he is the scariest thing I know. And I'm fed up running from him, from all of them. It never ends, running. It will never end unless we do something about it.'

'We?'

'I need your help; this town needs it,' said Joe, dropping to his knees. 'I am so sorry for leaving you. I didn't have a choice, and I am so sorry I didn't come back, but you're still you, I can see that. If you can hold onto yourself, there are people who want to go after them.'

'I could hurt people like this; part of me wants to.'

'Then use it on them, on the monsters that did this to you.'

Daisy sniffed, wiping the tears from her eyes.

'I don't know how long I can hold onto me. If we do this and I start…becoming more…you'll have to shoot me.'

'If it comes to that, we can think…'

'No,' snapped Daisy, her eyes flickering red. 'You shoot me dead. They may have changed me, but I will not become like one of them. Promise me.'

Joe stared at her, seeing no give in her eyes.

'Okay,' he agreed.

'Good. Now then, Rambo, what are you planning?'

Joe heard the old Daisy sarcasm in her voice and smiled. He told her his idea.

'You can make that?' she asked.

'Sure, my father was a military man,' he answered.

Chapter Five

My Father Was A Military Man

1

In the end, after all the avoidance, all it had taken for the dam to crumble was one simple question from Daisy: 'The scars on your wrist, was that your father?' Her tone was light, curious, as the wind buffeted through the Blazer's broken windscreen, rippling through her gold hair. He was driving them to the Teal property, his right hand on the steering wheel's leather, the mottled quality of the skin that encircled his wrist apparent even in the dark, seeming to reflect the goblin green glow from the dash.

'Yeah, that was him,' he said and then it all came spilling out in a flood: the abuse, the beatings, how sometimes he had been chained up inside the family barn for days without food or water for the slightest of slights. His voice wavered at times, but it never broke. In some ways it felt like he was reciting facts for an exam; other times it felt like he was baring his soul. He talked about running away, about his desire to be free, learning as he did that he never really had been. That caging everything inside, especially his guilt for leaving his sister, Harper, prevented him from being free, even though it had been six months since he had fled his home in the middle of the night, when the sky was black velvet above and the land was caked over with snow.

The act of telling freed him, at last, of the weight of his past.

When he had finished, Daisy twined her fingers through his, smiling at him through the dark. She bought his hand to her lips and kissed his knuckles, her touch like silk.

'Of course it takes a life-threatening situation for you to open up,' she remarked.

He smiled at her tightly. *I'm not completely free, not yet.* His thoughts were on Harper, some hundreds of miles away.

2

To his surprise, all the lights were on at the Teal property, including several lanterns strung along the porch of the main house. It was in this lantern light that they discerned a dozen armed individuals, their rifles pointed up.

Judging by the number of vehicles parked outside, Joe guessed the others had managed to gather more than their families to this haven.

Two figures were moving across the dooryard with their guns drawn, forcing Joe to slow the Blazer to a gravel-crunching stop. Through the destroyed windscreen, he could smell the spicy musk belonging to the dust kicked up by the tires. One of the two figures was the blonde deputy from the station.

A flashlight clicked on, its light aimed at his face.

'Had a change of heart?' Elaine asked.

She sounded smug, yet Joe detected a hint of relief in her voice. He looked to Daisy in the passenger seat. Elaine's flashlight beam drifted to her and he registered surprise in her face.

'Something like that,' he replied.

3

Inside the Teal farmhouse was pandemonium. The connected living room/kitchen, with its yellow wallpaper, was choked with bodies, mainly adults standing around looking like they didn't know what to do, while the few children, excited at the prospect of being up so late, chased each other through the forest of legs, giggling. Joe saw Bill Denton, who had cornered him that morning to say, 'I can't understand why Jackson hasn't thrown you in a cell yet,' sipping absently from a Budweiser can, his blue eyes vague and far off. He was surrounded in a semi-circle of men all drinking the same way with same haunted look. There was horror in their faces, but also uncertainty, as if they couldn't decide what they'd seen. Knowing what lurked on the edge of town, Joe wondered what things these people had experienced.

He was not surprised to see Deputy Mark Stone drinking on the arm of a sofa amongst them, still in uniform. A young boy of five was clutched to his chest, asleep with his arms around Mark's neck. The boy's straw-thin legs dangled over his father's left knee, ending in a set of white Nike Airs with a red swish.

'Everybody, can I have your attention?' shouted Elaine.

She said this in the kitchen area, her height and uniform giving her some natural authority so that everyone turned towards her as she stood, hands on her hips, her blue eyes sweeping the crowd until the din eventually died down. They were hard, those eyes, and glazed with loss.

He remembered the way she had reacted when he had announced Jackson's death and thought maybe there was more between them than work colleagues.

As she began telling the others the plan he had come up with, looking for volunteers - he doubted they'd get many - Len sidled up to him as he reclined against one of the kitchen countertops.

'How far did you make it out of town?' he asked in a whisper.

There was none of the malice that he had exhibited back at the station in his craggy features. It seemed that his return, alongside Daisy, was enough for the father of Lily Grey to forgive and forget.

There was also something else that radiated from him, something that Elaine had given off, too, as they spoke outside in the dooryard. It was a type of excitement, but not the bright glee a kid feels in seeing Christmas presents under a tree glittering with lights. No. This was duller, more a confirmation.

Joe looked past him to Daisy, who was closest to the kitchen door, reclining on the opposite counter. Her gold hair hid her features as she stood, head bowed, gazing at the floor as Elaine spoke. She must have sensed his look because she glanced up, her cobalt blue eyes staring through her fringe.

There was rage there, an unfathomable level of it.

'Not far, why?' he said.

'They've got the roads blocked all around town. Alan Marsh got ambushed heading north,' said Len, nodding at a middle-aged man in jeans and plaid beside Bill Denton. While he wasn't drinking, he had the same dazed look as the others.

'They had a trailer across the road. When Alan slowed down, they came in through the windows and dragged two of their party out. One of them was his daughter, the other her fiancé.'

Joe looked at Alan Marsh for support and found only despair there.

'This is all crazy,' announced Bill Denton.

Elaine, who had been speaking, fell silent.

'You sound just like your old man, Elaine Green.'

Joe had no idea what this meant, but he saw Elaine wince.

'Even if we did believe all this about...monsters, what you're talking about is an act of terrorism,' Bill went on, his cheeks flushed red. His eyes, tiny beads of blue within flesh that was sagged and lined, shone with irritation. In the kitchen light – like the wallpaper, it was a mellow yellow colour – the few remaining barbs of hair on his bald hair gleamed silver.

'Plus, we would be relying on this one to make the damn thing,' he said, pointing at Joe. 'Last time I checked, he was one of these carnies not that long ago. Hell, not only that, everyone in this room had him pegged as the kidnapper.'

'I didn't,' said Len Grey, raising his right hand as he did.

Bill's red face glared at Grey, his silver brows knitting together.

'And I'll have no problem building it. My father was a military man, we used to make them all the time back home,' Joe added.

'Are you all mad? I know you certainly are' – Bill pointed at Elaine - 'and there's no way I'm trusting you' – now he pointed at Len - 'and you're not even from around here.' He gestured towards Joe. 'That's beside the point. The point is, there are no such things as vampires.'

On the peripheral of his vision, Joe noticed Daisy's head shoot up. She was glaring at Bill

Denton, but not enough to make her eyes flash, he saw.

'What are we going after next? The boogeyman?'

Despite the haunted looks on the faces of those surrounding Bill, no one corrected him, nor did they join him as he laughed. They just stood, their vague appearance reminding Joe of mannequins in a store window.

'So you think we're lying?'

The question came from Daisy, stepping away the counter she was reclining against. Bill Denton stopped laughing, though his Cheshire cat grin remained as his beady gaze slid up and down her body as she stalked towards him.

His eyes didn't look irritated anymore, but happy. Happy to be listened to, to be in the spotlight.

'And here's the other tumbleweed that's rolled into town,' he said. 'What are you going to do, tell me some motivational story that's going to make me join your band of merry soldiers?'

As Daisy passed Joe, he got a waft of her scent. Not campfires and sun beaten skin; instead she smelled sweet, overly so.

'Do you think everyone is just gathered here for fun?' Daisy asked him. 'Have you given any thought as to where the family is that own this place? You know, the one that's in all the photographs on the walls? I don't see them here, do you?'

Bill's grin dipped slightly at the corners.

'Why, are you scared, just like everyone else here?'

'I'm not scared...'

'Yes, you are. I can smell it on you. You're scared and you have every right to be, but you're also a fool if you think you can hide out here and

336

not have them come after you. The things that took the Teals and Lily Grey.'

'Listen, girlie, there are no such things…'

Bill Denton was jabbing a finger at Daisy when she moved. The whole group gasped. Alan Marsh screamed, shrill and pained.

'That's one of them. That's one, that's one,' he shrieked

Bill Denton out weighted Daisy by a hundred pounds. That didn't seem to matter. She slapped his hand out of the way, gripped his biceps, pinching him between arms that were like pistons as she lifted him, all in the time it took Joe to leap from his reclined position against the counter. Len followed him.

Neither moved to stop Daisy as she slammed her forehead into Bill's, her eyes blazing scarlet.

'There's no such thing as what?' she shouted, her canines long and pointed.

4

'Well, that was something,' said Len Grey, taking a seat beside Joe.

They were on the porch, looking out on fields veiled in darkness. Somewhere in that murk was Daisy; she had run off after what happened. From inside the farmhouse came the agitated murmur of many voices in discussion. Joe could feel their hysteria as he sat, a barely controlled thing that flopped like a fish in their grasp.

He paid it no mind; that sense of confirmation, dull yet overwhelming, was guiding him, or more accurately propelling him, the way being locked into one of the carnival's rides would. Towards what? The fair? Death? He didn't know, nor did he seem to care. That confirmation was dampening any fears or trepidation he had, but it was more than that. There was a desire that was all his own to run towards something rather than away.

'Think she's coming back?'

'She will, she just needs some time,' Joe replied, examining the objects he had gathered from Philip Teal's tool supplies.

He just needed one more component to make it work.

'Montague did that to her,' Joe explained to Len. 'He had one of the others try to do the same to me.'

'Jesus,' said Grey and then added, 'Though if you were like her that might improve our chances.'

'I don't know, I'm not as strong as Daisy is.'

Joe studied the man beside him who he had, until tonight, begun to think of as The Grey Man on account of his dour countenance. There was none of that depressive vacancy in his appearance now; now he looked energized.

'You've changed your tune,' he said.

'How do you mean?'

'Before, with Montague, you were acting…'

'Crazed,' offered Len as Joe struggled to find an inoffensive way to say what he wanted to say.

'Well, yeah and before that, during the searches, you pretty much looked like a zombie.'

'Funny, my son said the same thing the other night,' he said, staring off into the darkness.

The night was still beyond the porch and not a breeze stirred, as if the fields beyond were holding their breath. Even the sound of the cows mooing in the barn sounded timid, as if they were hesitant to break whatever peace held their surroundings.

'I guess I know what the truth is now,' Len told him. 'I know what's been going on, what needs to be done and I'm content with that.'

Joe nodded, understanding.

'So, you're coming with? What about the kids?'

'I have to. Meryl is still with them. I'm a lot things, a sorry sack of shit for a husband being the primary one, but I'm not about to let my wife down, not this time. As for the twins, Henry, my eldest, is looking after them and he's doing a finer job of it than I would in his position. The kid is a saint; he gets that from his mother.'

'You think …'

'Yep, I think she's alive. I know she is, and I think those bastards will keep her that way. That little trick of putting your girlfriend in that car means they expect you to come back to them.'

'That's what I'm hoping,' Joe remarked.

'But they're scheming bastards as well, from everything that I've seen,' added Len. 'I think they'll have her alive still, just in case you turn up with the cavalry, all guns blazing. Is there anything more that you need?'

Len nodded to the apparatuses Joe had collected so far.

'There is one more thing.'

He reached to his left, the shovel's blade lifting from the porch boards with a metal chime and handed it to Len. Lily's father admired it, stabbing the blade into the floor as he did, right hand on the smooth wooden handle.

'I need manure, a whole lot of it.'

'No problem, I'm used to shoveling shit. It's part of my job. I might as well do it here; never knew I was training for something like this'.

'What do you do?' Joe asked.

'Why, I work on one of Launder's chicken farms,' he said, standing with the shovel. His knees popped like firecrackers as he did.

Footsteps approached them from around the corner of the house, the porch boards dipping and rising, recalling the sound a boardwalk makes stretching out over water. A tired Elaine Green came up to them.

'What's the verdict?' asked Len.

'It's just us.' The sorrow in her voice was palpable. 'They think they can wait it out here, stick their heads in the sand.'

Joe felt sorrow, but only for Elaine's disappointment. Searching his feelings, he realised that dull confirmation was at play once more, shooting them down a track in the dark towards the unknown. This task, the task of cleaning up Marybell, was theirs, the outsiders; even Elaine and Len wore those labels he saw now, Elaine for being the only female in a position of authority, and Len for how the town perceived him and his family. Offering the others a chance to aid them had been a token gesture at best. Joe found himself smiling, his grin grim, leaving him feeling like a lunatic.

'Four against forty,' Len commented. 'What was it you said about those odds, kid?'

'That was before you had me,' replied a voice in the darkness.

Daisy stepped into the light, no longer in the white dress. She wore blue jeans, a faded AC/DC t-shirt, and her cowboy boots. The boots had been the only item of clothing that the carnies had dressed her in. She had cut her hair as well, shaving it short, her fringe forming a blonde fin that affirmed her elfin look.

'If you leave your mouth open any longer something is going to fly in there and call it home,' Grey whispered loudly in his ear.

'Where did you get those clothes?' asked Elaine.

'Found them upstairs.'

'When were you upstairs?' This time it was Joe asking, knowing she hadn't gotten past him as he sat.

'There was a window open on the second floor.' Daisy shrugged.

The trio on the porch craned their heads upward.

Chapter Six

The Frozen Children

1

'How are you doing?' Joe asked, the chain of his handcuffs jingling as he shuffled in the backseat. They were locked tight enough that the metal bit his wrists.

There was a brief moment when Len had snapped them on him that he stopped breathing. Staring at the two rings of silver encircling his skin for a brief moment recalled the smell of old hay and rich earth and he had heard the sound of heavy breathing – not his own, because his windpipe and lungs seemed to have seized, were beginning to cry for air. This breathing belonged to a man calming down after a labouring task, the task of correction, of teaching. Then Daisy's fingers had curled around the chain that bound the two cuffs together, dragging his brown eyes to her blue ones as they stood as a foursome in the Teals' dooryard. He wasn't aware of Len or Elaine then; only the look on Daisy's face asking if he was okay.

In order to say he was, he had to breathe, so he did. Now he wanted to be there for Daisy as she had been there for him. So he asked, 'How are you doing?'

'I'm fine,' she replied.

Her voice was curt, preoccupied.

Daisy guided the Blazer through a silent Marybell, not that it needed much; the road from Teal's was a straight ribbon that became Main Street through town and beyond. The Blazer's tyres rolled with that seamless noise spinning rubber makes on smooth tarmac. Plus, the town was dead, its streets barren and silent but for the buzz of electric humming from the streetlights. A sound Joe could hear as the wind charged through the hole in the vehicle's windscreen, cooling them.

'You wouldn't tell me if you weren't?' he said in some poor attempt at humour.

There was a pause and then Daisy said in a hard voice, 'I slaughtered one of Teal's cows back at the farm. My blood was up after dealing with that disgusting man and I could feel the hunger gaining a foothold. I thought a cow was better than nothing.'

'Daisy...' he began, meaning to tell her it was all right, but she interrupted.

'They were scared of me ...the cows.' There was a tremble in her voice as she continued to stare through the remaining cracked glass. 'Even before I...they were scared. They tried to run. That dress certainly wasn't appropriate clothing; there was practically nothing left by the time I had finished.'

'So you changed. What about the new hairdo?'

'I wanted to see a little of the old me in the mirror is all.'

He considered this.

'That's exactly what I thought when I saw you,' he told her. 'The old you. I saw that in your eyes even when we were out on the road.'

They were zipping by the burning pyre that was the police station, the car filling with the greasy aroma of smoke, stinging their eyes until they watered. The roof of the single-storey building was gone, replaced by flames that licked at the sky; their fumes were a billowing tornado of embers like fireflies a mile high. Glass littered the parking lot in front looking like molten slabs of lava, reflecting the orange dancing light of the fire.

A horrifying idea occurred to him as they whipped by, of Marybell's people, the ones still alive hunkering down in the sanctuary of their homes, too afraid to step outside, suffocating as those firefly embers descended on rooftops baked dry after days of ceaseless sun. A part of him felt no remorse at the prospect, was even glad, yet a larger part of himself saw Lily Grey at the entrance to the fair, her straw-coloured hair blowing in the wind, her cheeks flushed with excitement. He felt a helpless rage, knowing he could do nothing except get revenge.

'Thank you,' said Daisy, pulling him from his thoughts.

'I was thinking if we get through this, we should just get in my station wagon and drive. Drive as far away from this place as we can, just you and me on the road with T-Rex playing on the dash.'

'Sounds good, sounds like heaven,' he said.

Daisy nodded to him through the rearview mirror, blinking back tears. Neither of them believed they would live to see their dream.

They were out of the town now, its buildings shadow shapes behind them, with the glow of the fire withering in the center. Launder's homestead sat off the road on the right, also wrapped in darkness. The carnival was easy to make out after that.

It was lit for business.

Only seeing it now at night, it seemed perverse, a mockery of its good-natured appearance during the daylight. The Fairway stretched out like some glamourized crucifix, bejeweled by its lights and stalls and rides. Calliope music played slowly, sounding like an insane funeral dirge. At the rear loomed The Whirl like some giant cataract over an eye that's gone sour with age and disease.

It frightened him. Looking at it made him feel like spiders were scuttling over his body. He wanted to squirm and itch at himself, wanted to tell Daisy to keep driving, that they'll just start their road trip now.

He didn't.

His anger was there, keeping him locked on the path, overriding his fear. He looked from it to Daisy in the rearview mirror.

'This is it,' she announced.

They could see the arch that proclaimed 'Welcome to Doctor Montague's Carnival of Delight and Terror'. Of the carnies themselves, they could see none.

Before he could say any more, Daisy yanked the wheel to the right.

2

They drove straight through the entrance arch, the Blazer's engine growling as both wing mirrors were smashed off. Daisy began beating down on the horn and screaming curses from the driver's seat window as they raced down the Fairway towards The Whirl. Already, Joe could discern shapes emerging from the shadowy alleys between the rides and stalls, cutting off their retreat. They moved silently and gracefully, keeping low to the ground like stalking predators.

'Oh god,' gasped Daisy.

He had been paying so much attention to what was behind them that he hadn't spotted what lay ahead. The headless body of Sheriff Jackson had been stung across The Whirl's central hub in a crucifix shape pointed downward. Blood from the frayed wound of his neck had stained the white metal carmine.

Joe understood the meaning of that symbol, that it was a joke meant to harass them. It worked, as his anger changed from a dull boil to a burning rage, his nails digging four bloody crescents into each palm.

Right then he didn't care if the plan worked or not; he only wanted to cause them pain.

There was another change as well: the black trailer, the one he had seen Lou Fritz driving on the day Lily Grey vanished, was blocking the direction to the left where the Fairway became a T. There was also another to the right. With the carnies swarming the grassy avenue behind them, they were being boxed in.

With no other option, Daisy slammed on the Blazer's brakes, bringing them skidding to a halt before the mighty Whirl. Hard enough that Joe had to reach out with his cuffed hands and stop himself from being flung into the back of Daisy's seat. As the car bounced on its springs, they saw Earl Porter in the control booth to the right of the ramp leading to one of The Whirl's cabins. Its door was open and inside, sitting cross-legged with a gloating expression of superiority, was Montague.

'What did you do to me?' Daisy yelled at him.

This was as she was exiting the car, slamming the door hard enough to make the big vehicle rock. If she was afraid, she didn't portray it – she appeared exactly as they planned: enraged.

From the rear, Joe saw the shapes of carnies closing in. From the front Montague stood, dressed in a black suit of such elegant design it could only be described as regal, his silver hair and beard gleaming in the chaos of the carnival's lights, stepping to the top of the ramp.

'Why, I made you into something more,' he said in a voice that boomed with authority and self-righteousness. 'I made you part of my family.'

'I didn't ask to be part of your family!' Daisy screamed up at him.

'Does a child ask to be informed about the realities of life? No. Does it benefit them to be told? Yes. You have been given a unique opportunity to live forever, to live above all over forms of being. How about I tell you what exactly it means to be one of us? Come join me. But first, is that a present I see inside your vehicle?'

She yanked Joe from the backseat to stand before The Whirl, not really looking at him. Her attention was on the carnival owner. Montague's eyes burned with joy at the sight of him, a growing smile spreading across his lips. There wasn't anything inhuman about that grin, yet it was somehow heinous.

'Finally, Mr. Cage has been returned to us.'

This was an announcement to the carnies who had gathered behind them, cutting off their retreat. Like with Carmen, he saw that their humanity had been stripped away, seeing only rage and hate and hunger in their faces.

It made him think of how Daisy had looked earlier with Bill Denton. There had been enough of *her* left to prevent herself from going too far.

How long would it be before she couldn't resist anymore? Before the hunger took over her completely?

'You didn't feast, my dear?' Montague asked.

'I thought I might need a bargaining chip to get here,' Daisy replied.

'My, my, that must have taken an unbelievable amount of resistance on your part.'

Joe looked at Daisy while pretending to be scared, which wasn't hard. She looked tense, the muscles of her jaw working as if struggling to resist.

Maybe she's further along than I thought.

'Join me. We'll go for a ride on The Whirl. Bring your gift, in case we get hungry.'

3

'Well, they're not dead yet, from the looks of things,' said Lwn, watching as Daisy and Joe arrived at the carnival.

'Rook,' muttered Elaine at his side.

'What was that?'

Elaine glanced nervously at Len, unaware that she had spoken out loud. Both of them were crouching, concealed by the undergrowth of the woods on the edge of Launder's property. They had a rear view of the fair with its gaudy twinkling lights and eerie music.

'Sorry,' she replied. 'I guess I just had a moment of sanity there. Detective Rook works for the state police. He's bringing a bunch of investigators to town tomorrow to help with your daughter's case. I was just thinking for a second that his job is my job and that if I were doing it right I would be arresting these people, not plotting to murder them all. Just thinking how insane my life has gotten in the space of a few hours.'

Len observed her underneath eyebrows that were thick and bushy. Hair the colour of steel. Sweat dripped down his temples; the air beneath the trees was seemingly stagnant, like a murky swamp of heat.

'My life has been insane ever since Lily,' he remarked. 'When something as crazy as this enters into it, you can't be blamed for having a crazy response.'

'I'm not worried about blame or going to jail,' she told him. 'I'm just thinking that the toughest part of my job used to be dealing with drunks on a Saturday night. Now, my town is burning down, people are dead, my boyfriend, Jackson, is dead, and it's all because what shouldn't exist, does.'

This news caused Len's eyebrows to slide up. Glancing at his wristwatch he saw that they didn't have much time, that they should be getting on, but he couldn't do that if he was with someone caught up in their grief. If he did, they were apt to both get killed.

'You still think of this as part of your job?' Len asked.

His question surprised her. Made her look at Len more closely as his words cycled in her head. Long enough that she was aware of how foul her uniform felt on her, how the beige shirt was stuck to her back from sweat.

'I suppose in a way it is, protect and serve and all that,' she answered. 'I want revenge, too and it feels like that should be a bad thing. Jackson and I had something I had never experienced before. They took that from me, but that feels silly, like some cartoon reaction from a movie. Really, I'm here to make them stop, to stop doing what they're doing because it's wrong.'

Len reached out to her, placing a hand on her shoulder. The dampness of her uniform made him aware of just how sweaty his own body was.

'You'd make a great sheriff, you know that?' he told her.

She grinned at him, her teeth a white line in the dim light. Len watched as she brushed back a strand of her blonde hair clinging to the side of her sweat-slicked temple back. A gesture that made her seem absurdly young to him.

From the field they heard the sound of The Whirl's motor, a puttering kind of belching that progressed into a drone as the wheel began to turn.

'I think now's the time,' she said, readjusting her grip on her Beretta.

'Joe said that if they were keeping Meryl anywhere, it was probably in Montague's camper, that one behind the Ferris wheel.'

'Lead on then.'

4

Daisy tossed him unceremoniously into a seat on the right, doing so with one hand while Montague resumed his at the rear of the cabin. The doors closed behind her with a swooshing noise, locking them inside.

'What am I?' Daisy asked as the cabin lurched into movement.

Neither of them paid Joe any mind as he recovered from the throw.

'You're a young woman of this decade,' Montague answered. 'I thought you were all brought up on a diet of pop culture. Don't you know the name Hollywood has for us? They call us vampires, my dear, creatures of the night, which is a preposterous myth taken from the old country on the other side of the east sea. It's marvelous how it has survived alongside our legend. I believe those desperate folks centuries ago created it out of a need to have hope. I mean, if your nights are spent huddling for warmth around the fireside when the wolf pack is howling in the mountains and the bears are roaring in the forests and there's us and we look like them but we are so much more, you would wrap yourself in lies too. History remembers lies more than truths; I suppose that's how it has lasted. Back then they called us the frozen children on account of how we do not age.'

'So I will… '

'Stay exactly as you are forever,' said Montague with a smirk.

His grey eyes slid venomously onto Joe. He stared back, couldn't not; it was like Montague held him by the eyes while his body clenched with fear. The man or creature or whatever he was exuded terror in waves.

'In those days it was near impossible for a human to kill one of us,' he said, his disenchanting tone becoming sharp.

His head snapped back to Daisy standing by the cabin's door. Joe took a breath, drinking in the hot night air; unaware he had been holding it.

'But the humans have a gift for creations and everything they create is designed to destroy in some way or other. Which is why I'm so glad you brought this one back to me.'

Despite the vulnerability he felt, Joe couldn't resist replying. 'You're nothing but animals. Lily Grey proves that.'

'Ah, yes,' remarked Montague, crossing his legs. 'The tragic tale of Lily Grey, the reason why we are all here, isn't it?'

'Lou Fritz murdered her, didn't he?'

Montague's head whipped up; his attentions had been on picking lint from his creaseless trousers.

'Lou?' he said, grinning wide. 'No, my boy. Adam Kavalier did.'

351

5

Elaine and Len found Montague's camper unlocked, darting inside as quietly as possible, guns at the ready. The interior was lit by lamplight, revealing an office/living room space complete with rich furniture. There was a hallway at the other side of the room that ran the length of the camper.

They tiptoed over to it, their steps muted by the thick carpet. Standing in the mouth of the passage they could see two doors along the right side before the hallway met its end at another doorway, which was partially ajar.

From what Elaine could see, it looked like a bedroom.

'What's wrong?' Len asked in a whisper, sensing her hesitation.

'If your wife is here then why haven't we run into someone?'

Len's eyes staring down the barrel of his Remington whipped around the living area, the shotgun's stock planted firmly into his shoulder. Despite the lights, there were still plenty of shadows for one of them to hide in.

'I'll go first, you cover my rear,' Elaine instructed.

She held her Beretta close to her body in her bad hand; bad because it wasn't her dominant one. That one was still injured; her wrist had swollen and felt filled with hot glass, even with the tablets she had swallowed back at the Teals'. She stretched out her right leg, her eyes fixed on all three doors, and took her first step into the hallway. Len shuffled behind, his back against hers, cradling the Remington in his hands.

Her ears strained for any sound that might indicate they weren't alone. Other than their breathing, she could make out a ticking clock.

They reached the first door on the right and with her gun aimed at its center, she nudged it open with her foot. The hinges groaned as it swung wide. The light from the hallway spilled inside for her to see a tidy bedroom.

She could see a double bed, though the invading light only reached halfway across it, leaving the far side in darkness. Elaine aimed her gun there, until all she was aware of was what she saw and her own lungs breathing. In and out, in and out, in and out; nothing stirred in the darkness.

She moved on, a floorboard creaking under the carpet where she placed her foot, until she came to the second door. This time she had to reach out with her injured hand and twist the door's handle, a painful ordeal that bought beads of sweat to her brow. Inside was a bathroom that looked unused.

That left the third door, the one at the very end of the hall.

As she neared it, she became aware that throughout all this she had been breathing air that was stuffy with dust from the carpeted floors. Outside the third door, she noticed a new scent, a slight tang of human sweat.

She nudged the open door wide, her eyes immediately locking with Meryl Grey's. She was sat upright in jeans and a blue polka-dotted shirt, her mouth gagged, her wrists strapped to the headboard of a huge bed.

6

'Who the hell is Adam Kavalier?' said Daisy.

The Whirl was halfway to the top, and like the ride, Joe's mind was spinning, only back in time. He was inside Journey Through The Crypt after Lily; his surroundings were hidden by smoke and darkness until a shadow began to grow out of the mist. The closer he moved the more defined the shadow became, until he was seeing a gravestone in front of him. The name written on it was 'Adam Kavalier' and the date beneath was '1253 - '.

'Tradition is an important part of our existence,' announced Montague, his grey eyes mischievous. 'This is something you will come to understand as a member of this family. Tonight, we are breaking a tradition that has protected this carnival for centuries traveling across the highways and backwaters of this land. I was not dishonest when I told each of you that we do not only endeavour to provide entertainment to people, but also memories for a small price.'

'When you say "price", you mean more than money, don't you?' commented Joe with disdain. The man's pompous words were making him feel sick.

'Now that you are privy to the truth of the matter, I can tell you yes.' In seeing his disgusted expression Montague shot at him, 'Shouldn't we be paid for our efforts in adding a little brightness to your dull, mundane, and limited lives?'

When he returned his gaze back to Daisy, he became pleasant again.

'We provide memories that will last a lifetime and in exchange, we take the strays, the runaways, the outsiders. If you want something to blame, blame this country itself. It sees its own people as either grandma's open purse or waste that needs to be disposed of. In taking what we need, we help with that waste deposal.'

'Like us,' Daisy snapped accusingly.

She had stood this entire time while listening, fury worming in her muscles, arms at her side. Joe saw that the nails of her fingers had elongated, to become white talons, and that she hadn't even noticed.

'No, you are exceptional and for certain exceptional people we offer them the chance to join us.'

'I don't remember being given much of a choice with that offer.'

Daisy's voice was lifeless when she said this, making his heart ache. In looking at her then, angry as she was, changed as she was, Joe felt sympathy and rage. The same rage that burned in him for Lily Grey now swelled to include the woman he loved.

'Of course not, my dear, because the change involves a significant amount of pain,' explained Montague. 'If a surgeon told you the truth about the surgery he was about to perform, very few people would actually agree to it.'

'I don't give a shit about the pain!' Daisy yelled at him. 'What I'm talking about is having a choice forced onto me against my will.'

Montague did not seem to have an answer for that. He reclined in his seat, air hissing from his nostrils as he contemplated Daisy's glaring gaze.

7

'Meryl!' cried Len, running over to his wife's side.

He placed the shotgun on the bed before hugging her. Meryl instantly burst into tears. Elaine wheeled away from them to take a position facing the hallway. She couldn't shake the feeling that there was something wrong.

'We'll get you out of here,' she heard Len say to his wife.

When he hissed the word 'shit,' she glanced around, observing that he had tried to untie her with his fingers and was now resorting to sawing the rope with his knife. A noise from the hallway caused her head to rotate back.

It looked the same as always; she could see the desk chair, upholstered in emerald leather, and part of the mahogany desk in the room that they had first entered into. The two doorways, now on her left-hand side, were still open.

The noise came again, the sound of something falling onto the carpet, and this time Elaine knew where it was coming from: the other bedroom.

She took another peek behind her – Len had almost gotten his wife's right wrist free – then set off down the passageway once more to investigate.

8

Len stumbled around the bed, hitting the frame with his knees, filling his lower legs with pins and needles. He saw Elaine moving down the hallway and thought nothing of it, his mind too concerned with getting his wife free. By the time he had limped around to her left side, she had clawed out the gag.

'I'm so sorry!' she cried out to him.

Her tears now bordered on hysteria. She reached out to him with her free arm, wrapping it around his neck, pulling him partially onto the bed.

'I'm sorry for everything,' she wept into his collar.

'It's okay, it's okay,' he repeated, whispering in her ear, stroking the back of her head. 'Everything will be okay.'

'I've ruined everything. The kids, are they okay? They...they're never going to forgive me,' she said in a wheeze.

'The kids are safe and there's nothing to forgive, okay?' He held her face in his hands as he said this.

Other than her tears and her soiled clothes, she looked unharmed. Her weeping suggested that she had suffered deeper hurts, hurts that he didn't even want to imagine, so he embraced her tightly.

In his head, he saw her throwing him that terrified look as she stumbled out of their house. He felt no anger or hate, only despair for not being strong enough to stop her leaving. Later, perhaps, those feelings may surface, but right now his one motivation was to get Meryl away from this situation.

'How did you get past the guard?'

Len's eyes snapped wide as he pulled out of Meryl's embrace.

'What guard?' he said to her, scanning her face.

'Len.' It was Elaine and her voice was shrill.

Meryl's and Len's heads snapped to the doorway to see Elaine being ushered into the room by a giant of a man. Len recognised him as The Russian Strongman, Youssef, someone who had assisted in the search for Lily. His left arm, as thick as a tree trunk, was hooked around Elaine's neck, which in contrast looked slim and fragile. In his right, he held the barrel of her gun against the side of her head.

'If this isn't a Hallmark moment, I don't know what is,' he said, his voice mocking and deep.

Len eyed the shotgun he had left on the other side of the bed. There was no way he would reach it in time. Before he could decide what to do next, the giant began to point the Beretta in his direction.

9

'I feel like we are getting off topic here,' Montague remarked.

Joe observed Daisy's eyes dart in his direction. He nodded his head ever so slightly while staring at the carnival owner, hoping she understood. According to his wristwatch, time was almost up; they needed Montague to keep talking.

'I was telling you about the importance of traditions, you see. For the longest time my family was led by another, Adam Kavalier, and his practices...well, they weren't as civil as mine. His idea of satisfying our hunger was to attack small, isolated communities, people who no one would miss. However, as the centuries wore on, it was becoming clear to myself and several of the family that as the human race expanded, the world grew smaller and it began increasingly hard to achieve this without drawing attention to us. It also became apparent that Adam did not care if we became known or not. He was ignorant. So it was decided that the family required a new leadership – my leadership. However, you simply can't destroy the head of a coven. The idea that a new leader was being sought was a change of such magnitude that murdering the old one was not acceptable.

Tradition, you see, can also be a trap. We have kept Adam alive for centuries; to this day there are still members of my family that hold him in high regard even though his days are spent confined inside that trailer you see below.'

Joe attempted to spy through the glass of the cabin to see, finding that they had almost reached the top of The Whirl. The carnival was lit with a million lights; he could see the carnies standing below, their necks craned. Hearing Daisy gasp behind him, Joe whipped forward only to find Montague's face inches from his. For a second Joe believed that the carnival owner meant to kill him then, to bite through his neck as he had done with Jackson. The creature stared at him with lunacy in his grey eyes.

'What happened to Lily Grey was an accident,' he said in a tone that was mournful and unsteady. 'Adam managed to escape somehow while Lou and Youssef were supposed to be looking after him. Before we could get him back inside his trailer, the deed was done. The girl was dead.'

Joe stared into those mad eyes. Before, he thought of Montague as having such power, but seeing him now, he was a tin pot dictator who was failing to keep those below him in control. Then that glimpse beneath the surface was buried beneath his smarmy, superior attitude as he shied away back to his seat.

Only now it didn't sit right on his face.

The frustrated, panicked madness seemed to lurk on the corners of Montague's features, wanting to overthrow his pretend calm disposition. Instead of looking like a friendly secondhand car salesman, he looked like a small-time politician about to lose his shit.

'Sounds like you don't always choose exceptional people to be part of your family,' Joe commented.

Montague chuckled. 'If I had had my way, Adam would have been killed long ago and this whole mess would never have happened,' he said and added with a shrug, 'Tradition.'

Joe glanced at his watch; they had thirty seconds left.

10

The carnies watched The Whirl rotate on its axis from below, heads craned upward like captivated stargazers. Most clustered around the beige Blazer that had once belonged to Sheriff Jackson.

Jack Clifton, the carnival's resident fire-breather, snorted sharply, his nostrils assaulted by some foul smell. He was the closest to the vehicle and was able to discern exactly where the awful odour was issuing from.

'Jesus, it smells like someone's shit themselves in there,' he remarked.

This caused several carnies around him to laugh. Some edged closer to spy inside the vehicle to see if what he said was true.

11

The compartment was curving to The Whirl's peak so that view from all four sides was of the dark heavens surrounding them. Joe remained bound at the wrists and seated, while Montague sat cross-legged, and Daisy stood.

'If events had played out differently, both of you would be embracing me right now.'

Joe couldn't help but scoff.

'Don't be so righteous,' Montague told him, his voice deepening, his grin growing as Carmen's had, revealing too many teeth. 'If things had gone to plan I wouldn't have had to kill you now for the murders of two of my most trusted allies.'

'You never did figure me out, did you?' Joe spoke without any idea what he intended to say, his brain telling him to drag out the time as much as he could.

Montague had risen at this point and was stalking towards him. At his words, his gait faltered slightly.

'Bah, what does it matter now?' he said, considering.

He began creeping closer again.

'It must get boring living for so long. I imagine when you do stumble upon a mystery, it can easily become consuming. You found out where I was from, that my father was in the military, and that he taught me how to disarm someone. He was discharged after rising pretty high. You never learned that or what he specialised in.'

'I don't care anymore,' sighed Montague, his face freakish now, the skin separating almost to his eyes, which were silver and empty. 'You're just trying to prolong your pitiful life.'

'I think you will care,' said Joe.

Now he was standing, putting as much space between him and Montague as he could by pressing against the cabin wall. He could see Daisy steeling herself.

'DON'T YOU MOVE!' bellowed Montague, pointing at her. 'You're one of us now, and we live by certain…traditions. Sometimes they must be paid in blood.' Montague turned his gaze back to him. 'Okay, Joe, tell me what this big secret is. What did your father do?'

'My father was a demolition man'.

As this information sank in, Joe watched as Montague's sneer sagged, the skin of his cheeks resealing, his eyes, confused at first then widening with horrifying understanding. The watch on Joe's wrist beeped; the countdown was over.

12

The Blazer bloomed outward like a red flower. The front bumper rocketed off, cleaving through the torsos of the four individuals in front of it. This was caused by the initial blast force, which turned fragments of glass and metal into projectiles. These shredded those nearest into gory pulp. Unhindered, the shrapnel continued on their outward trajectories, embedding into the carousel, the helter skelter, and various other surrounding structures. The black trailer was tossed into the air, its metal skin shredded like butter by the flying projectiles. Jack, the fire-breather, who had been peering into the trunk at the odd package that was there, had the skin from his face ripped off by the blast. He had little time to register this as flames engulfed him. The fire spread outward from a second wave from the bomb's immediate blast. It flowed like lava into The Fill Up, causing secondary explosions from the gas tanks. It raced forward and devoured the base of The Whirl. Earl Porter, who had been in the control booth, watched as the heat caused the windows to bubble before exploding inward and dosing him in flames. The mighty Ferris wheel groaned and shuddered. The blast kept going, striking Montague's camper with enough force to tip it over onto its side. Inside the motorhome, the bullet Youssef intended for Grey went wide, scratching his bicep instead of digging into his heart. The carnies left alive, thrown free by the blast, stared upward in disbelief. The Whirl was leaning over the carnival.

Chapter Seven

Up In Flames

1

The whole cabin lurched several degrees off center, causing them all to stagger. Joe gripped a bar of metal above his head while Daisy collapsed into the seat behind her. Their eyes met, seeing the same resignation in each other's face: they weren't making it out of this.

The cabin gave another lurch and this time they could see the carnival below, all in flames, as the metal struts bent further under the weight of the mighty wheel.

'You fucking children!' screamed Montague. 'What have you done?'

He had been slammed onto the floor.

'We're having a bonfire. Don't worry, it's traditional,' Daisy shot at him.

There was a series of snaps as the supporting wires ripped apart. Then an agonised groan issued from the metal as it bent as easily as paper.

The Whirl pitched forward onto the blazing carnival. It fell slowly, almost gracefully at first, for a structure of its size.

Montague had seized onto one of metal bars that formed the cabin's skeleton, his feet dangling in the air as the ride began to topple. Daisy was pinned against the glass below him while Joe clung onto the side, also hanging.

From their perspective they did not appear to be falling; it was more like the ground was rising to meet them. It did so with a mighty crash, the glass of their cabin shattering as it became embedded into the roof of a ride.

Daisy and Joe were tossed through the hole created in the cabin's glass front. Air billowed and pummeled them as they fell, reaching for each other the entire time, into what seemed like a void of darkness.

Then they hit the ground.

2

As the explosion rocked the camper, shifting the world to the left, Elaine drove her elbow into the giant's nose, hearing an enjoyable crack. She heard him scream at the same time that her feet slid out from under her, sliding over the camper's floor along with the ornate dresser that had been set to her left.

At the same time, Len was still spinning from the grazed bullet only to have his legs crunched between the bed and the right wall, which had now become the floor. A shriek erupted from his throat at the bright flare of pain in his calves as Meryl flopped onto him, followed by the bed's mattress.

The gun, get the gun! a voice in his head screamed.

Elaine had landed on the balls of her feet like a cat. The giant hung above her; he had lost her Beretta but managed to seize onto the doorframe to keep from sliding with them. His eyes burned red at her, his mouth a grotesque pit lined with brilliantly white teeth. He dropped to the floor beside her.

She scuttled away, trying to put as much distance between him and her as she could, only there was nowhere to go. The room had been tipped on its right side; the window there now looked out of the ground, and its one exit was above them. Her companions were useless. She could see Meryl trying to untangle herself from beneath the bed, her left wrist still secured to its frame by rope.

'Come here!' roared the giant.

To make things worse, she was backed into a corner.

'No escaping this,' it said to her, its jaws splitting wide, its tongue loping out and extending towards her.

The world filled with thunder. The beast shaped like a man staggered backward in a spray of blood and gristle. Its tongue flopped against the wall to Elaine's right, having been blasted from its body.

Her eyes wheeled round to find Meryl standing tall, shotgun clutched in her hands. She racketed the weapon, screaming, 'No escaping me!'

The beast lunged for her; its head peppered with buckshot fragments while its mouth had become a pouring wound of red. The shotgun thundered again, causing the beast to stagger down to one knee as its chest erupted into gore. It attempted to shamble to its feet and Meryl fired again and again and again until the air in the room was rancid with the reek of burnt gunpowder and the beast's blood.

By that time, Len was standing, hugging his wife as tears rained down her face. Elaine went to them, embracing them both.

3

Daisy's hands were on him, searching for any place that he had been hurt.

'Are you all right?' she kept asking.

With a groan, he asked, 'Can we go on that road trip now?'

When she pulled him to his feet he noticed that they had landed in a graveyard. He recognised it instantly; they were inside Journey Through The Crypt. Unlike before, the starry sky overhead had a hole punched through it where they could see the cabin they had been in. Montague was crouched inside, holding onto the metal frame, and glaring down at them.

'You've destroyed it!' he cried as flames licked the sides of the hole.

Smoke was beginning to enter through it along with a flurry of cinders, glittering like fireflies. Already, Joe could feel the heat from outside as the fire pressed against the building.

'My family, all I've built, you've destroyed it all.'

Both of them were coiled, ready for him to leap at them, when another voice ripped through the night air.

'So this is your modern world. It looks very much like the old one. All fire and death and blood.'

Neither Joe nor Daisy could see whom this voice belonged to; they could only witness Montague's reaction to it. His face became a picture of terror.

In seeing it, Joe thought, what do the monsters fear?

Montague was not looking at them, but at someone standing on the roof of the carnival's ghost ride. Joe heard him say the name 'Adam' before he vanished from his sight. From above there came the sound of a scuffle, except this was filled with animal-like shrieks of rage and pain.

'Let's get out of here,' he said to Daisy.

4

Joe led Daisy down the corridor of zombified hands into the forest room, feeling the heat at their backs now like a warm, dry palm.

'There's a fire exit over here,' he told her, dragging her between the fake redwoods, his hands still in cuffs.

They were in sight of the green exit sign when a portion of the ceiling caved in. They threw themselves to the floor, which was all fake plastic grass, similar to what they had landed on in the other room.

Amidst the falling paneling and the dust, they could see two figures fighting each other. One was Montague; the other was taller than him, dressed entirely in black, his hair the colour of coal, and slicked back.

For Joe it was hard to make out exactly was going on; both creatures moved too fast. Yet he associated what he was seeing with big cats mauling each other on their hind legs. They fought tooth and nail, the interior of the room ricocheting with sounds of snapping jaws and swiping claws.

'Come on, before they see us,' said Daisy, pulling him to his feet.

They moved towards the fire exit once more only to come to a halt. The corridor to the exit was blocked by another figure that neither of them recognised immediately, on account of his entire torso, plus the lower half of his face, having been burnt charcoal black. It was only in seeing his shaved head and glasses (the right lens sported a crack) that they realised they were looking at Earl Porter.

'Why couldn't you just lay down and accept what was going to happen?' he cried, his skin smoking, smelling like burnt fat.

Joe's eyes darted around the floor for a weapon, his hands limited by the handcuffs.

'Why did you have to cause such a fuss?'

Earl charged at them, the folds of his scorched skin cracking to show teeth that were perfectly white and elongating into fangs. Daisy shoved Joe to the side, causing him to fall, before swiping at Earl's eyes with her nails. He was too quick, jerking his head out of the way before shouldering into her.

Daisy was flung through a nearby tree, its plastered top half collapsing into the fake forest floor. Close by, the battle still raged between Montague and the mysterious new arrival who Joe assumed was Adam Kavalier.

The zombie corridor was now a smoking throat, tainting the air with the smell of burning plastic. The walls on that side were rippling with heat.

As Earl stalked after Daisy, Joe leaped onto his back, throwing his cuffed hands over his head until their chain caught around his neck. The smell of burnt flesh was like soot in his nostrils, making him want to gag. He planted his right knee into the nape of Earl's neck, pulling back on the handcuff chain. The effect was immediate; Earl's attention diverted from Daisy's crumpled form as he attempted to remove Joe from his back by spinning in circles, his claws trying to rake at him. He couldn't reach and Joe began to feel the chain cutting into the flesh of his throat, spilling blood in rivulets down Earl's front.

A pair of hands grabbed each of his wrists. Daisy had joined him, leaping onto Earl's back. They shared a glance and then Joe felt Daisy pull with her new strength, felt the chain sink through Earl's throat with ease.

The creature dropped to his knees as blood showered from the ever-widening groove they were creating in his neck. They held on, still pulling long after the choking sounds emitting from him stopped, until Daisy seized Earl's head by the temples and with a twist, pried it from his shoulders.

She threw it into the gloom, which had gotten a lot hotter. Joe observed that the zombie corridor was now in flames that were licking out at the walls.

'Come on!' he shouted, grabbing Daisy by the elbow.

She was strong enough to shrug him off easily and did so, but only as they reached the corridor. When he turned back he saw what had captured her attention. Twenty feet away, surrounded by a forest on fire, was Montague.

He had stopped fighting and stood bloodied and bruised before his opponent, who held his head tenderly between the palms of his hands. His eyes drifted from the face of the figure towering over him to them, distraught and filled with disbelief. Then the tall figure gripped his hair with one hand, jerked his head to the side, and buried his teeth into Montague's neck.

Montague's body barely twitched as the creature bore it to the floor.

The fire had swept the room like a tornado at this point. Everything was orange and yellow and white. All the moisture in the air had been burned off, replaced by smoke and floating embers. Some of these sizzled on Joe's arms, singeing his hair there. From overhead, there was a groan as more roofing collapsed into the inferno.

Gently, he placed a hand on Daisy's right arm.

'Come on, we have to go,' he told her.

She remained rooted in place, staring into the torrent of flame, her AC/DC shirt ripped in places. A tall figure rose amongst the fire and the smoke, his back to them. He seemed to be adjusting the collar of his shirt as if unperturbed by his surroundings. Daisy stared at him through tears.

'Come on!' Joe shouted at her, tugging her arm.

The tall figure turned and observed them. His face was narrow with high cheekbones and a peak of a forehead, his skin like alabaster. He viewed them with eyes that were as coal-black as his slicked hair, unconcerned.

A steel girder fell from the ceiling and clanged as it met the floor, causing an explosion of sparks to take flight like a swarm of angry hornets. The tall figure didn't react to this; instead, he nodded at them with the slightest tilt of his head. He disappeared a second later, stepping out of their sight.

Joe had Daisy moving then, retreating, back stepping before eventually turning and running the length of that dark, narrow corridor and out.

Chapter Eight

Olive

1

Olive woke to a tingling sensation on her right cheek and screamed as her fingers brushed away a spider the size of a silver dollar. Her hands clamped over her mouth a moment later as the events that had led her to fall asleep in such a cold, damp place came back to her. She listened, ears straining for the sound of a heavy, knocking tread coming to find her.

Those footsteps had come down the staircase last night after they had finished with her mother. She had curled up in a corner of the pantry, huddling behind a sack of potatoes, while trying not to breathe for fear of being heard.

Her mother hadn't screamed, nor cried out. Still, Olive knew she was dead; she had heard her feet drum out their last rhythm on the kitchen linoleum above. Then those footsteps had come down the cellar stairs.

There was silence beyond the pantry's door now, a pause as the carnival owner scrutinized the room from the bottom of the staircase. Then they recommenced, though not with the hard rapping they had made on the wooden steps, but with a dull clap against the cement floor.

Olive squeezed her nose closed with her fingers while the palm of her hand mashed against her lips. There was the scrape of a shoe. She froze, sides quivering, her bladder feeling heavy and full, her body leaking sweat.

There was another scrape as the person beyond the pantry door turned, walked back across the cellar and up the stairs. Olive tracked his steps with her eyes on the cellar ceiling as he made his through the kitchen into the living room, stopping only to begin moving, this time accompanied by a shuffling noise. She guessed that he was dragging her father away.

He dragged him to the porch, then his knocking tread went upstairs. When it came back down, it did so with her brother, shrieking to be let free.

Olive kept quiet, not wanting to be found out.

There were no more footfalls now, nor had there been overnight. Still, Olive hadn't moved from her position, the house feeling occupied somehow.

She hadn't heard him close the front door, which led her to imagine that the hidden pantry door hadn't fooled him and that he was waiting silently for her to try and leave, just to spring upon her at the last second. So she had waited, listening to the floorboards creak and the pipe gurgle until there was no more space inside her to be terrified anymore.

She was still scared, just not hysterical. That was when she had begun to cry for her mother, her father, and her brother. For not being brave enough to try and stop the monster that had entered their house as her mother had. Or for not trying to kick and punch at it as her brother had.

Eventually she slept, though it wasn't really sleeping, more like slipping under a black quilt of protection. She woke once to discover she had wet herself, before slipping back under with a shrug. The second time was to the sound of explosions shaking the entire house. The fact that explosions were occurring did not shock her in the slightest considering what she had experienced already. Waking now was her third time, the time of the spider.

Would she go back to sleep this time? It was like time travel, or more accurately, time-jumping. Don't want to deal with tensing at every single sound that might be a potential murderer lying in wait? Time-jump.

Except that wasn't going to work forever. Eventually, she would have to try and leave; she would head to the police station, not for any reason other than that's where her mind told her to go because it was a safe place where she could be looked after by people with guns. That seemed crucial.

The only problem was that to do that meant leaving the pantry. The pantry wasn't safe, but it was safer than the house above where her mother's corpse was stiffening on the kitchen floor beside her pie-making stuff all laid out.

There was also the journey into town to consider; she lived half an hour away from Marybell. She wondered if her father's truck was outside still. It had been last night before she descended the cellar stairs, but that didn't mean that the monster that had slaughtered her family hadn't taken it.

Plus, what if he was still up there?

At that thought Olive leaned forward, listening. Hearing only the heavy presence of an empty house, pregnant with silence.

'Okay,' she whispered in a croak.

Her throat was a dried out creek that she massaged as she stood. She snatched a garden trowel from a shelf and stepped towards the pantry door, her left hand stretching out timidly to grip the handle as if it were hot. It wasn't; it was icy due to the cellar's natural cold temperature.

A shiver ran up her arm and sizzled in the nerves of her spine.

'Okay,' she whispered once more, letting air out through her cracked lips.

She twisted the handle, pushing the door an inch at a time while aiming the trowel's point at the widening gap. The cellar was the same as it had been when she had flown across it, bar one change. Daylight streamed in through the windows, beaming rectangles on the floor.

Olive stared, open-mouthed at the light. It was the first indication that she had spent all night in her family's creepy cellar.

2

Nothing appeared at the top of the cellar staircase as she climbed it. Nor did a hand reach out between the steps to gasp her ankle. She made it to the top unharmed and lingered before the kitchen door, swapping the trowel between her sweaty hands in preparation for what lay on the other side of the door.

Eventually, she pushed it wide, saw her mother, and broke into tears. No preparation would have helped her cope with the sight before her.

Shirley Launder hadn't managed to scream because the monster that killed her had bit straight through her throat all the way to her spine. Olive could see the ivory bone amongst the chewed pink flesh. There was no way she could not see it; even though the light outside was of the pale early morning kind, the kitchen fluorescents were still on, humming faintly.

They offered no protection, no mystery.

Her mother's corpse lay on the kitchen floor just as clinically exposed as she would have on an autopsy table. Her blouse had been ripped apart, leaving her thin chest on display, including her plain beige bra. There were jagged circles on her torso, allowing Olive to make out individual teeth marks.

3

After carefully placing her mother's trench coat over her body, Olive poured a glass of water from the tap and drank deeply. She remained there in front of the sink, looking out the window, drinking glass after glass, thinking about how her mother's head wobbled now because the only thing supporting it was a cord of flexible bone. If Olive tried to lift her, she knew, her head would simply flop over until it was against her back, giving her staring eyes an upside down view. Eventually, her stomach began to ache with the tap water's cold chill.

She dropped the glass into the sink, shattering it, before moving on.

The living room was a rectangle space of upheaved furniture. There were blood spots on the walls and, to Olive's surprise, bullet holes. Then she remembered how her mother had used her .38. She had been so brave.

Olive counted five bullet holes in all, three in the walls, two in the sofa, and one that had blasted through the window. Shirley Launder was brave, but not much of a shot.

Outside, the sun was rising behind the woods, turning the eastern sky canary yellow while the west took on a pastoral blue. To the north lay the smoking remains of the carnival. Olive paid them no mind. Some part of her connected the explosion she had heard to what she was seeing, but the majority of her had entered into a state of shock.

She was just going through the motions that would get her to her intended destination: the police station. Other than that, even her fear that her family's attacker could be lying in wait still was forgotten. She was a zombie.

Her father's truck sat on four flat tires so she set off towards the barn where they stored their bikes. She hadn't even bothered to collect the truck keys from the rack in the kitchen, anyway.

The barn was cool and dusty, smelling of the horses the previous owners used to keep in it, a smell Olive loved. As she made her way to the bikes, she caught a glimpse of something small and white lying off to her right. It was a hand, and after closer inspection, she saw it belonged to her brother.

He was clearly dead, lying face down on the barn floor in a congealed pool of blood that now looked like dark jelly. She could see the massive rip in his shoulder. That wasn't all she could see, either. To the left, hanging from a beam by chains, was her father, also dead, his face frozen in a sneer.

Olive started screaming then, except it wasn't really screaming because she couldn't get any air to go down her windpipe. There seemed to be a block, so instead of a full-on shriek, what came out of her sounded like a yelp.

She grabbed the nearest bike without looking and jogged outside. She was a mile down the road before she realised that it was her brother's, because her sneakers kept scraping the road and her knees were too high.

4

The sun had risen higher by the time she reached the town, painting half the sky and the flat expanse of land around her in rich oranges and yellows.

She cycled over a bridge with a stream of muddy water, most likely runoff from her father's chicken farm. She passed the leftovers of a car crash; there were no bodies, but plenty of glass scattered all over the road and she wondered why hadn't anyone cleaned it up. Olive hadn't like the way the Pontiac doors were open, as if whoever had gotten out had just disappeared. There was blood on the car seats.

She saw the remains of an Alsatian lying by the curb, its intestines hanging out. She saw storefronts with broken windows. There was glass everywhere, and she was forced to skirt around it and cycle in the middle of the road.

At last, she arrived at the police station and she saw people.

5

'Well, this town is fucked,' she heard one of the survivors say.

That's what they were calling themselves, according to a scrawny bird of a woman who Olive later realised was the minister's wife. She had said this to her while clutching a crucifix between her two hands and staring wide-eyed at them all, yet she seemed not to see anything.

'The Lord has tested us and found us worthy. We are survivors, yes, yes,' she went on to say.

'Shut up, Miriam. You hid in a closest all night long,' her husband said to her, looking tired and dishevelled.

Miriam seemed to not notice.

This all occurred in the police parking lot because the building itself had burnt to a husk. Several of the surrounding buildings were fire damaged. The lot was full of similar tired, dishevelled, and shocked individuals, some of whom were receiving medical care from anyone with experience. Olive observed the local veterinary, Randal Mack, and two women, Susie Clayton and Barbara Walsh, who worked as nurses in the closest hospital, tending to a shrieking man with a bloody leg.

A loud yet familiar crash drew her attention away from them to the other side of the street. She saw Henry Grey attempting to break into a Coca-Cola machine while his twin brothers watched from a distance. They stood in the road itself, though no one seemed to be worrying over this.

Olive made her way to them.

'You might want to step off the road in case there are cars,' she said, tapping one of them on the shoulder.

Both twins looked to her, then up and down the road.

'There's no cars today,' said one of them.

It was the sheer conviction on his voice that made Olive's eyebrows jerk up.

'Boys, she's got a point,' said Len Grey, who had strolled over, limping slightly, his arm around his wife's waist. The other arm was bandaged.

The twins obeyed without protest and stepped onto the curb. Olive mimicked them by glancing right and left and seeing what they said was true. There would be no cars on today, not in the way there usually was, and maybe not ever again. Marybell felt dead to her.

'Come on,' muttered Henry, banging at the Coke machine.

'You're Glen Launder's daughter, aren't you?' asked Meryl Grey.

Like her husband, she had her arm around his waist.

'Yes,' answered Olive, knowing what question was coming next.

'Where are your parents?'

She gave no answer, simply held the red-headed woman's gaze.

'Oh …well …I'm sorry.'

Olive gave a nod in response.

'Yes!' cried Henry, loud enough that several heads turned in the car park across the road.

However, his cry wasn't as loud as the sound of Coke cans rattling out of the machine's low mouth. Some of them split and sprayed fizz onto the path, which made the twins laugh. Henry bent down and retrieved a handful; these he gave to the twins and then held one out to her.

'Thanks,' she said, accepting the can.

The drink was warm, but sweet. As she gulped half of it down, a police officer marched over to the Greys. It dawned on Olive that she had only seen two of them this morning and out of the two, people were looking to this officer for leadership rather than to the other.

'Any sign of Daisy or Joe?' the officer asked the Greys.

The name Joe pricked up Olive's ears; that name was familiar to her.

'How long do you think they'll keep the school closed for?' Henry asked her, sipping from his own can.

'I dunno,' she replied, listening to the Greys' conversation with the female deputy.

'They took off. I guess they wanted to get out of here before the news hit and those detectives you were talking about descended on this place,' replied Len Grey.

'They spoke about having someplace to be,' offered Meryl Grey.

Out of the corner of her eye, Olive watched the deputy stare down the vacant road.

'Think they'll be okay?' she asked the Greys.

The three were walking out of her earshot. Henry was looking to Olive, waiting for her to elaborate more. She did, but her mind was elsewhere, pondering why she recognised Joe's name and why the deputy was so interested.

Epilogue

Home

1

The house was a little way off the road down a dirt track, not unlike the homes where all this madness seemed to start for her. Staring at its pristine white paint with its navy tiles in the falling sun, she thought this is where the madness started for the man beside her, and it began a long time ago.

'Are you ready for this?' Daisy asked him.

Joe stared at the house from the station wagon's passenger seat. His cheeks had taken on a shrunken look as tension wormed into his features. His eyes were hidden behind a pair of cheap sunglasses.

They'd been on the road ever since May 13, driving across the heartlands to Indiana, driving him home. It was now the 20th of May. They could have arrived sooner; Daisy found she no longer needed to sleep anymore, not since the transformation. She could have driven them straight here, but they had chosen to take their time.

Before leaving Marybell, Joe had ransacked Montague's camper, stealing over fifty thousand dollars in loose cash, which they had used to spend their nights in the best suites their money could buy. They had made love a lot, though timidly at first, not because either of them hadn't wanted to, but because she had been afraid that at any moment she might lose control.

She hadn't. And the sex was good. The overindulgence of the suites, of spending long hours sharing bubble baths with bottles of booze, of telling each other everything about themselves, of driving with T-Rex blasting from the dash, of endless room service – it was all good. In some ways, the past seven days had been the best of her life.

In other ways they had been the worst because, despite all the goodness, all the laughs, and all the love, she was haunted now. There was a ghost inside her body, and like the phantoms she had enjoyed watching terrorize the four investigators staying at Hill House with Joe at a drive-in theatre one night, she was haunted by something unseen but felt.

There was never any warning when the feeling came upon her, a strange type of hollowness that demanded to be filled. On one occasion this had come over her as Joe slept and she had drifted over to him, her eyes fixed on the pulsating rhythm that throbbed inside his carotid artery just beneath the fragile skin of his throat. She could almost smell the coppery scent of blood. If it hadn't been for the splash of something warm on her chest that caused her to look down and see that she was drooling, Daisy didn't know what would have happened. She had fled immediately, not even caring that she was nude. She spent the night satisfying her craving by feasting on livestock.

By the time she returned, Joe was awake and worried. He took one look at her – she had been unable to meet his eyes, mostly out of shame, though partly because her head was swimming drunkenly from her night time banquet – and marched her into the shower. It wasn't until she walked past the hotel room's floor-to-ceiling mirror that she noticed she was painted red.

'As ready as I'll ever be,' Joe replied, pulling her out of her thoughts.

She saw that beneath his suntan, his skin had turned pale. Daisy put the wagon in gear and began to climb up the drive.

2

The dirt track expanded into a circular shape before the house. Now that they were this close, Joe could see the barn off to the right where his father used to chain him up in order to deliver his "lessons". That's what he called them, with all the reverence of a preacher about to perform a sermon.

Daisy parked the wagon on the left-hand side.

'Want me to come with?' she asked, staring at the two-storey building.

'No, I think I'll be alright.' Which was not what he actually meant. What he meant to say was that he felt it had to be him who went inside first.

Joe hesitated for another moment, then pulled the handle on the door and stepped out into the beaming sunlight.

The first thing he noticed was the smell of his mother's flowers that sat on either side of the porch steps: honeysuckle. Their cloying scent struck him with more nostalgia than a photo album.

His father's car wasn't here, a good sign. Not that it mattered. If he was here, Joe had the Beretta he had swiped from Marybell tucked into the back of his jeans.

He mounted the steps, pausing with his fist raised to knock only to realise this was the house that he had been brought up in. The knowledge didn't make a damn difference to the fact that he had always felt like a stranger inside it.

The front door wasn't locked and he slipped inside as quiet as a shadow.

3

The woman in the kitchen looked older than he remembered. In his head she was his mother; however, his eyes told him that from behind, she could have been his grandmother. She was drying her hands over the sink with a dishtowel when he entered the room, his boots knocking on the wooden floorboards. Her hair was entirely silver now, tied up at the back in a bun while a mess of stray strands curled around the flesh of her neck.

'You're back early, George. I ...'

She stopped speaking as soon as she turned and saw him. A look of shock that was almost revulsion showed across her face as her hands went to her diaphragm. The sight of him had knocked the wind out of her.

Tears began to well in her eyes.

'Hi, Mom.'

'I thought ...' she croaked, shook her head, and added, 'Your sister is upstairs. She'd love to see you.'

'I'd love to see her, too,' he said with a smile.

She returned it, albeit a watery, shaky kind.

'She's in her room ...And Joe, your father's at the store. He won't be gone long.'

Joe nodded at this piece of information before moving towards the staircase.

4

Harper's room hadn't changed much, yet the sight of its bare walls still struck Joe as being just as awful as anything he had endured in Marybell. Her bedroom was like a room in a show house: clean, neat, and bland. It held none of the personality of the girl who inhabited it, in the same way his own room had when he had lived here, which had made leaving easier.

He had been wondering if his family ever discussed him and he guessed from his mother's reaction that such discussions were prohibited, like a great deal of many things. Having his room so utilitarian must have helped.

It occurred to him as he stood in the doorway of his sister's room that Harper could just disappear as he had, without a trace. The walls were painted in the same beige colour that matched the sideboards. The room was furnished with a bed, dresser, and a book cabinet filled with religious texts.

Harper was currently occupying the bed, stretched out in the sun across its duvet, with a frayed Ray Bradbury book in her hand. It was one of the ones that he had stolen from the library and bequeathed to her before leaving.

'Which one is that?' he asked.

Her button-shaped nose remained pointed at the page.

'Dandelion Wine,' she replied, without looking up.

'My favourite.'

He still couldn't see her face, only her hair, which was chestnut brown. She was dressed in a long, navy skirt that reached down to her ankles and a plain white blouse buttoned all the way up to her neck. Her room was unbelievably hot with the sun beaming in, yet she showed no sign of discomfort in her heavy clothes.

'So you're back,' she remarked. 'I heard the car pull up. Who's the girl driving it?'

'She a friend,' Joe answered, leaning against the doorframe. 'Her name's Daisy. I think you'd like her.'

'I don't think so.'

'Why?'

'Because her arms are showing, and only whores wear clothes that show that amount of skin,' Harper replied. The words were all George Cage's.

Joe ran his tongue along the front of his teeth. 'Aren't you going to give your big brother a hug?'

Harper dropped the book onto the bed, allowing him to see her face. Her right cheek was ballooned to twice its normal size, looking like a tumour, the flesh there bruised purple-black. She glared at him with her left eye. Her right was swollen shut.

Joe didn't know how long they continued to stare at one another, only that he looked away first, to the window, hearing a car pulling into the drive.

5

George Cage stepped out of his pickup and examined the lime-coloured station wagon with the pink curtains parked in his driveway. It was empty.

He squinted at the house, his salt and pepper eyebrows becoming a frowning thunderhead over his brown eyes. He was a tall, well-built man dressed in jeans tied at the waist by a leather belt the colour of walnut, its bulky buckle reflecting the sun's light, and a plaid blue and white shirt. His hair, which was the same salt and pepper colour of his eyebrows, was shaved into a crew cut.

Though he had never seen the car before, he had a good idea who it belonged to. The Cage household was not one that had regular visitors; other than the occasional salesman, no one knocked on their door unless he had agreed to it first. His wife knew not to allow anyone inside.

There was only one person who he could think of that could make Audrey forgot the house rules, his rules. Briefly, George considered whether this had been preplanned, that perhaps his wife had already met with this unwanted visitor somewhere in town and organised a time when he was out for him to come by.

Mounting the porch steps in his boots, he shoved the idea aside; it would be better if he kept an open mind and not jump to conclusions. Jumping to conclusions would lead to jumping to dishing out punishment, and if there was one thing George Cage believed in, it was finding the right punishment for the crime.

6

'Audrey, I believe we have a visitor,' George said brightly to his wife from the hallway.

He could see her in the kitchen at the back of the house in shadow; still, his eyes adjusted quickly. She was repeatedly wringing a dishtowel between her thin, calloused fingers. Her eyes flickered to the dining room.

George approached the entrance to the room, his boots coming down on the wooden floorboards in hard clumps. To Joe, they sounded like the footsteps of a troll or a giant from a fairytale. He even looked like one, stepping into view as Joe stood at the head of the dining table. While his mother seemed to have wasted even further in his absence, his father appeared even more robust. Even with his shirt on Joe could make out the muscles underneath.

'He returns,' proclaimed George Cage, 'like some wandering pilgrim from the good book.'

Sweat was pouring between Joe's shoulder blades. His palms were slick with it.

'We know better, don't we, Audrey? Have you seen his car outside? It looks like a fag car, with those pink curtains. Did you steal it? I hope you did, rather than associating with those people. They have diseases, you know.'

As he ranted, his fingers unclasped his belt buckle, sliding its leather length out of his jeans before wrapping it around his right fist. Audrey Cage whimpered from the hallway, hugging the alcove frame of the room.

'That's what they get for being sinners.'

Joe's throat, which felt like it had closed and grown as dry as the Sahara desert, worked. His Adam's apple bobbed up and down. Seeing his dad twining his belt around his fist was such a familiar sight that for a few seconds, Joe felt like everything had been a dream, that he hadn't really left at all, and he had regressed into creating an internal fiction to cope.

Then he remembered Harper's deformed face. The swelling would go down, but the horror and damnation in her eyes would take longer to heal from, if at all. His father had never punished her while he had lived in this house.

'A bit rich coming from you,' he remarked in a dry whisper.

George Cage stopped twining the belt around his fist, his eyes looking up from it to his son with surprise. 'What did you just say?'

'I said,' answered Joe, his voice steadying, gaining power, 'talking about sinners is a bit rich coming from you. I've seen your handiwork upstairs in my sister's face.'

'Don't you go there, boy. Don't you talk back to me.'

'Fuck you,' Joe snapped and heard his mother utter a cry. 'You're so full of shit you know that? Lording over this house like some sort of tyrant spouting half-baked philosophies. Not a single person in this house has sinned as much as you, yet you're the person who never receives a punishment. Tell me why that is, Dad. Is it because you're afraid if you acted like a human being that Mom and Harper would realise that there's more to life than the insides of this house and they would up and leave you? Or is it just because you're one sadistic son of a bitch?'

'That's enough of this insubordination!' roared George Cage, stalking across the dining room in three quick strides.

As he barreled down upon him, his features as red as a traffic light, Joe saw that he didn't mean to just hurt him this time: he meant to kill him. There was no restraint in his expression, no thought behind his eyes, only murderous rage at being spoken to so indignantly within his own home. Like the monsters at the carnival, his mask had slipped to show his true character. Unlike them, it wasn't emptiness that existed beneath his surface. It was insecurity.

Joe would conclude this all later, but at the moment, there was no time to ponder, to label the emotions he was seeing on his father's snarling face. He just had time to put up his hands, his left jerking the Beretta out of his jeans.

The gun went off with a boom; however, that was because his left hand had struck his father's right, the one he had the belt looped around. The belt buckle, which had been trailing behind him, slapped against Joe's left forearm rather than his head, immediately causing a red welt to form and the flesh there to go numb. The bullet nailed into the ceiling with a crack, showering dust upon them. Joe caught his father's other hand as it swung towards him by the wrist; still, he only slowed its trajectory and his knuckles thumped into his jaw, leaving him seeing stars.

'Take that, you little fucker,' he heard his father say through gritted teeth.

Joe buried a knee in the man's balls. He didn't scream; instead, the air *woofed* out of him as he hunched in the middle.

His fingers seized onto the barrel of Joe's gun. Then both of his hands were gripping it, crushing Joe's left hand between them.

Yelling, Joe kicked out at his father's right knee, hearing a sickening snap. A high-pitched scream escaped his father as he collapsed onto one knee. His right hand still gripped the gun, while his left hand pulled back and drove into Joe's stomach. Suddenly, he couldn't breathe.

George Cage took advantage to finally rid him of the gun by throwing it into the living room. He threw Joe against the dining table before taking off after the weapon at a limp, his kneecap feeling on fire under the skin.

'No!' screamed Audrey as he picked it up.

When he wheeled around, aiming the gun at Joe, he saw his wife was covering him with her body, her expression wild and terrified. Even with her in the way, George thumbed the hammer back and steadied his arm.

Something hit him from the hallway on the left with the force of a locomotive, driving him against the fireplace. The gun went off, the bullet striking the wall with a crack, spraying more dust.

Whoever it was had seized his gun hand by the wrist; its other hand gripped his shoulder with nails so sharp they felt like knives entering the meat there. At the same time, he felt its legs wrap around his waist and squeeze, giving him an idea that whoever it was, it was petite, almost-child sized.

Harper, he thought.

Then there were teeth at his throat and like the thing's nails, they entered him as easily as a hot knife through butter. Pain, brilliant, searing pain, erupted there and made what had happened to his knee feel like a graze.

George Cage attempted to scream as his own blood splashed down his front and found he couldn't, that the thing had bitten through his vocal cords. And it wasn't finished there; it was still biting the flesh, urging the flow of his life's blood to continue to spill while sucking up the outpouring. His legs gave first, folding below him until he was kneeling on the hearth. The leech-like thing followed him down, still hugged to him, its powerful jaws now shaking him.

7

By this time, Joe had pulled his mother out of the dining room into the hall and towards the stairs where Harper was standing, staring over the banister.

Her one good eye was wide and staring at Daisy killing her father.

'Momma!' she cried. 'What's going on?'

Audrey Cage didn't answer, probably because she was in shock.

'That's my friend,' was all Joe could think to say as he grabbed Harper by the arm and half-guided, half-dragged both his mother and sister upstairs.

When Harper asked what was she doing to their father he replied, 'She's punishing him.'

8

It didn't take long before the sound of his father's feet shuffling against the floor stopped.

'Is your friend going to come up here now?' asked Harper.

'No, she won't,' replied Joe from the top of the stairs.

As he put one foot on the next riser down Daisy called up to him. 'Don't come down. I'll deal with this.'

Joe thought about it, then retracted his foot. He was tired, his jaw ached, and there was an awful clenched pain in his stomach where he had been punched.

'And Joe?' she called as he half turned towards his old bedroom. 'I love you, okay?'

'I love you too, Daisy,' he replied.

If he hadn't been so sore and tired, he would have recognised the finality in Daisy's voice. Instead, he peeked in on his sister who once again was drowning in Bradbury. His mother lay on her bed, snoring beside her.

It seemed the tiredness was catching.

He shuffled into his room and was asleep before he hit the bed.

9

It was night when he woke, his body aching, but his mind refreshed. Both the girls were asleep now, curled together in Harper's single bed.

Joe went downstairs, flicking on the lights. The area by the hearth where Daisy had murdered his father was clean. The living room stank of bleach and cleaning chemicals. He called out Daisy's name.

There was no reply.

He went outside to see if the station wagon was still parked by the house. It was, but all of Daisy's clothes were gone. Montague's money was still in its leather shoulder bag behind the driver's seat. He didn't bother to count it.

Turning, he noticed that the barn doors were slightly ajar. Inside, the barn smelled of rust and old blood. In one of the stalls, Joe discovered a section of the earth had been upheaved, as if dug up and filled in again. There was a shovel at its head, its blade stabbed into the disturbed earth.

He stared at it for a long time, thinking about setting the barn on fire. Then he thought that they had been lucky with the gunshots on account of the nearest neighbour being a mile away and them being used to his father shooting off. If he set fire to the place, they would only involve the emergency services.

Joe removed the shovel from the earth, returned it to its rightful position, and went back inside.

10

In the morning Joe shared a coffee at the kitchen table with his mother. He could see Harper, her back to them, through the windows before the family barbecue. Despite the fact that her body blocked most of his view, he could still make out flames as they licked the air, making it quiver and wave.

'I've been thinking about this,' Audrey Cage informed him, talking fast and sounding as giddy as a schoolgirl discussing her weekend date.

Joe thought she kind of looked like a schoolgirl, too. There was a warm light in her face he had never seen before that took ten years off her.

'I woke up in the middle of the night, my brain on fire with all these ideas. We paid off the house and the land years ago, there's that. Your father got his pension from the military and he took it all as one lump sum, which I have access to. It's not much – enough to live off maybe, but not enough to send you kids to the places you deserve. I was thinking about how much you wanted to go to college to study English and Harper, well Harper, should be able to have what she wants, as well. Holt Maddens, you know him, he owns the hardware store in town. I think he'd give me a job if I asked. Again, it wouldn't be much, but it would allow me to save for you both.'

She looked at him with pleading eyes that said *Please say that sounds good.*

'That sounds brilliant, Mom. But save that money for Harper. The idea of me in college …'

'You're not staying, are you?' Suddenly, her schoolgirl giddiness was gone, replaced by an expression of motherly worry.

'No, I'm not.'

'This is because of your friend?'

'Yes.' He wanted to tell her more but had no clue where to begin explaining everything that had happened between Daisy and him.

It turned out he didn't need to. His mother nodded as if she already understood, her grey eyes large and owlish.

'Anyway, that's great about the job. If you ever need anything else, I want you to have this.' Joe patted the shoulder bag that sat in the chair beside him.

Before his mother could ask what was inside, Harper entered the kitchen. 'I'd like to get some new books today,' she informed them.

11

He took her to a local bookstore instead of the library. When he pulled up in the station wagon she said, 'I can't go in there.'

Joe nodded and went inside alone. He came out minutes later, having cleared every shelf of anything written by Ray Bradbury. When he told Harper, she squealed with glee, snatching the first book from the bag he handed to her. It was a copy of *The Illustrated Man*.

Harper looked over its cover, seemed to drink it in, and then said, 'You're leaving, aren't you?' She sounded like she was doing her best not to sound hurt, but he still heard it.

'Not today. I want to make sure you and Mom will be all right. I'll be back, though.'

'Is it because of that girl, your friend? She left, didn't she?'

'Yes.'

'If she left, doesn't that mean she doesn't want to see you anymore?'

'Maybe. Maybe not. Daisy and I went through something that I can't begin to describe. She was there for me. I think it's my turn to be there for her.'

He watched Harper ponder this, her eyes casting to the bookstore's front through the windscreen.

'Promise to call us,' she said. 'And promise to come home for good.'

Joe stared into her eyes, which were the colour of chocolate, and deeply serious.

'I promise.'

They hugged, Joe breathing in the scent of her hair as they did. When they broke apart, Harper's eyes had already returned to the book in her hands. As he started the station wagon's engine, he heard her flip it open to the first page.

The End

Acknowledgements

Well, this has been one hell of a ride. The idea of this particular rollercoaster hit me while my wife and I where honeymooning in the US. We had just spent the day at a theme park, and it got me thinking about how terrified I used to be of rollercoasters when I was younger. I'd have very similar reactions to being in the queues of such rides as Lily Grey did in this book and it was that memory coupled with several curve balls my imagination threw my way that led to the creation of this story. I am immensely gratefully to my wife, Claire, as any spouse should be when their partner is forever challenging them to do better; this story wouldn't exist without her.

A special thank you goes out to Kelly Brocklehurst for doing a fantastic job editing this beast of a book. Your talent has no bounds. Thank you to Michael Goodwin at Dark Pine Publishing for providing such an eye-catching awesome cover. As well a massive thank you to Christopher Robertson for reading this book and writing such a generous foreword. I'd also like to thank Mark Watson, Dave Musson, Nigel Milner, Valeria Tsykunova and Sarah Read for being beta readers for this novel. All your advice and guidance made it even better.

I'd like to say a final thank you to everyone who's given up their valuable time to read something I've written, time being a precious fleeting thing. I hope I made it worth your while, I really do; if so, I encourage you to let your thoughts be known, whether that be through a review, a post on your social media or simply telling a friend. These type of actions are the life's blood of any writer in this industry as they encourage other readers to take a chance on their work. This, in my opinion, is the most important element of the publishing industry as stories are meant to be read far and wide and reviews help achieve this.

About the Author

Jamie Stewart is a horror author and editor. His books include PRICE MANOR: THE HOUSE THAT BLEEDS, I HEAR THE CLATTERING OF THE KEYS (AND OTHER FEVERS DREAMS) and MR. JONES. He has co-edited such anthologies as WELCOME TO THE FUNHOUSE for BLOOD RITES HORROR and THE SACRAMENT, which is coming this October from DARK LIT PRESS. His short stories can be found in various anthologies, podcasts and Youtube channels.

Jamie lives in Northern Ireland with his wife, Claire, and dogs, Poppy and Henry. He can be found on Instagram @jamie.stewart.33 where he reviews and promotes books.

Printed in Great Britain
by Amazon